RUTHLESS PRINCE

Dark Syndicate

KHARDINE GRAY
FAITH SUMMERS

Copyright © 2020 by Khardine Gray

Please note : Faith Summers is the Dark Romance pen name of USA Today Bestselling Author Khardine Gray

All rights reserved.

Ruthless Prince Book 1 of Dark Syndicate Copyright © 2020 by Khardine Gray

Cover design © 2020 by Book Cover Couture

Photography: Wander Aguiar

Cover Model- Christoph

No part of this book may be reproduced in any form or by any electronic or mechanical means, including information storage and retrieval systems, without written permission from the author, except for the use of brief quotations in a book review.

This work is copyrighted. Apart from any use as permitted under the Copyright Act 1968, no part may be reproduced, copied, scanned, stored in a retrieval system, recorded or transmitted, in any form or by any means, without the prior written permission of the author, except for the use of brief quotations in a book review.

This is a work of fiction. Names, characters, businesses, places, events and incidents are either the products of the author's imagination or used in a fictitious manner. Any resemblance to actual persons, living or dead, or actual events is purely coincidental.

The author asserts that all characters and situations depicted in this work of fiction are entirely imaginary and bear no relation to any real person.

No part of this book may be reproduced in any form or by any electronic or mechanical means, including information storage and retrieval systems, without written permission from the author, except for the use of brief quotations in a book review.

The following story contains mature themes, strong language and sexual situations.

It is intended for mature readers. All characters are 18+ years of age and all sexual acts are consensual.

RUTHLESS PRINCE

Dark Syndicate Book 1

USA Today Bestselling Author
Khardine Gray
Writing as
Faith Summers

Copyright © 2020 by Khardine Gray

All rights reserved.

No part of this book may be reproduced in any form or by any electronic or mechanical means, including information storage and retrieval systems, without written permission from the author, except for the use of brief quotations in a book review.

❀ Created with Vellum

DARK ROMANCE WARNING

Dear Reader,

Thank you so much for picking my book to read. I hope you enjoy it.

I just have to warn you that this book is a dark romance. It contains scenes that may be triggering to some readers .

Best of wishes xx

AUTHOR NOTE

Please note: Faith Summers is the dark romance pen name of USA Today Bestselling Author Khardine Gray.

WE WERE DESTINED FOR DISASTER FROM THE SECOND WE MET ...

Massimo D'Agostino is the heir to his father's empire.
Don't be fooled by his handsome face, or that piercing blue gaze.
He's no prince charming.
He's dangerous and feared, possessive and fierce.

Our first meeting began with a contract that forced me to marry him and sign my life away.
I was a debt repayment and a pawn in his game to exact revenge against my father.
The only way out is death.
I belong to him now.
Me, the Balesteri Mafia Princess.
Pure and untouched...
Owned by the devil who placed me in a gilded cage.

But something unexpected happened the moment our paths collided.

It made me want more of what he had to offer every time I lay beneath him.

Then the past came knocking at the door and dark secrets scattered at my feet.
Suddenly I don't know truth from lies.
Or, who the monster in this story is.
I thought it was my husband.
Now I'm not so sure...

RUTHLESS PRINCE

PROLOGUE

MASSIMO

17 years ago

"Earth to earth, ashes to ashes, dust to dust..." Father De Lucca mutters then pauses for a moment.

I gaze at him standing at the head of my mother's grave. The solemn expression on his face deepens, and the pinch in his brows tells me he feels our loss too.

I remember him telling me stories about my mother when she was little. He was the priest who gave her her first communion, and he married my parents. I doubt he thought this day would come.

No one did. Not this soon, or so sudden.

Father De Lucca pulls in a breath, looks around the gathering of mourners, and continues. "In sure and certain hope of the resurrection to eternal life through our Lord Jesus Christ, who is able to subdue all things. God has received one of his angels today... I commit Sariah Abriella D'Agostino's body back to the earth from whence she came, and I wish for a blessing on her beautiful, kind soul."

I stare ahead and note how my father looks at him on those final words. I wonder if Father De Lucca found it strange too. That my mother would kill herself.

Pa is standing paces away from him. A tear runs down his cheek as a light sparks in his eyes, probably from the kindness in the blessing.

The light fades a moment later, and he returns to being the broken man. I'm twelve years old, but I know what broken looks like. It's how I feel.

Up until now, I've never seen Pa cry. *Never.* Not even years ago when we lost everything and were thrown into the streets with nothing but the clothes on our backs.

My grandfather gives my shoulder a gentle squeeze. When I glance up at him, he gives me a reassuring look. The type that everybody else has given since this all happened.

Grandfather has one hand on me and the other on Dominic, my youngest brother. My other two brothers, Andreas and Tristan, stand at his other side.

Dominic hasn't stopped crying, not once since we told him Ma wouldn't be coming home. He's only eight years old. I hate that he has to go through this. We all teased him for being the baby and clinging to Ma. But then, we all clung to her in some way.

The only other funeral I've been to was my Nonna's. But at six years old, I was too young to understand death. Back then, I didn't feel the way I do now. Like the collision of numbness and anger inside me will rip me apart.

Maybe I feel like that because it was me who found Ma in the river.

I was the first person to see her dead.

I was the first person to confirm our worst fears after she'd gone missing.

I was the first person to know that the last time we saw each other was goodbye forever.

We all looked for her for three days. It was while I was walking by the riverbank at Stormy Creek that I saw her, just drifting there in the water amongst the cattail reeds. Her eyes still open, *glassy*. Her skin pale. Lips...blue. Her body rocking gently from side to side in the water. I'll never forget the way she looked. Like a lifeless doll with her white-blonde hair flowing out around her, her dainty features still looking so perfect. But lifeless. *No more.*

Inside I'm still screaming.

They said she must have jumped off the cliff. That's what I heard the grownups saying.

Suicide...

Ma killed herself.

It doesn't feel real.

It doesn't feel right.

I'm pulled from my thoughts when Father De Lucca nods his head and Pa takes a handful of the dirt to throw down into the grave. When he finishes scattering the dirt, he gets down on one knee and holds out the single red rose he's been carrying since we got here. We all have one.

"Ti amo, amore mio. I will love you forever and ever," he says. My parents always declared their love for each other. Always.

I know he feels the same guilt that surrounds us. We all blame ourselves for not being able to save her. As Pa casts the flower into the grave, Father De Lucca says a prayer and Grandfather takes my brothers to give Ma their flowers.

I remain where I am. I can't will myself to move. I can't say goodbye yet. I don't want to say goodbye at all.

I know what will happen next. We'll leave and they'll fill the grave with the rest of the dirt. Covering Ma up forever. My legs tremble at the thought and that weakness returns to my body.

People start throwing in their flowers too, one by one. Some look at me, others just follow suit dropping their roses: lilies, dahlias. Ma's favorites.

I've been holding onto the rose in my hand so tightly the thorns have cut my palms. I almost forgot I had it. I look down at the stains of blood on the stem and leaves. The rich crimson color stark against the dark green.

A heavy hand rests on my shoulder, startling me. When I look up, I find myself staring straight into the pale blue eyes of the devil. The man who took everything away from us. *Riccardo Balesteri.*

A man Pa used to call his best friend. That's who we knew him to be before things changed and he became a monster.

Pa doesn't involve us in business, but there was no one to shield us from anything that day two years ago when Riccardo came to our home with his men and threw us out.

I didn't know what happened, but I remember the arguing. I remember Pa pleading with him to be reasonable and Ma crying as she tried to get Dominic and Tristan out of bed. It was Andreas who took me and calmed me down when I tried to help. The men just laughed at me.

Now, this man is here at my mother's funeral with a smile on his face.

"Dear child, I'm so truly sorry for your loss," he says.

His words are similar to what has been said to me all day,

starting when we entered the church this morning and as we arrived at the cemetery. Everyone who said it, though, meant it. They were genuine. This man is not.

The *click-clack* of what I know is a gun steals my answer. Not that I would know what to say. I haven't spoken much since I found Ma in the river.

I look up to see Pa holding out two guns, aiming them at Riccardo. Grandfather places a protective arm around my brothers while the remaining guests stare on in terror.

The only person who doesn't look scared is Father De Lucca. His face is stern and becomes harder when Riccardo tightens his grip on my shoulder.

"Get your hands off my son," Pa demands, tilting his head to the side.

Riccardo laughs. The sound ripples through me. He squeezes my shoulder so hard I wince and my knees buckle.

"Giacomo, trust you to make a scene," Riccardo answers in a sing-song voice.

"I said get your hands off my son. *Now!*" Pa shouts.

In answer to his demand, Riccardo applies more pressure to my shoulder. His fingers dig past the fabric of my suit and burrow into my skin.

"Let me go," I growl, thrashing against his grasp. He's too strong though. I'm helpless. I can't do anything.

"So disrespectful at your wife's funeral," Riccardo taunts. "I wonder what Sariah would think if she wasn't six feet under. Maybe the disappointment you are as a husband made her jump to her death. Yes, yes. That must be it. Maybe she preferred death to being with you."

Enraged, Pa steps forward with his guns, but Riccardo retaliates by pulling his own, pulling me closer and placing the steel barrel to my temple.

I cry out, dropping my rose and gritting my teeth. That

makes Pa stop in his tracks. His eyes widen with fright and my soul shudders with fear. This man is the devil. Pa always told me to never underestimate. It will get you killed. So, I won't do it now. I won't underestimate or assume that Riccardo won't kill me.

Tears run down my cheeks when he smoothes his hand up to my neck and holds me tighter.

"You fucking dog," Pa shouts. He still has his guns raised though. "How dare you show up here today to gloat? Get your fucking hands off my son."

Riccardo smiles and leans closer, close to my father's outstretched guns, daring, as if he knows Pa won't kill him.

"Look at you, thinking you're hot shit. You can't kill me. You know that."

"Do you want to test me?" Pa snarls.

"*Fool*, if you could, you would have done it already. But... you know you can't. You know the moment you do, you're dead. Your boys are dead. Your father is dead. Your family in Italia is dead. Everybody you know will be dead. The creed of the Brotherhood protects me and mine."

Pa seethes. Defeat enters his eyes. The same defeated look he's carried for the last few years as one bad thing happened after another.

"Leave us," Pa replies.

"That's right. I thought so. You know you can't do shit to me. You're powerless and useless, helpless as shit," Riccardo continues to taunt. "You lost everything. She was the last good thing you had left."

He looks at the grave. Through my tears I catch the first glimpse of sadness in his eyes. He releases me and steps back, lowering his gun.

"Leave us, Riccardo. Go away. Go the fuck away," Pa says.

"Came to pay my respect to the angel you should never

have had. That's all," Riccardo answers. "And maybe to see your face. That look on your face as you accept you've truly lost everything."

With a crude, sardonic laugh, Riccardo turns and walks away.

Pa lowers his guns, puts them back in his holsters, and takes hold of me, pulling me in for a hug.

"Massimo," he breathes against my ear. "Are you hurt?"

I swallow hard. "No," I answer. He pulls back to look me over. Sees the rose on the ground and picks it up.

We stare at each other. The sadness in his eyes grips me so bad it hurts.

"I'm sorry, my boy... I'm sorry for everything," he says.

"Why does he hate us so much?" I ask, my lips trembling.

Pa shakes his head. "Don't worry about him. Don't, my boy. Today is not about him." He straightens and holds the rose out to me. "Massimo...give your mother the rose. It's time. Time to say goodbye. We will get through this. We will. Please... Never think your mother didn't love you. She did with all her heart."

I know it's true, but part of me wants to ask him why she would leave me without saying goodbye. Except I know the answer. Life became too hard after Riccardo took everything from us. That's why.

"Give your mother your rose, amore mio," Pa repeats, pushing the rose closer to me.

I take it, and then those steps I dreaded. My legs grow heavier with each one. I stop right by the opening to the grave and release the flower from my grasp. As it falls, my heart breaks all over again.

Riccardo was right. Ma was the last good thing we had left. She was truly an angel.

I gaze off into the distance and see the vague outline of him walking down the path leading back to the car park.

He called my father powerless, useless, helpless. He blamed Pa for my mother wanting death, but it's not his fault. Everything that's happened to us is Riccardo's fault. All of it.

In the moment the thought strikes me, I vow vengeance. As I watch his retreating back, I promise myself that I will fix this. No matter how long it takes me; I will spend the rest of my life if I have to helping my father rebuild. And I will make Riccardo Balesteri pay for everything.

Right now, we might be *powerless, useless, helpless*, but we will not be that forever.

It doesn't matter how long it takes.

He will lose everything too.

CHAPTER ONE

EMELIA

Present Day

"It's going to be our last night here for a while," Jacob states, looking around our little booth in the diner.

We've been coming here for so long that the place has become a second home.

"I know," I agree.

A wave of nostalgia washes over me as I think of all the times we've spent here and the years we've been friends.

This is also the last night I'll be seeing him for a very long time. Playfully, I toss a cheese ball at him. He catches it with his mouth. We both start laughing, and people at the nearby tables glance our way.

"Have you finished packing?" Jacob asks, setting his arm down on the table.

"I don't know what kind of question that is," I bubble, shaking my head at him.

He's my best friend. He should know better than to ask me something like that.

I leave for Florence in the morning in prep to start my sophomore year at the L'Accademia di Belle Arti. My dream is to become an artist. I've been excited to go to Florence since my father booked the tickets. I've always wanted to study in Italy, just like my mother did. Jacob and I finished our freshman year at UCLA a few weeks ago. My bags have been packed since.

If Mom were alive, she'd be really proud of me. Going to the Accademia is the last thing I'll do to follow in her footsteps. It's going to be amazing.

"Sorry, my mistake." Jacob chuckles. His large brown eyes sparkle. "It was more the case of me asking if you're ready to go. But you were probably born ready."

I laugh. "I was. I'll miss you a lot, but I can't wait to leave," I confess.

It will be exciting to start my classes because some of the best teachers in the world will instruct me, but I won't deny the chance to escape L.A. and my father's controlling hand doesn't appeal to me as well.

Although I'll have bodyguards accompanying me and I'll be staying with my uncle, this is the first time I'll be going to Italy without Dad.

"I get it. I just hope your old man doesn't have a heart attack." He smirks.

"I know. I keep thinking he's going to change his mind." Like he nearly did about me going to college.

I wanted to go away to study right from the get-go, but

Dad wouldn't hear of it. We only settled on UCLA because it was close to home. He wouldn't hear of me living on campus either. The best things about going there were the courses and getting to see Jacob.

It took the miracle of Uncle Leo's assurance that he'd look after me and profound begging to get Dad to allow me to go to Florence.

"Fingers crossed he won't. You worked hard to show him you'll be fine, and you worked hard for the placement." Jacob nods, looking proud of me.

"Thank you."

I know what it means to be a Balesteri, and specifically to be the daughter of a mob boss. My father is a powerful man. As such, he has enemies. I already experienced an eye opener when my cousin, Porter, was gunned down in the street a few years back. My family isn't average. Neither is Jacob's. We're both old enough and smart enough to know where we come from. Jacob's father works for mine, so we're well aware of the dangers we could face just for being who we are.

I love my father dearly and I know he just wants to protect me, but sometimes I feel like I'm living in one big gilded cage. Going to Italy will give me a chance to be free. Truthfully, I'm hoping that if everything goes well, Dad will allow me more freedom so I can travel around without constant supervision. Or his watchful eye.

"Your mother would be happy and very proud of you," Jacob intones.

I draw in a breath, nodding slowly, and he reaches across the table to cover my hands with his. Mom's been gone for three years now. Sometimes it doesn't feel real. Sometimes the grief comes back to haunt me, and I remember how she suffered during those last few months when cancer got the better of her.

I wasn't sure which killed her first—the rigorous sessions of chemotherapy or the disease itself. She didn't even look like my mother in the end. The only thing that remained was her beautiful spirit. She was watching me paint when she took her last breath. I'll never forget the way she looked after. Like she was proud of me. Proud for sharing her dreams in art, and proud for my desire to follow my own.

"That means a lot to me, Jacob."

"I know it does. I'm seriously going to miss you a lot."

"But you'll come and see me, right?" I ask, hopeful.

He releases my hands and gives me one of his cocky grins. "Every chance I get."

"You better."

"You know I will." He presses his lips together and I stare back at him as a sliver of awkward silence fills the space between us.

In his text earlier he mentioned wanting to ask me something important. I have a pretty good idea what that *something* might be.

He's been different since we started college. Different in a way that suggests he wants us to be more than friends. I pretend not to notice, but I do. I see it now as he stares back at me.

I might be an idiot not to want him too. Jacob is handsome and has always taken care of me. But to me he feels like a brother. I can't see us being more than friends, and I can't feel anything more than friendship either.

Besides...even though no one has ever said this, I know no matter how close Jacob is, or what ties bind our families, Dad would never allow anything more than friendship between us. Definitely not when he's told me I'll have an arranged marriage someday, the way he did with Mom to bring their family businesses together. That was the news Dad hit me with on my eighteenth birthday. It was a onetime-only business discussion that enraged me because I'm the hopeful romantic who wants true love. However, since I know my father, I knew that discussion was final. The same way I have no freedom, I have no say in regard to who I end up with. During that talk, it went without saying Jacob would never be a man Dad would consider for me. So, even if I did return Jacob's feelings, I know I can't defy my father.

"I...guess I should talk to you about that something, right?" he says, fidgeting and tense.

"Yeah, you should." I want him to tell me what's on his mind so I can be real with him.

"I was...thinking about us and the relationship we have," he begins. "We've always been great together."

"Yes," I answer, biting the inside of my lip. "We have."

"Emelia, you know I really value you."

I'm about to tell him I value him too—*as my closest friend*—when the door to the restaurant bursts open and Frankie, one of my father's guards, barges through.

The moment our eyes lock I know something is wrong. My nerves spike when he marches over with a heavy thud.

"Emelia," Frankie says, "you have to come with me now."

I look back at Jacob then back to Frankie. "What?"

"I need you to come with me, urgently."

Urgently? Oh God. The second my mind processes that word I'm overcome with worry.

"Why? Has something happened to Dad?"

This is similar to how I found out Mom had cancer. I was in class when Frankie came and told me she'd been in a car accident. She blacked out while she was driving and crashed her car. She was okay from the accident, but what followed next was a journey I'll never forget. I don't know what I'd do if I lost my father. I couldn't bear it. He's all I have left.

"Please tell me he's okay," I stutter.

"He's fine. He's requesting to meet with you. It's imperative we leave now."

I swallow hard. "Frankie, you're worrying me. Please tell me what this is about."

"Emelia, don't." He shakes his head firmly. "I said it was urgent and that's all you need to know. Now come," he demands with balled fists and a glare, reminding me that, while I might be the Balesteri princess, there are certain things I'm not privy to and he's under no obligation to tell me anything.

He answers to my father, and we both know when my father says I need to be somewhere that's where I have to be.

No arguments, no more questions.

I stand. Jacob does too. I planned to stay out with him for a little while longer. We didn't even get to finish our talk.

"I'm sorry, Jacob," I say with a slight shrug of my shoulders.

"No, don't apologize. I hope everything's okay," Jacob replies, but I can see the disappointment lurking in the depths of his eyes. I feel guilty for it because I know this is a conversation he's wanted to have with me for a while and I've avoided it with fear that my answer would ruin our friendship. "I'll see you in Italia."

"You better," I answer, throwing my arms around him.

"You have my word," Jacob promises with a smile but gives me a watery gaze brimming with worry. "Buonasera."

"Buonasera," I reply with a little smile.

"Come on," Frankie pushes, beckoning me to come.

When I move toward him, he places his hand to the small of my back then ushers me away.

"What about my car?" I ask, glancing over to the parking lot as we step outside.

"I'll have someone pick it up," he answers gruffly.

I'm led to the Bentley and see Gio, my father's second in command, at the wheel. Frankie opens the back door for me to get in, and once I'm strapped inside, he joins Gio in the front.

A lump forms in my throat as the car sets off down the road and I glance back at the diner, seeing Jacob watching me as we pull away.

This is weird, very strange, even for my father. He's never done this before.

Thirty minutes later, when we drive past the road that would take us to my home in Malibu, my heart squeezes. Dad was at home in his office when I left earlier. He never tends to go out once he gets home in the evenings, and definitely not on a Saturday.

My chest follows my heart, tightening with unease when we drive past the Balesteri Investments complex and carry on down the Pacific Coast Highway.

When we didn't go to the house I assumed I'd be meeting Dad in his office at work. That's the only other place he would be. Now I have no idea where we're going.

We continue down the highway for another hour, driving past the marina at Long Beach then taking the route to Huntington Beach.

We turn onto a road with gorgeous state-of- the-art-looking beach houses that look like they were pulled from a dream. Then we're back on another road where all I can see is the sea and the waves rushing up against the shoreline. As a large white wall comes into view and the car slows, tension knots my insides.

I have no idea where the hell I am or why Dad would be here, and at this hour. I've only been to Huntington Beach a few times and not in recent years. It was never to see anyone we knew. It was for fundraisers and I was with both my parents.

We pull up at a large metal gate that opens for us. When we drive through and I see ten Navy-Seal-type men guarding the entrance with machine guns, I know whoever lives here has to be either someone of great importance, or someone with a lot of enemies.

CHAPTER TWO

EMELIA

Gio mutters something under his breath to Frankie, who nods and shakes his head. I didn't catch what he said, but from what I heard it sounded like they had similar thoughts to me. Dad has guards, yes, but our home isn't guarded like this.

As we proceed down a lengthy drive, more guards appear and I take in my surroundings, noting how the beach blends in with the grounds. Off in the distance is a dock. There's a yacht and two sailboats moored by it. I just make out the outline of another boat but I can't quite see what it is from here.

Ahead of us, a mansion emerges. Against the dark velvet sky, its cosmopolitan beauty steals my breath away, even in my tension-filled state. Lit by the combination of the moonlight and the ground lights surrounding the front of the house, I can see the glitzy Mediterranean design that makes me feel like I'm heading to some lavish villa in Sicily as opposed to the uncertainty I feel brewing in my soul. The mansion is easily one of those ten-million-dollar homes you read about with the scenic beachfront view and acres of land surrounding it. I'm guessing the owner must be classy and like sailing, too, from the presence of the boats back at the docks.

Who is he, though?

As we get closer, I see cars parked on the drive and men with guns file out from the corners, snapping me out of my reverie and enchantment over the beauty of the house.

"Fucking hell," Gio hisses under his breath.

"Yes, fucking hell indeed. This guy is one serious motherfucker," Frankie mutters.

My father hates the men swearing around me. He's afraid it will taint me. To me it's foolish to worry over such things when there's always something bigger to worry about. Like what is happening now.

"Whose house is this?" I ask, but neither Frankie nor Gio answer me. They make a point of ignoring me by continuing to gaze ahead.

I grit my teeth to keep in my rage. They don't have to be such assholes. It was a simple question. One I'm sure anyone would ask. Since I don't want to feel foolish again, I decide against asking anymore questions. It's clear they won't be answered from these two.

We park and Frankie gets out of the car first. Both men come to my side when I step out, shielding and protecting me as they take me by my arms.

I allow them to lead me. My nerves spike when the guards with the guns come to us and urge us forward into the house. The temptation to look around beckons to me when we step inside, but even I can't be tempted now by its beauty. Right now, it wouldn't matter if the house was the most beautiful thing in the world because the ominous feeling prickling my nerves and the clench in my lungs are signs that whatever is going on is not good.

"This way," one of the guards ahead says, pointing to a room I can see must be the living room.

We go in and the breath I was holding onto releases when I see Dad sitting on a black leather sofa.

As he looks at me, I can tell from his pale skin and the sweat running down the side of his face that something is very wrong. Worry is etched in his entire body, and the daunting look in his pale blue eyes dims its usual vibrancy.

Dad actually looks scared.

The last time I saw him look anything close to this was when Mom got sick. That look just worsened with each treatment she had and hope of her survival slipped away.

Why does he look like this now?

What could have happened?

When he stands, I rush over to him and hug him. We pull apart and he takes both my hands into his then plants a kiss on my forehead.

"Dad, what's going on? Whose home is this?"

"Emelia...something's happened." His voice is shaky, another trait I associate with the time Mom was sick because, outside of that time, my father is usually a force to be reckoned with.

"What's happened?"

"Remember that discussion we had some time ago about what would happen in regard to any marriage proposals?"

My lips part and I narrow my eyes, unsure where he's going with this conversation.

"Yes... I do." Of course I remember that *marriage proposal discussion* very well. Coincidentally, I was thinking about it earlier when I was with Jacob. It hasn't been far from my thoughts so it doesn't take much to remember how upset I was after Dad and I spoke.

As I gaze at him, my breath hitches with trepidation as I consider why he's bringing up the subject *now*.

I've been brought to this home. A place I've never been before, to meet my father, who looks scared.

I shift my gaze from his to look around the living room and I bite down hard on my teeth to keep them from chattering. When I return my focus to Dad, I bring my hands together, *tight*.

"Whose home is this, Dad?"

"It's mine," comes a deep baritone voice from the far corner of the room.

I snap around and my gaze lands on the most handsome man I've ever seen in my life. He has a strong mix of raw masculinity and beauty I've never seen before. I'm not sure if it's right to call a man beautiful. This one is, though, with his striking appearance and those piercing, midnight blue eyes that capture and hold my attention.

He's tall, foreboding, and the white button-down shirt and black slacks give a full view of his well-muscled body. As he sets back his powerfully built shoulders, he exudes a presence that commands authority and obedience. I can feel it like it could be something tangible floating through the air.

I'm thrown by his looks and the strength in his presence, but it's the way he's looking at me that rivets me. He's looking at me like he can see straight through me, right through to my soul.

I'm only pulled from the trance when an older man who undoubtedly has to be his father steps up behind him. Apart from the eye color, they look too similar not to be father and son. I sense the same air of authority in the older man. Except he doesn't have that penetrating look in his eyes. I place him to be the same age as Dad and guess straightaway these are mafia men. They emanate the vibe.

Mr. Bianchi, our family lawyer, walks up next with some documents in his hands. When I see that, I remember what Dad said and panic surges through me.

"Floor's over to you, Riccardo," the younger man says, surprising me by calling my father by his first name. Only my father's friends call him Riccardo and I've never seen this man in my life. "Now that we're all here, you can finish what you were saying to her."

I don't miss the brief glance of admiration he gives me. In response, I tilt my head and try to look like I'm not fazed, although I am. I'm used to *men* looking at me the same way they used to look at my mother. She was very beautiful, and while I don't profess to possess the sort of beauty she had, people have told me I look exactly like her.

"Emelia, this is Massimo D'Agostino and his father Giacomo," Dad introduces them, pointing at the men respectively. At the mention of the name D'Agostino, I instantly wonder if the name has anything to do with D'Agostinos Inc., the oil company. I recall it because the name is unusual and not one I'm used to hearing. It's Italian, and they're Italian, so maybe I'm right.

I won't be an idiot with pleasantries and manners though. It's clear we aren't here for biscuits and tea. I look back to Dad and stare at him head on.

"Dad, what are we doing in Mr. D'Agostino's home?" I demand.

"Emelia, you're going to marry Massimo in a month's time," he answers, and my mouth drops wide open.

"What? No... I... No." I shake my head furiously in disbelief. "What? No."

"*Yes*," he confirms in that voice that shows the depth of his seriousness.

I blink back tears that well up in my eyes, willing myself not to cry. "Dad, this is outrageous! I can't marry someone I don't know," I gasp. "I didn't know it was going to happen this way."

This is a lot different to what he told me. He promised I'd get to at least meet the man I was going to marry well in advance and there would be time to get to know him.

"Dad, you actually agreed to this?"

"I have. Massimo wishes to take you from tonight."

The second he says that my heart sinks and I step away from him. My head feels so light I might faint. All I can do is stare at him in shock. "*Tonight*! What about Italy? I'm leaving tomorrow. What about school?" I knew it was too good to be true, but I never imagined something like this happening.

"You won't be able to go," he replies, and my heart breaks.

"My art... Please, please don't take my dreams away from me," I beg. "Please, Papa."

Papa...

The last time I called him that was years ago when Mom died. Literally moments after when I fell apart. I feel like that girl again.

"Emelia, I'm sorry." Remorse brims within his eyes but it's not enough to soothe me. He knew how much going to Italy meant to me.

"I worked so hard to get into the Accademia. Papa, it's the *Accademia* for crying out loud. You *know* how good you have to be to get in. They said I aced the test."

He reaches out and cups my face. "My child, I'm sorry. I'm truly sorry. This has to happen. I can't do anything about it." He presses his lips together and holds my gaze. "Please do not make this harder than it already is."

"How could you do this to me?" I counter, and he drops his hands to his sides.

Dad cuts Massimo a sharp glance to which he returns with a faint smile. That's when I get the impression that there's more at work here.

"Sir, are you ready for the contract?" Mr. Bianchi asks and I turn my focus to him as he holds up the document he's carrying.

"*Contract?*" I cut in before Dad can answer.

"This is a business contract. As my heir you will need to sign it," Dad explains and suddenly everything feels so much worse. There was never any talk of me signing anything of the sort before.

"What? I don't understand," I breathe out.

"I'm ready, Mr. Bianchi," Dad says, ignoring me, and Mr. Bianchi sets the document on the coffee table next to us then backs away.

"Mr. D'Agostino, please sign here," Mr. Bianchi says, and Massimo walks over to sign in the section he pointed to.

He's so close, too close to me, and the hair on the back of my neck stands on end when our eyes lock. When I see there's nothing there in his eyes, no soul, nothing human, nothing he wishes to give away, I feel trapped in the depths of his blue gaze. It's like I've been sucked into a black hole and all there is is darkness.

Massimo straightens up and keeps his gaze trained on me. "Mr. Bianchi, why don't you do Miss Balesteri the honor of reading the necessary parts of the contract so she's clear about what she's signing to."

There's a purposeful menace laced in his tone that catches my attention. It's mocking and I think it's directed at Dad.

"Yes, sure." Mr. Bianchi nods and retrieves the document. He gives me a look of sympathy before he starts and my skin flushes with icy fear. "It is hereby certified by this contract that Massimo D'Agostino will, as of this day, 1st July 2019, become the sole proprietor of Emelia Juliette Balesteri. She will fall part of all assets acquired from Riccardo Balesteri in an attempt to recover sums of the debt owed. She will belong to him, and marriage to him will bind all future business acquisitions and inheritance linked to her name—"

"Stop," I cry out, stopping him from going any further. My mouth hangs open, but since I can't form any more words I just stare at Mr. Bianchi in utter disbelief.

Bile churns my stomach. It rises into my throat, *burning*. My brain scrambles and my skin prickles with goosebumps. The situation is so much worse than what I thought.

Not going to Italy to pursue my dreams for my career is *bad*, the idea of marrying a man I don't know devastating, but this...

The words of the contract swirl around in my mind as I look at the men standing around me and focus on each one. Giacomo, whose face is stern, void of emotion. Massimo, who stares back at me in anticipation. Mr. Bianchi, who looks away in shame. *Him*, I give credit. He seems to be the only person before me who knows this is wrong.

When my gaze settles back on Dad, it all comes together.

Contract of ownership?

Sole proprietor?

An attempt to recover the sums of the debt owed?

Jesus Christ.

The reason why this isn't like what we discussed before is because it's not.

This is something else entirely. The kind of thing I've heard spoken of in hushed whispers in the circles we travelled in.

This is hell.

"You're selling me!" I gasp. My voice is shrill, rising several octaves as I speak, shaking as I tremble from deep within. "*Papa*, you're selling...*me?*"

Dad's face contorts and his jaw clenches but he doesn't answer.

He's selling me.

It's true.

I fall part of his assets.

A debt exchanged.

What the fuck happened?

My father is incredibly wealthy, so what the fuck *could* have happened?

"Me, Papa? *Really?* I'm your daughter. Papa, it's me, Emelia. You can look at me like I'm a thing and just sell me? When you promised Mom you'd always take care of me this was what you meant?" I'm shouting now and I can't help it.

I've never raised my voice to him before but right now I don't care to be the respectful daughter he's used to. The whole debt exchange part of this shit is what has thrown me for a loop. I can't even worry about the aspect of my inheritance since that was always going to be part of *business*.

"Emelia, I need your signature," Dad states.

"Dad...how could you do this? You're actually selling me," I croak, and fuck, the tears come hard now.

How could he think this is okay? How could he treat me like I'm property? *An asset.*

The urge to try and stand my ground comes and I back away from my father. But I hit a wall. No...it's not the wall. Arms steady me, holding me in place, preventing me from fleeing. I look up and see Frankie. He averts his gaze, though, and stares right ahead. He was right to think I would flee, but how far would I get?

"You will sign the document, Emelia." Dad glowers at me.

"No," I cry, and as the word falls from my lips I realize that's the very first time I've ever defied him.

Dad takes the pen from Massimo and the contract from Mr. Bianchi then rushes at me lightning fast. I gasp when he yanks me away from Frankie, pulling on my arm so hard I fear he's dislocated my shoulder.

Like I'm a petulant child, he marches me over to the coffee table, sets the contract down and takes my hand to place the pen between my fingers. Dad then squeezes my hand so hard I cry out from the pain.

"You will obey me," Dad rages, squeezing harder, shocking me. "You *will* do this, Emelia."

In all my nineteen years, he's never behaved this way. Never hurt me. Never mistreated me in any way. Desperation and rage mingle in his eyes and I have to correct my prior thoughts because he didn't look this scared when Mom died. I've actually never seen him look so terrified.

"You can't make me do this." I try to pull my hand away but he's too strong.

"Do it!" he shouts.

I'm shocked when a heavy hand lands on top of his, nearly covering both our hands, and suddenly Massimo has a gun at Dad's head.

All the blood siphons from my body as I take in the sleek steel barrel of the Glock pressed to Dad's temple. My head spins as my brain attempts to process what I'm truly seeing and I feel like I'm standing on thin ice that's about to crack any second.

Dad stills and his fingers loosen their grip over mine. He gulps and his eyes go as wide as mine feel.

"Emelia, maybe you require some encouragement. I'll fucking do it," Massimo says so casually and effortlessly he could be talking about the weather.

Oh my God... He's serious. He'll do it. He'll kill Dad. He'll kill my father.

Dad goes rigid, frozen with fear in Massimo's arms. Fear that only worsens when the hammer on the gun cocks.

Click-clack.

The sound fills the room and highlights the gravity of what I'm being faced with.

It's a sound that pulses into my soul.

It's a sound I don't think I'll ever forget.

It's a sound that reminds me of the darkness of my world. The world my father spent his life trying to protect me from.

It's here, staring me in the eye in the form of a beautiful devil.

That soulless look in Massimo D'Agostino's eyes is all I need to know that he wouldn't hesitate to pull that trigger and kill my father right in front of me.

"No, please...don't hurt him," I beg. "Please don't kill him."

"Sign the damn document then, Princesca, or you will not like what happens next," he answers.

I'm helpless against his threat. There's no point saying anything more. I have exactly one choice and it doesn't involve walking out of here and getting on that plane to Florence in the morning.

My gaze drops to the contract before me resting on the coffee table. Against the dark polished wood, the cream-colored paper seems to stand out like a light bulb.

With a trembling hand, I secure my grip around the pen and place the tip to the bold line on the contract next to my name where I'm supposed to sign.

Relief washes over me in waves when Massimo lowers the gun, but tears sting my eyes as I sign away my life and my dreams.

"Take her to her room," Massimo commands when I straighten up, shaking.

Someone takes my arm. I don't know who it is because those same tears blur my vision. I move, feeling numb inside, and I can't look at Dad as I leave.

I don't know what the hell trouble he's landed us in. All I'm aware of is instead of looking forward to my dreams, I'm walking to what feels like my destruction.

What else could it be?

I've been sold.

CHAPTER THREE

MASSIMO

I stare after Manni, my head guard, as he takes Emelia away. If I were finished up here, I'd take her to her room myself. Not him.

I already feel my blood boiling watching him touch her. Getting the first touch of what's mine. *The Balesteri princess.*

With her obsidian-colored hair, misty gray eyes, and a body like a lost pin-up model, Emelia Balesteri has been deemed a prize in the underworld since her father showed her off at the Syndicate's charity ball months ago.

She's a prize I now have. A princess who was locked away in a tower governed by her father's controlling hand. And I just moved the princess from one tower to another. The difference about this story is there will be no prince to save her. No one will come to give her freedom. She is the spoils of war, a trophy, and I won't be mistaken for a good man and feel sorry for her.

Beautiful and innocent as she is, Emelia is a piece on the

chess board and taking her from her father was only the beginning of the havoc I intend to wreak in their lives. I'm just getting fucking started with Riccardo Balesteri. The pale-blue-eyed devil who ruined my childhood.

My marriage to Emelia means when she turns twenty-one I get back what once belonged to my family. Balesteri Investments was my family's business. It was started by my *great, great, great*-grandfather decades ago and called D'Agostino Investments until Riccardo stole it from my father, setting off a chain reaction that caused us to lose everything.

That's what we want to do to his ass. Take everything he owns and leave him with nothing. *Destroy* the motherfucker.

When we found out about the shit he was up to I could have suggested demanding the business back, but I wanted to do more damage. That's why I wanted his daughter, because marrying Emelia also meant Riccardo can't make the money he hoped to by marrying her off or selling her to someone else.

Poor girl. I could tell she really had no idea who her father truly is. I'm sure she wouldn't have begged for Riccardo's life if she did.

I knew from the night of the ball there was no way she could know the real Riccardo Balesteri. Like most of the men in the circles we travel in, that was the first time I saw her. Riccardo led her in like an innocent lamb to the slaughter, dressed in black to declare her for sale. It was clear from the excitement on her face that she didn't even know why she was there.

That event was what we call a *Viewing*, a signal to start bidding. He displayed her like a piece of meat for sale, and she's been the talk of the underground since then.

Any compassion I could have felt toward her occurred at that moment, and it ended there.

I turn back to face Riccardo and find the fucker looking straight at me. The question in his eyes is one of shock. Under normal circumstances I'm sure a man who pulled a gun to his head would be dead before they could take their next breath. Not me, though, and the motherfucker knows exactly why I did it. And fuck me, was it ever one hell of a bitch of payback for that stunt he pulled on me at Ma's funeral.

"It's done," that fucktard Bianchi says, cutting into the thick fog of silence that's settled over the room. He applies the Balesteri family seal to the contract, closing the deal.

"Good," Pa says, taking back the lead.

Although I can feel Riccardo's heated gaze on me, I watch Bianchi as he gathers the contract and the other documents with our offer and starts placing them in a large manila envelope.

He's what I call a "yes man." An irritating, spineless piece of shit who does what he's told. Part of the vermin who has worked for Riccardo from way back when.

I stare the asshole down and wonder if he remembers me as a boy. I'm sure he does. He's been looking at me like he remembers me just fine.

Years ago, as he and his company of fuckers came to throw my family out of our home, I stared him down the same as I am now. Back then, he laughed at me and called me a foolish child. I was ten years old. Bianchi is not laughing now. He's shit scared, the same as Riccardo.

Now I'm twenty-nine, and I'm about to take over my father's empire. An empire my father built from the nothing we had.

With the handover of leadership, the repayment of Riccardo's debts will come to me. Unlike the foolish child I was called, I've exacted a well-thought-out plan that's barricaded Riccardo left, right, and center.

The leverage we hold over him will ensure he'll screw himself and everyone with the surname Balesteri if he even breathes the wrong way.

"May I go now?" Bianchi asks and I almost laugh. He looks like he's ready to shit himself.

Riccardo looks even worse for the fact that his beloved lawyer had to ask us permission to leave.

"You may," Pa answers. We don't need a lawyer for what happens next.

It's Syndicate business, and as such will be handled between us. It will be interesting to watch.

I continue to stare at Bianchi, who hurries out of here, scurrying away like the fucking rat he is.

"Leave us," I tell my men, and they follow. The two guards that brought Emelia here leave too, leaving the three of us in the room.

"Back to business," Pa says with a well-earned smug smile.

"How about we head back to my office?" I state motioning through the door we came through with my gun.

Riccardo bares his teeth before he proceeds to walk. Pa and I follow behind.

I left my office door open, so we walk right inside and each take a seat. I put my gun away and give my father the head chair because this next part is all on him.

This part is what you call the true art of war—knowing when to get your enemy exactly where you want him to be and striking not at the point where he's injured, but when you know he walks the line between life and death and only a miracle will save him. That is where Riccardo is, and the fucker knows it.

"You can't just take my voting rights," Riccardo says, trying to keep his tone under control. "They are what tie me to the Syndicate. What kind of member would I be without my rights to vote and make decisions?"

His voting rights are his biggest worry right now. Not Emelia. *Asshole...*

"That is not my concern. I want your voting rights, or the deal is off," Pa answers, and Riccardo just stares back at him, *defeated.*

My father is here with me to secure the very last thing this asshole owns: his voting rights in the Syndicate, the Brotherhood. Like Riccardo, my father is one of the Syndicate members. Voting rights equal power and control. They give control and take away control. This is my father's final act as boss. His final gift to me before he hands over the D'Agostino empire.

Our demand for Riccardo's voting rights was the shocker we dealt just before Emelia walked in. It was why he behaved the way he did with her. Shock and desperation consumed him from the fact that we discovered his secrets. All thanks to my brother, Dominic.

Dominic found out Riccardo was stealing Syndicate money to do business with the Sequina Cartel in Ecuador. The fool took a gamble and used their money, along with virtually all of his, to traffic containers of heroine to Europe. He lost millions when it got seized by the feds and had to turn to us for help. *Us,* his enemies.

He came under the pretense that he needed a business loan. Pa gave it to him and had Dominic check him out when Riccardo couldn't pay us back. It was then we discovered the truth and realized the asshole only came to us because he knew he couldn't turn to anybody else. Maybe he thought he could prey on the lost friendship he and my father once shared.

Seeing the road to destroy him open before us, we seized

the opportunity and made him an offer he'd be a fool to refuse.

The offer was this: his beloved daughter, with her inheritance and the new set of luxury apartments he bought at the start of the year, in exchange for the debt he owed Pa. In addition to that, we wanted his voting rights in exchange for our silence on his crimes to the Syndicate for breaking the creed.

"You will give it to me, or I won't hesitate to inform the Brotherhood of your gross errors. I doubt you want that on your hands."

Terror makes beads of sweat form on Riccardo's upper lip. *Bastardo.* He's an idiot for thinking we, of all people, will let him reason with us. He's lucky. That's what he is. Lucky that we *only* want to destroy him instead of just killing his ass. The motherfucker did the one thing you shouldn't do in our world: *underestimate.* He never thought anybody would discover his secrets.

"You are loving this, aren't you?" Riccardo sneers.

"Yes, I am," Pa answers, short, sweet, and succinct, knowing that Riccardo doesn't want the Syndicate on his ass. I bite back a grin as I watch a smile of victory dance across my father's lips. Power is a beautiful thing. It's so much better when you can taste it and feel it coursing through your veins. Unlike that day at the cemetery, Pa and I are so far from *powerless, useless, or helpless.*

"Giacomo, you people took my daughter," Riccardo reminds Pa.

"And with her comes a return of what was once mine," Pa answers, mimicking his tone. "We're not going over this again, *Riccardo.*"

"It's a serious matter."

"Of course, but one that is no longer up for discussion," Pa adds.

"I don't see how you think it's right to do this to me."

"I don't care what you think is right or wrong. This is the way it's going to be. Decide now. We don't have all fucking night. Shall I make the call now to the Brotherhood? Or will you be handing me what I want?"

Riccardo stares back, fury brimming in his eyes along with fear. The asshole truly thought he was untouchable, but everybody loses sometimes.

Apart from us, the Brotherhood of the Syndicate is made up of two other powerful Italian crime families and two Bratva families. They will not be pleased to hear how Riccardo has been benefiting from their investments for the last ten years and how much he's stolen.

He knows they'll kill him. They'll deal death exactly the way he threatened at Ma's funeral. It would start with him, then they'd kill his daughter, his family, then his friends. Everyone he knows from here and in Italia.

The Syndicate is a secret society of crime families set up to protect wealth and allow its members to flourish in more wealth. Cross them and break the creed, and it means death to all you know. There is no way out.

This selfish fucker, however, is just worried about himself. I know it. He knows we'll kill him too, and we'd be able to without retaliation for all he's done.

Death, however, is too good for him. He did exactly what we wanted. We wanted to watch the asshole fall and crumble. To see his face as he loses everything. It's interesting, though. I thought his daughter might have been his one good thing, but she isn't. Riccardo Balesteri values his money and power. The one good thing in his life was his voting rights in the

Syndicate. The man makes me sick. He's more aggrieved to lose that than selling his daughter.

"What's it going to be, Riccardo?" Pa asks and holds out another contract to him. That one would have the same wording as the one Emelia signed. But it needs to be signed in blood.

"You bastard. You had to take everything," Ricardo says and looks from Pa to me.

I've sat back and minded my place, allowing my father to talk. It's my turn now.

"Be fucking grateful we left you with the roof over your head and the clothes on your back," I answer, and he cuts me a sharp glance.

He won't say anything to me. I can tell he's still shaken from earlier. *Good*. Fucking good. I've been waiting for a long time to find a way to get him, and while I've seen this man several times since my mother's funeral, I've held back and waited patiently for the right time to strike.

"We don't have all night, Riccardo," Pa states in a menacing voice.

I retrieve a pen knife from my desk drawer and hold it out to Riccardo.

Grudgingly, he takes it and looks over the contract. A smile dances on my lips when he cuts the tip of his thumb and blood drips on to the dotted line.

"There. You have it all now." He looks at me. "*You* have it all."

"I do, and you have nothing," I answer. "It will be most interesting to see what happens next. Definitely interesting to see what happens when I marry your daughter, ruining your damn plans."

Boy, did this bastard ever have his fair share of plans for his daughter. I can just imagine how many bids he must have gotten for her at the ball, and since then too. The minute I saw her, I knew the fucker wanted to marry her off and secure some business arrangement with a marriage.

It all made sense when we found out what he was up to with the Syndicate and the trouble he was in as a result of all the money he lost.

"You will not get away with this," he warns. I'm amazed he has the balls to say that to me.

I lean forward and hold his gaze. "I think I already have." I reach for the contract and hand it to Pa, who takes it gladly.

As I look at this devil before me, I think back to the day at the cemetery when I vowed vengeance. This is only the beginning.

He's broke, has no daughter to secure any form of business marriage, no assets to sell, and Emelia's inheritance will come to me in a few years' time. Without his voting rights and with the dire financial situation he's in, he's useless as shit. That's one sure way to get thrown out of the Syndicate.

The Syndicate is a dream you hope to happen upon. From what we've predicted from his losses, Riccardo won't be able to rebuild. Once it's clear his business is going under, he'll be useless to them. What we want is for them to uninitiate him.

That is the ultimate goal. Riccardo isn't stupid. He'll know that's what we're gearing toward. Just like he did to Pa when we were younger. That was the start of how we lost everything and the hard life that followed. Pa was uninitiated after the Syndicate deemed him no longer useful.

An eye for an eye, a tooth for a fucking tooth. Once the Syndicate kicks his ass out Riccardo will have nothing, and he'll be nothing.

Pa clears his throat. "Pleasure doing business with you, Riccardo," Pa says. "I will contact the Brotherhood and make them aware of what's happening in terms of your rights. You may go now."

Ricardo stares back knowing he doesn't have a leg to stand on. He rises to his feet and leaves.

"We should have taken his home as well," I state as soon as the door closes.

"No, we have to leave him with a base so we can watch his next moves," Pa answers. "Home is where the heart is, even for those with dark souls. He'll be plotting his next moves there."

"Yes, I imagine so," I agree. I just wanted to truly leave him in the shit, put him on the roadside with a paper bag if I could. It still wouldn't be enough.

"He will try things. We've crippled him in a big way, but don't underestimate him."

"I won't."

Pa looks at me and pride swells in his eyes. To see that in a man like him for me is a massive accomplishment. My father is the kind of man who went through hell and back. He rules with an iron fist that shows the extent of his power. I've seen him at his lowest, cut down like grass, and at his highest. That is where he is now. A proud mafia boss; a powerful leader in the business world and the Syndicate.

I'm honored to fill his shoes. The fact that he picked me over Andreas is an honor I will take to my grave, bad as I feel about being picked to lead the famiglia over my older brother.

"You're ready to be boss. You acted like one today," he says.

I dip my head in reverence at his words. "My thanks to you, Father."

"I'll finish the asset transfer later today in prep for the ceremony. Then there's the Syndicate meetings. I will initiate you and spend the next few months training you. Then that will be it."

That will be it. And I will form a new leadership with my brothers.

"Thank you."

Pa rests his hand on my shoulder and nods. "Business discussion over. Do not keep your woman waiting."

"No, I won't."

His face hardens, and I know he has no compassion when it comes to Emelia.

"Make sure she knows who is boss now. Make sure she knows who she belongs to."

Ruthless. That's what he wants me to be.

I have no problem with that.

I have no problem with showing Emelia Balesteri who she belongs to. My fucking cock has been hard for her since I first saw her at the stupid ball.

I'll have no problem breaking my new toy in.

CHAPTER FOUR

EMELIA

True fear in its purest form hit me the minute I stepped in this room.

The men marched me up a wide set of stairs and up to the first floor, where we carried on to the room I'm in now. They switched on the lights then left me.

An elderly woman came in with a tray of sandwiches moments after I was dropped off. Although she said nothing to me I could tell she was curious.

Instead of eating the sandwiches like I'm sure she hoped, I sunk to the floor with my back against the wall and allowed myself to cry.

That was roughly half an hour ago, but it feels like forever. I'm not sure which is worse—being left to my thoughts by myself or being around these people. I think being left alone might be the winner because right now I'm so scared. Terrified, more like, and I'm just waiting to see what's going to happen next.

The room I'm in is massive; the floor is hardwood, has a four-poster bed, mahogany furniture, and an entire wall made of glass that has a stunning view of the sea and the rock formations against the beach. Off in the distance I can see a bigger sailboat. It's massive and quite unlike the ones I saw earlier. This one has white sails, and even from here I can see it's customized with a grand design that only a person who loves sailing would have. It screams of wealth. *Money and power*. Money and power enough to buy a person.

Within the glow of the silver moonlight everything looks like I'm glimpsing into a fairytale.

But this is far from anything of the sort. I feel more like I'm trapped in a Tim Burton film, stuck in a nightmare I can't escape.

I'm scared and I feel sick, like I'm going to throw up everything I ever ate in my life.

Whenever I was scared, I used to run to Jacob, or at least call him. Tonight, I can't do either. I can't leave this place, and I can't call anyone for help. My bag was the first thing to get taken. Inside was my phone.

The last time I felt this shaken was when Mom was sick and we knew there was nothing we could do for her. We knew she was going to die. It was Jacob who was there for me, because Dad dealt with his grief by shunning everyone. Including me. I think of Jacob and know that he will be worried. He will call me and get no answer, then worry some more. I'll bet, too, that he'll go to the house in the morning to check, just to be sure I'm okay.

Will Dad tell him what happened to me? I doubt it. Jacob would go crazy if he knew, and it would not be good for him if he did that.

There's a side to my father that I've caught glimpses of in the past but didn't see in full bloom until tonight as he squeezed my hand like he would break it if I disobeyed. I would never want him to hurt Jacob, or worse, for Jacob to try to rescue me. He's the kind of friend who would do that.

Not even a handful of hours ago my thoughts were consumed with going to Florence. Now, my dream is just that: a dream. A thing my heart wants. I have to push that all aside to think about what is happening to me here and now.

The reality of the situation is this: I'm supposed to marry and live with Massimo D'Agostino for the rest of my life. And I'm just supposed to accept that?

How?

I can't believe Dad would do this to me.

And realistically, what now? I'm in this bedroom. Is it Massimo's? It must be. Why would they take me to a guestroom if I belong to him? This room must be his.

No one spoke to me at all. No one said anything, not to me or each other.

They just deposited me here like the thing I am and left.

What will happen when he gets back? Will he take my virginity? Would he care that I'm a virgin?

Men like him don't care. They take. I'll be here for sex.

I won't be stupid enough to think Massimo will be mine too. Like Dad, he'll have his women.

Dad doesn't know I knew about his affairs. I don't even think he knew Mom knew. At least, to my knowledge, he didn't appear to be seeing anybody while Mom was sick.

I'm certain Massimo has his host of women. A man who looks like him definitely would.

I never wanted my life to turn out like this. When I married, I always hoped it would be for love. This is complete shit.

The bedroom door handle turns, and I nearly jump out of

my skin. The door swings open and there he is, standing in the hollow of the doorframe gazing at me.

My breath hitches in my throat and my heart races the longer he stares. Those piercing eyes seem brighter against his olive skin.

Terrified, I stand as he walks in and closes the door behind him.

I find myself wanting to look away, but at the same time his striking appearance commands my attention and rivets my gaze to him, making it difficult for me to focus. I think I'd find this easier if he weren't so ridiculously gorgeous. He's the kind of man who you would naturally stare at.

Paralyzed under the weight of his watchful eyes and the trepidation of what he's going to do to me makes me want to run. Run far away and never look back.

He gets closer but stops a few paces away, still towering over me. The scent of his aftershave fills my nose and I grit my teeth.

"There's a bed for you to lie on. You don't have to take to the floor," he says, breaking the silence.

Unsure of what to say, I decide not to answer.

"Unless you like the floor," he adds. His voice deepens as it drops, and my nerves scatter when he looks me over from head to toe, assessing me.

He feels like a giant next to me. He's about six foot four while I'm five two.

"This isn't right," I rasp. My voice sounds weak and weary, foreign to my ears. I don't sound like the strong woman my mother raised me to be. I don't sound like the woman I was earlier this morning when I woke and told myself I was going to conquer the world and be the best version of myself I could be.

"What?" The corners of his lips turn up into a smooth smile, revealing perfect white teeth.

Of course, his smile is also beautiful and disarming. Maybe that's what he uses to intimidate people.

"You can't do this. You can't have me," I answer, trying to steady my heart so it doesn't leap out of my chest.

"The piece of paper we signed says different, Princesca."

Princesca... He called me that earlier.

If he means that word in relation to me being a spoiled brat, he's wrong. I'm not that. I never have been. Yes, I may have never wanted for anything in my life, but that doesn't mean I was given everything just because I wanted it.

"You don't know me," I retort.

"I don't need to."

"You're right, you don't need to know me to know this is wrong. There must be some other way my father can pay you back. Let me go." I'm proud of myself for the little speech, but the pride fades when a deep chuckle rumbles within the walls of his chest.

"I'm the one the debt is owed. I choose how I want to be paid. I choose what I want to take."

"So, you picked me?" I give him an incredulous glare. "Why the hell would you pick me?"

As soon as the words fall from my lips, I feel completely stupid. I'm my father's heir. That's answer enough. My inheritance in the business alone is worth several million. Add the assets that fall part of it and I'm actually worth a fortune. That contract stipulated Massimo would get everything. Every single thing attached to my name.

"My dear Princesca, you really are living in the dark." He smirks, revealing the dimple in his left cheek.

"There must be some other way."

"I'm sure there is, except I've done exactly what I wanted to do," he answers.

My heart squeezes. It feels like a rug has been pulled from beneath me. This is the man I'm supposed to marry. While he looks like a fairytale prince, he's not.

My lips part, but I'm at a loss for words.

"So...you see, it can't be any other way, Emelia Balesteri. I marry you, and I get everything you own. You belong to me, and everything you have and will get belongs to me too."

"It's wrong. You must know that."

"Stop it," he orders. His smile fades. That cool, calm demeanor returns, and I realize then that this is his dangerous side.

"Stop what?"

"Stop trying to prey on my good side. I don't have one."

I tremble now as his gaze bores into me. He's telling me things I should know, but mostly he's saying I have no hope.

"Don't you have a heart?" My voice has reverted to the weak tone it took when I first spoke as I make one final attempt to reach whatever I see in him that might resemble something human.

"No," he answers. "I have no heart, Princesca."

"This has nothing to do with me. I don't know you."

"Massimo D'Agostino, age twenty-nine, soon-to-be owner of D'Agostinos Inc. Last check came up clean." He smirks, and my soul quivers. "We will be married in one month's time. You will live here, and that is all you need to know."

"You think that's enough," I lash back.

"It's enough because I say so. Enough nitty-gritty. I think I've given you enough answers to your questions. Now, take your clothes off."

CHAPTER FIVE

EMELIA

I can't control the whimper of shock that falls from my lips.

"No..." I choke out, shaking my head.

"Yes. I want to get a look at what's mine."

Oh my God. This is it. He's going to rape me, and there's not a damn thing I can do about it.

My survival instinct kicks in and I try to bolt past him, but one large hand clamps down on my wrist and brings me right back to where I was.

"Please, no..." I plead.

"Emelia, if you want to get along here you will obey me, or life will be very difficult for you."

"Obey you? Who do you think you are?" I must have some death wish asking him such a question. I'm not thinking straight. Who could in this nightmare?

"Don't make me answer that or repeat myself," he hisses. "Take your clothes off."

My God... he's serious. I'm going to have to do this. *Obey.*

What will happen to me if I don't? What is worse? To be willing and allow him to take me and do whatever he wants to me, or for him to take it violently?

He releases me, and the hardened gaze he gives me now tells me not to push him. If I do... I don't know what he'll do to me.

I can't believe I'm even having these thoughts. His eyes become turbulent, like a tempestuous sea, as his gaze rakes boldly over me like lust-filled invisible fingers.

Swallowing hard, I will myself to do this.

With trembling hands, I move the tiny strap of my summer dress down my left shoulder, then my right. I curse myself for choosing to wear this stupid dress because it made me look cute. It's also very easy to take off. The dress drifts to my feet the moment I slip off the second strap.

I'm in my bra and panties now. Those and my little ballerina pumps. That's all I'm wearing.

He gives me a nod, signaling for me to take those off too.

"All of it," he states, and his jaw tightens.

Which should I start with? My bra or my panties? While I decide, I bend and slip off my shoes...*slowly*. One, then the other.

No one has ever seen me naked. Not even this much. Nobody, not even my doctors.

I straighten and note the amused look on his handsome face. Amused at me for taking my shoes off and the slowness in which I did it. My hands shake as I reach up to the little butterfly clasp holding my bra together, and I fumble to get it undone. It's not actually that hard to undo. I just can't get my hands to work. My breath catches when the clip snaps open, and I wince when the heft of my breasts fall out.

I can't look at him. The hot blush of humiliation that sweeps through me leaves me breathless and lightheaded. I'm frightened and ashamed. I'm terrified and angry at what I'm being forced to do.

I take off my bra, and it drifts to the floor, joining my dress. My breasts bobble when I bend to push my panties down my legs. Once they're down, I step out of them and steel my spine, willing myself to be strong.

I keep my gaze ahead, staring at the white of his shirt, avoiding his eyes.

He reaches out and lifts my chin, guiding my gaze back to his. The brush of his fingers on my skin sends a shiver through me. A shiver of sexual heat that I hate. I shouldn't feel anything for this man. Definitely not anything sexual. No part of what he does next will be with my permission. Nothing. Nothing at all.

He holds my gaze and releases me, but not before brushing his fingers along my neck. Then slowly, slowly he walks around me, circling me the way a predator would its prey. His eyes have a lean, hungry look that grows hungrier, *greedier* with each passing second.

They touch me everywhere. My head, my chest, my stomach, right down to the smooth mound of my sex, where he lingers before his gaze flicks right back up to meet mine.

"I can see what the talk is all about now," he comments, but I don't know what he means. "*Beautiful...*" he adds, and my traitorous pussy clenches with need.

I've never had a man look at me the way he is. If they have, I wouldn't have seen them because they would have been scared of my father. I've also never had a man call me beautiful, either, for the same reason. Not even Jacob.

"Take your hair down for me," he adds.

I pull the band from my ponytail. As soon as I do, my long black locks tumble down my shoulders and gather at the small of my back.

The desire in his eyes is a tell that he's ready to strike. Fear lances through me like a bolt of lightning.

He takes one step closer, and I step back. One more step, and I'm completely pressed up against the wall. I wasn't far from it in the first place.

He places a hand right by my shoulder, blocking me in so I can't move. I can't stop shaking. The terror comes from deep inside. Deep inside my soul. I can't control it.

Massimo lowers his head until he's a breath away and smells my hair. Then he reaches down to touch a lock. His fingers brush over my nipples, making them hard. The contact makes arousal ripple through me, and my throat goes dry.

Allowing the ends of my hair to curl around his thumb, he watches, fascinated. Then, when he presses his hand to the flat of my stomach, I know this is it. He's going to strike. I just don't know if I'll survive it.

"Please...not this way. I've never..." I wince, hoping he won't laugh at me and make me feel worse.

"*Never*... Never what, Princesca?" he asks. His warm breath tickles my nose.

"I've never...been with a man."

At the declaration, the devilish smile that lights up his face scares me. It's unlike the one he gave me before. It holds an air of victory, like he just struck the jackpot.

"Fucking hell. I definitely did well," he breathes out and chuckles. "Are you on the pill, Princesca? I like to fuck bareback."

My mouth opens, but I can't speak. I'm not used to people talking to me like that. His dirty mouth shocks me but at the same time commands a response from my body in a way I don't like.

"Answer me," he pushes.

"Yes," I reply quickly. I take the pill for my skin. When my doctor prescribed them, I never even thought about sex.

"Good girl. Make sure you take them."

When the seriousness returns to his face, he releases my hair and runs his thick finger over the flat plane of my stomach, never taking his eyes off me. Pressing into the wall, I try to hold myself up to keep from falling over as he traces the line from my belly up to the deep valley of my cleavage. His fingers flutter lightly over the swells of my breasts then linger on my left nipple. It pebbles at his touch. Wetness gathers deep in my pussy. He smiles down at me like he knows. Then it occurs to me that maybe he does.

He knows his touch is arousing me. I gulp and fight back tears when he leans even closer and nips the lobe of my ear. It weakens me, and for a moment I give in and allow the arousal to claw through me. My breath comes out in a rasp as I try to catch it.

His fingers return to my stomach, then down he goes. Down, down until his hand cups my sex and his fingers slide over the smooth mound of my pussy.

I gasp when he slides a finger into my virgin passage and starts pushing in and out.

He moves back to my ear and whispers, "Wow, your pussy is so tight. I've never fucked a virgin before. I'm definitely going to enjoy you. You feel so good, Princesca. I can't wait to feel you around my cock."

My cheeks burn at his dirty words set to control my arousal and encourage my attraction to him. Then my throat tightens so much I think I might faint from the lack of air when he stares down at my pussy and starts pumping in and out *faster*.

The smile fades from his lips, and his handsome face takes

on that hard edge again, hardening as he finger-fucks me into the wall.

Arousal hits me, making me hotter. I moan with each thrust, embarrassed and ashamed that my body is responding to him in such a way. When a jolt of pleasure rockets through me, I lose control completely.

My hands leave the wall and grasp his shirt.

He gives me a wide grin, and I'm shocked when he bends his head to suck my left breast. He starts sucking hard and speeds his movements inside my pussy. Suddenly, pleasure bursts through me. I try to fight it, try to hide it, try to will the sounds of ecstasy away from my lips, but I can't.

I come. Hard. As I come, I moan so loud I can't believe the sound escapes between my lips. Wetness gushes from my pussy onto his fingers, and it's only then that he stops pumping and sucking.

Straightening up, he pulls his finger out of me and holds it up for me to see the glistening juice.

I'm shocked further when he places it in his mouth and licks it off.

The breath leaves me when he crouches down, pulls my hips to his face, and nuzzles his face between my thighs so he can thrust his tongue up into my passage. Arousal sparks inside my pussy again as he laps up the wetness that's gathered between my legs.

Shame fills me as I watch the gorgeous man who just bought me eat me out. I'm shocked and enraged at myself when my traitorous side admits that I like what he's doing to me.

When he stands up, he wipes his mouth with the back of his hand. A lock of his jet-black hair falls over his eye.

My gaze drops to the distinct bulge of his cock pressing against his pants, and I gulp back the fear.

"Well, isn't this interesting," he taunts. "Hope you liked the taster, Princesca. Next time will be even better."

"Next...time?" I mutter, my voice barely audible. I don't know if I should be relieved that it seems like he might not rape me, or worry over next time.

"Next time... I'm not that kind of monster, sweet, innocent Emelia. I'm not going to fuck you tonight," he says, lifting my chin and sliding his hand down my throat. "I won't take the cherry between your legs tonight. When I do, you'll give it to me willingly. You'll want me to take it."

Fury grips my insides at his confidence. I hate that he seems so sure of himself. He doesn't know me.

"No, I won't. I won't give you anything," I snap back.

He tightens his grip on my neck, widens his smile and nods with the same surety. "Oh, you will. You know why?"

I'm curious. "Why?"

"Because you already want to. Fear and arousal. I can smell it, even now. I smelled it before I made you come. You wanted me at 'hello'." He lets me go. I sink into the wall, my lips parted. "It's okay. I wanted you too."

He winks at me before he turns and walks away. I watch him as he leaves and the door clicks shut. A second later, a key rattles inside the keyhole. I'm locked in.

It takes a moment before I realize I'm not breathing, and the smoke clears from my mind.

This is crazy. I don't want him. I can't. He's the enemy. My enemy. I can't allow myself to be used this way.

There's only one thing I can do.

Escape.

I have to try.

CHAPTER SIX

MASSIMO

I can't remember the last time I jerked off.

It was so long ago, the memory of when it might have happened is a complete blur. And I'm pretty sure I was drunk.

The minute I left Emelia standing against the bedroom wall, naked and beautiful, aroused again for me, I knew the only release I'd have tonight would be in my shower.

Either that or head to Renovatio, my strip club, to pick up a whore for the night. I wouldn't be able to do that though. I'd gone too far with the obsidian-haired beauty to want anybody else. I'm used to getting what I want, and what I want is her. My cock wants to be inside her tight, wet cunt.

I lie down in my bed and rest my head on the stack of pillows, gazing up at the skylight. Licking over my lips, I smile. The taste of her is still in my mouth. It's a taste I savor. When that sweet nectar flowed from her pretty pussy into my mouth, all I knew was I needed more.

Fucking hell, I've been fascinated since this whole idea to marry her came about. At the ball, I thought she was another stuck-up princess, but this girl is far from that. There's a fire inside her that captivates me. It makes her think she can defy me. Tell *me* no? I can't recall the last time a woman uttered that word to me. The fact that it came from a powerless, defenseless being like her in her perfect nakedness is pure arousal.

I can see I'm going to be quite amused in this business venture.

Right now, I'm the happiest motherfucker. I have my enemy's daughter a captive in my house, and I'm on the precipice of watching Riccardo lose everything.

What must the princess be doing now?

I can just imagine my beautiful virgin Princesca still pressed up against the wall, mortified at what I did to her. I'll bet, with the way *Daddy Dearest* runs things, what I did to her was the most she's ever done sexually.

I had her checked out and learned that she has a guy for a best friend. Unusual, given who her father is, even if the guy's father works for him. Everything that man does is tactics. *Everything.* And I'm willing to bet that little trip to Italy she thought she was going to take was tactics too. I just don't know in what way. I didn't know about that until yesterday. That was one reason why we had to move fast. Riccardo kept that hushed.

Unbeknown to the princess, the only thing that separates our rooms is a passage. Hers is one of my guest rooms. I had the place prepped yesterday when Pa and I decided on what we were going to do. We'd been waiting for a few more details from Dominic before we enacted our plan.

My little brother can find dirt on anybody. Even when they think they don't have dirt, Dominic can find shit to use against a person. This time, he hit the motherload.

I have a plan for all my brothers, if they will join me. I know my ascension to leader has caused a stir. Before I got home, I got a text from Pa letting me know all transactions have been completed and transferred to my name. My brothers would have been alerted too. I wonder what they all think now.

My ownership of Emelia, too, might cause another stir. We were all at that ball that night when Riccardo presented her to the world. I know it wouldn't have just been me who liked her and wanted her. I just got to have her because I'm boss now.

Now, she's in my house, and I want to fuck her.

I'll wait, though. I meant what I said. I'm not that kind of monster. No matter how ruthless and heartless I am, I wouldn't force myself on a woman. I like to fuck, and my woman must want me as much as I want her. Even if we just met, that connection has to be there.

At my club, the women are always willing to give me whatever I want. I have my pickings. I don't have to try. The fiery beauty in my home, however, has given me a thirst for more of her. I got my taste, and I want more. *More* I will have, and like I said to her, she'll give me what I want. My cock hardens at the thought of breaking her in.

Attraction is there in abundance. I felt that the moment our eyes first locked. What I never expected was to be so taken with my enemy's daughter, like the call of a siren to a poor bastard sailor who's lost his way.

Desire and chemistry are what sparked tonight between us.

She felt it too. I know she did. I like that she's fighting it. I like a challenge.

I want her to accept in mind, body, and soul that she belongs to me.

On that note, I fall asleep.

When I wake, I resist the urge to see her. I'll get my maids to tend to her today and allow her to get used to being here. I won't let her out of her room yet though. Not just yet.

I grab breakfast and fire off a text to my brothers, asking them to meet me at the club in an hour. It's not open for business yet, but that's where we meet and hang out. I like to keep my business meetings at the D'Agostinos Inc. offices, but there are some meetings I hold at the club too. Mostly the ones for my rackets I like to keep under wraps.

I haven't seen all my brothers together since early last week when the shit about Riccardo started to come together. We had a meeting at the office with Pa, where he announced that he wanted to wrap up the transfer as soon as possible. That was when I noticed the tension again amongst my brothers. It rubs me the wrong way to think they might not want me to be in charge. Today when I meet them, I'll be the official boss on paper.

Tristan is already there when I arrive. He's playing pool in the lounge with a Cuban cigar slinked to the corner of his mouth.

My spirits lift when I see him. He sets the cigar down on the ashtray and a smile spreads across his face.

He meets me halfway with an outstretched hand and a curt nod.

"Morning, Boss," he says.

I smile. "Hello, brother," I answer.

I shake his hand, but he pulls me in for a hug. It's a rare thing amongst us, only done on special occasions. I'm glad he seems on board. Of all my brothers, I'm closest to him.

Perhaps it's because we're only a year apart. Andreas is two years older than me, and Dominic is three years younger than me. We're also very similar. We even look so much alike we could be twins.

"You look different, like a man in charge," he notes with a nod. "Or like a man who's taken charge of his woman." Mischief speckles his eyes. I chuckle knowing he must be curious to hear what happened last night.

"Not yet," I confess.

He shifts his weight from one side to the other and stares at me. "You're kidding. I purposely didn't message last night because I thought you'd be busy with your new toy. I know I would have been."

"Careful, I might think you're after my wife-to-be," I joke.

He rolls his eyes. "You fucker, you know every man in sight is going to be after your wife-to-be."

"Better not fucking be. They'll know better than to look at what's mine."

I'm possessive, and I don't care who I piss off. What's mine is mine. I know there's truth in his words though.

"Relax, I'm just teasing. In regard to me, I mean. Wouldn't do shit like that to you. Seriously, though, you did nothing with her?" He gives me an incredulous glare.

"No, didn't do shit. Virgin."

Now his mouth drops.

"Fuck, you're kidding. I'm not surprised, but still."

"Yeah."

"Not waiting for the wedding night, are you?" He quirks a brow.

"Fuck no."

He nods. "Good. How did it go with Riccardo? Did you make the bastard suffer?"

"I would say so. I would definitely say so."

"I have the men on watch."

I reach out and give him a pat on his shoulder. That's what he's in charge of. He oversees the soldiers and associates, so we keep things in line and under control.

I glance at the door as it opens. Dominic comes in carrying a tray of coffee from Starbucks. He also holds a pastry bag.

Dominic chuckles when he sees us. "Sorry I'm late," he states. "*Boss.*"

Good. He seems on board too.

"You know I won't beat your ass for lateness yet." I smirk.

"Don't worry, master. I thought I'd appease you with the best coffee in the world."

"You prick, you just wanted to grab some for yourself," Tristan scolds him.

"Yeah," Dominic confesses with a laugh.

I shake my head at him. When he reaches us, he sets down the coffee and the pastry bag on the little table. Instead of hugging me, he bumps his fist with mine and takes out a plastic container from the pastry bag. It has a slice of carrot cake inside it.

I press my lips together knowing what it means. Ma used to make carrot cake when we had something to celebrate.

"Thought you might like this. It almost tastes like hers," Dominic says. "*Almost.*"

I take it. "Thank you. I appreciate it, little brother."

Now he hugs me.

"Great, we're like a bunch of pussies gathering over coffee and cake," Tristan teases and plops himself down on the sofa.

"Hey, it's a rare day. Alright?" Dominic frowns and leans against the edge of the pool table.

I glance toward the door in anticipation, hoping Andreas

will come in next. Since he's never late, I'm inclined to assume he's not coming.

Seeing my sudden discomfort, Tristan and Dominic exchange glances.

"Any of you hear from Andreas?" I ask.

"Nah..." Tristan replies, sitting forward and resting his elbows on his knees.

"Maybe he's just running behind," Dominic states.

"Or he's not coming," Tristan intones and I cut him a sharp glance. "Come on, man, when is he ever late? Fucking never."

Dominic looks uncomfortable. He reaches for his cup of coffee and starts sipping.

"I guess I'll start, then. This was kind of unofficial. I just... wanted to meet with you and update you." I assume business mode, although I'm disappointed Andreas isn't here.

Disappointed and pissed. Unofficial or not, I'm boss, and if I've called a meeting, he needs to be here. I guess I really was right about the stir and tension. He's not happy I'm boss.

"You changing things up?" Tristan asks, giving me a curious but hopeful stare.

"Yeah, I am. *Everything*."

Dominic continues to sip on his drink but looks as curious as Tristan.

"Like what?"

"I'm splitting the company and the assets four ways," I answer. His skin goes pale. Dominic almost chokes but rights himself and widens his eyes.

"*What?*" he gasps, choking.

The two stare on in the shock I expected because we're all greedy mobsters at the end of the day. The only man I know who splits up his wealth is my old friend, a boss in Chicago called Claudius Morientz. As a result, he has a crew of his men who are loyal to him to the death. I want that here for us. I figured L.A. could learn a thing or two from Chicago. I also figured it should work better here because we're already brothers and we're close. At least that's what I thought.

"Jesus, Massimo," Tristan rasps. "Do you know what you're saying? Do you know how much the empire is worth?"

"I know. But...your loyalty is worth more to me."

It's been four months since Pa announced that he'd chosen me to take the lead. That came about after my grandfather's death. Pa said whenever that happened, it would signal the time to set up a new structure and he would return to Sicily. That's his plan.

Any of the four of us could have led the empire, but the competition was down to me and Andreas. Pa has been training me for the last few months and showing me the ropes. The next few months will be about the Syndicate.

It took Pa five years to find a new niche of business, and when he did, he hit it big. He went into the oil and gas industry. He went the legit route and set up an empire to rival every other. There's not a man alive who doesn't know the D'Agostino brand. The company and all that we own are worth billions.

Tristan and Dominic both look at each other and then to me.

"You are a better man than I give you credit for, Massimo D'Agostino," Tristan says. "You already had my loyalty, brother."

I dip my head in appreciation.

"And mine," Dominic adds. "You don't have to do this. You earned it. It was clear from way back that you would be the best option to take the lead after Pa. I don't want you to think you have to give us anything for what we should give you naturally."

"My thanks to you," I say. "The empire belongs to all of us. It's mine, and I want it to be yours too. I'll get the lawyers to draw up the ownership documents stating exactly that."

I have a feeling that was Pa's intention. That's another reason why he gave it all to me. He knew I would do this. We all work for the family business, and we each have our own side-business ventures, but at the end of the day, legacy is legacy. That is what D'Agostinos Inc. is.

"Thank you," Tristan says.

"I thank you too," Dominic adds.

"You're both welcome. I guess that leads us to the next matter of what we'll be as a structure." Pa never had the traditional hierarchy set up. He made us all capos. He was boss, and Grandfather his consigliere. I want to do something slightly different.

"Fuck, I've never seen you look so serious." Dominic chuckles.

"It's time to be serious," I answer. "I want Tristan and Andreas to both be underboss, and I want you to be my consigliere." I look at them both.

Now they're smiling.

"Fuck yeah." Tristan muses and grabs a cigar from the humidor. He lights up and nods his satisfaction. "I like that. I'm definitely in."

"And me, you trust me that much?" Dominic asks, pointing to himself.

That's a no-brainer question for me. "You know I do. There's not a damn thing that you can't find. Not a damn thing you can't do. You wouldn't lead me into shit, and right now I need a clear mind. I want to focus on the Syndicate, and I don't know how they'll react when they find out I have so much power."

I've been worried about that. They don't believe in having

a leader. No one is above the other. They don't want to make mistakes of the past, like some of the other syndicates. We're a six-family syndicate. Instead of having one person lead the group, each family has a leader to represent the family.

Five years ago, when D'Agostinos Inc. was declared a Fortune 500 company, Pa was approached by the Syndicate to rejoin them.

It's bad enough to be new in the sense of being re-affiliated with them for the last five years, and me personally being new, but I'll also be the youngest member there. Having the voting rights of two leaders is going to be a big deal. They won't like it.

"They're a bunch of old fucktards who need a good shakeup. You can't worry about them," Tristan says.

"I'm not. Not like that. It is what it is, and they'll have to deal with it. What I want is for them to uninitiate Riccardo. I want to focus on that. That's why I need to keep things tight with business."

I look at Tristan. Although I've chosen Dominic as my consigliere, I'll need Tristan for this next part of the plan as additional muscle. Traditionally, the leader of the family is allowed to choose an accompanying member who will attend all Syndicate meetings with him. I'm going to choose Tristan as that person for me and that will automatically make him my second in command.

"You,"—I motion to Tristan—"I'm choosing you to join the Syndicate with me."

"Me?" Tristan looks worried.

"Yes. You. It has to be you, Tristan." *In case something happens to me.* I always have to be mindful of danger. I look back at Dominic and know he already understands my drift. "Dominic, you keep our secrets, and you make shit happen. We're entering a new era. Things have to be different."

"I hear you," Dominic agrees.

"Andreas is not going to be happy about that. He'll wonder why you didn't choose him," Tristan states. He knows, too, that above everything, the Syndicate comes first. If shit happens to me, he'll become boss due to his link to the Syndicate.

"Tristan, don't." Dominic scowls at him.

"Fuck you, what do you mean by don't?" He raises his shoulders into a shrug. "I'm just saying what we're all thinking. If I were wrong, he'd be here, right?"

Someone clears their throat from across the room, and we all look to see Andreas standing by the door. He's holding a bottle of wine.

I straighten up, and while I'm happy to see him, I get that vibe that he's not exactly thrilled.

"I'm here," Andreas says. He walks to me and smiles.

His eyes are more like Ma's. They're ice blue while the rest of us have a darker shade. To me it makes it easier to see when something's off with him. Like I can now.

"Sorry I'm late, *Boss*." He gives me a smile.

"That's okay."

"Why are you late?" Tristan challenges.

Andreas snaps his head around and glares at him. "I was occupied, fucking two waitresses I picked up at the bar last night. I saw the message late. Do you want more details?"

"No thanks." Tristan grimaces.

"This is for you." Andreas hands me the bottle of wine.

"Thank you," I answer, taking it. He then holds out his hand and I shake it.

"Well done. I heard the part about you choosing Tristan to join you in the Syndicate, and yes...I am wondering why you didn't choose me."

I clench my jaw. "Because you're my second underboss, and I need you to focus on D'Agostino. That's why."

It's also because if I were to place my trust in anybody, it would be Tristan. Although, Andreas is what you call ruthless and heartless. He'd make a good boss, a great leader. He's exactly like me. It just comes down to trust, and he knows it.

He nods, and the corners of his lips curl into a smile.

"I understand, and my thanks to you."

My phone rings and I reach into my back pocket to answer it. It's Manni. I always take his calls, and I'll definitely take this because some shit could have happened at home with the princess.

"Yes?" I say into the phone.

"Hey, Boss, you're not gonna like this. They found Pierbo dead by the docks this morning. They said it was suicide. He hung himself." *Suicide.* My breath stills at that word like it always does. And like always, I think of Ma.

Pierbo was one of our enforcers tracking Riccardo's activities. It was only yesterday that I spoke to him. He worked solid with Dominic to gather intel. It was he who found out that Riccardo was mixed up with the cartel. Dominic did the rest of the digging. This is suspicious as fuck.

"You sure it was suicide?" I have to ask. In our world, people can make shit look any way they like. I have the attention of my brothers at the mention of death.

"Hung himself. And there was a note," Manni replies. "Sorry, Boss. I'll let you know more if I get anything else."

"Okay."

He hangs up, and I look back to my brothers.

Something's not right... Something's fishy as fuck. Pierbo was supposed to see me later. He said he had something he wanted to talk to me about in person.

"Who's dead?" Tristan asks.

"Pierbo. That was Manni. He said Pierbo killed himself."

The guys exchange worried glances.

"Really?" Dominic asks. I nod, but I don't believe it.

I'm so sick of having that feeling. Just like with Ma. I still don't believe it.

On this occasion, however, I'm going to check it out.

Although nobody can easily get to one of our enforcers, I wouldn't put it past Riccardo to start his retaliation sooner than we anticipated.

Fucker.

CHAPTER SEVEN

EMELIA

I knew I was going to feel like shit from the minute the sun came up.

I'm on the floor again. This time, I'm right by the window. In the gap where it meets the door to the en suite bathroom.

I've been trying to distract myself with the scenery before me, watching the waves crash against the shoreline of the golden beach. The scene has been my one companion. Either stare at it or go insane.

Stare at it or allow myself to slip away into misery at how fucked up this all is.

There's no clock in here, but I can tell it must be late morning.

The flight I would have been on to Florence has long left without me.

It's funny. When I imagined myself going, I could see myself at the Accademia, but I couldn't see myself getting on the plane. It wasn't part of the vision. It was missing. Maybe it's foolish to think of things like that, but it happened, right?

I never got on the plane. I'm here, and as the realization that that plane took off this morning without me onboard hit, I truly accepted that this nightmare was going to be my new hell.

I keep going over everything in my mind and wondering if Dad never saw something like this coming. How could he owe so much money? What the hell happened? *How* did it happen?

Then there was last night. I couldn't be more embarrassed at the way I behaved while Massimo touched me. I came. I *came* on his fingers, and I found myself savoring his tongue licking my clit. Although I did nothing with him, I felt like a slut. I couldn't even deny that I enjoyed it. The evidence was there in my moans, and the devil lapped up my flow and my dignity.

Shit. It's all fucking shit. And what will happen later?

He promised *next time*.

I glanced at the little tray of food that sat there on the table when I woke up. I assumed he brought it in. I haven't touched it. I don't want anything. I can't eat until I come up with a sound plan of how I'm going to leave this place. The beach is close, but I won't be able to get to it from here. There's a window, but surprise, surprise...it's locked, and there's nothing heavy enough in here that I can use to smash it. Besides, smashing it would alert people. I don't want that.

I'd rather not escape by sea, either, because I can't swim very well. When I was ten, a boy from my elementary school drowned. I've been wary of the water since. But...I'll swim if that's the way out.

I won't know my surroundings properly until Massimo decides to show me around. *If* he does. I don't know if he intends to keep me locked up in here or what the hell it is he's going to do with me.

The key rattles in the door and my heart squeezes. Unlike last night, I stand up, rising to my feet, and get ready for him.

When the door opens, the tension in my shoulders leaves when I see a guard and two maids in uniform. One is carrying a bag from Neiman Marcus, and the other a tray with croissants, a few other breakfast pastries, and pots of jelly.

Both maids are Italian. One looks to be a little older than me, while the other looks like she might be in her mid-to-late fifties. They enter the room, but the guard stays outside. A safety measure to make sure if I try to run away, he'll stop me. God, this is a nightmare.

"Good morning, signorina," the younger one says with a smile. "I'm Candace, and this is Priscilla." She points to the older lady.

"Buongiorno," Priscilla says, speaking with a hint of an accent.

"Hi," I answer, deciding they seem harmless. At least I hope so.

Candace looks at the untouched food.

"You weren't hungry?" she asks.

"No," I lie. I'm starving, but I think I might vomit and never stop if I eat anything. "You brought the food for me?"

She nods. "Yes. You should try and eat something."

I don't answer. They both seem like nice people, so I don't want to offend either of them.

"Won't you try these?" Priscilla asks.

I shake my head. "I don't want anything."

They glance at each other. I wonder what Massimo told them. How I got here and everything. Did he tell them the truth? That he practically bought me? Or is it more fitting to describe it as being kidnapped and held captive against my will? I imagine being in a courtroom scenario and the judge laying down the different sentences. I'm pretty certain any court of law would agree to all the above. I never agreed to any of this. All someone would need to do is open a door and I'd run far, far away, never to return.

"I got you some...um, clothes. Mr. D'Agostino wanted you to have these until your things arrive," Candace says, holding out the bag to me. Her smile fades when I don't take it.

I shake my head at her. Fuck pleasantries. *Fuck everything.* They're all in on it together. I don't want anything.

"I don't want any of it. He's kidnapped me and brought me here to live with him. I don't want anything. I don't need food. I don't need clothes. Definitely not when I have my own. I have more than my fair share of clothes. I don't need any new ones." The words reel off my tongue as I ball my fists at my sides.

They both look like they don't know what to say to me. I can't blame them since I wouldn't know either.

Priscilla's lips part as if she's going to say something, but she sighs instead.

"How about we leave them here?" Candace offers, placing the bag down in the corner by the dressing table. "Maybe you'll change your mind by lunchtime."

"I don't want lunch or dinner. I don't want anything. I just want to go home." I wince and look at Priscilla, who seems to offer the most sympathy.

"I'm sorry, dear. We've been told to make you comfortable. We can't do anything else," she says.

Great. Just great. Perfect.

I bring my hand to my head and will myself not to cry again. No more tears. I can't cry anymore. I did enough.

"When are my things getting here?" I demand.

"We don't know," Candace replies.

"Can I make a call?" I want to call Jacob. Calling the police would be the reasonable thing to do, but in my world, I know not to call cops. If you get out of a situation like mine, you head for the hills and pray the enemy never finds you. "I need to call my friend."

"I'm afraid that's not possible," Priscilla replies.

"I can't use a phone?" I gasp. The agony in my voice is evident.

"We'll speak to Mr. D'Agostino about that."

I get that lightheaded sensation again, like I'm going to faint. "Can I go outside? For some fresh air."

When Candace bites the inside of her lip, I already know what she's going to say. "Not yet," she says, confirming my thoughts.

"Where is Massimo? Where did he go?" My voice sounds withered.

"He's going to be in business meetings all day."

"It's Sunday," I point out, feeling stupid. Maybe *business* is code, like it usually is. Maybe it's code for screwing around. He's wealthy. Why would he be in meetings all day on a Sunday?

"We're gonna leave and give you some time. I'll come back and check on you later," Candace promises.

The two leave and the door closes. The key rattles and my heart squeezes.

I'm locked in again.

I walk over to the wall and throw a fist into it, hurting my hand. I don't care. It makes me feel something other than helpless and useless.

I sink back down against the wall, resuming my former stance of pathetic, and stay there.

The hours go by. Candace comes like she promised. She tries each time to speak to me, but I'm a shell. Priscilla comes too. I give her the same treatment. I don't eat either. I can't.

Night falls. I close my eyes, falling asleep in my new prison. I remember thinking of living with my father as being kept in a gilded cage.

That was nothing. I had it good back then. I just don't know why he would take care of me so well and allow this to happen. I blame him, but I know deep down that he was forced. That's the only explanation. The D'Agostino monster forced his hand, then forced mine too when he held a gun to my father's head.

But Dad sold me. That contract was all arranged before I got to the house.

Wasn't there another way?

I don't know what to believe and what to do. It all hurts me deeply, and every time I think of Italy, my heart breaks a little bit more.

I drift and float into a dream, then burning tickles my nose and I stir. *Smoke.* Tobacco smoke, like the type Grandfather used to have. Dad also smokes when he has company, but my grandfather would always have a cigar.

My eyes flutter open to see the bright sunlight. It's morning, and a gentle breeze caresses my skin.

Breeze.

My eyes snap wide. I twist toward the window but stop mid-movement when I see him.

Massimo is sitting on the window ledge—shirtless, smoking a cigar.

My breath hitches for two reasons. The first is the sight of him without his shirt. The next is fear.

I am afraid of him. I won't lie to myself or be a hero and believe I can overpower him. *I can't.*

He puts the cigar out and stands, giving me a better view

of his body. There are tattoos covering the whole left side of his abs and all over his arms. There's an angel inked on his left pec, and then what looks like Arabic writing all along the right side of his torso and left hip. I don't know what any of it says, though, and I'm not going to give him the pleasure of staring too long. Not when he looks pissed. I stand up when he moves closer and pray silently my heart doesn't beat out of my chest.

And that I won't die of fright.

CHAPTER EIGHT

EMELIA

"I've been told you aren't eating and you're refusing to wear the clothes I got you. Tell me why that is," Massimo demands, staring me down.

My lungs constrict, but I will my body to function and block out the fear. If I show my fear, he'll use that against me. He'll use it to try and control me.

Nothing about any of this is good, and if I don't stand up for myself, he'll push me around until there's nothing left of me. I can't let that happen.

"I don't want anything from you," I answer, lifting my chin in defiance.

A deep rumble resonates from his chest. I swear it sounds like a growl. Like the sound a bear would make, or a ravenous wolf.

"You think that is how this is going to work?"

"Where are my things? You've brought me here and expected me to just be okay with this shit."

"You think that is how this is going to *work?*" he asks again, with emphasis on each syllable, baring his teeth.

I'm pushing him. I know I am, but I have to say what I have to say.

"I want to make a phone call. Prisoners usually get that, don't they?" I keep my gaze trained on him.

"The person who needs to know you're here, knows. The next time you speak to your father will be at the fundraiser."

I don't know when that is, but I assume it's before this wedding we're supposed to have.

"I want to call my friend," I tell him and he chuckles.

"*Friend?*"

"Friend."

"You mean that boy? Is that what you call him? *Friend?*" His eyes narrow to slits. If I'm not mistaken, I catch a glimpse of jealousy. It momentarily throws me for a loop. I didn't expect that.

"*Boy?* So, what am I? Just a girl?" I challenge.

He steps closer, but I stand my ground. "Don't push me, Emelia. Don't. You will not like it."

Suddenly, fear weighs me down. "What would you do? Beat me?" God, what if he did? I couldn't bear to be with someone like that. "Is that how you would treat me?"

"What is your relationship with Jacob Lanzoro?" He holds me firm. I see now the flash of anger in his eyes.

"He's my friend," I answer.

"Do you fuck your friends?" he asks.

My mouth drops open. "No! What is the matter with you? I told you last night that I'm a…" My voice trails off as the memory of how I was with him last night comes back to me and my cheeks flush.

"People lie all the time."

"I'm not lying."

"You aren't calling him or speaking to him ever again."

"You asshole." The words fall from my lips. "How can you be so cruel? He's my friend. He'll be worried about me. He'll come looking for me."

I know Jacob will. He'll find out somehow what happened, and he'll come looking.

"If that little fucker knows what's best for him, he'll stay the fuck away. Wouldn't want his blood on my hands," Massimo sneers.

"You monster!" I cry. When he tries to grab me, I slap him across his cheek so hard it leaves a mark.

He snarls and reaches to grab me again. I jump out of the way and try to break away, but he catches me, lifts me up, and throws me down onto the bed. A scream tears from my throat when he climbs on top of me. All I can do is hit back at him but he grabs my hands and pins them over my head.

"You think I'm a monster, Emelia?" he growls. "Be grateful you ended up with me."

"Fuck you," I shoot back. "I was going to Italy. I'm an artist. I was going to live my dream, and you took it away. How dare you tell me I should be grateful? Bastardo."

I'm surprised when he laughs. "You are foolish if you think that's how your life was going to play out." He pins me down so I can't move. "You are just collateral to your father."

"Liar!" I cry and he gets up in my face. "You liar. He loves me. You forced him to do this to me. You held a gun to his head and I had to sign or you would have killed him in front of me. How dare you try to justify what you've done? *Monster.*"

"Yeah, maybe I am a monster. But I'm not a thief or a liar, and I don't double-cross my friends." He presses his hand into my stomach.

I'm aware there are things I don't know about my father,

but since Massimo has only shown me cruelty, there's no reason to give him the benefit of the doubt.

"You're all the same," I rasp, and I mean Dad too. I'm here because of him. No matter how desperate he was, I'll never forgive him for doing this to me. "Evil, all the same. Whatever you think my father is, you are the same."

Of all the things I've said to him, that seems to grip him the most. I can see it in his eyes.

"I am nothing like your father. He's the devil," he growls.

"You fucking dog!" I lash back. "What do you think you are? A damn saint? Fuck you."

He answers by tearing off my clothes. The dress rips right off me in one swift move. Then my bra comes off too. He tears off my panties and seconds later I'm naked beneath him. I scream and try to fight back, but he holds me down.

Massimo then flips me over onto my front, and before I can take my next breath, a heavy hand lands on the bare skin of my ass, jolting my body forward. Another scream rips from my lips, and another slap comes down hard on my ass. And another. And another. And another.

"Stop it!" I cry. "You're hurting me."

In the reflection against the glass wall I notice he was gearing up to spank me again, but he stops at my cry. When his hand touches my ass again, it's a gentle caress of his fingers running over my skin.

There's a moment of nothingness as I stare at our hazy reflection. Me naked, pinned to the bed with my hair falling over my face, and him half-naked. Too close to me.

I keep still. I keep very still, but my poor heart can't take this. It's beating so wildly in my chest I think it might explode.

His fingers flutter over my ass, and it's only then that I notice how much the skin burns.

In the glass I watch him bend his head, then I feel his lips pressing against the stinging patches of skin. Six kisses for the six times he spanked me.

Before I can process the shock of that, he grabs me and pulls me into his lap. Slipping one large hand behind my head, he cups it and holds me close, bringing me forward until our lips almost touch.

I'm naked, pressed up against him, with our eyes and our lips close. With no words spoken and just the sound of my heavy breathing, the tension is thick in the air. The myriad of thoughts that race through my mind twists and scatters. My lungs tighten and the air dispels, leaving me breathless the longer he stares at me with those tempestuous eyes.

The only things I'm aware of are my shaky breath, my racing heart, my skin touching his, my nipples pebbling against the hard wall of his chest. The wetness gathering deep in my core stirs, growing only for him. *Arousal.*

Maybe I've gone crazy. The last forty-eight hours have made me crazy, because how can I feel aroused after what he just did? He ripped off my clothes and spanked me. No one has ever laid a hand on me and hurt me like that.

How the fuck can I be aroused by that?

Now, what is this?

Is he going to kiss me? Is he going to steal my first kiss away from me too? It's so naïve and child-like to think that way. *Foolish.*

When he leans forward and brushes his lips over mine, electricity sparks deep inside me and pulses through my body, but instinct makes me turn my head away. Instinct to protect something that seems more passionate to me than him claiming my virginity. I can't give him my first kiss. I won't allow him to steal it...yet.

Yet is the word I need to bear in mind because I can't fight him. I'm weak and defenseless against his strength, and...this thing that seems to screw with me every time he touches me. This is the second time I've been naked in his presence, and look at the way my body responds to him.

What will happen next time?

"So pretty, so pure, so innocent. You've never been kissed, have you?" He breathes and I look back at him.

I try to pull away from the invasion of my space, but he latches onto my hair and holds me still.

"Answer me," he demands.

"You just accused me of fucking my best friend. Why are you asking me about something as simple as a kiss?" I challenge.

I don't know where my strength or courage comes from to talk to him with such defiance. Maybe it's an enhanced version of fear talking, but I feel a small victory when annoyance spreads across his face. The victory is only momentary, though, because he presses his cheek to mine and gets close to my ear.

"Answer the question I asked you, Emelia. You've never been kissed before, have you?" His voice is crude and demanding.

When he tugs on my hair, I press my hand to his chest. The taut skin and deep ridge of muscle tighten under my palm, and he runs his fingers over my ass.

One hand on my head, the other on my ass, making sure I know I'm locked in, paralyzed against his hold.

"No. I have not," I answer.

"Your kisses belong to me now. Your arousal is mine, your fantasies are mine, *you* are mine. Nothing is yours. You don't fuck with me, and I won't fuck with you either."

And just like that, he picks me off him and sets me back down on the bed. When he stands up my gaze drops to the bulge in his pants. It's more pronounced against the joggers than what he wore the other day.

He smiles when he sees me staring and smiles wider when he reaches for the remains of my little dress. He gives it another tear, and another. He rips it up like paper and reaches for my panties, which he pockets.

"Don't want my clothes? Well, then you won't wear any," he snarls.

"You asshole. You can't leave me in here naked." I shuffle against the bed and straighten up.

"Watch me," he answers, reminding me that I'm about to marry a monster.

Massimo stalks to the corner of the room where Candace left the bag of clothes and picks it up.

"If you ever want to wear clothes again, you'll do as you're told," he warns.

"You're seriously going to keep me locked up in here naked?" I can't believe it.

"Yes, I am. When I think you've learned your lesson, I'll let you know when you can wear clothes again."

"What the hell is wrong with you?" He's crazy. No one behaves this way.

"Don't push me, Princesca. Unless you want another spanking. That was a punishment, not for pleasure."

My cheeks heat with embarrassment.

"I hate you," I rasp.

He gives me that disarming smile and takes a few steps closer so he can loom over me. "No, you don't, but that's a subject for another time."

My lips part to tell him he's wrong, but my voice catches when the flicker of something deep within his eyes catches and holds my attention, throwing off my thoughts.

"How do you expect me to love you if you treat me like shit!" I wail.

The wild smirk on his face is another tell that foolishness has fallen from my lips once again.

"I don't expect your love. That is not what this is about." His gaze becomes a stony glare. In the depths of his piercing eyes I see this whole ordeal isn't just about money. There's more to it.

He has money. He has power. What I see when I look at him is a thirst for revenge. Revenge against Dad.

What did my father do to him? What did Dad do that would have such a repercussion on me?

And, why the hell do I have to pay for my father's sins?

When he turns, I see the massive dragon tattooed on his whole back. Dark and inky, filling up the space. He heads to the window, locks it with the little key, and places it in the same pocket he stored my panties. Then he leaves me. Once again naked.

Naked and thinking of how the hell I'm going to get out of here.

I need to find a way to escape.

How though?

Massimo will make sure I don't get the chance.

CHAPTER NINE

MASSIMO

She's right. I am a *monster*.

I just acted like one.

Is that who I am though? The man I've become? Has the thirst for revenge changed me into something I never wanted to be? Have my years of waiting for an opportunity to destroy Riccardo made me the kind of man who would prey on an innocent woman?

Woman... Fuck. She's barely that. She's nineteen, and I'm twenty-nine. Ten years apart. I should know better. My fucking cock might stir for her, and I might have wanted to fuck her senseless, but truth is truth. She's a virgin in every sense of the word. Never been kissed and never been touched, until I defiled her with my dirty mobster hands. *Dirty Sicilian*. If anybody witnessed what I did today and called me that, they'd be well in their right.

I'd agree. And I might do it all over again and feel shame all over again just to feel her lush ass jiggle beneath my palms.

It was wrong. All of it is wrong. She's innocent in this mess, but she's a necessary part of the plan to destroy Riccardo. Taking his heir will destroy him in more ways than one.

She's my stolen virgin bride. I took the princess, stole her from Daddy's nest and watched him sign her away to me. Phase one complete.

But fuck... She's driving me crazy. The woman is driving me crazy and fucking insane, if I can bring myself to admit to feeling an ounce of jealousy over her pathetic friend.

I'm drawn to her, attracted to her. The fact that she's attracted to me too wasn't really in the cards. It's screwing with my mind, and I realize I didn't plan for this part.

I'm turned on by lust and my dominance over her. Two days in, and I can't seem to control myself. The lust is like a thirst for blood that leaves me wanting more. I shouldn't fucking feel this way.

I head down the corridor and walk past Candace as she polishes the table on the second floor. She watches me as I deposit the bag of clothes in the room I use to store things. It's two doors down from Emelia's.

Usually, Candace would talk to me, but she says nothing. Not even good morning. Most bosses of my caliber would consider that insolence and kill her for it. We have a different relationship here.

Candace and Priscilla are the only two members of my house staff I treat like family. They're also the only members of my house staff who aren't terrified of me.

They know I won't kill them if they cross me because their families have worked for mine for generations, right from Sicily.

Candace in particular knows she's special to me. We grew up together and our families were close enough for me to class her as a younger sister. That's why she's acting the way she is now, by giving me the silent treatment. It's because of that relationship we have why I can't stand when she's not talking to me, so I stop by the end of the corridor and glower at her, forcing her to acknowledge me.

"What?" I demand.

The flush in her cheeks suggests she probably heard Emelia's screams. We weren't exactly quiet or mindful of anyone hearing us, and her room is just down the hall. Candace would have definitely heard, and it would have sounded like I was torturing her.

"Nothing, *Boss*. I can see you're in full asshole mode this morning so it's best I keep quiet." She runs the duster over the railing and shakes her head at me in dismay.

She's worked for me for years, even though she knows she doesn't have to earn her keep. When she goes off in one of her moods and mouths off to me like that, I play along.

"Fuck yeah," I answer with a smile that pisses her off even more. "That might be best if you don't want to piss me off."

With a hard stare she turns away and focuses on what she was previously doing.

I proceed down the corridor, leaving her. I walk by Priscilla, who just looks at me.

She was my nanny when I was a boy and is the kind of woman who does what she's told without asking questions or showing any emotion. When I got in last night with blood on my hands, she didn't say shit to me one way or the other. She just handed me a rag and a bowl of hot water, no words spoken.

It was Priscilla who messaged me to let me know what was going on here yesterday. Emelia refused everything.

I can tell she must have heard Emelia too and isn't happy about it.

Maybe it's best she doesn't talk to me today either. I wouldn't know what to say, anyway, and I don't want to end up confessing that I took out my frustration on Emelia over the recent shit with Pierbo.

I thought having Candace and Priscilla tend to Emelia would be a good idea. Candace is twenty-five, so not that much older than Emelia, and Priscilla has that motherly presence. I guess I was wrong.

I don't wish to talk to *anyone* right now, except the guy waiting for me in the hall. When I get to the doorway, I see him. Tristan is standing by the massive fireplace, looking at my favorite painting Ma did.

Emelia is an artist. My mother was an artist too. Ma painted only for us.

When we all got our separate houses, Pa split up some of our favorite paintings so we could each have some. I got the majority because I have the biggest house.

Tristan turns when he sees me and raises a brow.

"Jesus Christ, what the fuck happened to you? You look like you've been bitten by wolves," he muses and laughs.

I run my hand over my cheek and feel weal marks where Emelia slapped me.

"Don't ask," I seethe.

He shakes his head at me. "Like fuck. You have to tell me what happened." He smirks.

"She slapped me," I answer.

He laughs. "You're serious? Does she have claws?"

"Tristan, please. Don't. It's all shit. Come, let's go outside." I need fresh air to help me cool off.

I walk on ahead through the double doors that lead onto the terrace. I was out here earlier working out and I left my T-shirt slung over the patio chair. I grab it, shrug into it, and sink down into the awaiting seat. Tristan sits opposite me and pulls out a document from the inside pocket of his leather jacket.

"What is that?" I ask.

"Shit that suggests we're right. It suggests Pierbo didn't really kill himself." He hands me the document. I scan over it.

It's an itinerary for a package holiday booked for a weekend. Next weekend. At the top of the page, in the column with the contact details, is Pierbo's name along with a woman's. Sheila Carmichael.

"Sheila... Who's she?"

"The woman who is carrying his child. He was going to take her away for the weekend. According to the preliminary autopsy records from the coroner's office, he spoke to her a few hours before he died. Sheila said he called to tell her to pack sunscreen." He frowns and straightens up. "That doesn't sound like someone who would kill themselves a few hours later, does it, Massimo?"

"Like fuck," I answer.

The thing about this is I don't know where to go from here. We spent the whole day yesterday trying to find answers. While Dominic and Andreas did their own checking around, Tristan and I took to the streets. I hated going to the morgue and seeing a guy I could trust dead on the slab. *Lifeless.* I hate it more that there was a ninety-percent chance that his death was caused by Riccardo.

No proof, though. All damn day, we moved from one area to the next, talking to one asshole after another, getting blood on my hands when I had to kill a prick who tried to stab me.

"What now? We've come to a dead end," Tristan states.

I shake my head. "I don't know. We gotta go with what's on paper for the moment. Just until something says otherwise. Clearly, Riccardo got to him out of spite, but fuck, Tristan. It's Pierbo. How does anybody get to a guy like that?"

"I don't know. And it doesn't sit well with me. Nothing adds up to anything more than what they're calling it."

I tuck a lock of hair behind my ear. "We need to focus and stick to the plan. There's too much going on to lose focus." Especially for me.

I have big things happening over the next few weeks. The first is the Syndicate meeting where I'll be initiated. After that will be an official family dinner where Pa will give me the ring and declare me to the family as boss. We have family flying over from Italy for that and other members of the D'Agostino clan attending. It's a big deal. Then there's the damn fundraiser I'd rather skip but have to attend because it makes the company look good. Riccardo will be there too. I'll be taking Emelia to that, which will be the next time she sees him. That's three weeks away. The week after is the wedding.

Anything could happen in the space of that time, so I need to keep my eyes open and my ears to the ground. I don't doubt that Riccardo will be plotting some way to get Emelia back. I know he will.

"We can't lose focus. That would be a big mistake. Andreas and I will sort things out for the company and keep an eye on Riccardo. Dominic will do his stuff. Everybody knows what they're supposed to be doing, so don't worry. You just be boss. It's not an overnight job, especially doing the Syndicate business."

He's right about that. If it were only about learning how to run business for D'Agostinos Inc., it wouldn't be too bad. Pa prepped all of us to do that. The Syndicate is different, and my initiation will just be the start. The Brotherhood is a whole other ballgame of power, the next level of unimaginable wealth. Wealth I never dreamed of having. Definitely not when we had nothing. Those guys talk in billions, not even millions. That's why Riccardo is screwed. He couldn't even scrape together a million dollars to give us, let alone the twenty-five owed.

"Thanks, I appreciate it, brother." I raise my fist and bump it with his.

"No worries. So…you look shaken by this girl. What's going on, Massimo? Where is she?" He smiles.

"Locked in her room." *Naked.* I won't tell him that part.

"Gonna keep her locked up forever?" He quirks a brow.

"Tristan, I don't know what to do with her, and I don't need to be told this is crazy. It is."

"Of course it is, but I sense you like her…" He gives me a curious stare. "The marriage was your idea."

"It made sense. How else would we screw with the whole aspect of the Balesteri inheritance?"

"Fucking fuck the inheritance. Don't give me that bullshit, Massimo. You liked her at the ball." He nods and I incline my head to the side.

This is what happens when people know you too well. Tristan isn't just my brother; he's my best friend. Nothing gets past him.

"Didn't everybody?" I say as a final attempt. The way I remember it, every man with eyes who wasn't happily attached at that charity ball was looking at her. They all wanted her.

"Fuck, who cares about everybody? Massimo, no one would fault you for acting on *what* she is instead of *who* she is." He nods.

I have to laugh. "It's the same fucking thing. Who and what."

He shakes his head. "Nah. It's not." He gives me a wicked smile. "She's Riccardo's daughter. That's *who* she is. The enemy's daughter. But she's a woman. That's *what* she is. A very beautiful woman who belongs to you. Don't tell me you didn't notice that part."

I sit back in my chair. "I noticed just fine." *And so did my cock.*

Two times I've had her naked pressed against me, and both times I've wanted to devour her. *Both times,* I was very well aware that she's a goddess with the body made for the way I like to fuck.

Tristan smiles. "So that's it. You'll marry her, and it will be shit? Or are you going to live at the strip club? Noticed how you didn't go last night. Or maybe you got your dick wet here."

"Tristan, drop it. This is business."

"And what business is business without a little pleasure mixed in? When you have the kind of money we have, you're king. You can do whatever shit you want."

Footsteps echo against the pavement, and my next words fade.

Priscilla walks toward us with a stiff smile that attempts to hide her disapproval. Beside her is the woman who's probably the closest I could have called to a girlfriend. Gabriella Mineola. Her platinum-blonde hair looks like a halo on top of her head, and the smile on her face is filled with the mischief we always get up to when she's in town.

Tristan leans over to me. "Oh, I see. I didn't know you were still getting your dick wet with *her,*" he states, voice filled with disdain. He can't stand her.

"I'm not," I answer just before Priscilla and Gabriella reach us.

Tristan and I stand. Priscilla simply gives a quick bow of her head then departs. Gabriella looks from me to Tristan, and her smile brightens, reaching her large green eyes.

"Massimo and Tristan D'Agostino. I think it's been awhile

since I've seen the two of you together," she states, putting out her hand for us to kiss her knuckles.

Being polite, *for me*, Tristan gives her a handshake. I don't touch her.

"I'm going to run," Tristan states. "Remember what I said," he adds, eyeing me with sharp seriousness.

He's talking about Emelia. I give him a nod before he leaves us. I return my focus to Gabriella, who is already looking at me. Her gaze turning more seductive by the second.

"Gabriella. Haven't seen you in a while," I state.

"I was travelling."

It's a fucking lie. The truth is she had an affair with Senator Braxton. His wife found out and he kicked Gabriella to the curb, instead of leaving his wife like she thought he was going to. I'll pretend I was born yesterday, though, like she believes, and accept that she was travelling.

"Sounds good."

"Look at you. How do you get more sexier every time I see you?"

"Don't know."

She runs her finger over my chest but keeps her gaze trained on me. "Remember the last time we saw each other?"

"I do." I remember well. She stayed the whole weekend here, and we never left my bed.

Her father is the head of the Mineola family. They're incredibly wealthy and have wanted to invest in D'Agostinos Inc. for many years. Every time they made an offer, Pa declined. He's strong that way. Knowing when to accept an offer and when to reject because of the shit that might follow. Me, not so much. I've never been able to decline this woman my bed, or...wherever desire might take us. She just hasn't ventured to my parts in close to a year.

She chuckles and presses a perfectly manicured finger into my chest. "Me too. It was nice. So, there was news abroad of your ascension to leadership. And your engagement."

That would have gone out yesterday. News travels fast in our circles. I can just imagine the talk about it. Me, the ruthless D'Agostino prince, and the sweet Balesteri princess. Two families people know to be former enemies. Two families only certain special people know to belong to the Brotherhood. What a stir we must have created.

"Yes, I'm getting married." I answer to that alone because she would have heard about me being boss months ago. That's old news and nothing that would send her here.

She gazes out to the beach and lifts her head, signaling for me to look.

"Won't you take me for a walk on the beach? It's such a lovely day. Just want to get one last fill before the lady of the house takes her reign." She gives me a saucy smile. One I don't return.

I'll walk with her on the beach, though, because we should talk, and I know that eyes are watching us. I'm certain Priscilla is watching from somewhere, and I don't want more judgment today.

I wave my hand, and we head down the path.

The beach was what I loved about this property. I've always loved living near water. It was a given that I'd be the brother to choose the beach house because of my love for sailing out on the open sea. There's not a boat I can't sail, and no water too turbulent that I can't captain my way through.

While we grew up near water, my brothers live more inland. Tristan, however, loves the woods. He likes being away from people.

As soon as we take the last step down the path, we're on the beach. It's a private beach that came with the property. I have two miles of it before it connects with the rest of Huntington Beach.

Gabriella's hair lifts in the wind. It looks like strands of sunlight. She turns to face me when we get farther out.

"Are you going to invite me to the wedding?" she muses.

"We haven't decided yet who we'll be inviting." That's the nicest anybody will get from me. She knows the answer is no.

"Maybe I'll get a different invite. I can't imagine you with an inexperienced girl," she says and circles me like a cat marking its territory. "I heard she's pretty," she states.

"She is," I answer.

I plan to be very straightforward with her. In times like these, no one can tell friend from foe. Just because we used to screw around doesn't mean she's here to get back in my bed. Or maybe she is. This was how it started in the past. We'd meet and we'd fuck, then we'd leave. Until next time.

"It figures. I always wondered what the Balesteri princess looked like. Riccardo kept her away from the world. No one ever knew who she was."

That's exactly how it was, but most crime families are like that. It's how I'd be if I ever had a family. I'd keep them out of business. At the first sign of shit, your enemies come for you through your weaknesses. Women and children. In that order.

"You seem keen," I note, looking her over.

"Relax..." She smiles. "I'm here solely to know if we'll still be fucking around after your nuptials, or maybe before." She giggles and tilts her head to the side.

"Gabriella, we won't be playing that game anymore," I answer, and the smile recedes from her face.

"Oh please, don't tell me you've suddenly turned into the doting husband." She laughs. "How can you with that sort of shit show for a wedding? *Arranged.* It's so obvious. I just don't know what for."

I lean in closer, and she laughs.

"You know a lot. Did Riccardo send you to check on his princess?" I ask, boring my gaze into her.

It would be a clever idea since anybody else would have been shot dead before they could get to the door.

"What if he did?"

"*Did* he?" I demand. My blood heats.

"No. I know what you mafia men are like. It's always about pussy in the end. I'm just offering it up to you."

I'm usually good at guessing when people are lying, but thanks to the last few days, my emotions are screwed—from worrying over my brothers and what they think of my leadership, to the sexually charged encounters with Emelia.

"You weren't offering it well before the news," I answer, probably showing more emotion than I intend.

I thought about her. I thought about being serious, and she knew I was just before she hopped in bed with Senator Braxton. I've never been serious about anybody, but she made me consider it.

That's probably why Tristan can't stand her. He knew how I felt. I didn't have to say it.

The smile that lifts the corners of her mouth is shaky. She raises her hand and touches my cheek, lightly running her finger along the graze Emelia left there.

"Such a beautiful man you are, even when you're scarred. Makes you look better. I wasn't into serious then, Massimo. I am now." She drops her hand and runs it down the length of my chest and down to tug on the waistband of my pants.

I catch it just before she can grab my dick and smile down at her.

When her eyes shift from mine and she stares off in the distance, over my shoulder, my nerves prickle. It's then I feel it. Eyes on us, *on me*.

I'm so used to being alone and walking around on this side of the beach by myself that I forgot. How sloppy of me. We're standing about forty feet away from Emelia's bedroom.

I turn around knowing it could only be her watching, and it is. She's standing by the window I was smoking at earlier. Wrapped in the bedsheet with her obsidian hair wild and tousled, she looks like we spent the night together. Even from here I can see the dewiness in her skin and those misty gray eyes. Striking against the darkness of her hair.

Pretty isn't the word I'd use to describe her. She's beautiful. She is beauty. And the most beautiful thing about her is that she doesn't know.

We're in her direct line of sight. I don't know what to be more impressed by—the way she stares me down or the fact that she hasn't moved. She's been caught watching me with a woman on the beach she doesn't know, and she's still standing her ground. Clearly pissed as fuck at me.

Jealous.

Good.

I can see it. The same way she sparked jealousy in me when she asked if she could call her friend.

My cock hardens when my gaze drops to her breasts hidden away from my sight with the sheet. I remember how her nipples pebbled with arousal against my chest and how she tasted the other night when I got my first suck on her tits and her pussy.

She's going to let me do that again. Next time, I'll get a good suck and make sure I get my fill of her pussy before we start to fight.

I look back to Gabriella and note the hard line of her jaw.

She's never been a woman to like competition, and never a woman you tell no. It's different with me, though. I call the shots. When she thought she was using me, she couldn't have been more wrong.

"She's pretty," she states.

"I know," I answer and fury flashes in her eyes.

"I can already tell you'll be bored quickly too. Call me when you want to fuck a real woman who knows how to please you in the bedroom."

She walks away, and I allow her to.

My gaze returns to the princess watching me from the window in her bedroom. My cock's hard, ready to fuck her as I think of what she is.

A woman who is mine. A woman I doubt I'll get bored of because I'll be too busy teaching her how to please me.

She's a girl I can't wait to turn into a woman.

I gaze back at her now and realize I want more than her obedience.

The spark of attraction that's rippling in this space between us tells me she wants more too.

This is going to be very interesting.

I turn away from her and continue down the beach, planning for later.

CHAPTER TEN

EMILIA

Is this what it will be like?

He'll have his women while I'll be stuck looking in from the outside. Or rather, the inside of this room. I'll be stuck watching my husband with some woman running her hands all over him.

I continue watching Massimo walking down the beach. I watch him until he disappears from my view then I blink against tears.

It's not jealousy... Okay...maybe it is. But not in the conventional sense of being jealous. What's grating me is being forced to feel this way because I'm in this situation.

I wouldn't feel this way if there was any part of this whole fiasco that was normal, because I wouldn't choose to be with a man who cheats on me.

The way she touched him, although brief, spoke in abundance of them being together. She looked like his type. Like the kind of woman who knows what to do in the bedroom, or wherever. *Not a virgin.*

Although they were far away, I noticed the way he was around her too. She is blonde and pretty, has an enviable body. Definitely his type. Probably the kind of woman he wouldn't treat the way he treated me.

So, maybe this is it. We'll get married, and he'll have her and maybe others like her. I shouldn't feel anything close to jealousy, but I guess it was wrong for me to hope that, whenever the day came for me to get married, I'd marry someone who loved me.

I can't believe the way he treated me earlier. He spanked me and ripped off my clothes, then he said he didn't want my love. How stupid of me to say such a thing, though, when he had whatever meet-up he had with a woman who looked like a Barbie doll.

I move from the window and wipe away a tear with the heel of my hand. I almost trip over the fucking sheet I've had to wrap myself in. Walking to the bed, I sit on the edge, looking around the room. It's going to be another day of nothingness. Another day of shit.

The only difference between yesterday and today is that I have more shit on my mind.

The woman on the beach with Massimo pissed me off, but what I've been thinking about since he left was what he said about Dad.

Massimo spoke like he knew my father very well. He spoke with confidence in his words.

I want to know what Dad did to him. To them. The D'Agostinos. In his living room the other night were both Massimo and his father. His father would not have been there if he didn't have some vendetta against my father too.

So, what was it?

What happened?

When did it happen?

Massimo called my father a liar and a thief. What did he lie about? What did he steal?

And is Dad broke if he owed a debt that could only be paid by exchanging it for me? He must be. I know this whole thing with me would never have happened if he wasn't broke. His behavior back in selling me was that of a desperate man.

He's done his best to keep me out of business, so I don't really know much of anything. I know what I'm supposed to know because it's most often what I'm told in terms of safety and what Jacob told me, but that's all.

To my knowledge, Dad's supposed to be a multi-billionaire. I must have been wrong and truly living in the dark because there was also what Massimo said about my life.

He said that my life wouldn't have turned out the way I wanted. That I was collateral to my father. I don't believe that. I'm stuck on that part because my father has always been so protective over me. He loved me. You would only protect someone the way he protected me if you loved them.

He even got worked up over guys I might have been interested in dating. Behold, that's why I've never been kissed. And shit, my life was probably comparable to living in a convent. Minus the nuns. I had Jacob, but there was always a constant supply of people watching and making sure I was safe.

Massimo must have been lying. There's no way I'm going to believe a monster over what I know my father to be. He was just telling me bullshit to piss me off.

But if it was all bullshit, then why do I feel deep down that there's some element of truth to it?

The keyhole rattles and I tense right up. Like Pavlov's

dogs, my poor body has now been conditioned to become anxious when I hear *that* sound.

The door opens and I instantly relax when Priscilla comes in with a tray of food. Before she can say good morning, my stomach rumbles loudly, making her smile.

I'm not surprised to hear my stomach griping. I haven't eaten anything since that pizza and the double-chocolate shake I had with Jacob. That was two days ago. I've had sips of water. That's all. I'm so hungry now I could eat a cow.

Priscilla smiles wider when I offer her a kind one.

"Good morning, signorina," she says.

"Good morning."

She looks me over wrapped in the sheet. I wonder what she must think. If I were her, I'd probably assume correctly that I'm naked under it, but then my mind would race over why I might not have clothes on. Maybe she thinks I spent the night with Massimo.

"Yesterday, I was easy on you. I don't plan to be anything of the sort today," she states, and her accent becomes more pronounced. "You need to eat something."

"Okay... I will."

Priscilla sets the tray of food down on the little table by the dresser. I see she's prepared some treats like she has previously and added a stack of large chocolate chip cookies on the side.

"I hope you do. It's never wise to stop eating. It makes things worse," she points out. "I thought you might like something sugary. My specialty here is pastries. Do you like pastries? I don't know anyone who doesn't."

I can see she's trying to be friendly and make me feel comfortable so I decide I won't be the bitch I was yesterday. Truthfully, I need someone to talk to, and the worst thing I could do in my situation is make enemies with the house staff.

"I like pastries," I reply. "Those look great. Thanks for making them for me."

She looks pleased and relieved at my answer. "You're welcome. I think you'll like the macaroons. They're actually an old recipe from Mrs. D'Agostino, Massimo's mother. She loved adding cinnamon."

His mother... What must she be like?

"When do I get to meet her?" I ask. Better to ask questions like that to someone like Priscilla, because talking to Massimo is like talking to a wall.

The crestfallen look on Priscilla's face, however, suggests I've asked a question I shouldn't have.

"I'm sorry, dear. You won't. She died many years ago. But we keep her spirit alive in our memories and all the things she loved."

I press my lips together as a pang of guilt sweeps through me. "I'm sorry. I didn't know. I don't know much about the D'Agostino family," I confess.

"That's okay. I've...worked for the family for a long time. I knew Massimo and his brothers when they were little."

"He has brothers?"

"Three. I'm certain you'll meet them very soon."

She speaks fondly of them. *Very fondly.* If she's been with the family for such a long time, she must know the ins and outs of what they get up to. As I look at her, I try to think of what Massimo told her in relation to me.

"Do you know why I'm here?" I ask in a small voice.

She nods uneasily. "Yes. I do know. News has travelled that you will be marrying Massimo in a few weeks, but I was informed on the day of your arrival."

My breath catches when I think of that type of news going out to everyone. Family. And Jacob.

He never got to tell me how he felt about me and now he's heard I'm getting married. What must he think?

She walks up to me and rests a hand on my shoulder. "Eat. Just eat and take it from there. I'll be back in a little while with some shampoos and accessories you can use in your hair. It will help you to...get used to the place."

I nod my thanks. I don't ask anything else because I know there's no point.

No point in asking if I can go outside. No point in asking when my things will get here. No point in asking if I can call Jacob.

When she leaves, I walk to the food, and the minute I take one bite of a cookie, my taste buds open and I find myself scarfing down everything. One cookie after the other disappears down my throat, and all the pastries too.

The tray probably held food enough for three people, but I ate it all. When I'm done, there's nothing but crumbs left. I'm so full I have to lie down.

Priscilla returns a little later with a basket of nail polishes, shampoos, and all sorts of things I would normally indulge in on the regular from Bath and Body Works.

I spend the day distracting myself with the contents of the basket. I wash my hair and spend hours in the bathtub, soaking my wounds from Massimo's ruthless hand.

When night falls, I lie in the bed for the first time and find myself thinking about him as my head hits the pillows. I wonder where he is. It must be well into the night now because the days are longer during the summer months. In L.A. we can have daylight right up until eight-thirty o'clock.

Is he with that woman?

Is this how I'll spend my nights? Alone and wondering whose bed he's sleeping in?

Maybe he's here and in his bedroom. I don't know. I don't even know where his room is.

Is she in there with him?

Will she be at the wedding? I saw the way she looked at me. I was too far away to see her face properly, but I saw enough to note the scowl and vindictive expression that wrinkled her pretty face. She saw me watching before he did, which was when she started to touch him, like she was marking her territory.

Bitch... She wouldn't know that I couldn't care less.

The hours pass and I can't will myself to sleep. I keep thinking he's with her. Or someone else. Why wouldn't he be? He's gorgeous. The kind of man to melt you with his arresting good looks and a face that Hollywood would pay millions for.

I don't know what woman could resist him, or who wouldn't react to him the way I do. Every girl I know at UCLA would die if a man like that even spoke to them. And they'd be completely envious of me.

My mind tracks back to my first night here, how he touched me. My skin heats at the memory, and my pussy clenches with need.

I'm an idiot for thinking of this shit. I'm an idiot for not being strong enough to resist. Gorgeous as he is, the man is a monster. I shouldn't feel anything for him.

What I should be thinking of is how I'm going to leave this place.

The door opens and I jump, startled. I was so lost in my thoughts that I never heard the key rattle.

I have the light turned down to an amber glow. It bathes over him as he walks into the room and locks the door behind him.

His eyes meet mine, and I straighten up on the bed.

He's shirtless again, just like this morning. He has a black towel slinked over his shoulder and his hair looks damp. Damp like he just took a shower, or like he was working out.

My gaze drifts down to his boxers and those long athletic legs, each muscular and, like his abs, covered with tattoos. I realize that the only parts of his body that I have seen that haven't been inked are his face and neck. He doesn't have any on his forearms, either. It's enough to carry the illusion that he has none when he's wearing a dress shirt. Was that done on purpose?

My previous worries over him being with that woman are replaced by the icy fear that's crawled right back inside me.

What does he want now? Is he ready to have his way with me? Jesus, I'm going crazy here not knowing what will happen next. I'm on edge from one minute to the next.

"What do you want?" I ask.

He tilts his head to the side and regards me with those piercing eyes. "Is it wrong for a man to want to spend the night with his bride-to-be?"

My breath hitches, and warmth flushes over my body. *Tonight.* It could be tonight. It could be now that he comes to claim me.

I'm not ready.

He sets the towel on the chair by the bed before he comes closer. The scent of musk and soap tickles my nose, confirming he just showered.

"Nice to see you in the bed," he states, pressing one knee on the mattress, which sinks in from his weight.

"What do you want?" I ask again.

"Relax, I'm not going to fuck you," he answers. I feel silly that I must visibly look relieved at his words. "But I'm sleeping in here tonight. We don't see enough of each other."

"I thought you might be occupied with someone else." I

want to ask about that woman and who she is to him, but I think better of it.

The corner of his mouth lifts, and a smile slides across his lips. "Don't spy on me, Emelia. You might not always like what you see."

My blood heats. "I wasn't spying. I simply stared through the window and there you were. *With her.*"

"I guess that's true."

"Does she come here often?"

He smiles, revealing perfect white teeth. "Be careful, Princesca. I may start thinking you're jealous."

"I have nothing to be jealous of," I snap, answering too quickly. "You can be with whoever you want."

"Really? *And*...you'd be okay with that?" He narrows his gaze and climbs fully onto the bed, studying me.

"I don't care what you do. This is business, and I fall part of the assets, right?"

We stare at each other for a few seconds. Then he tugs at the sheet. I lash out to smack his hands away when he tries to pull it down from my breasts, but he catches my wrists.

"Don't touch me."

I wince. He, however, tightens his grip on my wrist and lowers his head to press his lips to my ear.

"I can touch you whenever I want, Princesca. You belong to me. You just said it yourself. You fall part of the assets. You remember signing your name, right?"

Enraged, I try to pull my hand from his, but he just holds on tighter. "I was forced. That's not the same thing as me giving myself to you."

"Interesting choice of words." He holds up my hand and plants a kiss on my knuckles.

"They are just words."

"Maybe so, but I think...you're curious."

I flinch and raise my brows. "What am I curious about, Massimo?"

He runs his finger over the back of my palm. "To see what it would be like to give yourself to me. To see what it would be like if I hadn't stolen you away from your father. Curious to see what it would be like to be with me, for you to give in to desire."

"No..." I mutter, swallowing past the lump that's formed in my throat as the desire he speaks of quickens my pulse.

"Take the sheet off," he commands, his tone level.

"Why?"

"I want to see you." His gaze drops to my breasts and my entire body blushes at the wild sexual flames that dance in his eyes.

"You saw me already."

"I want to see you again."

"What if I don't want you to see me?" I challenge.

"That's not up to you. You don't follow instructions well, do you, Princesca?"

"Are you always such an ass?" I throw back.

"Yes."

"You like humiliating me, don't you?" I say in a small voice.

"Sweetheart, when a man asks you to strip, it's not because he wants to humiliate you. It's because he likes looking at your body." His lips lift into a mutinous tilt, and he gives me a disarming grin. When his eyes cloud and darken with that wild sexual haze, it grips me, and the stir of arousal swirls deep in my core.

He comes closer and hovers over me with that smile and that look, snaring me further. "Emelia... When a man asks you to strip, it's because he wants you, Princesca."

The strangest thing happens to me on hearing those

words. I forget. Just for a moment, I forget...*everything*. Shame and desire mingle hot in my throat, and the raw power of attraction holds me at its will.

I drop my guard. He sees the moment I do. This time when the devil tugs at the sheet, I allow him to.

He pulls it right off me, exposing my nakedness to him once more. My nipples pucker at the hungry look in his eyes, and my body heats when he runs his finger from the tip of my chin right down to the valley between my breasts.

The urge to tell him to go away fades away, blending into the air when he climbs closer.

"Lie back and spread your legs for me," he commands. The mellow baritone of his voice is laced with sexual heat. Husky with desire.

My breath quickens. I swallow hard. The question enters my mind again through the haze. What is he going to do to me? The build of pressure rising inside my body terrifies me because I'm not sure I would put up a fight if he decided to take me.

"What are you going to do?" I whisper.

"Play with you," he says.

"*Play?*"

"Play. Tonight, we play. So, lie back and feel me."

My heart races. He's watching me in that predatory way again. Eyes focusing on my every move, my every action. Smiling when I obey and lie back on the stack of pillows with my legs spread so he can play with me.

He gets on top of me fully, locking me into the cage of that wild sexual energy. His breath tickles and tantalizes my nose as he lingers there before me, looming over me, looking at me.

"Stop fighting it," he says, as if he can read my mind. When his fingers flutter over my pussy lips, I flinch and try to

I move away, but he pulls me back. "I'm not going to do anything to you that you don't want me to do."

I tremble under the weight of his stare. I don't want him to be able to see straight through me. He can, though. That smile on his face says he can.

Brushing his nose along mine is the start. Then he presses his lips to my cheek and kisses my skin. He avoids my lips, but it's like I can feel him there too. His lips trail down to my neck, slowly, so slowly. Desire warms my insides.

One kiss follows another, and another, until my body comes alive with the scatter of heat. Kissing my neck, he travels down to the huge swells of my breasts and kisses my nipples, licking at the tips then teasing with his tongue.

I grab the sheet when he sucks my left nipple. My pussy clenches from the jolt of pleasure. He stops sucking, and that devilish smile from the other night returns to his face, scaring me.

"Have you ever allowed a man to suck your breasts before, Princess?" the devil asks, holding my gaze.

"No..."

"Do you like it?" he whispers in my ear.

I look away as embarrassment fills me, but he catches my face and guides my gaze back to his.

"Answer me... Don't be afraid. Tell me if you like it." His grip tightens on my jaw.

"Yes..." I hear myself say. I can't believe I said that.

Satisfaction lightens his eyes from the dark molten heat. He lowers his head to suck again. Sucking hard while he reaches to my right to capture the nipple between his thumb and forefinger.

Conflict rides through my soul when I start feeling good. His mouth sucking my breast feels amazing. His fingers caressing me feel like nothing I can quite describe. I can't control the mindless moan that escapes my lips, no more than I can control the arch of my back as he starts sucking harder. He moves from one breast to the other, sucking and swirling his tongue around my nipple.

The pleasure that rushes through my veins becomes too much. I groan out a loud moan when a greedy orgasm takes me over the edge. I allow myself to give into the call of pleasure, and he takes full advantage of my weakened, aroused state to move down to my pussy and start lapping up my release.

He spreads my legs wider, buries his face right there between my thighs, and drinks.

He drinks as he runs his hands over my ass, which still stings, and holds me to him so he can suck the sensitive, swollen nub of my clit. My body takes over. Somehow, my hands move to his head, encouraging him to continue. He does. But not before looking up at me and smiling at my defeat.

I couldn't resist him. I still can't. He has me right where he wants me: wanting him to continue his feast on me.

When I start moaning again, he reaches up and grabs my breasts, massaging the mounds while he eats me out, taking me to the height of pleasure again.

Raw ecstasy shoots through me, sizzling every part of my body, and I come again. I come hard, harder than before, so hard I can't catch my breath.

He drinks again, taking it all until there's nothing left and I'm drained.

Drained and panting, I can barely focus when he rises and licks his lips, taking the last traces of my arousal into his mouth.

My hand falls to the bed, limp, but he catches it and positions himself on his knees so I can see the massive bulge of his cock pressing against his boxers. Shock spreads through me when he brings my hand to the bulge and clamps my fingers over his hard length. He makes me rub up and down on his cock and holds my hand to him so I don't let go.

"That is what you do to me, Princesca," he confesses. I feel hot all over again. "Do you want to know a little secret?"

A secret?

There are so many floating around. Too many.

Knowing one would lessen the burden of not knowing anything.

"Yes."

A smile dances across his lips. "I'm curious about you too. I've been curious since that night I first saw you. *You,* Emelia Balesteri—my enemy's daughter."

As I stare back at him and take in his words, I know he's not talking about Saturday. What he's referring to sounds older. Like it was a long time ago.

If I'd seen this guy before, I'd remember. When is he talking about?

"What night?" I ask.

"The ball."

"The charity ball?" He was there?

"You can call it that. It's best you call it that, Princesca. The truth would hurt you too much, and I don't want to hurt you that way tonight," he answers as he moves away from me.

My skin flushes when I realize I was still holding onto his cock. I push the embarrassment away and stare back at him.

What did he mean? *I can call it that.* I thought the charity ball was exactly that.

I was nervous but so happy to finally join Dad at one of his events. It was the first time he'd ever taken me to anything like that. That ball was a few months before I turned nineteen. I felt so grown up and like a representative of Dad and the company. He even introduced me to one of the investors. It was a good night for me.

"If it wasn't a charity, what was it?" I ease up onto my elbows.

"No. No, Princesca," he says, lying next to me. He reaches out and pulls me closer, setting the sheet back over me then him. "I like you like this. Innocent and untainted. Unknowing."

Thoughts from earlier return as we stare at each other. Once again, I know he's referring to Dad in some way. He keeps saying things to make me question what I know. Making me question Dad.

Making me question him, and myself, and what we just did.

It's all going to drive me crazy.

If I stay here, that's exactly what will happen to me.

I'll lose my mind. And I'll lose myself too.

CHAPTER ELEVEN

MASSIMO

I'm on my way to see Andreas and about ten minutes away from his place.

I tear down the road on my motorcycle, riding way past the speed limit. I need the speed and the feel of that edge of danger racing through my veins to clear my mind.

I've been opting for my car over my bike for the last few weeks. No particular reason. I just like it. The same way I felt like riding the Ninja X2 bike today.

I think I needed that buzz to take my mind off everything.

It's been four days. Exactly four days since Emelia has been in my care, and the woman is growing on me. I know well enough not to divulge too much information to her that won't matter. Part of me thinks it matters, though, because I want her to hate her father the same way I do. I want her to see him for the devil he is.

Riccardo set Pa up. Pa was in charge of the family business. Back then, it was investments. Same as Riccardo's. In those days, the Syndicate was low level. When Pa and Riccardo joined forces, he set up a pump-and-dump scheme, hired people to cash out and ruined Pa.

That was after Riccardo set up Balesteri Investments and stole all the clients Pa had obtained for years. That left Pa bankrupt. All his money and assets were seized to pay debts, and because some of the members of the Syndicate and their families were clients, it was easy to get him out. The whole plot was a carefully woven plan to destroy.

Sometimes I still feel the press of his gun against my temple. My mind tracks back to the day of my mother's funeral and I'm that twelve-year-old boy again, unable to do shit to Riccardo to defend myself. I hate that prick so much. The thought of Emelia thinking the sun shines from his ass makes me sick.

At the same time, she's dirty by association to him. She's his daughter. It's enough for me to destroy them both. It's enough for me to want to cut them down like grass. His empire, and his precious daughter along with it.

If only I didn't want her.

Four days, and this is me.

Last night, when I mentioned the charity ball and watched confusion settle onto her pretty face, I felt sorry for her. Sorry for her and more disgusted at Riccardo for taking her to something like that. The Syndicate is a band of powerful men. They have a shitload of money. When you have money like that, it comes with certain privileges. Dark, arcane powers that normal people would never have access to, or ever conceive.

The charity ball was an example of that. Dressed to look like a fundraising event where members of the associated companies can indeed raise money for their sponsored charities, it also masks other activities. Things people class as dark and label the Syndicate as such.

Activities like auctions of virgins and the sale of young women are just some examples. Take your nineteen-year-old daughter to an event like that and dress her in black and that opens the floor for bidding. While the Syndicate provides the facilities for darker tastes like that, they don't monitor it. So, Riccardo could have dealt with anyone. The kinds of men who normally purchase women from the viewing are never good. An observation as such coming from a man like me, with a soul as dark as mine, is enough to guess the types of sick fucks Riccardo must have dealt with. Emelia shouldn't have been a part of that.

I woke this morning with her still pressed up against me. Naked and perfect. My cock is still hard from the memory of her. My heart still warmed from the way her fingers fluttered over my chest as she curled into me, her hair sprawled out on the pillow, like we'd spent the night having wild sex.

I was being serious when I said I was curious about her too. I shared a secret I shouldn't have by telling her that.

For things to go the way I want, I can't, under any circumstances, show emotion. This whole ordeal is a war between families that started years ago. The moment her father thought he could steal from mine and try to ruin his life.

The thing is, doing all this won't change the past. Not a damn bit. It won't do shit. It won't bring my mother back. I know deep in my heart that my father's life was ruined the moment he knew my mother killed herself.

Riccardo is the enemy, and so is Emelia, so I can't allow myself to feel for her.

I park on Andreas' drive and get off my motorcycle. This visit was a long time coming. I should have made it already. Things are not okay between us. I can feel it, and I can't allow the shit to continue if I want to be the kind of boss I hope to be.

Setting my helmet on the handle, I make my way past his convertible, which is open. Inside I notice a pair of panties.

He lives in a condo. He has the smallest house of all of us because he's never in. When he's not working at D'Agostino, he's sailing. At least we share that similarity with our love for anything to do with the water.

I walk up the steps to the door and notice that it's open. It's fucking nine in the morning, and he's got his car and door open without a guard in sight.

Given the circumstances, I feel for my piece in my back holster. It's not like Andreas to be so sloppy.

I make my way upstairs to his bedroom and instantly regret opening the door the moment I do.

In his bed are two naked women, fast asleep on top of the covers. Standing beside them is Andreas, getting a blow job from a naked blonde woman.

"Fuck!" He winces when he sees me. I back away, closing the door.

Shit. I'm already in his bad books. Fuck do I know how to make a situation worse than it is.

I walk into the kitchen and stand by the door, noticing bottles of wine and other bottles of liquor. Some empty, some full.

He comes in minutes later wearing a pair of joggers and one of his old college T-shirts.

"I'm sorry," I apologize quickly.

"Don't mention it," he replies and looks over the mess in the kitchen. "What's going on?" he asks.

"Came to see if you were alright."

He chuckles. "I'm fine, brother. As you can see, I'm living

my best life. Two women in my bed and another sucking my dick. What could be better than that?"

It's like watching someone who strived for excellence fall in shit. "It's not like you to spend the night with whores."

"Don't you have a whorehouse?" He raises a brow.

I bite the inside of my lip. "That's different."

"How? Massimo, please, whores are a natural part of the package. We all have them. You have them in abundance. And I know this marriage shit isn't just going to suddenly change you overnight. You're not wired that way. So, that aside, I'm sure there was a purpose for your visit, *Boss*." The corner of his lips curl and his eyes darken.

"Andreas..." I start, but I don't know what to say to him.

Sorry Pa chose me over you? Sorry I chose Tristan to be part of the Syndicate, not you?

He must be pissed as fuck.

"What? Massimo, what? You know as well as I do that there's nothing to say. It is what it is. No more, no less. Pa chose who he wants to take the lead, and you chose who you want to support you. It is what it is," he says with a nod.

"You aren't okay with it," I state, cutting to the chase.

He chuckles. "Brother, I have to be okay with it."

"I want you on board, Andreas."

He reaches out a hand and holds my shoulder. "You are my brother. I will back you in whatever you do. That's all you need to know. Doesn't matter if I look like shit and act like shit. I'm just...licking my wounds. You'd do the same if you were me. And I'd be in your shoes, going to your place to sort you out."

He releases his grip on me.

"I just want to know you're okay."

"I'm fine. I guess sometimes I get stuck in tradition. The oldest son usually gets to be boss. But hey, if Pa were traditional, maybe the right person would never get chosen." He gives me a curt nod.

I won't say anything against Pa. He's a fair man and my fucking idol. I don't care if I sound like a pussy thinking that, but it's true. The man laid the cards on the table and gave his four sons a chance to shine. That's what he did. I won the leadership fair and square.

I just hope it hasn't cost me my older brother.

"I need you to take care of business at D'Agostino," I say to him.

We never got to go over what I'd talked to the others about because we went on the streets to look into Pierbo's death. The most I got to tell him was that I was splitting the business four ways. That was all.

Andreas is a man like me, though—he doesn't care about money. He cares about power.

"And I will. You can trust me. I'm proud of you, kid." The light returns to his eyes.

I ball my fist to bump his. "Thank you. That means a lot to me."

He nods and gives me the first real smile he's given me since Pa announced I'd be taking over. "She'd be proud too. Ma. I know she would. You're like him. More than me." He chuckles. "Now, get the fuck out of here. I need to get back to my women."

I smirk. "Okay. See you later."

He tips his head, and I make my way out. I understand him and understand where he's coming from. The only guy who worked as hard as I did for the position was him. I'd feel like shit too if I didn't get it.

CHAPTER TWELVE

MASSIMO

By the time I got back home from work, two things had arrived for Emelia: the ring I'd ordered and her things.

Her stuff was sent with one of her father's lackeys, and the jeweler I commissioned to sort out her ring for me on short notice was waiting for me in my living room.

The ring is beautiful and actually looks like her.

It's the kind of ring I'd get if this were real between us and she were my doll. My girl.

I put it in my back pocket and head to the hall where all her stuff is. I'm going to go through all her things personally. Never can tell what that old fucker might have put in here. I was surprised when he agreed to have everything sent over.

It's everything she packed up for Florence. It was already packed, so I don't know why that fucker took four days to send it when I requested it the day after the meeting.

There were over twenty suitcases and five smaller bags she

was supposed to carry on her flight, plus four large boxes that were supposed to be shipped over.

Typical princess with too many bags. Ironic how she packed up to move to a different country and ended up with me.

It takes me a little over an hour to go through her stuff. I sorted through her clothes first. Then I got lost in her art. She'd packed up all her art supplies and ten paintings that I have to admit are breathtaking. She's good. She's really good, and definitely right to call herself an artist.

She was going to the Accademia in Florence. I know they don't take any old person there. You have to be good. And because of who runs it, money can't buy you a place with them. You have to earn your spot.

She seems to do a mixture of landscape and dark fantasy. Ma was a landscape person, and she liked doing portraits too. She loved painting people and did many paintings of us.

When I checked out Emelia, I had to admit that the first thing to strike me about her was her talent. Now I've seen it.

It's after seven. Dinner is being made. I have plans to change things up a little bit with Emelia. Now that I have the ring, I think it's time. I look at the elegant little black dress she wore to the ball resting on the arm of the sofa and nod to myself. She will wear this tonight. For me.

I grab it and some of her underwear, then head to my room to get showered and changed. I throw on a black long-sleeved dress shirt and black slacks, then trim my beard just to clean it up. Once I'm done, I make my way to Emelia's room with the little dress and the bag with her panties, knowing she's going to bitch at me for going through her things.

She's sitting by the window when I walk in, still wrapped in that sheet.

She sits up and gives me that look a lot of women give me that I've grown used to. On her, though, it piques my interest, especially when the fire of fury fills her eyes. I love that she tries to stand up to me. She thinks it's courageous, but all it does is turn me on.

"Do you plan to leave me locked up in here for the rest of my life with no clothes?" she snaps, returning to her former stance of defiance.

"Do you want to be locked up naked in here? You look comfortable sitting over there, and maybe I like the idea of having a naked woman in my house."

"Find a different one. The blonde you were with the other day seemed eager to please," she hisses.

Good comeback. I know she's jealous of Gabriella. She shouldn't be, but I like her jealousy. It makes her look prettier, and when her lips pout like that, I imagine them around my cock.

"Come here," I say and she tenses.

"Why?"

"Fucking come here now, Princesca. If you make me get you, you won't like it." Or maybe she will.

Maybe another spanking is in order, although I hope the next time I do that it will be more for pleasure than punishment. I think of how she yielded to me last night and my mouth waters. I want her just like that again, but next time, I want to be inside her.

She likes me. She likes me and doesn't know what to do with the attraction that ripples between us any more than I do.

She gets off the window seat and makes her way over. She smells nice, just like yesterday. I know Priscilla got her some stuff. I'm glad she did. That sweetness compliments her natural fragrance.

When she reaches me, I hold out her dress. Her eyes widen when she realizes it's hers.

"My dress. My things are here?" Her eyes search mine and I almost feel like a prick for depriving her.

"Yes. Your things are here."

"Can I have them?" She raises her brows.

"Eventually." I smile.

"Ugh." Her shoulders slump. "Why? Why can't I have them now? Do you know how weird that is?"

"There are a few things I need you to do for me." It's time to lay down the law.

"What? What more do I need to do than I've already done?"

"Aww, so much more, Princesca. I want your obedience." I spell it out because I haven't said anything of the sort yet.

"Obedience? What the hell do you think I am?"

"Like fuck. You better understand me and agree, or you'll stay locked up in here naked until the wedding. Hit me or strike back in any way, and you'll know what being locked up means. Do you understand me?" I ask, holding her gaze.

"I understand."

"The only way you leave this property is if I say so. And when I buy you something, you wear it. When I tell you to do something, you do it."

"Why didn't you just get a dog?" she throws back. "There's a reason they're a man's best friend."

I catch her face and pull her close. She gasps. "That smart mouth of yours is something else. So pretty I want to kiss it, and so hot I want to fuck it. You don't talk back to me. Baby, if I wanted a fucking dog, I'd have one."

I release her and she catches her breath. Biting back a whimper, she looks at me, disappointed. "You're like two different people."

I know what she means, but it has to be this way.

"This is what you get. Now, put the dress on, come to dinner with me, and we'll talk about you getting your things."

"Dinner?" she asks.

I smile.

"You want me to have dinner with you?"

"I want you to have dinner with me."

"And you want me to wear the dress I wore to the ball?" she notes and looks me over curiously.

I bite down hard on my back teeth at being caught out but smile that she was so observant.

"I do," I answer. "What can I say? I liked the way you looked in it."

It represents a time when I couldn't have her. She was untouchable, just like her father. I was the boy again, poor in a different sort of way, looking on at something I couldn't have. I'll admit it.

If circumstances were different and she wasn't who she is, and her fucking father wasn't who he is, I would have bid on her. I would have bid on her and made sure I got her.

But look at me now.

"Why didn't you talk to me at the ball?" she asks. The question completely throws me.

I chuckle, deep and low. "No..." I shake my head at her.

"No to what?" She narrows her eyes, confused.

"We're not those people. I'm not a man who will fight for you, Emelia Balesteri. Your father kept you in the dark. But you are just as evil as he is to me, which makes you nothing. Do not make the mistake of thinking we're anything more than what we are. We are not. *You* are not."

Her eyes brim with tears. I feel like shit, but needs must.

"Take off the sheet and put on the dress," I instruct, and for the first time, she listens and doesn't argue.

She allows the sheet to fall from her, revealing her nakedness to me. My cock hardens as I look her up and down. I've never seen a more perfect woman. Everything about her is perfect. *Everything.* Including her soul. I don't know how Riccardo created such a being. She must take after her mother.

I smile when she looks at me. Her cheeks flush. Her nipples turn hard, and the heft of her breasts bounces as she bends down to put her panties on.

She puts on the bra and then her dress. Then the shoes. Her hair is in a ponytail, though. I want it down, just like it was at the ball.

"Take your hair down," I say.

Again, she does as she's told and the tumble of shiny dark locks flows down her shoulders. She tucks a lock behind her ear. I thought that was the style, but it seems to be something she does out of habit.

I put out my hand to her and she takes it. My hands swallow hers right up and she feels small next to me.

We leave the room. I realize this is the first time we walk together in this hall. Manni brought her here on Saturday night, and the only interaction we've had is in that room.

Despite the hold I have on her, the dullness in her mood, and the way I tainted anything we shared last night, she seems taken with the place.

She looks at the design and the décor of the corridor. On this side of the house, I have a balcony that overlooks the ground floor and the entire ceiling is made of glass.

The floor is marble throughout the whole house but changes to stone when we step out to the terrace.

As we step into the night, the cool night air lifts her hair and it caresses her skin.

The long dinner table by the fountain is set. Both Priscilla and Candace are standing by, waiting to serve us.

The feast on the table looks amazing. It's all my favorites. I hope Emelia doesn't give me any hassle tonight.

Priscilla smiles when we approach, and Emelia does too. It's the first time I've seen her smile. It's a pretty sight.

"Wow, look at you," Priscilla beams. "You look absolutely stunning," she adds.

Candace nods her agreement.

"Thank you," Emelia replies.

They both look like they want to continue conversation with my bride-to-be, but when they see the stern expression on my face, they know they mustn't. The mood shifts instantly as they both look at me.

"Well, if there's nothing more you need, we'll go," Candace says.

"There's nothing more I need. You may take your leave," I dismiss them, and they leave us.

I pull out a chair for Emelia to sit. She does but doesn't look at me.

"Thank you," she mutters, her voice barely audible.

I sit at the head of the table right across from her. It's too far away, but it works. I want to look her right in the eye when I talk to her and tell her what's happening next, then I'll give her the ring.

She scans her surroundings and gazes over the sea. In the moonlight it looks like one of her paintings. I wonder what it is she sees when she looks at it. Ma used to say that a real artist sees the world through different eyes.

"What is it?" I ask, startling her.

She returns her focus to me and shakes her head. "Nothing. It's nothing."

"No? You look like you saw something."

"I did. I just don't wish to share my vision with you," she answers and straightens in her chair.

"Eat."

She starts to serve herself food. It's not a lot, but at least she's taking it.

When her plate is full, she sets down her fork and looks at me, her lips parted, readying to ask me a question I know I probably won't answer.

"What did my father do to you?" she says.

I was right. I won't answer that question. "That's a matter for another night."

"Why? Don't you think I should know why I'm here? I think I deserve to know why my life was stolen from me and why I deserve this. You know stuff about me, don't you? You know who I am and what I am. You know who my friends are. Heck, you knew I was heading to Italy last Sunday and stopped me in my tracks. I worked so hard to get into the Accademia. I worked so hard...and the best thing happened to me when they accepted me. You took it all away. I want to know why."

As the words fall from her lips, I ask myself that question again. Of who I am and what I've become. What kind of man have I become to do this to an innocent?

As I look at her, though, as I take in her beauty, I remind myself of the mission and the plan. That same beauty is part and parcel of all Riccardo Balesteri owned. The beautiful woman before me is indeed an asset.

"What did he do to you?" she asks again, her voice demanding.

"He took everything from me and made sure my family had nothing," I answer, speaking words I've never had to share with anyone. Anybody who knows us already had a good idea of what happened, even if they didn't know the gory details.

"So, that's my fault, and I have to suffer for what he did?" she retorts.

"Art of war. Sometimes things happen and the good have to suffer for the bad."

"That's bullshit. How dare you say such a thing to me? Look at this place. You have so much. You took so much, and now you've taken me to screw with my father. How could you be so wicked? You have so much money."

"Money is not everything, Princesca. It can't bring the dead back," I answer and she swallows her words. "Enough. We aren't talking about this anymore."

I don't want to, not with her. Not with anyone.

I stand up, walk back to her, and pull out the box with her ring inside it. She winces when she sees it, but I don't miss the way her eyes sparkle with surprise when I pop the box open and she looks at the ring inside.

It's the beauty of it. Even she can't resist looking at it for what it is.

"Give me your left hand," I say and her features become stony. "Emelia, don't make me ask again."

She puts out her hand. I take the ring and slip it on her ring finger, feeling the tremble in her soft skin.

She stares at the ring, closes her eyes tightly, and when she opens them, tears again stream down her cheeks.

"I don't understand why you'd get something so beautiful for someone you think is nothing," she states. I grit my teeth, pushing aside the emotion that's threatening to break free and crack the wall around my heart. "Can I go back to my room, please?"

"You haven't eaten."

"I'm not hungry," she breathes. "Can I go?"

"Yes."

She stands, readying herself to flee, but I catch her wrist and hold her in place.

"You'll pick your dress tomorrow. The seamstress will be here at midday. Make sure you're ready."

I release her. She doesn't answer. She just walks away, and I stare after her.

I wanted to be firm with her tonight, but I feel like the ruthless, heartless bastard I've trained so hard to be. I should congratulate myself. I made it.

I should be proud.

I just don't feel it because I like her too.

CHAPTER THIRTEEN

MASSIMO

Tristan walks into my office with a stern expression on his face.

He messaged an hour ago requesting we meet as soon as possible. I had a meeting with some of our top investors, which I rearranged because I know when my brother requests to meet like this, it's serious.

He skips past pleasantries and stalks to my desk. From the inside of his black biker jacket he takes out a white envelope and sets it down before me.

"You need to see this," he states with a firm nod.

I open the envelope straightaway and pull out a picture. My hands tense up when I see who's on it.

It's a man called Vlad Kuznetsov. He's a Bratva assassin who belongs to a group called the Circle of Shadows. More importantly, he's supposed to be dead. I should know. I helped kill him, or so I thought.

"Where did you get this?" I ask.

Tristan pulls up a chair and sits. I expect the ashen look on his face. It was he who pulled the trigger. One lone bullet to the heart that should have killed the bastard who murdered his wife. Why am I looking at a picture of this man? A very recent photo, given the fucking date.

"Dominic," Tristan says, running a hand over his beard.

The one-word answer is enough because Dominic can find shit you don't even know is happening. Like this.

Tristan sighs and straightens up. "Our guys found Pierbo's stuff in a dumpster near the docks. Some burned, some not. A camera was amongst them. Smashed and burnt to a fucking crisp. Dominic was able to get the image from the chip. Massimo, look at the date when the picture was taken."

I do again. My eyes snap wide when I realize it was Saturday. The date Pierbo supposedly killed himself.

"*Fuck.*"

"Yeah."

Vlad and his band of assassins are known enemies to anyone in the Italian Mafia and those in the Bratva who don't fall part of his circle. Those of the Bratva who link up with them are few and far between.

"If he's here, someone hired him," I point out.

"Don't I fucking know it. Fucking hell, Massimo. This knocked me for six. I thought I got this guy. I thought I killed his ass, yet here he is. I already felt like shit because he was the hand that dealt the blow to my Alyssa. But I never got the man who ordered the hit on her."

I feel his pain as he speaks. Although five years have passed, the murder of his wife is not pain that will ever go away, especially not when her head was delivered to him in a box.

Mortimer Viggo is the elusive leader of the Circle of Shadows. It was he who sent Vlad to kill Alyssa. None of us have ever seen him, and nobody knows how to find him.

Tristan and Alyssa had been together since high school, but she became a debt repayment to Mortimer when her father owed money. Mortimer was going to give her to Vlad. However, when she and Tristan got married, defying the agreement, Mortimer sent Vlad after her to punish her. The demon waited until her wedding night to dole out that punishment.

He took her, killed her, and sent her head in a box to Tristan, gift wrapped, the very next day. We then found her body in parts, scattered all over L.A. That's not something you get over.

"Tristan. We looked everywhere we could for Mortimer."

"I know."

We searched all four corners of the globe for two years and found nothing. Now Vlad is back from the dead and he's here in L.A. That could only be happening if Mortimer ordered it.

"Fuck, Massimo." He balls his fists and seethes. "I can't tell you how screwed I feel right now."

I get up and walk around to him and rest my hand on his shoulder. "We'll get to the bottom of this. Please do not do anything until we have more information." I want to tell him not to do anything stupid but think better of it.

I can't say that to him. Whatever he chooses to do would not be stupid in regards to retaliation and making sure the dead stay dead. He's a man like me. Vengeance is his when he decides. He hates feeling helpless or being in the dark about anything.

"I know if you were me, you'd do something about it," Tristan points out.

"I *am* going to do something about it." I just don't want to lose my brother. Rest assured, that is exactly what would happen. I'd lose him. "Tristan. This guy has been a ghost for the last five years and suddenly resurfaces. Clearly, some plot of shit is happening."

"Right under our noses," he intones and I press my lips together. "Massimo, Pierbo died because he saw him. Vlad wouldn't have wanted our guy to find out he was alive and back in our city."

"No, he wouldn't," I agree. "I can't allow him to do whatever it is he's doing, though." The last five years were his get-out-of-jail card.

"You'd be rocking the nest, Massimo," Tristan states. Worry fills his eyes.

"I know." Of course I know. Rocking the fucking nest would stir trouble. I'm boss, and if Pa were still boss, he would say the same as me. "We'll look into it, get our best men out there, and try to find him no matter where he is. We'll kill his ass and make sure we cut off his fucking head this time. For Alyssa."

He releases a sharp breath and nods. "Thank you, brother. It's a hard thing for a man to accept he was useless to the one person who needed him the most. Vlad and his band of fuckers stole her from me, and I never knew until it was too late. I keep remembering how it happened. I took her to the cabin. We were supposed to be leaving for our honeymoon the next day. I just went into the kitchen to get the champagne, and when I came out, she was gone. That was it. The one thing I had to hold onto was killing him, but Vlad's not dead."

"Tristan, let's stay focused and get this guy. He declared war by coming back here."

―――

Before heading home I decided to go back to the Vincent Thomas Bridge. That is where Tristan and I thought we killed Vlad.

We were fighting on the bridge. Blow for blow, bullets flying. There were four of us in the end. Me and Tristan. Vlad and Aleksei, his right-hand man.

I stabbed Aleksei right in the eye and ended him. At the same time, Tristan shot Vlad. I saw it happen. They were paces away from me. That bullet went in his chest, and he fell. He fell right over the bridge and even hit the panels before he went into the sea.

The bullet should have killed him instantly, but if that didn't get him, the fall should have. The drop is three hundred and sixty-five feet. So he should have been fucked either way. Yet Vlad is alive. Pierbo saw him and got caught.

I thought Riccardo had Pierbo killed. Now it makes sense. Pierbo was a force to be reckoned with. Only a man like Vlad Kuznetsov and the Circle of Shadows could take down a man like him. So now I have more shit on my hands.

More things to get me dirty, and those close to me. Tristan said it well when he talked of rocking the nest. I would be doing exactly that. Rocking an ants' nest. The thing about that, though, is that they don't bother you until you disturb them.

When you do, they all come for you.

They come for you and wipe out whoever is with you.

Right now, we have the advantage. Vlad doesn't know we know he's alive. He must think he got us good with Pierbo's death and destroying the camera.

There's no way I'm going to be able to keep the fact that we know he's alive quiet, though. To look for him, I'm gonna have to ask questions, meaning he'll know we're looking.

That's the risk I'll have to take.

I make my way home and walk into Emelia's room. She's asleep, and I don't plan to wake her. The lights are out, with just the moonlight spilling in onto her ethereal body.

She even looks like a princess in her sleep. Graceful with her dark locks flowing over the pillow and her hands rested at her sides.

The report on her today was that she was quiet. Priscilla said she barely spoke and did what she was told to do. She tried on her wedding dresses and didn't like any. I don't know if that means she was being difficult or if she genuinely didn't like them.

The seamstress is coming back tomorrow. I don't want to be a bastard and pick a dress for her. I already feel bad enough about the ring.

She stirs, as if she can sense me concocting shit. I back away quietly toward the door.

Emelia will be my wife in a few weeks.

Five years ago, I didn't have anybody like that.

Now I do.

Rocking the nest to find Vlad means I'll involve her too.

CHAPTER FOURTEEN

EMELIA

My heart squeezes as I gaze at my reflection in the long mirror.

This wedding dress I'm wearing is beautiful, very beautiful.

It looks like it was pulled from a fairytale. Definitely fit for a princess. Its sleeveless bodice hugs my frame, accentuating my breasts and the tiny curve of my waist. The endless length of fabric flowing from the body creates that magical effect, flirting with my legs as I move.

I can imagine all eyes on me on the big day. I've tried on ten dresses today, and this one looks the best.

I really didn't like the ones yesterday, but if I'm honest, I wouldn't have liked anything with the mood I was in. Trying on wedding dresses for a disaster wedding couldn't have been more depressing to me.

I always felt, when I saw the dress I wanted, I'd fall for it the same way I fell for the guy. He'd be the one, and the dress would be the one too. That's if it was real.

If it were real, I'd pick this dress. This morning, I thought I'd make things less difficult on myself by pretending it was real. I knew if I sent the seamstress away again today, Massimo would think I was being difficult and punish me for it or some shit.

The dress sparkles against the sunlight beaming in from the long French windows of the hall. It's truly, truly perfect. It's probably the most beautiful thing I've ever seen.

Just like the ring on my finger, however, it doesn't feel like it belongs to me. It feels like it doesn't belong *on* me.

Both remind me of poison. The same way poison works its way into your body and slowly kills you. Both the dress and the ring have that effect on me.

Both are designed to hurt me.

Both are a poisonous reminder that I am owned.

I belong to Massimo D'Agostino, and just like one of his many assets, I am property. That is all I am to him, nothing more.

"How's it going in there?" the seamstress calls out from the other side of the curtains. The hall was set up so I'd have some privacy to change.

"Good, I...like this one," I reply. I give myself a once-over in the mirror and make my way out through the curtains.

The seamstress gasps, along with Priscilla and Candace, who came to help me. I swear Priscilla looks like she's going to cry. It makes me think of how I imagined my mother to be during this time. I tear up at the thought.

"My God," Priscilla says. She walks up to me and holds out her hands to take mine. I give them to her, and she gently squeezes. "Emelia, you look truly beautiful."

"Thank you. Thank you so much," I reply.

"My dear, you are one of the most beautiful brides I've ever seen," the seamstress states, bringing her hands together. Candace nods her agreement. "I second that. You look amazing."

"Thank you all. I guess this is the winning dress, then," I reply.

"Definitely a winner," she agrees. "It's perfect. I think we just need to take in the top here a little bit." She tugs on the edge of the binding.

"Okay."

"And may I suggest having your hair up to show off the back design? And a tiara, unless you specially want a veil."

"I like the idea of my hair up and the tiara," I agree completely. When I first saw the dress, I already thought the back needed to be displayed. It has scallops going down the curve. It's as beautiful as the front.

"Perfect. You're an easy bride to work with," she beams, rubbing her hands together. Her green eyes sparkle with delight and the crow's feet at the corners crinkle as she smiles wide.

If there's one thing I've noticed so far, it's that everyone who's been in contact with me since coming to live here has been really nice.

"Thanks, I'm glad to hear."

"Okay, go change, and I'll work my magic. I'll come back in a few days, and we'll talk about shoes and accessories."

"That sounds great." It sounds like I'm talking by default. Like the words are coming out of my mouth, but I don't know what I'm actually saying.

Candace seems to notice. I can tell from the sympathetic look she offers.

I duck back behind the curtains and place a hand at my heart when I look at myself again in the mirror.

I wish I could be happier.

I wish this moment could feel better, that I weren't marrying a man who has this effect on me I can't explain. It hurt me to no end when he called me nothing. I can't quite explain how it hurt me when he said it. It felt worse than feeling like a thing. Now, I'm not so sure where I am in my mind. What I am is stuck.

I change into a pair of jeans and a camisole. *Clothes.* My actual clothes.

When I woke this morning, there were two things in my room that I didn't have yesterday. The first was my suitcases and bags I was supposed to take to Florence, and the second was a little bit of freedom. The door was open. It wasn't locked. I could walk around outside the room, and I could open the window.

It was clear that Massimo had specifically come into the room last night while I was asleep and done all of that. I just knew it was him. The scent of him lingered in the air.

What wasn't there were my art supplies and paintings. I don't know if that was because Dad didn't send them, or if they are here and Massimo decided not to give them to me.

By the time I unpacked my stuff and changed, it was time for my dress fitting.

I pull my hair back into a ponytail and head out again with the dress. The seamstress takes it from me and places it in a bag.

Candace walks up to me and taps my shoulder. She isn't wearing her uniform today. Instead, she's wearing a long-sleeved T-shirt and a pair of jeans. Her hair is braided to the side, and she wears a pair of Converses that make her look trendy.

"I'm hanging out with you today," she says. "How about a walk on the beach?"

I smile at that. "I would love to."

"You girls get back in time for lunch," Priscilla says.

"We will," Candace replies. I just smile because it's not like I have a choice.

We leave the hall and head down the same corridor I walked with Massimo last night, but instead of taking the stairs leading up to the terrace, we go down another set of stairs. The door opens out right onto a patio that leads to the beach. As Candace opens the doors, the salty scent of the sea washes over me and I feel alive.

It's amazing what we take for granted in life. Small things like feeling the hot sun on my skin as the languid breeze lifts the ends of my hair are things I've missed so much over the last few days. I smile and savor the feeling, savor the freedom.

And since I absolutely love walking on the beach, I take off my shoes so I can feel the sand between my toes.

Candace chuckles. I smile back.

"Are you sure you want to do that?" she asks.

"Oh yes. I always take my shoes off when I'm on the beach."

"Maybe I'm too used to it," she answers. "Let's go this way."

We walk down near the rock pool and sit on the sand where it offers a scenic view of endless sea. It reminds me of Italy. Of the beach in Tuscany Dad always took me and Ma to when we went on vacation.

"Let's stay here for a while, then I'll show you around the rest of the place and maybe give you a tour of the house," she says.

I guess she must have been given the okay to show me more than the beach.

"Thank you. This is beautiful," I say. "I love it."

"Me too. Reminds me of Sicily."

"Yes," I agree. "I used to love walking along the beach when I visited my relatives there."

"When did you last go back?"

"A few years ago, with my mother. Just before...before she died." It's still hard to say the words that confirm her death.

She looks sad to hear that. "I'm sorry."

"It's okay. It was a few years ago. I still miss her so much, but death happens, doesn't it." I sound braver than I feel. Those words mask the truth of what I feel deep inside. I still cry for her. That sadness never ends, and I know if she were alive now, this wouldn't be happening to me.

"Yeah...death happens," she replies. Sadness clouds her eyes. "Both my parents are dead. It was an accident."

"I'm sorry to hear," I sympathize.

"Thanks."

"My mom had cancer. That last trip to Sicily was her last visit to her homeland. We painted... That's what I do. I paint."

"What do you paint?" She sounds intrigued.

"Everything. Anything my imagination conjures up."

"That sounds cool. I write poetry. I stuck with it after college."

"*After?*" I thought she was close to my age.

"After. I'm twenty-five." She beams.

"You look a lot younger."

"Thank you. I think it's my youthful spirit." She giggles. "I studied English literature. I wanted to be a teacher, but I guess I'll get myself together eventually. It can be tough out there trying to get started in your career."

"Yeah," I agree. My launch into my career has been tough for a reason I'm sure most people never encounter, and it looks like it's never going to happen for me. "How long have you worked here?"

"Years. I've known Massimo all my life, though." Her face shows that fond look I've seen on Priscilla's face. I hope she isn't going to sing his praises or do anything like that. I don't want to hear it.

"If it's okay, I...don't really want to talk about him," I say. That's the best way I can put it without sounding too rude, although I probably do sound exactly that.

"You don't have to." She nods. "I'm not here for that. I thought maybe you could use someone to talk to. Or just hang with. If you do want to talk about him, though, I swear everything you say will be strictly off the record. I mean that."

I gaze at her, wondering if I can let my guard down and trust her. She and Priscilla have been nice to me, but that doesn't mean anything when it comes to loyalty.

I learned well from dealing with people who worked for my father. In the end, they would always answer to him. Maybe, though... I could just talk about the things on my mind that she must already be aware of.

"It's hard, hard being here. Hard...doing what I'm doing. Marrying a man I don't know," I explain. Suddenly, I feel like I want to spill my heart.

She nods, understanding. "I know. I can only imagine. I could see it as you tried on one dress after another. You look like you want to be happy because the dresses and your ring are so beautiful, but the situation spoils it."

She hit the nail on the head. "Yeah. All my hopes and dreams crushed just like that. My life stolen. I don't know how I'm supposed to live like this. There's no escape for me."

She looks down at the sand, stares at it for a moment, then her gaze flicks back up to meet mine.

"Emelia..." Her voice trails off. "I feel sorry that this has happened to you. I confess that I don't agree. I'm paid to do a job, but I see many things I don't like. Your father did a lot to

Massimo's family, but I don't agree that you have to suffer for it."

My interest piques at her words. She sounds like she might have answers.

"I don't know what he did. I don't know anything. Up until last week, I never even knew my father knew the D'Agostinos."

"Yeah, that figures. Women and children are kept out of business. I wasn't so lucky. Just like Massimo, I saw the ugly side when I was far too young. It changes you forever."

As she speaks, I get the impression that there's more to her story than just her parents' accident.

"What happened?" I ask.

"I...can't talk about my story. Not yet, anyway. Maybe someday." She gives me a nervous, shaky smile. "Massimo, though... Things changed a lot for him when his family lost everything. My family has served the D'Agostinos for many generations. Being the help's daughter, I heard things. I saw things. I know things I probably shouldn't."

My chest tightens. "Like what?"

"Have you ever heard of the Syndicate?"

I shake my head. "No. Never."

"Good. They're a secret society, for the most part, although they don't keep their existence secret. If you know, you *know*. What you don't know is how they operate and what they do, but it's not hard to figure out they're untouchable. They're made up of six powerful crime families. Two of the current leaders are your father and Massimo's."

My eyes widen. "My father?" I can't imagine that I wouldn't have known about them.

"Yeah. I'm not surprised that you didn't know. Membership is only made up of men. So, maybe your uncles or someone like that would have dealings with them."

Uncle Leo is basically Dad's right-hand man. I'm sure he knows. "I see."

"You get initiated based on wealth or resources. Whatever you can bring to the table that's valuable. They live by a creed they sign in blood to protect each other to the death," she explains, hugging her knees to her chest. "Your father and Giacomo D'Agostino used to be best friends. Your father stole the business you now have from him and wiped him out. Left him with nothing. And because he had nothing, he got uninitiated from the Syndicate. That is worse than having nothing. It's often worse than death because you aren't supposed to be in a situation where you can share information about the Syndicate and its secret plans and plots."

Jesus Christ. I can't believe what I'm hearing.

"What happened to them?"

"Everything bad. They lost their home. At one point, they were living in a trailer park. Just barely. Fifteen years ago, Giacomo started his oil business and flourished. The wealth was like wildfire, but it never made up for their biggest loss of all. They lost all they owned during that terrible time, but they lost something worse when Massimo's mother died."

"What happened to her?" I ask.

"She killed herself when Massimo was twelve. He found her."

"Oh my God." I bring my hands up to my cheeks.

"I know. It was so sad because she was like this perfect being. She was always so nice to me. Called me the daughter she never had. I was always hanging out with the boys. Massimo never said as much, but he blames your father for her death."

My eyes grow wide as I recall what Massimo said about not being able to bring the dead back to life.

"This is a nightmare."

She smiles without humor. "It's worse than a nightmare, Emelia. This war began long before we were born. Massimo blames your father for her death and the hard life they were forced into when he was growing up. But his father blames your father for so much more. The thing about hearing too much is having to bear the responsibility of knowing when to keep quiet. The reason why their fathers fell out was her. Massimo's mother."

My breath hitches in my chest. "What do you mean?"

"They were both in love with her," she answers and a steel weight drops in the pit of my stomach. "That's all I know, but it makes you wonder, doesn't it? Makes you wonder what else happened."

Secrets and lies, that's what my world feels like it's based on. I stare at her long and hard and wonder why she's telling me so much.

"Why? Why are you telling me all of this, Candace?" I ask.

She raises her shoulders into a shrug. "Maybe I feel bad that you have to be dragged into a battle that isn't yours to fight. Maybe I feel bad that your life will be stolen from you if you marry Massimo. Maybe I'd just hate to be you. Or... maybe I'm trying to justify my reasons to help you, breaking loyalty to a man I think of as a brother."

My nerves scatter. "What are you saying, Candace?"

Will she help me? How?

She leans in close. Her eyes turn glassy as tears well within them. "He trusts me the most. That's why I get to hang out with you. Me and Priscilla. But he's not the boy I grew up with. None of the brothers are. It's not their fault, though."

No, it seems to be my father's.

"Candace, are you going to help me?" I ask, cautiously. We both look around nervously.

We're far away from the closest guard, who's stationed on

the terrace. He can't hear us talking, but it's understandable given the circumstances that fear and paranoia would set in.

Candace nods when I look back at her. "If he finds out I was disloyal in any way, I wouldn't blame him if he killed me."

"Then don't. I couldn't bear it." I wince, shaking my head.

"Evil will always continue to have its way if good people stand by and watch, Emelia. Evil will always win if good people sit back and allow it to happen. I would never forgive myself if I didn't help you, but please think before you act." She holds my gaze as I consider her words.

Think before I act...

A chance to escape is worth gold to me right now, but I know what she means. If I get it wrong, it won't just be me who will be punished.

She looks ahead of us and carefully points to the end of the beach where the boats are docked.

"Do you see that section at the end of the docks?"

"Yes." From here it's almost a blur, but I can see the end of the boardwalk. The waves crash against the rocks, and the area looks like it cuts off after that point.

"The cameras don't work there. Just past the area with the palm trees. There's one camera on a lamp post. That's it. The rowboat is the only boat without an alarm on it," she explains.

I can't believe my ears. She's just given me the answer.

"Oh my God, Candace," I gasp.

"Don't even try to take any of the other boats. Massimo keeps the keys on him at all times, and even if you could get it to work, he has a security system on it that he can control from inside the house. It will alert him the second the boat engine switches on. So, your only choice is the rowboat."

With trembling lips, I nod. "Okay... I'll go for the rowboat. Candace—"

"Emelia, it's dangerous," she interrupts. "That's the most

important warning I'll give you. Dangerous waters. You're right in the heart of it on that side, but there's a port about five miles out. Getting there in a rowboat is the hardest part. You have to be careful."

God... I know nothing about rowing a boat, let alone rowing one on dangerous waters, but this is a route to escape. A chance for freedom. A chance to have my life back. I would be a fool to miss a chance like that even with the risk involved.

"I'll be okay. I have to be."

"Then, please...make sure you flee and never look back if you do it, because if he finds you, he'll know it could only be me or Priscilla who told you how to escape. So...please think properly before you try it. He's given permission for us to show you around. It's up to you to gain his trust for you to walk around without supervision and the guards on constant lookout." She reaches out and takes my hands. "Please think about it before you do anything. That's my one request."

"I will," I promise.

I look ahead, see freedom, and I almost taste it.

How do I get Massimo to trust me?

Obedience.

Do what he says.

Being his.

CHAPTER FIFTEEN

MASSIMO

I stand, look each member of the Syndicate in the eyes, and raise the ceremonial blade.

All eyes are on me.

Apart from Pa, Riccardo, and his brother, these are men I've never seen before. All men of power with incredible wealth totaling twelve, including me.

They all sit around the long rectangular table in the boardroom and watch me. Me, the youngest, newest member getting ready to initiate myself and sign the blood oath to the creed.

They will not speak to me until I take the oath. And we have much to speak about.

As I slice the tip of my forefinger, I rivet my gaze to Riccardo's. I glare at him long and hard, making sure the other members of the Syndicate can watch me and take note that I have a problem with him.

They'll know the story. They'll know the past. It doesn't

sit well with me that these are men who could have killed me and my family on Riccardo's word, but this is the next phase of power.

Drops of blood drip onto the contract. One similar to the document we gave Riccardo.

This one stipulates that I share my resources, power, and life with the members. One body, one power, all to pursue wealth.

My blood on the contract is my signature. It's a serious thing, because to sign the creed means you sign your life away. The only way out is death, or like I've witnessed with my own father, disavowal.

That will not happen to me.

When I place the knife back on the table, Phillipe, the chairman, nods his approval. I saw the way he looked at me when I walked in. He and the two Bratva leaders exchanged glances. Curious glances. There's a spark of endorsement in his eyes now as he looks me over.

They all know I have Riccardo's voting rights.

What they don't know is what will happen now that I have them. This sort of thing is not something that's ever happened before. Taking voting rights for a debt. Questions we won't answer will be raised.

I sit. Pa gives me the final nod. I'm a member now, just like him.

This is where it will all begin. The next generation. When Pa leaves, I'll be here with Tristan the same way the leaders are with their counterparts. Riccardo is here with Leo, his brother. They both look at me from across the table. Seething.

Powerless, useless, helpless...

I could almost laugh. I would almost laugh if not for the image of his daughter in my mind.

Powerless, useless, helpless. It describes her too.

I haven't seen her in four days.

I've been busy with my men on the streets, looking for Vlad. I'm sure to shit the rats have whispered to him that I know he's alive and I'm on the hunt for his ass, because there's no trace of him. I'll also admit that I've been avoiding Emelia. I thought it was better to, but not seeing her has grated on my nerves.

Phillipe gives me a nod and clears his throat. His tanned olive skin looks stretched when he smiles. Like he's stayed in the sun too long. It makes his light blue eyes appear more intense.

"Wonderful," he says. "It's great to have a powerful man like you among our fold. You are just like your father."

"I take that as the highest compliment." It's the truth. I do, and more so because Pa became a titan without them.

"You should," he states. "Now, on to business."

"Fire away," Pa says.

"Taking a leader's voting rights is rendering him powerless in matters we need to agree on as a group. This is the first time such a thing has happened. We'd love for you to shed some light on the matter."

Phillipe is no fool. I'm certain it's as obvious to him as it is to Riccardo what we mean to do. We're devils come out to play. Everyone has questions. We'll decide how we answer.

Pa steeples his fingers and leans forward onto the table. "He owed a debt to me, and that is one of the ways I chose to be repaid. It's as simple as that."

"Let's be real, shall we?" Phillipe states, shifting his gaze to Riccardo. "Losing voting rights better be worth it. I'm also aware that a majority of your assets now belong to Massimo in his ascension as boss of the D'Agostino family. All but Balesteri Investments, but if I'm not mistaken, your heir will receive that. News has spread abroad of her engagement to Massimo. Meaning that's practically his too. It is not my place to question you on matters outside the Syndicate, but if I'm pushed, I will. My question is, what now?"

I like this guy. He cuts straight to the shit. These men aren't stupid. They're gonna know that we must have one hell of a debt over Riccardo's head to demand so much. I'm sure they'll most likely guess that Emelia fell part of the repayment plan. It's not hard to figure out things like that in our world.

Riccardo tenses, as does his brother. Backed into the proverbial corner. Right where we want him.

"I'm aware the situation is shit, but allow me time, and I will sort it all out," Riccardo replies.

"You better hope so. We'll give you eight weeks to sort yourself out, then we'll meet again to discuss this further. However, that still leaves the matter of the tip in the balance of power." Phillipe looks back at me. "Massimo, regardless of what happens to Riccardo, you will hold the voting rights of him and your father. What do you plan to do with it?"

It's my turn to talk. Everything I say now will be the guide for my future.

"I do not plan to rule over you." They all look at me with enquiring eyes. "The Syndicate is about brotherhood and unity. The creed that protects us binds us together. When it is abused, the structure crumbles, so I won't be using the extra vote unless the situation arises and I have to. If I have to, I'm sure we'll discuss what will be fair and reasonable and for the benefit of the group, if and when the time comes."

When Phillipe nods, I know he's satisfied with the answer, but he's not stupid. None of them are. They'll know revenge made us want Riccardo powerless.

"Very well, then. Welcome to the Brotherhood, Massimo D'Agostino."

I bow my head with reverence. Then they continue talking about business.

The meeting goes on for another hour before it closes. Throughout that whole time, I could feel Riccardo's eyes on me. I wonder what he's thinking about the most. What I'm doing to his precious daughter, or what I'm going to do to him?

When the meeting ends and Pa and I walk out to the car park, I expect Riccardo to come after us, so I'm not surprised when he does.

He calls my name. I turn to face him. Pa stops next to me and squares his shoulders.

"You better not be hurting my daughter," he seethes.

All I do is stare at him.

"You animal. You dirty animal. The two of you," he adds, looking from Pa to me.

"You aren't that bright, are you? Coming to talk to us when we've barely left the building," I retort.

"This is an outrage. A complete outrage. But this is what you wanted." He looks at Pa. "An eye for an eye."

"Fuck you, Riccardo," Pa tells him. "I don't know why you keep making the same mistakes. You don't get it, do you? We have the upper hand. I can destroy you with one word."

Riccardo balls his fists and glares at us, his face contorting with rage. "This is not over. You." He points at me. "I remember how you looked at my girl at the ball. You had to tie me down to beat me. Knowing there's no way in hell you'd get her otherwise. You fucking piece of shit. She will never want you. You can do whatever you want. She won't want you. You will always be *nothing*."

His words should roll off my back. They shouldn't mean anything, but I want to beat the shit out of him.

"Nothing," he repeats. And that's it. I lose my shit and grab him by his neck.

Motherfucker. I don't know who the fuck he thinks he's talking to. I hold on tight to his throat and squeeze hard. We're the same height, but I have more muscle. I'm built like a tank while he's an old man. He yelps, trying to wrench my hands free, but I keep hold of him.

"Get off me," he shouts.

"Fucking dog. I am walking on thin ice, ready to snap and kill you fucking dead, Riccardo Balesteri. Believe me, I'm ready to kill your ass dead. I just want to see you suffer, but my oh my, death might be better," I snarl.

It's Pa's hand on my shoulder that snaps me out of the haze of anger.

"Let him go, son. He's just rattled because he can't do shit to us. His words are just that."

The thing is, his words are just words indeed, but they got to me, and he knows that. That's why he said them.

Lifting my head, I see Phillipe and the Bratva leaders ahead of us, watching. That curious look is still on their faces.

They want to know what really happened. They want to know how it is I'm marrying my enemy's daughter, and why I have control of his power. They want to know how we got a man who was supposed to be untouchable backed into a corner.

They would rip Riccardo apart if they knew what he did.

Then they'd come for her too. *Emelia.* They would kill her without hesitation just for sharing the same blood, uncaring what she is to me.

I think of the other night when I went to her room. When I thought of what Vlad did to Alyssa, I thought of protecting her. That same force compels me to do the same now. The Syndicate won't be different from Vlad. Minus the creepy, unsavory fascination he has with women, they'll be brutal about the way they kill her if they ever find out Riccardo was stealing from them. We'll get more than just her head in a box.

My temper is drawing attention to us, and to her too. I can't allow my hatred for her father to get to me.

I release Riccardo on that thought and step back. He notices Phillipe and the Bratva leaders watching and at least has the good sense to tamp down his rage.

"Don't fucking talk to me unless you have business with me," I hiss. "See you soon, *Dad*," I add with menace in my tone and a crude chuckle. *Motherfucker*. He hates me calling him Dad to no end.

Pa and I leave him standing there, stewing in his rage.

That fucker. I wish I didn't have to see him. Ever. There's the fundraiser and then the wedding. Other than the Syndicate meetings, that will be it. I don't want anything to do with him, and I don't want him near Emelia either.

"Hey," Pa says, touching my elbow as we stop by my car. "You okay?"

"Fine."

"He got to you. I can tell."

"It's alright, Pa. He always gets to me."

"How are things at the house with Emelia?"

Shit. Everything is shit. "Showing her who's boss," I reply, because it's the right thing to say. I can't tell him otherwise.

"Good. Those people deserve what they get. I'll see you in the morning."

I nod and watch him go.

I gotta get this girl out of my head. That's what. I can't

give anyone ideas that she might be a weakness to me, let alone someone like Riccardo.

I have to keep my head screwed on and follow the plan. Marry her and take her fortune. It should be as simple as that.

She's just pussy. The spoils of war. A woman to warm my bed and serve a purpose in the grand scheme of things.

That's what I have to tell myself, no matter how taken I am with her.

CHAPTER SIXTEEN

MASSIMO

Getting home at four on a weeknight is extremely unusual for me.

Usually, I'm either at D'Agostinos Inc. or the club. But after my encounter with Riccardo earlier, I couldn't focus on being at either.

At the club, I can chill, but that usually involves fucking. At D'Agostino, I'd be handling some type of paperwork that I can't afford to mess with in my unfocused mind, so I got Andreas to fill in for me.

I'm home. Deep down I know why I'm here. I just don't want to accept it yet.

Fucking Riccardo. That motherfucking dog always knows how to get under my skin. *Always.*

Always knows what to say to rub me the wrong way, even when I have the upper hand. His fucking words about Emelia got stuck in my head.

All damn day, I tried to rid the insults from my mind. But

I can't shake them. I never knew the bastard saw me looking at Emelia at the ball. I never even knew he would have given two fucks about me at an event like that.

That was my fault. My mistake. I dropped my guard and allowed a moment of weakness, oblivious to the fact that my enemy could see me.

But why should it matter?

Why should I care?

Emelia belongs to me now, no matter what.

She's mine. Nothing can change those signatures on the contract.

So, why do I feel like this? Like it does matter.

Like I want her to want me.

Do I?

Fuck... Since when do I try to lie to myself?

Cards on the table. I fucking know I want her to want me. I have since that damn ball. That's why I'm here. That's why I've been avoiding her.

The marriage was my idea, but I was being a ruthless bastard when I thought of it.

I do want her to want me, but I shouldn't. The second that takes precedence in my mind, I'll start to care, then I risk this opportunity to screw with her father.

There are essentially two parts left to fulfill in this plan. Marry Emelia, then watch the Syndicate sling Riccardo's ass out the door.

I slump down on my bed in exasperation and gaze through the floor-to-ceiling windows to the sea pulling in and out of the shoreline.

The bright sunlight hits the water, sparkling across the surface like diamonds being scattered over it. Then, like a fantasy, Emelia emerges from the water, making me bolt upright.

My wife-to-be rises with the waves and makes her way to the shore.

Wearing a turquoise bikini, that body of hers is on full display, reminding me how much I want to dirty the virgin up and get nasty with her.

We must be a good thirty feet apart, but I can see her golden skin glistening. Radiant against the sunlight.

I watch her. And I want her. I want to touch her and taste her. Consume and devour her. Lust is overriding my ability to think straight or control myself. I don't want to resist. I want to give in and feel that attraction and chemistry that sparks when I'm with her.

Pushing to my feet, I loosen my tie and make my way out onto the terrace, going after what I want—*her*.

Fury fills me when I see Manni walk up to her with a little bag and she hands him something she carried from the sea. Rage consumes me when he says something and she laughs. I've never heard her laugh before, and I certainly never expected to hear the sound being elicited by another man.

To add insult to injury, his fucking eyes are all over her body, lingering on her ass when she bends down to pick something up she dropped. While I've known Manni for close to ten years, I feel like ending him right where he stands. He knows better than to be gawking at a woman who's mine. Lusting after her. What the fuck is he even doing with her?

I make my way to them, not caring that I look like a jealous bastard who's ready to kill. What I hate more is that Emelia seems fascinated by him. It's only when my shoes crunch against the sand nearby that they turn and see me.

Manni looks like he's ready to shit himself while Emelia gives me a hardened stare. The same one she gave me after she saw me out here with Gabriella.

"Boss," Manni says, dipping his head for a reverent nod.

"What are you doing out here?" The indignation in my tone tells him his answer better be good.

"I was just keeping Miss Emelia company. She can't swim very well, and we thought it would be a good idea for me to be out here just in case something happened," he explains.

Fucker. He's telling the truth, but he must know I saw the way he looked at her. Knowing the only punishment I dole out is death, his eyes plead with me not to kill his ass. The length of time he's worked for me and the fact that I've been able to trust him more than most will not make him immune to my wrath.

"Get out of my sight. Next time, if Miss Emelia wants to swim and needs someone to watch her ass, I'll do it," I answer, much to Emelia's embarrassment.

Manni knows what I'm talking about, though, and that I'm not mouthing off about shit.

"Yes, sir," he answers.

"Give me that," I order, beckoning for him to give me the little bag. He does and practically flees.

I glance into the bag and see that it's full of seashells. I then look at Emelia and see how upset she is. Because she has her arms crossed under her breasts, though, all I can focus on is the massive swell of her tits and the depth of her cleavage.

"What is the matter with you?" she snaps. "He wasn't doing anything wrong."

"Do not question my actions. You did not see the way he looked at you."

She smirks without humor and brings her hands up to her cheeks. "Unbelievable. Who cares how he looks at me?"

My eyes snap wide, and I have to bite down hard on my back teeth to tamp down my annoyance. It seems that my absence has loosened things up a little too much, and people, including her, have forgotten she's mine.

"*I* fucking care. Besides, why are you out here dressed like that? You don't have a one-piece bathing suit?" I realize how ridiculous I sound. She does too.

"Massimo. I'm wearing a bikini. People wear them all the time. But hey, if we're playing this game, I should ask where you've been for the last four days."

My lips part and I gaze down at her. Barefooted, she seems so much shorter. I tower over her. The truth of my absence surfaces to my mind, but I will it away.

She mistakes my hesitation for something else, and her eyes cloud with something I don't quite recognize.

"You were with her, weren't you?" she says, and I instantly identify the emotion in her eyes as jealousy. And hurt.

It takes me a moment before I realize she's referring to Gabriella. Before I can answer, though, she starts walking away, back to the house. I catch her arm.

"No," I answer, pulling her back. "I wasn't with Gabriella."

"*Gabriella...*" she repeats thoughtfully. She didn't have Gabriella's name before. Maybe telling her was a mistake.

"I was working," I continue.

"I don't care. You can be with whoever you want," she scoffs with disgust.

"Jealous much?" I taunt.

"Why the hell would I be jealous of her? She's not locked up twenty-four seven and ruled under the thumb of a condescending prick."

Prick? And a condescending one, at that. *Jesus.* This doll certainly has balls. I can't remember the last person to talk to me like that and live to tell the tale. Yet here she is, with her foot practically tapping against the sand, calling me a prick.

A chuckle slips from my lips. "Did you just call me a condescending prick?"

"Yes."

I dip my head briefly then smile at her. She tries to bite back a smile but fails and looks away. I catch her face and guide her gaze back to me.

"You're prettier when you smile," I tell her, and there's a noticeable shift in her mood. Her gaze softens and her shoulders loosen. The defiance isn't so strong.

"Is that you being nice?" she asks.

"I don't do nice."

She pouts, and my gaze drops to her lips. Those lips of hers have me thinking of how perfect they'll look around my cock. That smart mouth of hers will do more than amuse me eventually.

My eyes flick back up to meet hers, and I find myself momentarily in that state of flux again where I'm not sure what to do. I should walk away or send her to her room, but desire has already started to infiltrate my mind.

She sets her hands on her hips, drawing my attention to her body again, and the perfect idea comes to me about how I can reacquaint myself with my wife-to-be.

"Come, let's go clean up," I say.

"*Clean up?*" She arches her brows.

"Bathe." I almost laugh at the deer-in-the-headlights look she gives me.

"*Me*...and you?" Her back becomes rigid, and her entire body tenses. Apprehension fills her eyes. However, instead of the way she looked the other day when she was scared I'd deflower her, there's something else that lurks beyond her gaze that I definitely don't miss. *Lust.*

Invisible fingers of lust reach out to me and as I release her; her cheeks flush.

"Yes, me and you."

"No," she replies.

I give her a grin, and her beautiful eyes become narrowed slits.

"Princesca, I wasn't asking you. I was telling you." I lean closer and brush my nose along her ear. "Stop acting like you don't want to."

"It's not an act."

"No?" I gaze down at her nipples pressing against the sheer fabric of her bikini top. They're hard distinct points that weren't there before.

I smile, reach out, and rub my finger over the taut peak of her left nipple, much to her shock.

"Your body betrays you, Emelia. Come, you just got out of the salty sea, and I just got home from *work*." I yank on my tie, emphasizing the word *work* so she knows I was being serious about where I was. "I haven't played with you in four days. I wouldn't want you to forget what it feels like for me to touch you."

Her face turns red, and a flush creeps down her elegant neck.

Placing my hand at the small of her back, I guide her to the house and take advantage of the moment to run my fingers over her perfect ass.

I usher her to her room, deciding I'll go back to mine later and lock my door. She didn't see where I came from earlier. *Good.* The night I decide to show her my room is the night she'll stay there and move right into my bed.

I walk her into the bathroom and inhale the sweet scents of strawberries and vanilla. I smelled it the other day, but it's stronger inside the bathroom.

I close the door once we're inside. She turns to face me, hesitant, and her eyes take me in as they run over my body.

Nervously, she brings her hands together. I know that all

important question hangs heavily over her head. *When am I going to fuck her?*

I'm surprised I haven't done it already. I won't say anything. It adds to the mystery. It adds to desire.

"Take your clothes off," I tell her, and she obeys. I like that she's become submissive. But maybe it's not that. Maybe it's that she wants to.

Maybe she wants to, like I want her to.

She takes off her top first. My eyes go straight to her tight nipples and the swell of her breasts, round and perfect with the little pink tips begging to be sucked.

When she bends down to push her swimsuit down her legs, her wet hair falls over her face and her breasts bobble.

As she straightens up, that look returns to her eyes, and her hands tremble when I look at her pretty cunt right there, waiting for the taking.

I step forward. She steps back but looks up at me with fear all over her face.

I smile and brush my finger over her jaw. "I told you. I'm not that kind of monster. I'm not going to hurt you."

"Why should I believe you?"

I move in, press my lips to her cheek, and linger by her ear. "Princesca, you'll believe me because I haven't given you any reason not to. You've been in my home for almost a week. If I were that kind of monster, I would have fucked your brains out the way I wanted to that first night."

I know she's wet. If I felt her tight little pussy now, I know she'd be wet from my dirty words. When I move back, she tries to assert that defiance again but fails. I smile to myself.

With that, I unbutton my shirt and slide it down my shoulders. I shed my pants next, along with my shoes and socks. The curious look on her face as she watches me undress is classic. She's watching with fascination she's trying to hide. *Fascination*, which becomes more evident when I get down to my boxers, push them down my legs, and my cock juts free, perfectly erect and ready to fuck her.

She's looking exactly where I want her to look, and I hope she answers the next question I have in the positive.

"Is this the first time you've ever seen a naked man, Emelia?" I ask.

Her eyes meet mine. "Yes..." she answers hesitantly. It sounds like music to my ears.

I'm still in two minds about that best friend of hers. I don't know much about him off paper, but I have this feeling he wanted more than friendship with her. Looking at her, I don't know what man alive wouldn't.

"Come here."

She moves closer, and I open the door to the shower and guide her inside.

I get in next and turn the shower on a light spray to sprinkle over us. Placing my hands either side of her, I watch the water trickle down the side of her face.

"What are we doing?" she asks. "What are *you* doing?"

"Can't a man bathe with his bride-to-be? Especially after a long day at work."

"Don't you have Gabriella for that?" she throws back.

"No. Told you I'm not a liar, so stop with the questions about her. You're a clever girl, Emelia," I taunt and run a hand through my wet hair. "You know who I am. You know full well if I wanted Gabriella, I wouldn't be standing in the shower naked with you. You know full well that I'm exactly where I want to be."

When I move back and stare at her, I get the answer I've wanted all fucking day. She wants me too. I wish like fuck Riccardo could be here to see his daughter look at me the way she is now. I don't have to take anything. She wants to give it to me.

I grab the shower gel and the washcloth, squirt the gel on the cloth, and rub it over her breasts, cleaning the sand from her skin. She turns when I urge her to face the wall, and I run the cloth down her beautiful back.

"Why do you work so hard? Why, when you don't have to?" she asks.

I linger at the small of her back and look at the smooth skin.

"It takes my mind off shit," I answer, sharing a little piece of me.

"Shit like what?"

I move her hair out of the way, pushing it over her shoulder. "Shit I hope you never have to deal with." There's too much to say more than that.

She glances over her shoulder and looks at me. "That tells me nothing. Is this what it will be like every day? You gone for days while I don't know where you are because you have shit on your mind?"

Her question surprises me, so I stop and turn her to face me. She presses her back against the wall, her gaze clinging to mine.

"No, it won't be like that."

"What will it be like, then? I imagine being ordered around like a child and being cooped up here like an animal waiting for its master to return."

I deserve that.

Once again, she strikes a nerve. The same nerve that made me feel like an ass after I gave her the ring. It's like she brings out the person I was before I saw darkness. The person I try to suppress.

"No, it won't be like that. I'll take you everywhere I go. Here in L.A. and in Italy."

Her face brightens at the mention of Italy. "You would take me to Italy?"

"Yes. And show you off so people know you're mine."

"Oh...of course, the trophy wife," she sneers. "The thing you took from my father. You would show me off so people know you conquered him." She nods with sarcasm.

Lowering my head again, I hover inches away from her lips. "No..." I sound like an echo. "That's not why I would show you off, Emelia. I would do it because you're the kind of woman you show off."

She blinks then focuses on me, surprised by my words. Her eyes become more open, less guarded, the longer she stares back, and the twinkle of desire sparkles back at me.

My eyes drop to her lips again. This time, looking at the plump flesh makes me think of kissing her. Taking her first kiss, stealing it.

Or maybe...she'll give it to me...*willingly*.

When I move to her lips, the innocence in her eyes dissipates into thin air and the beauty moves toward me too.

CHAPTER SEVENTEEN

EMELIA

When I first saw Massimo on the beach, my thoughts immediately jumped to my escape plans. Get him to trust me, and it would open the door to freedom.

All the ideas that came to me over the last few days came rushing back to my mind, and I saw my chance to put them into action.

I was still playing the game, until he spoke those words.

You're the kind of woman you show off...

That's what he said. As he spoke, desire flickered in the depths of his eyes, compelling and magnetic, reeling me in like bait, and I could no longer bridle my curiosity or the attraction I felt for him. I no longer felt like the *nothing* he described me to be that night he gave me my ring.

Now, he lingers before me, inches away from my lips, waiting for me to give him my first kiss. Something I know he could take. Something he could easily steal from me.

What I'm looking at is a door. A door that could open the

path for me to leave. Be *his*, get him exactly where I want, then leave. Just like Candace said. *Flee and never look back.*

The door is open, but what I see inside, on that path that could be my freedom, is something else that lures me and entices my curiosity.

I see want and desire *for me.*

He wants me. That's what I see.

Massimo wants me, and not because he wants to screw with Dad, or even to screw with me.

I've never had a man like him look at me the way he is, and I've never been able to look at someone and see so plainly what they truly desire.

The confirmation of the thought sends a shiver of arousal spiraling through my body. It sparks my nerves and ignites wild heat through my entire being.

He moves even closer, beckoning me to come to him. When I do, everything in my mind is replaced by the desire to taste him.

It's me who closes the space between us. Me who gives it to him—*my first kiss.*

As my lips touch his, fire burns straight through to my soul.

Massimo is forbidden to me. *My enemy. My captor.* But, when our lips meet, it feels as if I should have always been kissing him.

Pleasure rouses passion, strong and unrelenting, making the kiss turn hungry, then greedy, in seconds. That's when I lose my mind.

Lust burns my brain and I moan into his hard, searching mouth. He takes advantage to sweep his tongue over mine and passion sings through my veins.

We're kissing.

We're actually kissing, and I don't want him to stop. I

want him to keep kissing me. When Massimo smoothes his hand behind my head to deepen the kiss, I don't want him to stop touching me either.

I savor him, deep down, knowing this forbidden moment is one I shouldn't enjoy.

His hands roam over my face, then down my neck, down to my chest, where he squeezes my breasts, making me moan out so loud the sound embarrasses me.

My naked flesh touches his, and as I kiss him, he feels like mine. Massimo feels like he belongs to me too. Whenever I imagined what my first kiss would be like, I didn't imagine this.

And when I imagined what it would be like to kiss this man, there's no way I thought I would feel like this. Like part of me has lost my damn mind, while the other part... That part of me craves him so much I ache.

The ache resonates from deep inside my core and cascades over my body, making me want more.

We kiss until the world fades into the background and everything goes with it. All I feel now is pleasure, and a primal need for him to take me. The rawness in the need seems to hit him too, but he pulls away from me, backing out of the kiss.

Massimo stares at me as dazed as I am, and I look back not knowing what to say.

I don't know what I expect him to say either. Or do. It's definitely not what he does next. His face hardens, and he becomes the beast again. The Massimo I'm used to. Not the man I just gave my first kiss to.

He moves away and leaves me standing there. I don't know what I did wrong. As reality returns to me slowly, I don't know what the hell just happened either.

Conflict constricts my lungs then races through my body.

The powerful effect is mind numbing, telling me that, even though I'd love to lie to myself and believe the kiss was *just* a kiss, I know it's not true.

It's then it hits me that if I can think like that, then it means I may be crossing over the line of mere attraction. *How the hell did that happen?*

What about him, though? He left me.

Why?

I barely slept through the night. That kiss in the shower played over and over in my mind and was the first thing I thought of when I woke this morning.

A kiss is supposed to be just that. *A kiss.*

Even if it was my first kiss, it definitely shouldn't mean anything at all to me or carry any form of sentiment because of our situation.

I'm not supposed to enjoy any part of this crazy arrangement Massimo and I have. It's a contract of shit that I have to live with for the rest of my life.

Live with it. Or try to escape.

Escape...

I can't live like this. I certainly can't live with a volatile man I can't wrap my head around. But now I've gone and shocked myself because my emotions betray me every time I'm with him. There was no acting yesterday. Everything I did with him was real. So, how do I start *pretending?*

Maybe the thing to do is allow things to play out. That's how trust might come. And since I doubt I'll earn it before the wedding, I'm guessing everything will happen according to the grand plan. I'll have to marry Massimo and represent the symbol of defeat for my father.

I wish I could speak to Dad. I know there's little point because all is said and done, but I feel like I need more context. I wish I could talk to him outside all of this and away from everybody else. I don't know if he'd tell me anything, but I'd try to get what I could out of him. My only chance to do that will be the fundraiser, and I don't know if Massimo will even allow me to speak to Dad.

God... This is such bullshit.

I don't know what I did to deserve this. It's so damn unfair.

The day goes by while I feel like a ghost in the house. When night falls, I start wondering where Massimo is. I'm not sure if I believe that he hasn't been spending his nights with *Gabriella.* Typical, her name would be that. *Gabriella. God. Christ,* listen to me.

I swallow hard as the thought of him in bed with her pulls at my heart in a way I hate.

Truthfully...I *am* jealous. I am. I hate to admit it, but damn it, I know I am, and lying to myself has never done me any favors whatsoever.

I was jealous that Gabriella seemed to be Massimo's type, jealous of her perfect body, and most of all, I was jealous that she looked like she knew exactly what to do with a man like him to please him in the bedroom. Not like me, who's never seen a cock until yesterday.

At ten I find myself sitting on the balcony on the second floor, gazing out at the beach, wondering where Massimo is. I'm so stupid. He could be here with Gabriella and I'd be none the wiser. I wouldn't know shit.

I still don't know where his bedroom is. During my tour of the house, that part was left out. There are parts of the house that I haven't been to. No one said anything regarding those areas. I noticed them but didn't venture there, not even by myself. I assumed the doors would be locked anyway.

I turn when I hear footsteps and see Candace approaching me, carrying a little plate with cookies on it.

"Hey, there," she says. "I was hoping you wouldn't be here so I'd have an excuse to have these all to myself."

I smile the first real smile of the day. "You can have them. I'm not hungry."

"Nah, I wouldn't want to be greedy or lie to Priscilla. You didn't come down for dinner, and you haven't been around much all day."

"I've just been wandering around," I answer. I know I can't really talk to her about what we spoke of on the beach. Not in the house, anyway. I won't be fool enough not to factor in that these walls definitely have ears.

She gives me a worried look, sets the plate down and sits next to me.

"What's going on in that head of yours, Emelia?" she asks in a hushed voice.

"All sorts of things," I answer, lowering my voice too.

"What we spoke of the other day?"

"Yeah, there's that."

"I can't really talk here..." She shakes her head.

"I know." I nod.

"Are you going to do it?"

"I want to. It would be stupid not to try. But I don't know what could happen at the other end."

"That is definitely something to worry about. Massimo looks like he's starting to trust you," she points out.

"Do you think so?"

"I do. However, if there's any doubt in your mind, don't do anything," she cautions.

"I won't. Besides..." I lower my voice and look down

to the garden where I can see Manni lighting up a cigarette. "...there's always someone watching me. It's going to be difficult to know when things will finally ease up." Right now, it seems like something that might never happen.

"I would have come and seen you, but the few times I got a glimpse of you, you looked like you wanted to be by yourself."

"No, it would have been okay to see me." The thought to ask her about Massimo's whereabouts enters my mind. "Candace, where is he?"

"Massimo could be anywhere. He's like that. Here a lot, then not."

"Where does he go? There was a woman here the other day called Gabriella. Is he with her?"

A smile tips the corners of her mouth, and she raises her brows. "Emelia, you're worried about him being with Gabriella?"

My cheeks flush. I'm so silly. I must seem so obvious asking her something like that.

"I just wanted to know."

"Okay... Here's what you need to know about Gabriella: *nothing*. She's bad news. Stay out of her way. She would have definitely heard about the wedding, which is probably why she was here the other day. If you see her, don't engage in any conversation."

"But—"

"No, Emelia, trust me. Sometimes the less you know, the better. So, I'm going to tell you to focus on what you want most and take it from there. I don't know if he'll be home tonight, so don't wait up. Please don't ask me more than that." She hops off the balcony. "Call me if you need anything else to eat."

As she saunters away, my stomach knots with the damn anxiety that's eating away at my insides.

Candace said to focus on what I want most and take it from there. My freedom should be the thing I want more than anything. But yesterday, my body wanted Massimo.

I wanted him and I haven't stopped.

That part of me wants to go to the dark side.

As badly as I want my freedom, now that I've had a taste of Massimo D'Agostino, I want more.

CHAPTER EIGHTEEN

MASSIMO

Dominic rests his beer on the table and smirks at me.

We've been drinking, but not enough to get drunk.

I try not to drink too much when I'm at Renovatio anyway, and definitely not when I have to ride my motorcycle home. When I'm here, I have this awareness about me that I don't think I'm wrong to adhere since my club attracts all sorts of men. Those who come to enjoy the naked women...*and* those who come to spy on me.

We're sitting in my private booth where I can see all: the girls on stage stripping; the usual crowd of wealthy, sophisticated businessmen; and the other kind of men you know from the look are dangerous.

Pa was pissed at me when I first set up this place. He loathes it and all it stands for. He said it suited Dominic or Tristan. Not me, although of the three of us I'm definitely wilder when it comes to women. My excuse was it helped me loosen up.

What could be better than having an endless supply of women to fuck when you want to? I used to practically live here with that *endless supply* of whores who were always willing to please me. Some are still here. Some are here tonight and watch me with hungry eyes, hoping tonight will be the night they get back in my bed.

I pick the best girls with the best assets. Big tits and big asses. They're all beautiful, and more importantly, they're girls who aren't afraid to strip down to nothing and fuck if they have to. My club is of the risqué variety. It's not a sex club like the infamous Dark Odyssey my friends the Giordanos own in Chicago, but we have *special* rooms and *special* girls who don't mind being paid extra to go all the way. It's pussy heaven.

I came tonight for the distraction I usually get out of the place, and thought I'd meet Dominic because he's always here anyway.

People say the best way to get one woman out of your system is to fuck another. However, they never tell you what the fuck you're supposed to do when you actually can't think of fucking anybody else besides the one woman you want.

I've felt off since I left Emelia in the shower. It's been two days and I'm still in that state of flux. Thrown off my game from the effect she had on me from one kiss.

One damn kiss that sparked something in my cold heart.

As her soft lips moved against mine, all I wanted to do was claim her sweet, innocent, forbidden flesh. Hunger clawed through me, making me want to push her up against the wall and fuck her senseless.

I've never lost control of my emotions like that before. It was a dangerous thing because it showed she had power over me.

Power. That was the problem. There was a shift in power.

In that moment, I gave myself to her and succumbed to my need for her.

Need and want are two different things. I can deal with wanting her. Needing to have her is something that blindsided me and pierced past the cover of reality.

"Jesus, bro, you're miles away," Dominic says, pulling me from my thoughts when he waves his hand in front of my face.

"Sorry. I was just thinking."

"Yeah, *obviously*. I was saying I'll continue checking out the streets," he states, setting his shoulders back. "It's only a matter of time before that asshole does something and we'll be able to get a lead."

We've been talking about the situation with Vlad. I've been listening and doing my best to follow the conversation but my damn mind is definitely fucking miles away.

"Thank you. Dom, I don't know what we'd do without you." I wonder that sometimes, because I know the reality is we'd be flying blind half the time.

"Don't worry about it. You know I'm happy to help."

"I know."

It might not be good to put all my faith in him, but in times like these I can't help it. Especially because of Dominic's expertise. He went to MIT for fuck's sake and graduated with two degrees, one of which he did because he was bored with the first and needed to fill out his day with something else. *Fuck,* I don't know anybody who would do shit like that. I went to Stanford and was quite content to do the one business degree.

"I just wish the situation was different," I add.

"I can't disagree. This is not a good situation to be in, Massimo. I hate when shit's brewing and we have no clues to track, but at least we have a heads up. We know there's trouble on the horizon, even if we don't know what it is."

"Yeah, fair point."

He eyes me with curiosity and tilts his head to the side. "Massimo, good as it is to hang out with you in light of recent shit, it's not like you to want to talk business out here like this."

I take a swig of my beer and set my bottle down next to his. "I needed a different scene," I reply. It sounds like bullshit and I don't have to guess if Dominic can see straight through it.

"Oh yeah?"

"Yeah."

"What's wrong with the scene at home? When last I checked you had a beautiful woman to look at." He chuckles.

"Please don't remind me."

"Why the fuck not?"

"There's more serious things to worry about than her."

"What happened?" he asks with narrowed eyes, cutting to the chase.

"Nothing."

I look down at the stage when a loud cheer ripples through the air.

Donna, my best stripper, just stripped naked and she's just leapt on the silver pole, running down the center of the stage to give the men a show.

I can already see men working their way out to the booking office to book her for a lap dance.

I look away and catch sight of the brunette on stage who's had her eye on me since I got here earlier. She just took off her bra, and her massive tits bobble as she runs her hands up and down the pole behind her, like she would if she were holding my cock. That should turn me on...but it doesn't, because *I'm fucked* and my damn mind is on my fucking *wife-to-be*.

Releasing a sigh of frustration, I return my gaze to Dominic. I'm about to steer our conversation back to Vlad but grit my teeth when I see Candace walking up the steps leading to the lounge. She's carrying a plastic folder in her hand.

Shit. The only other person who can't stand this place more than Pa is her, so I'm not sure why she's here.

Dressed in a little summer dress, she looks quite unlike her usual self. Her hair is braided to the side in her usual style and the permanent scowl that's taken up residence on her pretty face since Emelia arrived is very much there.

Dominic turns to look at her and I don't miss the once over he gives her, nor the way he schools himself in that habitual manner, like he's trying not to be attracted to her. I don't know if he knows I notice every time he does it, or that he's been doing that for more than a decade.

The last time she came here, she didn't speak to me for over a week. I never get her to meet me here. I *wouldn't* because of the nature of the place. When she gets up to us she glances down on the stage at the stripper, looks back to me and shakes her head. I don't know why she's looking at me like she expects better from me. She's the girl I grew up with so my dirty secrets and habits are nothing new to her. I might treat her differently to everybody else, but that's because she is who she is.

"Buonasera, *Angel*," Dominic says, tipping his head at her. He's called her Angel since we were kids. Sometimes she seems enamored by the endearment because, unknown to him, she likes him too. At other times, like *now*, she looks pissed. "And how are you on this fine evening?"

"Don't buonasera me, Dominic D'Agostino."

"Baby, you sound mad at me. What did I do? I'm just sitting here having a drink with my brother." He holds out his palms, feigning innocence, and she rolls her eyes at him.

"You couldn't have chosen a better venue?" She eyes him dangerously.

Candace has this meek personality that's always respectful toward us, but she can switch out easily and show the fire beneath all that sweetness. It tends to happen when any of us do something to disappoint her.

"Candace, what are you doing here?" I say, cutting in to save him from answering that question.

"You were supposed to pick this up from church today," she replies, practically shoving the folder into my hands. "Father De Lucca needs those signed and faxed over by tomorrow morning if you want the church booked for the wedding. He's been trying to reach you all day."

Fuck. I totally forgot I was supposed to meet with him.

"Thanks, I'll sort it out. You didn't have to brave coming here to give these to me." I raise a brow.

"Massimo, you've been AWOL, and I don't want to be the cause of messing up your plans, and not when you asked me to take care of Emelia."

At the mention of Emelia, my stomach clenches. "Is she alright?"

"*Really*, Massimo? And seriously, the least you could do is let her know when you'll be off with Gabriella."

"I haven't been with her," I argue.

"Of course not. I don't know who you think you're fooling. It's certainly not me and I have no time for foolishness, because my car just broke down and I need to get my dry cleaning before the store closes."

"I'll give you a ride, Angel," Dominic says already getting to his feet.

"I wouldn't want to interrupt your enjoyment of the show," Candace snaps at him.

"Nah, I wasn't even looking. I was going to leave in a minute, anyway, to get home in time to say my prayers. Tomorrow is Whit Sunday."

Jesus, I have to hold in the laughter. I'm surprised Dominic even knows what Sunday it is on the Christian calendar. At least he has Candace laughing.

"Do you know how ridiculous you sound?" she snaps smacking him in his chest.

"It's true, baby, you'd be proud of me." He chuckles. "Come on, let's go. I'll get you that tea you like."

Before she can say anything more, he slips his arm around her shoulders and ushers her away. With a heavy sigh I stand, deciding to leave too. There's no point staying here.

I jump on my bike and ride home. It's eleven when I walk through the doors of my office. Quickly, I sign the documents for the church and fax them over to Father De Lucca so I don't have to worry about them in the morning. When I'm done, I make my way to Emelia's room. The princess is asleep on her bed but fuck me, she's wearing a little nightie made of silk and lace, and she's lying there uncovered.

It's been hot for the last few nights so the window is open. A gentle breeze filters into the room, caressing her delicious body the way I want to.

I stare at her for a few minutes, taking in her perfection, noting the beauty that radiates from her inside and out.

As I remember the feel of her lips on mine, I find myself wanting to taste her all over again. I find myself wanting to take her and taste her everywhere, wanting to fuck her.

It would be so easy. All I'd need to do is wake her up and get her on her hands and knees.

So, what's stopping me from fucking her?

What am I waiting for? It's not like we both wouldn't want it. And fuck, since when do I consider things like that?

The second I think that, the answer comes. It's because she's a virgin, and I know a devil like me doesn't deserve her innocence.

I know as badly as I want her, that part of me that felt compassion for her at the charity ball has come back to bite me and screw with my mind. I know she doesn't deserve this, but the selfish motherfucker I am won't do anything different to what I'm doing outside of my plans.

I make my way to the window bay and lower to sit. Resting my back against the wall, I ask myself the question she asked me in the shower. *Is this what our life is going to be like?*

Is this what I want? I'm man enough to admit that, while my answer was true, in the moment I spoke those words I wanted her to be mine outside the contract.

I look at her now before me, like the virgin she is, laid out on the bed ready for me to take, and I want the same now.

Her.

CHAPTER NINETEEN

EMELIA

I stir when I feel the presence of someone in the room with me.

I was so tired last night that I fell asleep the second my head hit the pillow. As I open my eyes, my gaze lands on the man I was thinking about before I drifted off.

Massimo is sitting by the window just like he was last week. The only differences are he's fully clothed and, instead of watching me, he's looking through the window at the oncoming sunrise. He's got something shiny in his hands that he circles between his fingers.

I'm not sure what to say to him when he looks away from the window and gazes at me, so I sit up and try to guess why he's here.

Is it to play with me again?

Or make me crazy?

God knows I've been going crazy wondering where he's

been. I don't even think there's any point asking the question, because now I don't want to hear the answer.

"Good morning," I say, cutting through the silent tension.

"No," he replies, and I narrow my eyes.

"No to what? I was saying good morning. I guess it's not quite morning yet, though." I glance out to the dark sky and the red streaks of the oncoming sun threatening to pierce through.

"I know what you were saying, and I meant it's not going to be a good morning." He points out the window and shakes his head. "Red sunrise. It means the day ahead will be dangerous. *Red sky at night, sailors' delight; red sky at morning, sailors take warning.*"

I stare back at him not knowing which door of this crazy alternate dimension I've just walked through. He's talking to me like a normal person and I can't feel that angst that normally hangs in the space between us.

As he watches me, I feel like we could just be two people...*talking*.

"I've never heard that before."

"It's true. It's a sailor's rhyme." He looks away and tosses up a coin. That was what he had in his hand. It doesn't look like a normal coin, though. It looks more like a rune, of sorts.

Something draws me to him and I find myself getting off the bed. When I walk over to him, I have his attention again and his gaze travels over my body, bringing back that sexual vibe I can't resist.

I feel like I'm approaching a beast with every step I take, but I continue toward him anyway and sit opposite him on the ledge.

"What's that?" I ask, referring to the coin. "Is it a rune?"

"Yes. My mother gave it to me. It's like a talisman that's supposed to protect you when you're out on the waters."

"When do you sail? You're always at work...or out."

"Last Sunday of every month. I'm away for the week and I take the big sailboat out."

"Do you take people with you?"

"Yes."

My cheeks burn as I imagine him with Gabriella on the boat.

"Oh," I rasp and look away.

"My brothers," he says and I look back to him. "Women are not allowed on that boat. It's bad luck."

I smirk. "Do you really believe that?"

"I haven't tested it yet, and I don't plan to. I'm an old-fashioned mariner. I don't believe in challenging the sea...or fate."

"So you'll just disappear for the week and I won't know where you are?"

"Are you going to miss me?" He asks the question like a challenge.

"No," I answer, but even I don't believe that answer, and it's clear that he doesn't either.

His face becomes stern and we stare back at each other. His eyes are so guarded I can't tell what he's thinking.

Massimo breaks the connection by placing the coin in his pocket. When he looks at me again, the same lust that brimmed in his eyes the other day comes back, allowing me a glimpse into his thoughts.

"Come here," he says, putting out his hand to beckon me to him.

My breath hitches. Once again the path opens for me to gain his trust, but that's the last thing I'm thinking about when I move to go to him.

He reaches for me and pulls me into his lap. Then, before I can take my next breath, he smoothes his hand up the back of my neck, lacing his fingers through my hair and cupping the back of my head so he can guide me to his lips.

Remembering how he tastes, I go as willingly as I did that first time.

As our lips meet, my brain empties. Our tongues tangle and tease and I want him to take me. Our bodies touch, and I get that feeling again of never wanting him to stop touching me.

When he pulls away, I worry he's doing the same thing he did the other day, but he's not.

"Relax, Princess, I want more from you this morning. So much more," he taunts and I know this is it. He wants to take the last part of me he can take. Steal.

Take...

Steal...

He can't steal something that's given to him.

He picks me up and takes me over to the bed where I allow him to take off my clothes.

Massimo removes his shirt and returns to my lips. I run my fingers through his hair. He travels from my lips to my breasts, suckling on my nipples and, with his free hand, pushes his way into my pussy with two fingers.

"I'm going to fuck you so hard you won't be able to walk," he promises and a shockwave ripples through me.

He's about to undo his belt when the door opens and a very shocked Priscilla stands there watching us.

Quickly, I grab the sheet to cover myself and Massimo's hands still on his belt.

"Oh my God, I'm so sorry, I wouldn't disturb you, but it's urgent," she says. "Nick and Cory are here and they need to speak to you."

"Okay, I'll be out in a minute," Massimo answers and Priscilla leaves us, locking the door.

Massimo backs off the bed and grabs his shirt. When he shrugs into it and looks at me, my whole body heats.

What I see in his eyes is the same fear I feel for wanting him.

The difference between us is that he has power over me and I have none.

I feel even more helpless when he walks away, leaving me once again with nothing. Nothing but the desire for him that weakens me and all that I am when I'm with him.

I thought I was stronger than this.

But, I'm not.

It's just gone mid-day and I'm not going to spend the day wondering where Massimo is or spend it waiting for him.

I'd decided the other day that I wasn't going to be a ghost in the house or become the animal waiting for its master to return. I certainly won't do it today; definitely not after this morning.

It's been two whole weeks since I was pulled from my life. Two weeks I should have spent in Florence. I would have started the summer school in prep for the official start of the term in six weeks.

Being in this house has thrown me out of sync with myself. Not knowing what to do from one day to the next has forced me into this frame of mind where I'm waiting and counting down. It's not even like something good is going to happen at the end of the countdown. Like I'll be free.

At the rate things are going, I'm going to be stuck here for a while. A very, very, long time. I can't even come up with any form of escape strategy that doesn't involve landing myself in more trouble than I'm already in. Everywhere I look, there's a guard.

I've just walked down the stairs with my notepad and pen and I'm gazing ahead at two guards in the corridor by the front door. I can see more outside through the glass windows. They're just standing there, like I'm actually dumb enough to try and run past them.

It's a foolish thought since I'm sure Massimo didn't put them there *just* for me. I know it's because he has enemies, and whatever called him away this morning is part and parcel of who he is.

This morning was crazy and I won't try to explain my actions. I won't try to deny, either, that I wanted him to claim me. And I won't explain the desire as insanity. I'm not crazy and I haven't lost my mind. What I've lost is control of my emotions.

I make my way into the living room. I wanted to go out on to the terrace and draw the scenery. Nothing special, just the beach. It's an odd day, looking like it might rain, and a heaviness hangs in the atmosphere with the anticipation of a storm. So I guess Massimo was right. *Red sky at night, sailors' delight. Red sky at morning, sailors take warning.*

When he shared that with me it felt like something more had changed between us, something that drew me to him. Something as dangerous as temptation masked in purity designed to fool me. Like a fool, I went to him.

I take one step into the living room and stop short when my gaze lands on Gabriella sitting in the sofa by the door leading out to the terrace. She's flicking through a copy of Vogue and looks at home with her feet up.

I glare at her, instant rage filling me at her audacity, and she lowers the magazine to look at me with a cat-got-the-canary smile. Just like the other day, she looks perfect, and now that I've seen her close up, I can't deny that she looks like she belongs on the cover of that magazine.

As she gazes back at me, reality punches me in the gut with warning flags telling me this is the woman my husband-to-be will be spending his time with. She'll be the mistress. He'll be in her bed, and I'll be nothing more than a joke.

The thought strikes me but I steady my heart knowing it would not be wise to show any form of weakness or insecurity around this woman.

"Well look who it is," she cajoles in a sugary voice. "Aren't you the darling girl everyone is talking about."

Bitch.

I dreaded this day and almost knew she'd say something like that. It was a feeling I got when I first saw her on the beach walking with Massimo and she looked at me.

"Can I do something to help you?" I ask, keeping my tone even. I think it's a reasonable question given the fact that she's here and Massimo isn't.

She laughs, to my surprise, and straightens up. "Wow, cutting straight to the chase. I like that. I'm also assuming you must know who I am from the resting bitch face you're throwing my way."

"I know who you are; what I don't know is why you're here." There I go again sounding more ballsy than I feel. At least my voice isn't shaking and I sound believable.

"If you know who I am then you should already know I'm here to see Massimo. He and I have unfinished business we need to discuss. *Business* I seriously doubt the likes of you would understand." She flicks her gaze over me with scrutiny, like she's already made up her mind that she knows me inside and out.

A terrible idea forms in my mind. One that pops into my

head and reaches my tongue before I can hold back or think about it.

"Try me. Maybe I could help with that business, seeing as he doesn't seem to be here."

Again she laughs. This time her tone is more mocking. "You can't help me, Emelia Balesteri. The business I'm talking about is in regards to the bedroom. When you're riding cock for as long as I have, you want to make sure a man like Massimo gets what he wants. It keeps them coming back for more."

The urge to tell her to get out incinerates my blood. There's nothing more I'd love to do than that because it would be all I could do, but this isn't my home. I might live here, but being held captive in a house doesn't classify it as a place of abode.

Humiliation claws through me that I wish I could bridle, but I have no more control over that than all the emotions screwing with me. And while I'm wishing and wanting, I'm gonna wish that my life was different. A simple wish I won't get because it's a snap shot of what is to come.

"You should see your face," Gabriella taunts. "Look at the princess stuck for a comeback."

"Oh, believe me, it's not that at all. It's just that I don't usually speak to skanks."

The smile falls from her face and a surge of triumph races over my skin.

"How dare you—"

"That's enough," Massimo cuts in.

Gabriella and I both look over to the other entrance of the room to see Massimo and Candace standing in the archway.

Gabriella rises to her feet with the grace of a swan and a

smirk on her face, and I hate that I hate the way she looks at Massimo.

"Hello friend," she coos and his face hardens. "Don't worry, I'm gonna head out. I like you better when you're in the mood to play."

Friend...

Play...

It's a juxtapose on words and I'm not sure which is which. I'm not stupid enough to believe he hasn't slept with her.

"I think that's best," he answers, and Gabriella picks up her bag and walks past with her head held high and a broad smile of victory on her face.

I watch her, and I don't stop looking until she turns the corner and I can't see her anymore.

When I look back to Massimo, I think of this morning and my skin flushes with the heat of the wild sexual flames that scorched me as he kissed me.

"Candace, please accompany Emelia to wherever it was she was going," he says and Candace nods.

"That won't be necessary, I'm going back to my room," I say before Candace can move, and I turn away from them both with a heaviness in my heart that makes my legs feel like lead with every step I take.

He's not mine.

That's what that little encounter showed me. Massimo isn't mine and I shouldn't want him to be.

I shouldn't give into the entity that takes over whenever I'm near him. It's wrong on so many levels. I know that as much as I know hating him would be easier if I felt nothing for him.

But I do...

CHAPTER TWENTY

MASSIMO

I walk back into my office and throw myself down on my chair. It's after nine. Fucking late to be at work at this hour, even for a workaholic like me.

That visit from Nick and Cory yesterday led us all back on the streets when we found out some of the men we ally with were seen talking to guys who looked like Shadow members.

By the time we got to them most had scattered, and the two that were left behind couldn't tell us shit.

It's all so elaborate. Everything done in a way that's so hushed men like me can't break through and get to the culprits. Considering who I am, that's near impossible.

Now I'm here at work when, truthfully, I should be home. I've taken the coward's way out because I need to think, and I can't do it when I'm around Emelia.

Yesterday was... *Jesus*. It was just one of those up-and-down days, and Gabriella's presence at the house didn't help. I never wanted her to meet Emelia.

What happened is exactly what I thought would happen, except Emelia grew a pair of balls I never saw coming. It shouldn't have surprised me, because she's a fighter.

What stayed with me was that look in her eyes after Gabriella left. It was a mingle of want and hate from the confusion of what we are, and what we're not supposed to be.

I'm surprised when a knock sounds at my door. Everyone who would need me here has gone home for the day.

"Come in," I call out, and I couldn't be more surprised to see Gabriella when the door swings open.

"Gabriella, what the hell brings you here?" I ask. It's a foolish question. I look at her and know exactly what she wants. It's the same thing she said the other day. She wants to get back in my bed. Back on my cock.

That's why she was at the house yesterday and why she's here now.

Fuck...

She smiles. "I was looking for you. I went by the house again and was told you were still at work. I figured I should come and provide some much-needed stress relief."

She floats into my lap and I instantly remember the last time I had her. Those bright green eyes flicker as she runs her hand over my chest and wiggles her ass over my cock.

"You're hard," she says with a wicked smile.

"Not for you," I answer.

"Doesn't matter, you're still hard." Seduction ripples off her in waves.

I stare back at her, holding her gaze. This has to be a new one for me. A new record. This is the second time I've been in the presence of this woman and had to think twice about whether or not I should be with her.

The first time I was pissed and in this weird frame of mind. What am I tonight?

Gabriella runs her fingers over my chest again, pulling me from the stupor of thought.

"Come. Let's play around," she urges, lowering her head to whisper into my ear. "Let me take care of your needs."

I should do it. Fuck her and get Emelia out of my head.

Maybe that would do the trick. Maybe it'll work if I'm with her and not some random whore I picked from the club.

If I were going to be with anyone, surely a woman I considered mine once would move the desire I have for Emelia out of my mind.

Even as I think that, though, Emelia's beautiful face fills my thoughts. I see the pleasure on her face as I touch her, and the look of adoration in her eyes she tries to fight. The damn look is always there, even when I've pissed her off.

I imagine her soft skin and the gentleness in her kiss.

Emelia gave me her first kiss, and to me it felt like it was my first kiss too. It was certainly the only kiss I've ever had that made me feel passion.

I close my eyes when Gabriella runs her hand down my chest and shuffles so she can grab my cock and stroke my length.

"Do you have a condom?" she whispers into my ear. Her lips then brush along my neck.

"Yeah," I answer. My voice sounds far away, like I'm hearing it on the edge of the wind.

A smile of triumph lights up her face. "Then fuck me," she says, beckoning me with the crook of her finger.

She leans forward and kisses my neck.

When her lips touch my skin, I freeze up again thinking of Emelia, and I know I can't do this. I know I can't because it's her I really want.

Fucking hell... This wasn't supposed to happen. I want her, and I can't do anything with Gabriella or anybody else because of that.

"Gabriella, stop."

"What's the matter?" she asks, straightening up.

"We're not doing this," I reply and lift her off me as I stand.

I step away from her but she grabs my arm. I glare at her in a way that should remind her who I am. She takes heed and releases me, righting herself.

"Why?" she challenges. "Because of *her*? Your trophy bride?"

I'm not ready to admit that to anybody, least of all her. I loom over her and she shudders under the weight of my stare.

"Watch it, Gabriella. Be careful. Remember who you're talking to. I don't want you tonight."

She backs down and takes a step back. With that, I leave her.

My body moves on its own accord. Like I'm being summoned home. Home to Emelia.

I drive back thinking of her and yesterday. I think of how much she wanted me too. It's not that late when I get home, but I don't know if she'll be asleep. Her bedroom door is open. When I approach, I stop and wait by the door when I see her kneeling on the floor. Before her are some little pots of makeup and white copier paper that she's drawn on.

I make out swallows flying over a mountain. The sky is smudged with shades of blue and violet. She dips her fingers into one of the pots of eye shadow and smears it all over the areas that haven't been touched.

I held back her art supplies because I had plans for them. Plans for her. Nothing malicious. It was just an idea, but I actually feel bad now as I watch her make use of whatever she could find to do what she loves.

She shuffles around onto her hands and knees so she can reach across for a large fan brush. Doing so gives me a view of her perfect ass in those short shorts.

It's not until she shuffles back around that she sees me and jumps, startled.

The worry she usually exhibits when she's with me instantly settles on her beautiful face. She stands up, readying herself for whatever I might have up my sleeves tonight.

We gaze at each other in silence for a few moments. She looks better than she did in my imagination, and what I conjured up was pretty damn good. What's different is that longing, lurking beneath her stare. It reaches out to me and tells me she's been thinking about me too.

I walk in and close the door, locking the latch so no one will disturb us. The staff will know that if they turn that handle and the door doesn't open, they mustn't knock. I don't know what I plan to do to her yet. All I know is that I have to touch her.

I move closer and do exactly that. I touch her cheek, her soft, soft cheek, and she steps back, away from me.

"What now?" she asks.

My gaze drops to the rise and fall of her chest and the pulse of her heartbeat quickening.

"I wanted to see you," I answer. As the words fall from my lips, I sense that part of me again that's been locked away for years.

Locked away since that day when I found my mother in the river and saw her wide terrified eyes gazing back at me as if she were calling for my help from beyond the grave.

I look at Emelia and feel like the person I was before that happened. The man I could have been if I hadn't been burned.

Her misty eyes narrow and brim with the disappointment I saw nights ago when she looks at my shirt.

"There's lipstick on your collar," she states.

Jealousy.

It's all over her. Jealousy and hurt. Unlike the other day, however, I don't want to taunt her about it.

"Is it hers?" she demands, staring me straight in the eye. "*Gabriella's?*"

"Yes," I reply. The hurt in her eyes deepens. I've never had a woman look at me like that before. Mostly because I've never given them the chance to believe we could be anything more than screwing around.

"Who is Gabriella to you, Massimo?"

"A friend," I answer cautiously.

"A friend you sleep with?"

"Yes..." I answer and she looks visibly crushed at the declaration. Her chest and shoulders cave. Her brows pinch and her lips tremble.

"Get away from me," she rasps and backs away.

I follow her until she backs right into the wall, unsteady. She makes a move to slip away, but I place my hands on the wall on either side of her, fencing her in.

"Get away from me, Massimo," she mutters again.

"No," I answer, and in that moment, I remember what Tristan said.

Think of *what* she is, not *who* she is. I said it was the same thing. It's not. She's a woman I've been attracted to for months. I got drawn into her. The same way I am now.

"I don't want to do it tonight," she says, shaking her head.

"Do what?"

A tear tracks down her cheek. "Listen to you tell me I'm nothing. I don't want to hear about your night with her. I don't need to be reminded that I'm with a man who isn't mine. Now get out, get away—"

I don't allow her to finish. Before she can say another word, I crush my lips to hers, capturing her pretty mouth. The second I taste her, all the desire I felt for her comes flooding back to me.

The taste of her—her sweetness, her innocence, everything—drives me fucking insane. I get drunk on the taste of her need for me.

It's the same as mine.

The shock pulls me from the trance of the kiss. I move away slightly and take in her stunned expression and the desire in her eyes. It unlocks the restraint I placed on myself and compels me to tell her the truth.

"I didn't sleep with her," I tell her, shocking myself further. I explain myself to no one. Not my actions, nor my motives for doing anything. Yet this woman compels me to make her the exception. Especially when she does the unexpected thing of reaching up her dainty hand to touch my cheek.

It's the first time she's willingly touched me. It feels like being touched by an angel. A woman too pure for the likes of me. A woman who's unbroken and uncorrupted.

She's like having something hallowed in my presence, while I'm the devil waiting by the door to lead her down the path of temptation. She knows this. She's completely aware of who and what I am, but she's looking at me like she wants me. In her gaze, I see the path to redemption. Redemption from the vengeance I've sought for so long.

Suddenly, I don't give a fuck about wanting to prove Riccardo wrong. It doesn't matter, because as I look at her, I see who she is too. She's just Emelia, and right now, I don't care if she's my enemy's daughter.

When the beauty guides my face back to her lips, I go, answering passion's call, pushing aside everything past and present so I can savor her.

Raw passion pulses from me to her when I feast on her delicious tongue. When she moans into my mouth, I smooth my free hand up to cup her left breast. Emelia responds by pressing against me, gripping my shirt.

With my lips still trained on hers, I move with her to the bed and set her down in the center. I only break from her lips to whip my shirt off and take hers off too.

Much to my satisfaction, she's not wearing a bra underneath her top, so her beautiful breasts spill out. Instead of the terrified woman she was the other week, she gazes back at me with arousal brimming within her beautiful eyes.

"I want to fuck you, Emelia," I husk and a crimson blush darkens her skin. Her chest rises and falls. Her breathing grows heavier. I want to fuck her so hard she'll be screaming my name all night.

"I want to fuck you, Princesca. Please let me," I add. It sounds like a plea.

"Yes," she replies. "Fuck me."

Hearing how I've already tainted her has me smiling.

I back off the bed. She lifts herself up onto her elbows to watch me as I strip off the rest of my clothes. When her eyes settle on my cock, I feel it harden all the more, and the bead of precum on the tip shows how much I want her.

I move to her and take off her shorts and her panties in one move, exposing her pretty pussy.

I want to bury my cock deep inside that virgin pussy and make her mine. Brand her as mine. Claim her in a way that when anybody looks at her, they'll know just from the look in her eyes that she belongs to me. I know that I have to be careful, gentle. I've never fucked a virgin before, but I know everything will be new and scary for her. I don't want her to have any fears tonight.

When I move back onto the bed and loom over her, she rests her hands on my shoulders.

"I don't know how—" she begins, but I kiss her words away.

"You trust me. You trust me with your body," I tell her.

Watching trust come into her beautiful eyes is a delight I never thought I'd see.

"I...trust you," she says, moving in to kiss me.

I kiss her hard, then catch her face and stare at her, taking back control.

"Spread your legs for me." I release my hold on her, and she obeys. My mouth waters as I watch her part her legs for me, her delicious globes bobbling as she moves, the rose tips hardening under my gaze. "Good girl."

I nuzzle my face between her thighs, pushing my tongue into her tight cunt to warm her up.

Fuck, she's already wet for me. I want to bring her to orgasm once before I take her so it will be easier on her. Easier and more enjoyable.

I lick over the hard nub of her clit, making her moan. When she holds onto my shoulders, I push in harder and suck on the little bud until she throws her head back and cries out my name.

My name on her pretty lips has me lifting my head to watch her come undone in my arms. I take in the image of pure pleasure on her face and commit it to memory. That's how I want to remember her. That's *what* I want to remember, no matter what happens.

"Massimo," she gasps, reaching for me.

"It's okay, Princess. That's only the first taste of pleasure." I dive back in and circle my tongue over her clit, inhaling the sweet feminine scent of her, lapping up my first taste of her juices as they begin to flow into my mouth. She comes hard, bucking and thrashing against my face, but I hold her ass and press her to me so I can take all that I want from her.

I lap up enough of her juices and leave just enough to guide me into her entrance. Getting back on my knees, I hold her thighs open. Our gazes tangle as I reach for my cock to guide it into her.

I never expected to be gentle about this. There's nothing gentle about me, but I want to try for her.

I rub my cock over her pussy lips and push into her entrance, working my way in, inching into her virgin passage. I pause as her walls squeeze around the tip of my cock. *Fuck*, she's so tight it's almost painful, yet it's fucking pleasurable at the same time.

"Massimo," she gasps.

I run my fingers over her slender hips. "You'll feel good soon, I promise." On my word, I push past the tightness. She gasps when I slam through her maidenhead.

Emelia cries out again, and her eyes fill with a wild combination of pain and pure pleasure. All for me.

It's now that she truly feels like she belongs to me.

CHAPTER TWENTY-ONE

EMELIA

I feel like I'm being impaled on his length when the bolt of pain spears through my body, but the sweet pleasure has my soul spinning right back into the arms of passion.

Pleasure cascades over my body, flowing over me like a waterfall.

Pleasure in its purest form ripples through every fiber of my being, setting me on fire. It comes in overlapping waves. My body curves at the sensation, yielding to it. To him.

Massimo grips my hips, riveting his eyes to mine as he rocks his hips forward, starting a slow, steady pump.

"*Fuck*... Emelia, you're so tight," he growls. The thick vein at the side of his neck pulses, making my stomach twist into knots.

The lust thickens in my throat so much so that I can't talk. Instead, I moan into the rise of more pleasure, this time feeling different than when he first entered me, different to the way I've felt when we did other things.

My toes curl and my back arches against the cool satin sheets beneath my skin as he pumps in and out of my body. Then convulsive waves hit me again and again as Massimo increases his pace, fucking me like he owns me.

I search out his eyes, wanting to know what he's thinking. I can't tell. From the strain on his face, though, I think he's holding back. Then something changes with the rise of pleasure. It becomes stronger, wilder, hot and carnal with a ferocious hold neither of us can control. He feels it, too, and grits his teeth.

His balls slap against my ass as he drives his cock deeper into my passage, hitting my G-spot. He plows into my body over and over again. Another orgasm builds and rises, pushing me to the edge. A growl roars from his lips as his thrusts become harder, surer, faster and faster. It's too much, and he takes me right over the edge once more.

The explosion of passion and pleasure sweeps through me with a vicious force, and I fall into another, wild, earth-shattering orgasm. My bones tingle and my soul shivers in pure delight that consumes me, leaving me gasping and inhaling the scent of us as our bodies slap together.

"Massimo! Ahhhh..." I moan out loud when he starts rutting into me. My walls tighten around his cock from the intensity of the orgasm, making the friction of his driving beats slash through my mind.

He fucks me right through that, his eyes giving him away. Massimo pants and mutters a series of inaudible curses in Italian, then jackhammers into me as his release floods my passage. Hot cum coats my walls and the new sensation arouses me all over again. It warms my entire body and fills me with a luxuriating sensation that leaves my nerve endings tingling.

His shoulders slump forward, and his breath comes out in

uneven rasps. Against the drumming in my ears of my pounding heart, I hear it more than I do my own.

He pulls out of me. The instant his thickness leaves my passage, I feel sore and raw. I notice the smear of blood on his length mixed with his cum. He doesn't seem to care about that though. He seems more fascinated with me.

Massimo bends down, resting his elbows on the mattress to brush his lips over mine. I lift my hand to touch his cheek, feeling the roughness of his beard, and he brings my hands up to his mouth to kiss my knuckles.

"Are you okay, Princess?" he asks in a low husky voice still filled with the passion we just shared. He rubs his thumb over the top of my knuckles and gazes down at me.

"I am..." I whisper and smile at him. The smile comes natural to me, as if I'm supposed to give it to him after what we just did.

There's a twinkle in his eyes that I wish I could capture. The look and everything we just did confuses me, but I push away any thoughts that can break this moment I want to remember forever. There's a noticeable difference between us.

"You call me Princess when you're less mad at me for being who I am," I whisper. He presses his lips together.

"I shouldn't be mad at you for that." He runs his finger over the ring on my finger and twists it from side to side. "When I saw this, I thought it suited you."

"Thank you..."

As we stare at each other, I allow his words to sink in. I know that's as close to anything sentimental I'll get from him. I think it might be an apology for the way he gave me the ring.

I don't know what this thing is between us. I don't know what we're doing, but I don't want to resist the entity that's drawing us closer with each passing minute.

He gets up and pulls me to sit. As he does, a mixture of blood and cum flows from my core and leaks down my thighs, running onto the sheets. My cheeks burn with embarrassment, but he lifts my chin to focus my gaze on him.

"You're mine. It means you're mine. Whatever happens, you're mine. You belong to me, Emelia, with or without a contract."

I gaze at him and feel the power in every word as he shows me glimpses of his true self. Even though that wall of vengeance is still up.

Looking back at him, I wish I could see beyond the wall. I'm stripped bare and naked inside and out. I've given him everything. The most precious thing I owned belongs to him now. I gave myself to him.

"Do you understand me, Emelia?"

"I do." How ironic that it should sound like an acceptance of a vow.

"Let's go take that shower we never had the other day."

He scoops me up, and I slip my arms around his neck.

The bright morning sunlight wakes me.

As my eyes flutter open, I remember last night and everything I did with Massimo.

We had sex three more times. Once in the shower and two more times in this bed.

I roll onto my side and see that the spot where he lay when I fell asleep is now empty. I drifted off with his arm around me and my head resting on his chest. We fell asleep like we were lovers and held each other like it was habit.

Now he's gone.

I reach for the satin pillow and bring it to my nose,

inhaling the musky, masculine scent of him that still lingers on the fabric. As the scent fills my nostrils, I conjure up the image of the perfect, godlike man who climbed my body all night. He took me ruthlessly, over and over again. Beautiful and dangerous, temptation at its finest.

God... What the hell am I doing? What have I done? My emotions are all over the place. Yesterday I was hell bent on escaping. Yet by the time the sun went down, I was jealous of Massimo and Gabriella. Hours later, I found myself tangled in bed with him.

Despite the fact that my father sold me to pay off a debt, I feel as if I betrayed him by sleeping with the enemy and craving the enemy's touch all over again.

If I'm going with the story that Dad was forced to do what he did to me, then I have betrayed him. I'm not supposed to feel this way for a man who wants to destroy my father.

But then there is the other side of the coin, the part I still don't know about Dad. The vague information I've been given is exactly that. *Vague.* It's not enough to form any conclusion regarding me personally.

So...w*hat do I do now?*

What do I do about Massimo?

I pull the covers close to my chest to cover my nakedness. Sitting up, I look around the room and run a hand through my messy hair. It's bright outside so I'm guessing it must be late morning.

Once again, I don't know what shape today will take.

Deciding to get up, I take a shower and wash last night from my body.

The area between my thighs is very sore, and as the water cascades over my pussy, it feels raw and burns. It's a good burn, though, that I can't say I'm unhappy about.

I get out, change into a little summer dress, and pull my hair back into a ponytail.

A little rap sounds at the door just as I was about to do my makeup. I already know it's not him. Massimo wouldn't knock. He's never knocked.

"Come in," I call out. Priscilla opens the door. Candace is behind her carrying a tray with toast and coffee.

"Morning," they both say.

"Hi there," I answer.

Candace looks at me. I blush when her eyes twinkle with something that makes me think she senses what Massimo and I got up to in here last night.

"We are not having another day like yesterday," Priscilla proclaims. "It's nearly midday, and you haven't come down for breakfast."

My eyes bulge. "Oh my gosh, I didn't realize the time." There's no way I would have thought it was so late. I'm not the kind of person to have a lie-in. When I lived at home, I'd be up early to paint.

"You will eat this, and we'll be back in ten minutes," she answers.

"Massimo arranged something nice for you today," Candace beams.

I can't imagine what that might be. "What is it?"

"Something you'll like, dear," Priscilla answers. The corners of her eyes crinkle as she smiles.

I bite the inside of my lip and try to look happy. It's probably more wedding stuff. I know they both liked helping me pick out dresses the other day, and when the seamstress came back, we did everything else together as well. Other people to do with the wedding have come by, and as far as I know, there isn't much left to worry about because it's all being taken care of.

"Eat, and we'll be back to show you." Candace looks pleased. That heightens my curiosity.

"Okay," I agree.

I'm curious to know what this could be. What has Massimo arranged? In my heart I pray it's not something that will remind me why I'm here and spoil last night.

Once they leave, I quickly do my makeup and eat. Ten minutes later, Candace returns. The suspicion in her eyes makes me think she came back alone to question me.

"You ready?" she asks.

"Yeah."

"We're going to a different part of the house."

"Are we? What part?"

"It's on the left wing," she answers. "You look better than when I left you last night," she notes.

"Do I?" I ask, feigning innocence. I know full well what she means. Earlier, when I looked at myself in the bathroom mirror, my skin was glowing like a light bulb.

"Yeah, in a good way. Are you okay?"

When I nod, she gives me a reassuring smile. That's all she does. She doesn't ask me anything more.

We walk across the atrium and then head down the wide marble steps leading down to the hall where I tried on my wedding dress. We get to the hall and continue down the path to another set of stairs. These are stone and lead to a large set of oak wood doors that have always been locked. Whenever I've seen them, I've thought they led outside. Apparently not. And the doors aren't locked today. Candace opens the door wide, revealing a hall. What I see inside steals my breath away.

Art.

That's the best word I can use to describe the scene before me.

Art.

Art in abundance. There are oil paintings all along the walls.

We walk in, immersing ourselves in the glorious artwork that makes my nerves spike and tingle. The paintings are a mixture of landscapes and people. Because I love landscapes so much, I'm drawn to those more. I recognize some of the places. They're in Italy. Florence, Verona, and Sicily. All so beautiful.

"Oh my God," I mutter and turn back to face Candace. "These are amazing."

"Yeah. Massimo's mother was quite the artist."

Surprise rushes over me. "His mother painted all of these?"

"Yeah, she was incredible. That over there is me when I was little, playing with the boys," she says, pointing to one of the larger paintings to our left.

On it is a little girl, four boys, and a golden retriever running through a meadow. Playing.

We move closer to it and she points to the boy nearest the dog. "That's Massimo. He must have been eight there. Maybe seven."

I notice the way the blue of his eyes sparkles. The bright smile on his face, though, is something foreign to me.

"These are all truly amazing," I say.

"They are. I guess Massimo must have thought you'd be more at home inside here. He came in here early to finish setting up the room for you," she answers.

My mouth goes dry. "What? He set up the room for me?" I stare at her in disbelief.

"Yes. It was more of a storage room. He never invites anyone in here. But he brought those in the other day, and I helped him clean the place up."

She points over my shoulder and I turn to see a stack of boxes by the large archway overlooking the beach. Next to them is an easel.

The boxes look familiar so I move closer to them and gasp when I recognize them. They're mine. My boxes I packed my paintings in, and all my art supplies. Everything I was going to take with me to Florence. The realization makes me rush right over. The boxes are open and set up so I can finish arranging the contents. Candace gives me a bright smile when I look back at her.

An uncontrollable tear tracks down my cheek as I rasp out a ragged breath.

I didn't realize just how much I missed my art. Having my clothes was nice and eased my mind. But...this calms my soul.

"Hey, there," Candace says when I wipe away the tear with the heel of my hand. "You okay, Emelia?"

"No," I answer because that's the truth. I'm not okay.

This act of kindness has placed me in a tailspin, a whirlwind of flux. I don't know right from wrong, or who to trust. It would be easier to hate Massimo if he behaved like the monster I first met. The same monster who held a gun to my father's head and locked me in my bedroom naked to teach me a lesson. It would be easier if he were truly awful. Him doing this for me makes me wonder how I'm supposed to feel.

"Be strong, Emelia. Be strong and listen to your heart."

"I don't know about that, Candace. Listening to my heart would make me betray my father." *God...I've probably said too much.*

She shakes her head. "Think of yourself. Nobody else. In the end, that's what you have to do to survive this game. You can't think of anybody else. The moment you do, you lose yourself." She taps my shoulder and gives me a reassuring smile. "I'll leave you to get reacquainted with your stuff."

She gives me a curt nod and I get that sensation again that she's leaving because she doesn't want to say more.

I watch her go. The door closes, and I'm left to my thoughts and the beauty of the art surrounding me.

Pulling in a deep breath, I decide to look around at the paintings on the walls. I want to see what kind of woman Massimo's mother was before I dive into my own painting.

I walk to the painting Candace showed me earlier and find myself staring at Massimo, at his eyes. I can tell from the way his mother painted that she worked with emotion. It's embedded in the brushstrokes of the painting. The hues and gradients she used in the background texture all work together to create its own story. This was a happy day she painted.

Massimo said my father made sure his family lost everything. This was a day before that happened to them.

What must my father have really done? What cruel thing did he do? The more I think about it, the more I realize I don't know him. And I don't know who the monsters are in this story.

I thought it was my husband-to-be.

Now I'm not so sure.

I really am the princess in the tower if I continue to pretend that I think my father is a saint. I know he's gotten his hands dirty. I know he's done bad things.

He must have committed pure evil, however, for Massimo and his family to hate us so much.

In the deepest corner of my heart, there's a place that doesn't want him to hate me.

CHAPTER TWENTY-TWO

MASSIMO

I walk into the hall and see her.

I was right. She looks at home in here. The same way Ma's paintings look like they belong.

Emelia is so engrossed in her painting that she doesn't hear me walk in.

My mother was the same. She'd get lost in her work. I'd seen examples of Emelia's work when I looked through the boxes the other day, but watching her create something live is another thing.

She has a large canvas set up on the easel. On it she's painted a stormy sea against the darkness of night and a midnight-black horse with vapid wings riding the water. It's a dark fantasy.

She gazes out momentarily to the sea outside. Against the night it moves in shadows, looking nothing like her painting. But that's what she sees, what she still sees as she continues to gaze out the archway.

My gaze travels over her body as her little dress rides up her ass, and I think of all the ways I took her last night. I could have kept going, but I wiped her out. I left her bed this morning in a state of conflict and must have watched her sleep for a full hour before I got up and came in here to sort the place out. I had the idea the other day, but I wasn't sure I was ready to share this piece of me yet.

Now that I see her in here, I'm glad I have.

I stop paces away. She's still oblivious to my presence. I don't like that because anyone could sneak up on her. Not that it's likely to happen here.

"There's a horse in the water?" I ask as calmly as possible, but she jumps, startled, and turns to face me, clutching her chest. I don't know how, but she looks more beautiful today than when I left her this morning.

"Didn't mean to frighten you," I add.

"You're home," she breathes.

"I'm home. See, you don't have to wonder where I am. Came straight home from work." That's a little white lie, but she doesn't need to know details like that.

I was with Tristan and Andreas, questioning a few people who we knew had links to Vlad. Out of the five we questioned, one lived, but I'm sure he's very close to death. That happens when you're left to bleed out. All five were the worst kind of sick fucks anybody could come across. Right when we happened upon them, they'd kidnapped a young girl who I was sure could be no more than sixteen, and I know they were all getting ready to rape her. Pierbo's death aside, that was enough for me to end them.

"You came straight home," the beauty repeats, pulling me from my thoughts. I focus my attention on her because I want a repeat of last night.

"I did."

"Thank you," she says. I know she's not talking about me coming home. She's talking about what I did in here for her. It's completely out of character for me.

"For coming straight home?" I ask anyway. That smile I wanted to see appears on her face. The smile just for me.

"No. For this. I didn't know my art stuff came too. This is perfect."

Here is where I should crush that lightness in her presence toward me. I should place her back in line and stop her in her tracks from feeling for me. But I decided I don't want us to be that way. Taking her last night was exhilarating because she gave herself to me and allowed me to do what I wanted to her body. Tonight, I want to fuck her hard, the way I like to fuck. That won't work if she's scared of me.

I move closer to her, and she sets the paintbrush down.

"Perfect enough for you to see to paint?" I ask, and she nods. "Is that what you see outside?" Ma used to talk like that.

"I do. I see this stuff all the time. It just presents itself in my mind. Sometimes I think I can touch it."

"Black Pegasus rising from the waters." There's a spot that she hasn't finished, but she's started painting an orange glow on the water's surface. "What happens next, Princesca?" I ask, placing emphasis on *Princesca*. She was only half right about what she said last night. About me calling her that when I was mad at her.

She tenses at the word, and the smile recedes from her face. I catch her face before that pretty little mind of hers starts wondering.

"I like calling you that. That's all. I'm not mad."

"I'm not a princesca, though."

I chuckle. "You are mine. Now answer the question." I motion back to the painting and release her.

"It's a portal in the sea. The horse is going back to the land it came from. Beyond the portal is a reflection of this world. Mirror images of itself."

I gaze back, fascinated by what I hear. "That's impressive."

"Thank you. Your mother's paintings are beautiful."

"Glad you like them."

"My mother was an artist too. That's where I got it from. We used to paint together all the time."

"You're very talented."

"Thanks." She looks like she appreciates the compliment.

Enough talk now, though. I need to taste her. "Come here," I say.

She steps closer, coming to me willingly.

I brush my finger over her cheek, and as we stare at each other, the air thickens with desire.

Pressing my mouth to hers, I kiss her, and she kisses me back. She opens her mouth, allowing our tongues to tease and tangle as we taste each other.

She knows what I want. So she doesn't stop me when I lift the hem of her dress and cup her pussy through the satin of her panties.

The doors are open, but few venture down here. I've waited all day to have her. Now that I'm with her, I'm going to have her right here. I don't care who's listening. If they hear us, it's warning enough to stay the fuck away.

I deepen the kiss and slip my hands into her hair to pull it from the ponytail. I like her hair down. I want to run my fingers through the velvet strands while I fuck her.

I devour her mouth when she tilts her head back and the band slips from my grasp. Her luscious mane of locks tumbles down her shoulders, pouring over my fingers like liquid silk. I love it, the same way I love the feel of her willowy body in my hands. Fragile and delicate, but tempting with the dip of her curves and the mounds of her breasts.

I manage to move the little fabric away from the crotch of her panties so I can finger her pussy. She jolts, gripping my shirt. She moans against my lips, and a shudder of pleasure runs through her when I slide my fingers deeper into her passage. Her pussy walls convulse, and she pants, her lips now trembling.

Pulling my fingers from her juicy cunt, I pause my assault on her lips to taste her wet desire. The sweet nectar covers my fingers, evidence of her arousal for me. Surprise tickles her cheeks pink when I place my fingers in my mouth and lick off every drop.

"You want me again..." I state.

She looks at me like she doesn't know what to say. I get it. After all, we both have the same problem. We're supposed to be forbidden. This isn't supposed to be enjoyable, but here we both are, craving each other like a rare exotic dish.

I smile at her, and the beauty does the strangest thing. She slides her finger up my jaw and traces my lips. I allow her to, wondering what she's doing.

"What?" I ask.

"A smile that's not mocking me," she whispers. Her voice quivers.

As I look at her, I know she doesn't deserve any of this. She doesn't deserve to be with a man like me who's full of hate and death. I shouldn't have caged her like a wild bird. She deserves to be free.

I take her fingers and kiss the tips. The beginning of a smile lifts the corners of her pretty mouth. When seduction fills her eyes, though, the urge to be inside her comes rushing back.

I lean close to her ear and whisper against it, dirty words I know will curl her toes. "Is your pussy still sore, Princess?" I mutter and chuckle as a flush runs down her neck.

"I'm okay," she replies.

"I've been hard for you all day, Emelia. I want to fuck you properly. Hard, just the way I like it. Can you handle my cock?" It's time to take this to the next level and train her to please me.

My lips are close to hers now, and the sparkle in her eyes is a tell that she more than wants me to take her. More importantly, she'll allow me to do whatever I want to her.

"I can handle it," she says, confirming my thoughts.

Good... This is good. The only good thing about this day.

"Take your clothes off." I like watching her.

"The door is open, Massimo. What if someone comes in here, or hears us?"

"If they want to live, they'll leave quickly." I'm serious as fuck, and she knows it. She also knows I don't like repeating myself.

She pulls off her dress, leaving just the bra and panties. Her beautiful breasts fall out when she takes off her bra. She steps out of her panties and becomes the naked goddess of pure perfection standing before me.

I take off my jacket and unbutton my shirt, shrugging out of it and pushing it to the floor. Her eyes take me in when I undo my belt and pants and push them down my legs. I reach for her with one hand and my cock with the other.

Holding her close, I drive my cock inside her tight pussy. She gasps, reaching for my shoulders. She holds on so tight her nails dig into my skin, digging in so sharp I know they're going to leave a mark. I don't care though. I love pain sometimes. Especially when accompanied by pleasure. She'll learn that, too, when we explore some of my darker tastes.

She's so tight it hurts again. It's almost like I wasn't inside her last night. The look on her face is a mix of pleasure and pain too. I know I must be hurting her, but she's taking it.

I pull out slightly then plunge back in, deeper this time. She cries out loud, throwing her head back. The sight of her makes my cock harder. The sounds she makes turn my greed for her insatiable. That look in her eyes fills me with selfish desire and I start to fuck her hard. Hard and fast, just the way I wanted to last night. I held back then. Right now, I wouldn't be able to even if I wanted to. I want her so damn much it physically hurts. I want to take everything from her.

We both groan and moan as the sounds of wild sex fill the room. There's no way that anyone passing nearby won't hear us. I imagine people would hear us even if they weren't near because of the way sound travels down the corridor.

Fuck, she feels too good. Her walls tighten deliciously around my cock as a wave of orgasm claims her. That feels fucking good too. I'm not about to allow it to make me lose control though. I want more.

Deciding just that, I pull out of her again in the height of pleasure and pick her up. She wraps her arms around my neck.

"Hold on tight, Princesca. You're about to have the ride of your life," I tell her with a wink and impale her on my dick at the same time.

Her slick, wet pussy is hot as fuck. It fills me with hunger. I move us to the wall, knocking over the potted plant. It clatters to the floor, breaking.

Pushing her right up against the wall, I plan to devour every piece of her. Fingers dig deeper into my skin. Her cries become louder. Pleasure and pain combust into one delicious cocktail as I start rutting into her body at a furious speed, angling her so I can keep my promise of fucking her properly.

When I'm done with her, she won't be able to walk, and

she won't forget tonight. As long as she lives, she won't forget this moment. Never, because I won't.

Again, I don't care that she's Emelia Balesteri. In a few weeks, she'll be Emelia D'Agostino. All mine, in every law of the land and in the eyes of the great beholder when we take our vows in front of the priest.

The walls of her pussy throb, squeezing my dick like a glove, too tight. She feels too good. And as much as I want to continue, I know when I've reached my limit.

One last cry from her gorgeous mouth and the arch of her tits in my face has me blowing my load inside her. Fuck, my damn knees buckle. The pleasure is so intense I almost fucking fall over.

She milks the cum from my dick and takes it all, leaving me drained.

Drained, yet still wanting more.

CHAPTER TWENTY-THREE

EMELIA

Massimo's skin feels warm against mine as he takes both my hands into his.

The caress of his fingertips on my skin renews the swirl of delight I've been floating in for the last few days.

"One more step, Princess." He smiles, and his eyes sparkle in the moonlight.

I gaze down at him, floating in the still salty waters of the sea. I'm already waist deep, and I know one more step will take me away from the sandy floor. Taking me out of the bounds of safety, placing me in a position where I'll have to trust him.

"It looks deep," I breathe, and he smoothes his hands over mine.

"It is deep, but you won't learn to swim in shallow waters." He smirks, inclining his head, and a trail of water runs from his slick, wet hair down the side of his face.

This little idea was his. He wanted to go swimming in the

moonlight. Ironically, we're around the corner from the place where I was planning my escape. We're on the other side of the beach near the caves and jagged rock formations that look like small shadowy mountains against the night.

"You'll be fine," he adds, releasing my hands so he can take hold of my waist.

"Massimo, if you let me drown, I'm coming back to haunt you," I warn playfully, and he laughs.

I like him like this. I love that sound. The sound of his laughter. It fills me with something I can't quite describe every time I hear it. It's a good something.

"Princess, I'm not fucking letting you drown," says the man who wants to destroy my father. Except tonight he doesn't look like that man.

Massimo hasn't looked like that man in days. What he looks like is the man I'm fast becoming closer to in ways that I've never been with anybody.

I guess that's what happens when you give yourself to somebody and they have that part of you that no one else has claimed. It's trust.

He tightens his grip around my waist and I feel safe. On that thought, I take that step, and like I anticipated, the water engulfs me. However, I'm reassured quite quickly when Massimo holds me and I secure my arms around his neck, holding on as the cold water covers my shoulders and immerses my hair.

He smiles at me. "I got you, Emelia. Just relax and feel the water."

"I'm trying."

"Relax," he repeats. "All I want you to do is hold onto me."

The compelling magnetism of his stare pulls me in as I gaze back at him and allow his words to seep into my mind and my soul.

Hold onto him. I want to, but not the way he thinks or the way I should be. What I want to hold onto is this version of him.

"I will," I reply.

"Good girl. Tonight we'll just get used to you being in deep water. Try to move your legs slowly against the waves. But that's all."

"I think that's all I can do, Massimo. The rest of me is too afraid to do anything else." I wince and push myself up onto him as a wave splashes against my shoulders.

"Don't be afraid when you're with me," he says, as if I could trust him enough to take care of all my troubles no matter what they are.

Massimo secures his grip on me with one powerful, muscular arm, and with the other, he wades through the water.

We move away from the shallow, floating until we're bobbing up and down with the subtle waves, and it feels like we could be the last two people on earth. We're in the sea, swimming in a world of our own, existing without the details of who we are and how we came to be.

It feels good. The distance we've gone is the farthest I've ever been in any kind of water. There's something freeing about facing such a fear.

"You okay?" Massimo asks.

"Yes, but it feels weird not being able to feel the sand."

"It will at first, but you get used to it." He grins, and I look around me. "You know I'm going to ask why it is you can't swim, right? Our fathers came from the same place in Sicily. Everybody I know in San Leone can swim. My parents practically lived in the water, and we grew up like it too."

He's right. Everybody I know in San Leone can swim too. It's a seaside town and port south of Agrigento. Whenever I visited relatives, there wasn't a day that passed where they didn't spend it by the sea. I'm just a little different.

"My mother tried to teach me, but I saw something once that put me off."

He studies me. "What did you see, Princess?"

"When I was ten, I saw a boy from my elementary school drown." The instant I say that, concern fills his eyes. Another emotion I'm not used to seeing.

"How did that happen?"

"It was a school fundraising activity by the beach. He fell off the pier, and no one could get to him in time. It was awful, and I've been wary of the water since. I wasn't exactly fond of it in the first place. When that happened, I stayed away."

"I'm sorry that happened and you had to see death in such a way."

"It was awful. I didn't know him personally, but I saw him at school all the time. I had a hard time trying to unravel him from my mind after it happened. He was one of those kids that brought life and laughter everywhere he went."

His name was Jamie Scottsman. He played in the little league team, and because of that, he was very popular. I remember his face well. Him alive. It took me a while to shake the image of him lying on the sand, *dead*, after people tried to revive him and couldn't. I remember Dad taking me away from the scene as I cried, knowing what was happening.

"The sea can be a dangerous place, but it can also be magical."

"Magical?" I smile at that and try to imagine it as such.

"Yeah. Magical. Look around us. I'm sure you'll see things differently to me. I can't see a winged Pegasus on the water like you did the other day." He grins. "If you think the way you do when you're painting, you'll be able to shift the fear out of your mind."

I believe him because I've overcome many things by relying on my creative abilities. Deciding to take his advice, I look around and focus on the sliver of moonlight that kisses the water's surface. It shimmers and sparkles like it's truly been touched by magic.

"What do you see, Princess?" he asks, and I allow my imagination to run wild.

"Mermaids," I answer. That's what I imagine. In my mind's eye, I see four of them, beautiful and enchanting, just like in the fairytales and depictions people have illustrated over the centuries. "They've just surfaced in the moon's path, and they're singing."

He chuckles, and I look back at him. "Mermaids? I like that."

"Do you?"

"I do. My mother liked mermaids. She painted them too. It was her who taught me to swim, but as you know, sailing is more my thing. That came from my father."

I like it when he shares things about himself and his past. "That's cool."

"Yeah. My dad's family is heavily into it. And they're very old school."

"Like how?"

"*Superstitious.*"

"Like no women on the boat?" I raise a brow. The other day when he'd said it, it sounded like something you'd hear in a pirate film.

"Like no women on the boat, but I think I might have to make an exception and brave the curse for you."

That sends a thrill of arousal through my body. The thought of him doing something like that for me makes me feel special. It makes me feel like it's something he'd do *only* for me, and not someone like Gabriella.

"Would you, now, Massimo D'Agostino?"

"I would, Emelia Balesteri."

As I gaze back at him, I want him all over again, and again. I know I shouldn't, but whatever magic he thinks is here has me under its spell.

I lean closer and brush my lips over his. It's a brief touch that intensifies in seconds, turning hot as we kiss and our tongues tangle with the wild desire that always takes us.

He pulls back with a seductive glint in his eyes. "Lesson over."

"What are we doing now?" I giggle.

"Something wild. It's time to play with you again."

Play...

I like playing...

Before I can say anything more, he starts swimming backward with me, splashing the water as we go.

As we get closer to the beach, my feet connect with the sand and he takes my hand.

We walk out of the sea and head over to the large stone walls of the cave. I'm about to ask him again what we're doing when he pushes me against the wall and recaptures my lips.

The way that Massimo kisses me speaks of what we'll be doing tonight and *where* we'll be doing it. The latter becomes all the more apparent when he runs his fingers over the edge of my bikini bottoms and I feel the monstrous head of his cock pressing into my belly through his shorts.

His fingers find their way into my pussy, and I moan against his lips when he starts a low steady pump.

He pulls his fingers out, moves away from my lips, and slides his fingers into his mouth to lick off my juices. That always, always turns me on in a way that drives me closer to the insanity that takes over when I'm with this man.

Every nerve in my body tingles when he leans in close to my ear and runs his hand over my breasts.

"I'm going to fuck you right here against the wall of this cave, Princess."

My stomach does a crazy somersault, and the flames of desire licking over me beckon me to allow him to do whatever he wants to me. Outside though? *Jesus*...

"Out here, Massimo?" I whisper, and he catches my face.

"I'll have you wherever and whenever I want. You're mine." His gaze holds mine with that last word.

Previously when he'd told me that it sounded like destruction, like captivity, no freedom. Tonight I relish it.

When he takes hold of me and positions me to take his cock, I no longer care that we're outside. There are probably guards patrolling on the path above us, and they'll most likely hear us, but I don't care.

As he cups my sex and slides his thick cock into my passage, I most of all no longer care about who we are and how we came to be.

His lips press to mine as he starts moving inside me, and I know I'm falling for him.

CHAPTER TWENTY-FOUR

MASSIMO

Two fucking days...

That's how long we've stayed in bed since our rendezvous on the beach. Two days.

It's Thursday morning. Tonight is the ceremonial dinner where Pa will give me his ring. It will be a true symbol of his retirement as leader of the D'Agostino family.

In attendance will be my brothers, my two uncles and their wives who flew in from Italy, and my eight cousins, two of which have wives.

It's a big deal. I'm supposed to take Emelia to this dinner as a symbol of our family conquering the devil. She's supposed to be the trophy, *a prize*.

However, what I see as I watch her sleeping is the woman who's filled my every waking thought for the last few days.

Scratch that. It was since the night of the charity ball when she floated in on her father's arm and I knew I had to have her.

I woke before the sun rose and resumed my post by the window to watch her. Watching her yet again as I smoked. I seem to have fallen into this ritual of *watching, pondering, assessing*. All attempts to figure out what I'm going to do next.

Looking at her balances me. She's so peaceful in her sleep. In this room we've been trapped in a fantasy. Her and me. The two of us lost in the throes of passion, where nothing exists besides the attraction and chemistry that draw us to each other.

I forget the past when I'm with her. I don't know if that's a good or a bad thing, since my rage toward her father is sated and I find myself just thinking of her.

The sun casts its radiant rays over my sleeping beauty, hitting her in all the right places. The sheet is at her waist and she looks like the goddess, again with her breasts exposed. That gorgeous mane of hair is sprawled out on the pillow and, like the moonlight the other night, the soft sunlight spilling over her body caresses her skin the way I want to. The way I always want to.

Maybe I watch her because I want to capture it all before she wakes and we become the people we're supposed to be. *Enemies.*

Even though my family and I have this massive vendetta against her father, she doesn't have to be my enemy. I don't want her to be.

Things are changing. We can't stay in bed for another day. Out of duty, I can't stay in playing house with my doll because I can sense things happening on the streets, which doesn't sit well with me. I should have called Tristan by now, too, just to check in on him. I know he's not doing too well, and it's up to me to watch his back and make sure he's not doing shit to find Vlad by himself.

As I watch my girl lying in the bed across from me, desire to keep her safe fills me.

My girl...

Could she be?

Having a wife out of convenience is different than being with someone you want to be with.

I don't know what this is, but I want to explore it. I certainly want to savor it for whatever it is and play with my doll whenever I want to.

There's something I have to give her, and when I do, it's going to test my patience because she's going to ask me shit I don't want to hear.

When I shuffle to grab another cigar, she stirs. Her eyes flutter open and she looks at me.

Watching her wake up is the best thing ever. She pulls the sheet over her breasts as a smile inches across her beautiful lips. I need those lips on my cock soon. She gets off the bed, wrapping herself in the sheet, and walks over to me, settling down in my lap.

When she does things like this, I think of her bastard father and the shit he said to me. He'll have a fucking heart attack when he sees the way she looks at me next time. That's in a few days, when we gather at the fundraiser. It will be like a déjà vu of the ball, except she'll be on my arm.

She kisses me and I almost get sucked into the wild thrill that's had us in its claws. Instead, I press my nose to hers and hold her close. It's time to set pleasure aside and get back to business. Right now, she's in the same haze that clouds my mind. She's forgetting who we are, who *I* am.

I'm a mafia boss, and there's no reality that would see a sweet girl like her with a guy like me. Under normal circumstances, she'd run from me and the darkness that comes from being me.

"I have to go to work today," I begin. "But I'll be back by six to pick you up for the dinner. I want you to be ready."

The minute I say that, tension so thick it could stifle us both fills the space between us. I snake my arm around her waist and feel her trembling, probably worrying about how my family will treat her. The thing is, I don't know how they'll receive her.

"Do I have to go?" she asks.

"Yes. As my future wife you will be expected to attend." While everyone else may understand if I make up some shit like she was sick or something, Pa won't accept that.

He'd have me drag her down to his house vomiting and heaving if I had to, if she were sick. He's not a heartless man, but when it comes to anything to do with Riccardo, he becomes someone else entirely.

"What should I do? What do you want me to do?" she asks nervously, pressing her pretty pink lips together.

"You will stay by my side." I know if anyone will show her any form of compassion, it will probably be Tristan. Both Dominic and Andreas can be assholes when they want to be. "What I need you to do is behave." She has a smart mouth on her sometimes, and these aren't the people to mess with.

"Behave?" she asks, biting the inside of her lip.

"Yes, behave. Only speak when you are spoken to. No shit comments."

"And if someone talks shit to me?" Her eyes narrow.

"That won't happen." I don't think that will happen. It's not their style. The women aren't even the standard type of mean you'd expect in a situation like this. Although, I don't know what to really expect. They can be jealous, and Emelia is very beautiful.

"They'll all hate me, even though they don't know me."

She's right.

In defeat, her gaze flicks down to where my hand touches her tiny waist. I lift her gaze back up to meet mine.

"Anyone who dares to show you anything of the sort will have me to deal with," I promise.

I don't know what I'll do, but I feel some duty toward her to make sure she feels comfortable wherever we go. This is for life. Till death do us part. They will accept her as my wife from now on, and I expect them to treat her with the same respect they show me. It doesn't mean it will happen. The last thing I want to do is get into a fight over it.

"Do you mean that?" She studies me.

I smile at her. "Princess," I say, knowing she likes it when I call her that. "You're a clever girl. You know I don't say anything I don't mean. Which brings me to this."

I reach down and pull up the little bag with her phone. It's her actual phone. I didn't buy her a new one. She looks at the bag and her eyes widen when I pull the phone out.

She takes it when I hand it to her, and emotion swells within her eyes.

"Oh my God," she breathes and holds it to her chest. "What does this mean?"

"I'm giving it back to you. I don't have to tell you to use it wisely." By *wisely*, she knows what I mean.

"Are you going to tell me who I can and can't speak to?"

"Do I need to?"

She eyes me dangerously, her gaze sharpening. "Please don't spoil this, Massimo." She shakes her head. Her eyes pleading with me not to taint the last few days.

"Emelia...this is not about that," I reply, sounding like a broken record. I've said those words to her far too many times.

"What is it about? Can't it just be about us?" Her eyes cling to mine.

I want to say yes, but I can't. I can't say no, either.

"Watch it," I warn, tightening my grip on her waist. I'm aware I've spoiled it with just those two words.

"Can I call my father?" she asks, ignoring my warning.

"No, not until after the wedding." I'm leaving myself open giving her that phone.

"I can't call him before? We'll see him at the fundraiser. Will you forbid me to speak to him then, too, if he wants to speak to me?" She slips off my lap, and I allow her to.

I don't want her speaking to that bastard at all, but even I can't be that cruel.

"You can for five minutes. I don't want him filling your head with shit."

She holds her tongue on her next words. Since her hands are fisted by her sides, I can only imagine what she was going to say to me.

"What about my friend? Jacob. Massimo, he's my best friend. We've known each other since birth. He's going to be worried sick about me."

"*Friend?*" Okay, I'll do this. If she gives me the right answer to my next question, she can call him all she wants. "Has your friend ever shown any interest in you? Has he given you any inkling that he wants to be more than friends? Answer me truthfully, Emelia. I'm a motherfucking bastard, but I have never lied to you. Don't lie to me."

When her eyes cloud, I already know the answer to my questions.

"Answer me," I demand. She jumps at my raised voice. I'm pissed as fuck that I was right.

"Yes."

"Yes, what?"

"Yes... I think he wanted us to be more than friends."

"Well, then no, there will be no calls or messages to *Jacob*."

"How can you be such a prick? He's my friend." She seems more enraged about not being able to talk to this Jacob than her father. I won't ask her how she feels about him. I don't want the answer to that question.

"He's a friend who wants to fuck you. This discussion is over."

"I'm sorry, were we discussing? It sounded a lot more like you telling me shit."

I seethe and get up so fast she jumps out of my grasp when I reach for her. I get her, though, securing my arms around her middle. The sheet falls off as she tries to hit me. I take her right back to bed, lay her down and pin her hands over her head, laying her out like a delicious meal with her gorgeous breasts on show.

"Let go of me. Get away," she cries, but I hold her down.

"Emelia, this is bullshit."

"How is it bullshit? I just want to talk to my friend."

I have a mind to mention Gabriella and ask her if she'd be alright with me talking to her, but it's not the same thing. Gabriella is a former bed friend. Jacob is not, and I know that for certain. It was me who took her virginity, not that prick. I bet he wanted to though.

She's naïve and innocent. She doesn't know the dirty shit a man can conjure up. I'm doing it now as I watch her struggle beneath me in defiance and I have a hard time resisting the urge to fuck her into submission.

"I'm not going to be okay with you talking to a man who wants my girl," I say. It's only then she stops trying to fight me.

I release her hands and back off the bed, away from her. She eases up onto her elbows and stares at me.

"I could have put a tracker in that phone, or some shit to keep tabs on who you speak to. I could have given you a new one with a new number. I chose not to because I wanted you to have some element of privacy," I explain. "When it comes to those two people, however, the rules change. You will not call either of them. You ask me not to spoil this. I'm asking you the same. If you betray me, you will not like it, so don't do it. You don't want a problem with me."

I walk out and leave her on that note, staring after me.

She was quiet the whole journey to my father's house, just as I knew she would be.

She barely spoke back at the house when I went to pick her up. I was too absorbed in how she looked to note that she was pissed at me.

She looks beautiful in a strapless cocktail dress that accentuates her breasts and her curves. Her hair is down, just the way I like it, and her face is made up in a way I've never seen it before, with smoky eye shadow.

As I park the Bugatti on my father's drive and look out to the other parked cars, I get nervous too. It's an important night for me. I will be boss over these people. Today is the first time I need to garner that respect.

It starts with her and the presentation of her.

I look across at her sitting next to me and notice how anxious she is. "You look beautiful," I tell her, and she faces me.

Her face softens from the anger she exhibited this morning. "Thank you."

"That all I get, Princesca? No kiss?" This is the most playful she'll get from me. She knows I was right about Jacob, but she's pissed because she can't call him. I need her to shake off that funk though.

I lean in closer to her, and she kisses me briefly. It will have to do.

I take a lock of her hair and watch the ends curl about my thumb. "We'll finish that later."

When the twinkle returns to her eyes, I know I have her back, if only to calm her from our disagreement.

I get out of the car and open the door for her. When she steps out, I take her hand. This is the first time we've been out together. We look like we're going on a date. I'm wearing a suit and a dark shirt underneath, while she's in her dress. I catch a glimpse of our reflection in the car window. We look good together.

I glance across at her and see she notices too, but she looks away.

As we walk up the rest of the drive, it feels like I'm carrying her to the electric chair. I'm always happy to visit my old man. This is the first time that I wish I could reschedule.

As usual, Mario, Pa's butler, opens the door before I can reach it. He was our butler when I was a boy. After we lost everything, we had to let go of our staff, but the first things Pa found when we got back on our feet were those people. People like Mario, Candace, and Priscilla.

"Buonasera, Master Massimo," he welcomes me, dipping his head for a curt nod.

"Buonasera, Mario. This is Emelia, my fiancée," I say. It's the first time I've introduced her as such.

"Buonasera, signorina. I hope you enjoy your stay," he says to her. I'm glad for his kindness.

Our house staff always act like they don't know what's going on, but I know they do.

"Thank you so much, and buonasera," she replies. He nods his head.

"Everyone else is here. They arrived early." It's a warning to keep my head above water.

They want to see her. Emelia. They're curious and probably wanted to be there to watch us enter the dining room. Tonight is definitely going to be interesting.

"Grazie, Mario."

He walks on ahead, and we follow. He continues on without us when we get inside, and I make my way to the dining room with Emelia on my arm.

It will be dinner first, then mingling.

I hear talking in the dining room. It ceases in a hush, however, the instant we reach the door and everyone notices us.

Emelia tightens her grip on my arm. They're all looking at her and not even doing anything to look less obvious.

Pa is at the head of the table. There are two empty seats next to him for us. On his other side are my three brothers, sitting in order of rank. This is the first time this has happened. Tristan is right next to Pa and Andreas sits between him and Dominic. Everyone else can sit in whatever manner they choose.

"Good evening, everyone. I hope we aren't late," I say.

"Never," Pa answers, tipping his head at me. He looks to my hand holding Emelia's and a deeper curiosity fills his gaze. When he stands, everyone looks at him. "I wish to extend a welcome to my son, the new boss of this family, and his fiancée, Emelia Balesteri."

I didn't expect him to do that. Doing so, however, has set the tone for everyone else's behavior tonight.

"Thank you, Father," I say.

"Thank you," Emelia croaks, her voice coming out in a rasp.

"Come and sit," Pa invites.

We do. All eyes follow me.

I pull out the chair for her to sit and lower myself next to Pa. I set the tone, too, when I set my hand on the table, beckoning her to take it so everyone can see.

She looks at me but takes my hand, and when Pa looks at me with newfound admiration, I feel better.

I feel better about tonight, even if there are still a million things for me to worry about.

CHAPTER TWENTY-FIVE

EMELIA

I've never been so nervous in my life.

At the same time, I've never felt so strong. The minute Massimo reached for my hand, there was a shift in the atmosphere. The tension almost evaporated, although the shared curiosity exhibited by everyone was still there.

I watched as his father gave him the family ring. He looked different to me. He was in charge before and had this power. But as he put on the ring, he looked more like a leader.

I still can't get over how much he looks like his father, and his brothers all look like him too. They have the same tall, dark, and handsome features and eyes that are so striking you want to stare. Andreas has the only slight difference. His eyes are bright blue, not as dark as the other three brothers. Almost like God decided to change things up, or just make him different. He's the eldest. I'm amazed he isn't boss. My family isn't traditional, and it would be different for me because I'm a woman. However, in most Italian families, I know the oldest son is who takes the lead. I guess it must be different here. It's definitely not something I'll question. Andreas looks scarier than Massimo.

We ate a wonderful meal I was actually able to enjoy, and I got stuck talking with a few of the wives who wanted to introduce themselves to me. They took me away from the men and gathered in the sitting room to talk. They're talking now about vacations. I can't join in because right now, this is a vacation for me. They've been nice, although I can imagine it must have been difficult because they know who I am.

They know, yet they've tried to make me feel welcome. Again, it makes me question who the monsters are.

When Aurora, the youngest wife, starts talking about babies, the others start fussing over her. I don't know what the heck I'm supposed to say, so I keep quiet.

"Massimo needs you," a voice says behind me and I turn to see Andreas.

"Oh, thank you," I answer, feeling nervous to talk to him. The women quiet their conversation in his presence. I've noticed the respect everyone has displayed around the brothers.

"This way," he says, motioning his head for me to follow.

I do, and he leads me out into the hallway. Massimo isn't there, though.

"Where is Massimo?" I ask.

"Relax, you look like you needed saving when they started talking about babies. Unless I was mistaken?" He raises a brow, and my nerves spike.

"No. And, oh...thank you. You're right," I agree.

"Oh good. I wouldn't have liked to be wrong."

I smile, but my nerves are still on edge. I don't know what it is about him, but I feel more awkward in his presence.

Maybe it's because he's older and would have probably remembered my father's cruel hand more than Massimo. Or maybe it's because I know that I'd be with him if he were boss. What would have happened to me then? I truly doubt I would have faced the same fate as I have with Massimo. That's saying something, since I don't exactly know where I stand with him, except that I'm to obey and behave.

Andreas studies me. I'm not sure what he's thinking, so I don't encourage the conversation in case I say the wrong thing.

"I hope my brother is treating you well," he states.

"Yes," I reply.

"Well, you two look good together," he mutters. Those eyes of his pierce into me. "I hope he continues to treat you well."

Someone clears their throat. It's Massimo. I look at him and am surprised to see he has that same possessive air about him like when I was talking to Manni on the beach. I didn't think he would be that way with his brother.

"Just saving your girl from the talk of babies," Andreas explains. He called me Massimo's girl.

All day, I've been thinking about when Massimo said something similar this morning. Though I've been upset about him refusing to allow me to speak to Jacob, I did savor being called that.

"I hope that's all you're doing," Massimo states.

Andreas narrows his eyes, walks over to him and lays a heavy hand on his shoulder. "Relax, kid," he says and takes Massimo's hand with the ring. "The ring looks good on you. Proud of you as always."

I don't have many friends. Sure, my father kept me on a leash, but I didn't have many friends because a lot of the schools I went to housed snobs who were jealous of what I had. If it's one thing I'm able to spot, it's a fake compliment.

What Andreas said about the ring was off. I don't really think he was okay with not being chosen to be boss, and I don't really think he's as proud of Massimo as he says. Did Massimo notice that too? To me it was obvious.

"Thank you, brother," Massimo answers, giving him a one-shouldered hug.

"I'll see you in the morning."

"Be safe."

"Always. You too." Andreas gives him another tap and saunters away.

Massimo returns his attention to me and moves closer. "Ready to go?"

"I am," I reply. "Are you always going to be like that when men talk to me?"

"Yes."

"But that's your brother, and he was being nice," I counter. I don't know what the story is but I'll give Andreas the benefit of the doubt. It must be tough being the oldest and not being chosen to lead the family.

"My brothers are like sharks, Emelia. In their eyes, until we say 'I do,' you're still on the market." He's being serious.

"Oh... Well, then I'm ready to go."

Placing his hand to the small of my back, he guides me out. I feel like I should have said goodbye to the ladies, but it's okay.

Giacomo didn't speak to me. I didn't expect him to. I think I wouldn't have known what to say if he had.

We get into the car and head back to the place I'm now calling home. When we pass the diner, my heart aches and I think of Jacob. I couldn't lie to Massimo earlier. I wanted to lie because, truthfully, Jacob has never told me how he felt about me. It would have been easy to lie and say I had no knowledge of him wanting to be more than friends. I couldn't do it though. And I think Massimo would have seen straight through me.

When we're about halfway to the house, the silence gets to me. I want to at least have some idea of what his father thought of me. The guys were off talking for a long time. It feels awful when you know people are talking about you. While I don't mean to be self-centered in thinking they spent the whole time talking about me, I'm sure I was discussed. It's a given that I would be.

I turn to Massimo and take in the outline of his sharp features against the mingle of moonlight and the soft amber glow from the lights inside the car. Sometimes I find myself looking at him because his features are so striking. Other times, I look at him because he's a mystery and a wonder. A man who can change like the wind in temperament, but also one with secrets. Many secrets.

"What?" he asks. The deep baritone of his voice pierces through the blanket of silence.

"I was just thinking," I begin. "Thinking about what your father thought of me."

"He didn't say anything," Massimo says. I'm not too sure how I should take that. Is that good or bad? It can't be good, surely. "Don't read too much into it, Princesca. That's how he is."

I consider that for a moment and think back to when we first arrived at the house. Giacomo didn't have the same malicious vibe I'd witnessed when we first met. I'd say tonight almost felt like Massimo and I could have just gone to a family dinner.

"It was nice of him to introduce me," I state. It's true. He didn't have to, and I could tell it set the flow for the way everyone else should treat me.

"It was."

As it starts to rain, Massimo reaches out to the ornate dashboard of his car to switch on the radio. He finds a jazz channel and settles for it.

I take note of little things like that because this man is the definition of a closed book. I was surprised days ago when he shared so much about his mother. Now I know he likes jazz.

"You like jazz," I state and feel better when the corners of his lips turn up into a sensual smile.

"I do. It calms the soul. Just like my car."

I chuckle. He turns fully to look at me. I notice whenever I smile or laugh, he always gives me a look of fascination.

"Your car calms your soul?" I ask, trying not to laugh.

"My car calms my soul."

"How? I get that jazz does. I like jazz, but how in the world would your car do the same thing?"

A deep chuckle rumbles in his chest and, like every time I've heard him laugh, I savor the sound. "It just does, Princess. This one does." He taps the dashboard.

"Does it have anything to do with the fact that it's a big ol' Bugatti? A sure sign of wealth?"

He smirks. "I don't fucking care about that. If you got it, flaunt it. I like nice things. I didn't always have wealth, so I guess I indulge when I want to."

I think about that, about him not always having wealth, and try to imagine what it must have been like for him. Not everyone had the privilege of living as lavishly as I have all my life. I think it would be hard to go from having everything to nothing, then having to rebuild.

"A Bugatti is a good make," he states. "I look at it and remember how far I've come. It's a trusty car."

He's about to say something else when the car stalls and jerks. There's a screeching sound, and then the car slows down. Massimo steers it over to the roadside, where it cuts out.

"Fuck, what the hell is this now?" he snaps and tries to restart the car. It doesn't work. The hazard lights switch on, but that's all.

I don't know much about cars, but I can take an educated guess that this car won't be moving anywhere tonight. The electronics seem to be gone, which means it needs to go to a mechanic.

"What's wrong with it?" I ask.

"I don't know. I'm gonna check it out." He gets out and the rain splatters in, sprinkling all over my legs until he closes the door.

I watch him fumble around, lifting the hood of the car and doing all sorts until he comes back around to me and rests his wet head on the edge of the door.

"The car's busted. It's gonna take AAA two hours to get to us." The tempestuous hue of his eyes matches the midnight blue of the sky. "Fuck, I change cars regularly to avoid shit like this."

"How long have you had this car?" I ask. When I drove, I had my car for three years, and I had no plans to change it.

"Two months."

I press my lips together and try not to laugh, but I fail after two seconds.

"Why are you laughing, Emelia?"

"Because that's ridiculous. Wasn't it you who said how great this car was, *how trusty and well made?*"

He gives me a stern expression before he laughs too. "That's not funny. It's supposed to be trusty."

Deciding to get out and join him, I open the door and

step out. The rain isn't too bad now, although it's drizzling. Something I like, feeling the rain on my skin. Especially when the weather is hot, like it is now.

Massimo watches me keenly as I walk over to him. "My Miata never did this, and I've had it for three years."

"Doll," he says, leaning against the car door. "Can you see me driving a Miata?"

"At least it wouldn't break down like this car. Miatas are *trusty* cars."

He looks at me and studies my face. "Come here," he says, tilting his head to the side.

I move closer to him. He reaches for my waist, pulling me right up to him to close the space between us. His lips find mine and we kiss.

Every time this man kisses me, I find myself forgetting everything. Every time we're together in any kind of intimate way, all that exists in my world is him and what we are in those moments.

It's dangerous for me to think like this.

This whole day has been a big reminder to me, and a warning that I can't allow myself to fall for him. It's just hard when he kisses me like he wants to consume me.

Pulling away from my lips, he catches my face and looks me over.

"Smart mouth."

"It's true. Miatas are trusty cars." I run my fingers over his chest and his eyes roam over my body.

"We're about a mile from the house. Let me call a taxi. I want you, and the road's too open for me to strip you naked right here and fuck you on the hood of this car."

My cheeks burn in response to the image of him doing exactly that to me.

"What if we walked? It's going to take some time to wait for the taxi. We could just walk together."

His eyes narrow. "You want to walk with me?"

"Yes."

"In those shoes?" He looks at my heels. He's right. They'd be a nightmare to walk in for longer than ten minutes. Tonight, I was grateful that I didn't have to move around in them too much.

"I'll manage," I say because it would be nice just to walk. "Then we could talk some more about what we like."

He looks at me like the idea is odd, but then he nods. "I have a better idea," he says. I gasp when he suddenly scoops me up to carry me.

I laugh, and he does too.

"You're going to carry me home?"

"I am, Princess."

I circle my arms around his neck, and he smiles down at me.

"I like Bugattis, even though that one just made me look like a fool," he says, kicking the door shut with his heel.

"I like Miatas. They're trusted cars," I repeat.

He starts walking down the road. "I ride a motorcycle."

"Really?"

"Uh huh," he answers and then starts talking about his Ninja X2.

He actually talks to me like we could have always been this way. A couple. And, I'm so taken with his words and the way his face lights up as he speaks that all I do is listen.

CHAPTER TWENTY-SIX

EMELIA

Before I know it, we're back at the house. The gates open before we even reach them, and the guards at the gate watch us, watching him carrying me.

No one says anything. We just continue.

The doors open for us too, and I expect him to set me down, but he doesn't. He continues carrying me. We head toward my room but branch off down a path I haven't been shown.

"Where are we going, Massimo?"

"My room. I want you in my bed. You'll be in my bed starting tonight. I'll move your stuff in tomorrow."

The spontaneity of that decision should throw me off kilter, but it doesn't. Instead, I'm looking at him. I'm treading those dangerous paths again, not just as a thought in my mind, but my heart. I'm placing my heart at risk because I keep forgetting who we are.

The idea of being in his bed has my head spinning, and my soul along with it, right into the arms of temptation.

We reach a door, and he opens it. Once he steps inside, he puts me down, and as the lights come on, I'm stunned to silence at the elegance of his room.

It's as big as an apartment. I can see how he'd be MIA for days and not be seen anywhere. A person could live in this section of the house. There's a chill-out area with a black leather sofa and a fifty-inch-screen TV on the wall. To our left is an archway that leads into the actual bedroom.

Massimo takes my hand and leads me through the archway.

As we walk in, the décor reminds me of a classic European home. Exactly like you'd find in Italy.

A king-sized mahogany bed rests in the center, with all the furniture matching the bed. A wrought-iron chandelier hangs over it. The ceiling is high, and the walls are cream and navy. All except one wall, which is made of glass.

I can see the beach from here and realize that from what I'm looking at, the room can't actually be that far from mine. There's a door at the side, and I'd be willing to guess that it must lead to some sort of corridor that would go to my room.

There was a door in my room, too, that was always locked. I assumed it led outside. I think it comes here.

"This room is close to mine," I state.

"Yes, it is. You look like you're deciding if you should be mad at me or not."

"I'm not mad."

"Good, I don't want to waste time disciplining you tonight. Unless you want me to. You were quite wet after that spanking the other week." He smiles, and my entire body blushes from his scandalous words and the look he gives me.

"I didn't like that," I answer. He's right to look back at me in disbelief because I was wet. The evidence was there that I was aroused in some way by what he did.

"Don't worry. Next time, I'll make it more pleasurable. You have the perfect ass for spanking." He chuckles as I swallow hard.

I keep my gaze trained on him as he runs his tongue over his bottom lip and moves behind me. Warmth graces my skin as he unzips my dress, and we both watch it float down to my feet. My strapless bra follows. He reaches forward and fills his palms with my naked breasts, squeezing then kneading, making me moan in response to his touch.

"The dress looked great on you, but I prefer your naked body. And I love playing with your gorgeous tits," he mutters into my ear, his hot breath tickling my skin.

I moan with pleasure as he continues to massage my breasts. Pleasure claims my mind. I'm ready to kiss him when he flips me around to recapture the kiss we shared on the road.

Our lips meet, and I decide tonight will be different. Usually, I'm like a doll in his house, a toy for him to play with, but I want him too. I want to explore his body the way he explores mine. I want to enjoy it.

I tug at his shirt, freeing it from the waistband of his pants, and undo the bottom button. I'm about halfway up in my pursuit when he catches my greedy hands and clasps his over mine.

A dark smile lifts the corners of his mouth when he moves away from me to get a look at my face.

"You want me. Say it," he demands with a stare that makes me melt.

"I want you," I answer. Shame fills me.

He moves in close in a predatory way, as if he's going to take me whole. Fright momentarily fills me.

"Be careful, Emelia," he warns. "My Princesca. Be careful what you want. If you're not careful, you just might get it, and it won't always be a good thing. I'm the big bad wolf, the devil." He leers at me, but when I look at him, I only see the Massimo my heart wants. The man I'm drawn to, the man who makes my heart beat the same way it does when I think of my dreams.

"Still want me?"

"Don't you want me to want you?"

"No. Because you deserve better." I think it's a lie. I think he wants to believe that, and it's true, but it's a lie. His eyes darken to that of an afternoon sunset as he gazes long and hard at me. "I'm a selfish bastard, Emelia. You must know that by now. So I want you to want me whether or not it's good or bad."

I take charge now and finish undoing his buttons. I take off his shirt, and he allows me to. I start undoing his belt while he runs his thumb over the hard peaks of my nipples.

"What are you going to do to me?" He smiles.

"I want to suck your cock," I answer. My ears burn at my words. I've never said that before, and I've never done that before. I know he's wanted it. I have too.

His lips part as he watches me.

"Do you, now?"

"Yes," I answer.

I push down the band of his boxers once I've unzipped his fly. As I do so, his cock springs free and I run my fingers over the length. He's completely erect and ready to be inside me, but I'm having him first.

I lower to my knees and lick off the precum on the tip of his mushroom head. It tastes salty and masculine. It's the taste of him.

I secure a grip on the base and pump up and down, then

take him right into my mouth. He groans with pleasure I've never heard come from him.

I have no idea what I'm doing, but there's no way I'm not going to do this properly. I don't want him thinking of someone like Gabriella when he's with me. Or comparing. I suck harder when I imagine her doing this to him, and he laces his fingers through my hair.

"Fucking hell, Emelia, you are fucking perfect."

I take that as a sign I'm doing a good job, so I continue sucking hard. He thrusts into my mouth, fucking my face. He goes deeper, and I take it. He tightens his grip on my head, and I take it. He pumps so hard I think I might choke, but I take it because I know I'm pleasing him.

When I start to massage his balls, he groans out loud but stops pumping. He runs his fingers through my hair, and I stop sucking.

"I want to play with you in a different way tonight, Emelia, and finish inside you," he groans, pulling me up. The pleasure-filled expression looks beautiful on his face. Pleasure I gave him. "I want to be dirtier, darker with you tonight, Princesca. Let me."

He's still erect and looks like he's ready to blow, but exhibits enough control to kiss me so hard my lips burn.

"What are you going to do?" I ask. There's something dark indeed lurking in his eyes that hardens his face with raw desire. It intrigues me to find out what he means by dirtier and darker.

He moves us to the wall with the wardrobe, releases me, and pulls on a curtain I assumed covered the window. As the curtain opens, I see it's not a window.

My mouth falls open when my gaze lands on a large metal St. Andrews Cross unit by the wall and a little table that holds an assortment of restraints. Chains, handcuffs, ropes, and a whip.

BDSM. That's what this is. That's what I'm looking at.

Sheltered as my life has been, I haven't been deaf to the risqué conversations I've heard on campus many times, nor the secrets and plights amongst the company of wild friends Jacob keeps. It's stuff like this they talk about all the time.

In only a few weeks, I've given away my first kiss, lost my virginity, and now look at me. What am I doing now? What am I agreeing to?

"Are you scared, Princess?" he asks. My gaze drifts from the cross to him. "I want to tie you up and fuck you. I want to live out a wild, dark, reckless fantasy I've had of you since I saw you at the charity ball."

The thought of a man like him fantasizing about me is what hooks me and pulls me into the fantasy of allowing him to tie me up and do whatever he wants to me.

"Does that frighten you, Princess Emelia?" he asks again.

"No," I answer. I'm not sure if I meant to say that, though, because truthfully, I'm frightened and everything inside me should be telling me to run away. It's just not. My brain isn't working more than to tell me to say yes.

Say yes and agree. Agree to everything this man wants to do to me.

The flame of satisfaction lights up his eyes. Desire blazes deep within them, with molten heat so hot his stare burns me up.

"Will you allow me to tie you up?" He moves away from the curtain and takes my hand. Lifting it to his mouth, he plants a kiss on my knuckles. "You can say no. I give you freedom to tell me to fuck off because this is too much. But I want you like this."

I want him to want me.

"I...want to," I answer and swallow against the desire that burns the back of my throat.

"You have to trust me. This is us. It would be as simple as that. You and me."

"Yes," I answer. It's the easiest yes I've ever given because I want that too.

"Your safe word is *red*, Princesca. I will not hurt you, but if I do anything you don't want me to do or you want me to stop, you say *red*. Understand?"

"I understand."

He closes his hand over mine and ushers me to the cross. While I look over the structure, he takes a pair of leather cuffs from the table and secures one cuff to the left side of the cross, pushing the chain through the little hoop at the top.

He holds out his hand to me, asking for mine. I give it to him. He then secures the cuff to my wrist and repeats the same thing on the other side.

Before securing my ankles, he takes off my panties. When he's done and I'm tied up, I realize I'm completely at his mercy.

I've more than given over my body to him. I've given him my choice and my mind. My heart made me do it.

He steps out of his pants and boxers, shedding his clothes so we're both naked.

Walking over to me, he crouches down and buries his face between my thighs to start a slow suckle on my clit. He sucks, and the slow softness makes me more aroused.

The chains on the cuffs on my legs are slightly longer so I can move just enough and he can position me how he wants to eat me out. The cuffs around my wrists are long enough so I can bend forward. All are adjusted to move me into whatever sexual position he wants me to be in. I shuffle against his ruthless tongue as he thrashes over my opening, tantalizing my body.

"Oh God!" I cry out, throwing my head back. "Fuck." I come before I can pull in another breath. Wetness flows from me right into his mouth. As he drinks, he reaches up to massage my nipples. With the restraints on me, I can't move in the way I would to take the pleasure. It feels good but painful in a strange way because of the overload of intense pleasure.

"Massimo!" I scream. He answers with a dark chuckle.

"Scream my name, Princesca. Scream until you can't talk. I'm not finished with you yet."

I rasp out a breath when he dives back in and continues feasting on me. This time, his tongue feels amazing, and the fact that I can't move more than what I am holds me in the grip of pleasure to take what he's giving my body.

Dirty, dark, dangerous pleasure I'm now drunk on and greedy for when he feeds me more. I come again, screaming. No words come out, just a sound that tears from my lips, of raw, primal pleasure.

Massimo gets up and licks his lips, licking up the nectar from my pussy that dripped down the side of his mouth.

His cock looks like it's bursting, but he still emits that air of control. I want to touch him, but he's in charge of what we do next.

He moves behind me, grabs my hips. Lining his cock up with my entrance, he plunges into my pussy. I gasp when my body jerks forward.

He starts to fuck me. It feels so damn good I can barely breathe. I feel so amazing that I forget I'm restrained.

He pumps into me hard, and I take his hard thrusts. He grabs a fistful of my hair and pounds into me, making our bodies slap together. The sounds fill the room and our groans and moans join the orchestra of hot sex.

Another orgasm takes me, and he lets go of my hair. He rocks my body with his deep, rough strokes as I writhe against him, chains clinking.

The warmth of his fingers moves across my back like a trail of fire and circles over the tight rosette of my asshole. When he pushes his fingers in, my knees buckle, but he holds me up and slows his pumps.

"Baby, please let me take you here. Let me," he groans. I know I should be mortified, but I want to give everything to him. So I do.

"Yes," I answer, and he pulls out of me.

He coats my asshole with my juices, working his finger inside and around the area. Hyped up on pleasure, I'm only mildly aware of what he's doing until I feel the fat head of his cock pressing against my ass.

My eyes widen as he inches in. It feels so strange.

"It's okay, Princess, I promise you'll feel good really soon," he soothes me and strokes my back gently. He's so gentle I can't believe it's him.

I groan and he stops. "*Red* yet, Princess? You can say *red*. You're the boss of me tonight."

His words grip me. I try to look back at him, but my hair falls forward.

"No. I want you to..." I rasp, and he strokes me again.

Slowly, he moves in until he's deeper. A blast of pleasure races through my blood. *Holy shit,* the new sensation feels amazing.

What feels better is when he starts moving slowly inside me and goes deeper. That's when I mewl so loudly I'm sure everyone in the house and the surrounding areas can hear me. *Shit.*

The sound seems to encourage him because he starts pumping harder. I've adjusted to take his thrusts, so as he fucks my ass, all I feel is raw, undiluted pleasure that shatters me from the inside out.

I come again, and as I do, he floods me with a fierce cry, sounding like a warrior in battle. The warmth of his cum sprays into me, claiming that part of me like he did when he took my virginity. There's nothing left to claim. This man has taken it all.

We calm but I'm completely spent and drained. There is nothing left of me. The heaviness of exhaustion has come to take me whole.

He holds me up with one hand while he undoes the cuffs. One at a time they go, releasing me from the mercy of his fantasy. I know he enjoyed it, but the pleasure he gave me was unlike anything I've experienced. Like a drug, I crave more. More of him.

He scoops me up and carries me to the bed. I'm so drained I barely register that he's left my side. It's only when he wipes a warm rag over my mound that I figure he must have left me to get it. After he cleans me, he gets in bed next to me and I manage to roll into his arms so he can hold me.

"Are you okay, Princesca?" he asks.

"I'm tired."

"I'll take care of you." It sounds like a vow.

Is it?

I hold his gaze. It's like I'm seeing him for the first time. There's a sparkle deep in his eyes. It's the same as what I saw in the painting his mother did. It's his soul. That's what she painted in his eyes. She provided a window to his soul, and I see it.

"I see you," I say.

Slowly, he shakes his head, and just like that, the sparkle is gone. "Don't…"

It's good advice.

Don't.

I could apply it to anything, but I know what he means.

Don't fall for him, that's what he's trying to tell me.

I've thought about my heart a lot tonight. Cautioning myself the same. He's collected pieces of me. I thought I had nothing left to give.

I do. I have my heart and my soul. That's what I have left.

He doesn't love me. I don't think he can.

So, I must never allow him to take the last two things away from me.

CHAPTER TWENTY-SEVEN

MASSIMO

I step out onto the terrace and gaze up at the stars as memories of last night come back to me.

It was the twinkle in Emelia's eyes and the way she looked at me the whole night that I'll always remember.

I see you...

That's what she said to me. I knew what she meant. She could see inside me, past the wall I built, see deep down to the real me.

Just like at the ball, I dropped my guard. At the ball, when I first saw her, she was so striking I couldn't keep that wall up. The same thing happened last night. I allowed her in.

But I ruined it. I squashed the connection like a bug. Crushed it before it could take full bloom, suffocating the blossom of the feelings people share after they do what we did.

She trusted me with her body last night when she allowed me to tie her up. What she didn't realize was that she trusted me with more than that. She trusted me with trust. The element of trust. People don't think of it as a concept that's as important as love, friendship, compassion. It's the same.

We had sex twice before morning when she woke in the early hours. It felt good to have her in my bed finally, but there was something different about her.

Did she heed my warning? *Don't fall for me.*

I mustn't fall for her either. It wouldn't be hard to fall. I'm already on the edge.

There are, however, so many reasons why I can't love her. So many reasons why I shouldn't. And she mustn't give me her love, either.

We're a contract. Love is a weakness I can't afford. Women are just women in my world.

The women at the house last night were good examples, although I admit it's clear that my cousin Matthew is in love with his wife. That's his choice, and I'm happy for him. All the other men there with wives cheat. I hate it, but what did I think I was going to do? Marry Emelia and accept her as my wife the way you should, or would I have women on the side like most of the men in my family?

Pa was not like that with my mother, and while my brothers are sex-crazed animals, I know if they love, they would love hard. The same way I would.

That's why I can't do it, and I know that's why they don't either.

Love burned my father. Love burned Tristan.

The last thing I want to do is fall in love the way Pa did and lose my girl.

With Emelia, it would be hard if I lost her or if I failed her in some way. I can't live my life in fear.

Fear makes you weak. As boss and as a member of the Syndicate, I can't be weak in any shape or form. Emelia was a plan that is unfolding nicely. The wedding is over a week away. Things are in motion. I'm about to have it all.

I make my way back inside when my phone buzzes in my back pocket. Pa's here. He wanted to see me.

I just got back from doing the accounts at the club. Emelia hasn't seen me yet.

Pa's already lighting up a cigar in the sitting room when I get down there.

I walk in and close the door. He wants to talk to me in private, but I need to talk to him too. The situation with Vlad is rubbing me the wrong way.

"Hey, Pa," I say, sitting opposite him.

"Son, you look like shit." He smirks, looking me over carefully.

"I've seen better days."

"Talk to me. I'm all ears," he offers.

I sigh and run a hand through my hair. "I don't know what to do about Vlad. I'm not sure if he's still in L.A. He doesn't normally stay in one place for too long."

"There's every possibility that he's left. At the same time, he could still be here. It's all a matter of why he's here. He and the Shadows."

"I know, and there's no way of finding that out," I answer.

Pa looks at me long and hard. "You're worried about her," he notes. "Emelia."

"I should protect her if she's with me." I'm going to find it hard to talk to him about her without giving too much emotion away.

"You practically declared her yours last night. I saw."

He's not questioning me. He's stating a fact.

I run my hand over my beard. "I wanted her to feel comfortable," I answer, and his expression softens.

"I could see that, but there was more. She's not like him, Massimo. Not like Riccardo."

"No, she's not." I glance down at the floor.

"You feel for her," he states. My gaze climbs back up to meet his.

"I'm... I'm just doing what I'm supposed to. That's the deal, right?"

He smiles at me. "Massimo, you're marrying this girl next week. She's been with you for the last three weeks, and the marriage was your idea. A brilliant idea that I would have agreed to either way, but I noticed the way you snapped when Riccardo pushed you about her at the Syndicate meeting."

I bite the inside of my lip. "He just got to me."

"Your eyes gave you away, son. I saw the way she looked at you at the dinner, and I saw how you looked at her. You're protective of her. The same way I was with your mother." He straightens up and stares at me.

I gaze back, not knowing what to say. If there's anyone I can be real with, it's him. It's just hard because we're talking about our enemy's daughter.

"I don't want anything to happen to her."

"I understand." An uneasy look settles in his eyes. "Massimo... I feel like the time has come to share a thing or two about the past with you. That's why I wanted to see you."

My interest piques. *What is he going to tell me?*

He draws in a breath. "I'm sure you've always wondered what happened to make Riccardo hate me, hate *us*? I told you we fell out. We did, just not the way you think."

"What happened?" I've been consumed with hate for so long from all that Riccardo did to us that I never needed to concern myself with the fine print.

"We started out as three best friends. Me, Riccardo, and your mother. I always loved her. *Always.* I just never thought I was good enough for her. As we got older, I shied away, and he stepped up."

I straighten, unsure of where this conversation is going. I knew my parents knew Riccardo when they were younger and practically grew up together because their fathers were in the Syndicate, but it sounds like Pa's about to tell me something about my mother I never factored in.

"Stepped up to do what?" I narrow my eyes.

"Be with her. She was with Riccardo first."

My lips part. "What are you saying to me?" I ask, and I wonder who else knows this.

"I was the coward. I could never muster the courage to tell her how I felt. Then I did it one day. I couldn't stand it. Watching him with the girl I loved, knowing he knew I loved her more than he did." He pauses, brings his hands together, and continues. "I told her how I felt and asked her to think about it, about me and her. After all, I was about to break up my two best friends. It just so happened to be that the next night, Riccardo proposed. But she...couldn't say yes. I was there when he asked her, right there in front of everyone we knew, and she couldn't say yes. Instead, she looked at me, and I knew she chose me."

"Pa, you've never told me this," I rasp in shock.

"It's a bad story, son. We decided to be together. Of course, that ripped us all apart. It wasn't until after you were born that Riccardo came back into our lives. He saw a business opportunity we could both get involved in and be stronger together. I agreed because I felt guilty for what I did. That guilt made me make a lot of mistakes. I gave him too much power. Then he screwed me over."

"It was like he changed overnight," I add.

"He's only ever behaved like that when it came to your mother. Except at the time he did it, there was no reason to.

Years had passed since they were together. So, I think something happened."

"Like what, Pa?" I don't know what to think. Mom would never cheat on Pa, and not with Riccardo.

"Son, I accepted him back into our lives, but I kept one eye open for the eventuality that he might try to take my girl. My guess is he tried to move in on her, but she chose me again, and it infuriated him. At that time, he had power and didn't need me anymore."

"My God," I breathe.

He raises his hands. "He turned the Syndicate against me and took everything from us. He hated me because I had her. I felt you needed to know. It provides more context to the story."

"Thank you for telling me."

"You can't help who you have feelings for, Massimo. It's just something that happens. So...if you feel for this girl, it won't matter who she is or where she came from. Don't be afraid to show her your heart."

I listen to him and note how he knows me so well. He knows my heart is the one thing I keep locked away from the world and the one thing I'd keep away from Emelia.

I placed a wall up around my heart. Every time I'm with her, pieces of the wall fall away. I fall too. For her.

This wedding might be part of the contract, but I know what I'm starting to feel for her is real, and that scares the fuck out of me.

CHAPTER TWENTY-EIGHT

EMELIA

Today marks exactly one week until the wedding.

We have a morning ceremony, so by this time next week, we'll be married. I'll be Emelia D'Agostino.

I've been thinking about the wedding a lot since yesterday. It dawned on me that the buildup was now over and this was the last part. The countdown.

We're on our way to the fundraiser. This time, we're in the back seat of a limo.

Things have been weird between Massimo and me since the other night.

There's a noticeable strain that was the result of stepping too far over the line. He's been distant. I feel like I intruded and saw too much, saw what he never wanted me to see when I recognized that glint in his eyes. The glint that vanished straightaway. A sign that we'll be close physically, but he'll never give me his heart. A sign that I must never give mine to him either.

When I told him I could see him, he said *don't*. That one word held so much meaning and carried a lot of weight. It snapped me out of the trance, or whatever spell I'd been under since our first kiss.

That damn kiss bamboozled me.

We've been in this limo for over an hour, and Massimo hasn't looked at me once.

The limo pulls up in front of the building. The guards are already waiting to escort us out. It makes me nervous. Not even Dad had this many guards.

A man with so much protection is one with a lot of enemies.

Massimo is at my side when we step out of the car. A beautiful woman with auburn hair looks at him like she wants him—or maybe it's that she's had him and wants him again.

He sees her watching and takes my hand, but he doesn't look at me.

The fundraiser is being held at Stanford Hall, a place reserved for the rich and the famous. Tonight's fundraiser is similar to the charity ball I went to at Easter. This one is in aid of the Children Society.

We walk up large stone steps with pillars going up to the doors. When we step through the large oak doors, Massimo takes me aside to a little break room near the foyer, probably to lay down the law on me again.

"We're not going to be here for long," he begins.

"I thought we'd stay for the night."

"No, an hour, tops. Maybe less."

I didn't know that he planned to leave so soon. "Why?"

"You ask too many questions, Princesca."

"Can't we just go out on a normal date?" I throw back and he looks at me, surprised.

"This isn't a date. This is a business arrangement."

"I'm sorry, are you talking about the fundraiser or me?" Why did I bother to ask? As if I don't know the answer.

"Watch it, Emelia. I'm not in the mood tonight to argue about shit. Like I said, we're here for an hour, tops. You have five minutes with your father. No more. Other than that, you mustn't leave my side."

He always has a way of spoiling things.

I don't bother to encourage this argument because I know I won't win, so when he reaches out his hand to me, I take it. We leave the room, and Tristan approaches us.

"Hey," he says to Massimo, but to me he offers a kind smile and tips his head reverently. It surprises me.

"Hey, there," Massimo answers him.

"Riccardo is here. Arrived ten minutes ago," Tristan informs us and glances at me cautiously.

Dad is here. I can't believe I've been in the States for the last three weeks and haven't seen him.

"Massimo, there are a few undesirables here too. Nothing we can't handle. Just thought you should know."

Massimo's brow creases. Instantly, I wonder if there's trouble. "Tristan, if shit happens, you take Emelia and go."

I glance up at Massimo, surprised by the protective nature in his words.

"Don't worry, I will," Tristan says and, with a nod, leaves us.

I tug on Massimo's hand. He looks at me. "Is something happening?" I ask. Maybe that's why he's been so tense.

He reaches out and touches my face briefly. "No. Nothing to worry about."

When we enter the hall, I see Dad. He's the first person my eyes go to. He's standing by the drinks table in the far corner talking with a tall, bulky, Italian man who looks like he could be a wrestler. Dad sees me too, and I can't deny that my heart lifts at the sight of him. It lifts, then falters in the same breath as I recall how he sold me and ruined my dreams.

Massimo and I walk toward the middle, and so does Dad. We stop when we meet. I notice the way Dad completely ignores Massimo for as long as possible until he's forced by the awkwardness to look at him.

"Are you at least going to allow me to speak to my daughter, or is this a display of power?" Dad asks.

Massimo doesn't answer him. Instead, he focuses on me and says, "Five minutes. I'll come and get you in five minutes."

I nod, agreeing, and he leaves us.

"Come, I wouldn't want to waste the little time we have," Dad sneers in a mocking voice.

I look at him, really look at him, and try to see him as the father I always knew, but really, I want to rip into him and ask him what the hell happened.

We head to the balcony, where we can talk in private. There he takes hold of my shoulders.

"Look at you," he says, voice heavy with emotion. He seems more like the father I know now. "You look so much like your mother. Please tell me you aren't hurt."

"Not physically, no. I'm not hurt that way. In other ways, yes."

"I've been trying to get you back," he mutters and something like hope fills my heart. Those few words seep into me, and I feel valued again.

"You have?"

"Of course. Of course, Emelia. Sweet girl. I got myself in deep trouble. The D'Agostinos taking you was the massive price I had to pay."

"What happened, Dad?"

"I can't go into it. You have to know that that night I was just doing what I had to do to keep us both alive. I would never give you up willingly. No way. And I would never break your heart and spoil your dreams intentionally. In those few moments, as I watched my baby being taken away, everything came crashing down in my world. Everything I wanted to protect you from. I was ashamed to call myself your father, ashamed I couldn't keep my promise to your mother to take care of you."

Tears run down my cheeks. All these long weeks, I've floated from one emotion to the next, not knowing what to believe about him.

"Oh, Dad." I wince and throw my arms around him. As he holds me, I enjoy being held like I'm his little girl all over again.

"God, Emelia, I've been so worried. We all have. Jacob is beside himself with it. I've been doing all I can to stop him from doing something stupid."

"Jacob..." I mutter.

I never knew that last time Jacob and I saw each other, I'd be walking into this reality where I can't even call him. I knew he would be beyond worried over me without contact. When I switched on my phone, there were over a hundred messages from him. Messages I couldn't respond to on Massimo's command. He said he didn't put a tracker in the phone, and yes, I could delete a message after sending it, but I'm sure there are ways he would be able to retrieve it.

Dad hugs me hard. The moment, however, breaks when we pull apart and I stare back at him. The sentiment in his eyes falters as he looks back at me.

"Has Massimo hurt you? I've been terrified that he has."

I bite the inside of my lip and think about how to answer the question. I know what he's really asking. The look in his eyes suggests he wants to know if Massimo has forced himself on me.

"He...hasn't done anything I didn't want him to do," I answer with the truth, knowing my answer gives away some element of my feelings.

Dad's eyes cloud, and I'm sure he knows. Dad takes both my hands and sighs.

"Emelia, you are very young. You don't know how men like that operate. They break women like you. Young and innocent in this mix. You can't trust him. You cannot. You will never be number one in his life. You will just be a thing. Please believe me on this," he pleads.

What he's saying...I know it's true. I've worried about it and saw what I wanted to see through the moments spent with Massimo where I saw his soul.

"He will never love you," Dad adds, and I have to hold back tears. I hope he can't see my inner turmoil because I feel that sensation of betrayal again.

What hits me hard, too, is that in these few weeks, I allowed myself to fall for the monster. I fell, and I'm not sure I can unravel those feelings or bleed them from my mind.

"I know," I answer and dip my head briefly.

"I'm still trying to get you back," he declares in that low voice again and glances over his shoulder.

"How? Will you do something with the contract?"

"No, that way won't work." He lowers his voice. "I'm working on an escape plan."

Escape plan? Jesus...like the plan I had?

Escaping with Dad's help would definitely be betrayal.

"Escape," I whisper.

He nods. "I know it's not ideal, but I'll do what I have to," he promises. "His house is heavily guarded. That's where the problem lies."

I have a way. If I'm going to use it, now would be the time to tell him. I won't get this chance again.

"There's...a way," I start and his eyes widen.

"What?"

"There's a boat I can take. There's no surveillance at the end of his docks. He won't see me, but I'll need help once I get out to sea."

"God, Emelia. Are you certain of this?"

I trust Candace. She told me about the boat and the way out because she could see everything that was happening was wrong.

"Yes. But I don't know when I could do it. I'm practically watched all the time when I'm not with him. I have my phone, but if I use it, I'll have to use it that one time to call you and have the plan ready."

Nothing will happen before next week. The look on Dad's face tells me he knows that too.

"I'm sorry. We can make this happen. We have to try."

"Yes," I say, but my stomach twists into knots.

"I'll gather more allies and make sure they don't come after you. We need to do this as soon as you see a clear path," Dad says.

"Okay."

There's something I have to know first though. I have to hear the truth from my father's mouth. The truth of the past. I want his story.

"Dad. I heard some things. Is it true that you destroyed their family?"

When he nods in confirmation, I know I can trust him.

"I did, Emelia. It's not something I'm proud of. Please... don't hate me. I'm doing my best to fix things."

"I don't know if this can be fixed." They hate him, and the hate has rubbed my way too.

"It doesn't matter. It doesn't. What matters is I won't

allow you to suffer for my mistakes," he says with determination, then sternness returns to his pale blue eyes.

The curtains pull open, and a chill runs down my spine when Massimo appears.

Dad releases my hands.

"Time's up," Massimo says, directing his words at me, ignoring Dad completely.

Massimo puts out his hand for me to come to him, and I do, leaving my father's side. I tremble, and my legs are so shaky I fear they might shatter beneath me.

I glance back at Dad as we walk away. Rage changes his features.

I don't question Massimo when he says we'll be leaving. I keep quiet and allow him to take me back to the car, guards at our side. I follow him like a puppet being guided by its master.

What I do as I glance at him out of the corner of my eye and watch the beautiful outline of his profile is think of my escape.

Betrayal fills my mind as we set off down the road. Massimo is always saying, "it's not about that."

I'm going to borrow his phrase and apply it to myself.

Me escaping wouldn't be about betrayal.

This was all wrong from the beginning. I was taken and made to sign my life away to a man who wants to control me. I have to do what I have to do to get my life back.

The hard part is hardening my heart and making the first attempt to close off any feelings I have for Massimo D'Agostino.

Especially any love.

CHAPTER TWENTY-NINE

MASSIMO

DAMN IT TO HELL...

The last thing I wanted to do was leave the fundraiser so soon. I said an hour tops because I didn't want to be in the same room with Riccardo for too long when I didn't need to be.

Little did I realize that trouble would come knocking at the door.

When Emelia went to talk to Riccardo, I went to see Tristan, then I got a call from Manni about Bill Taglioni, another one of my enforcers. A guy who used to work the streets with Pierbo.

The minute Manni said Bill's name I knew he was dead. I just knew it. Hearing Manni confirm it made my blood boil.

We left and I saw Emelia home, then my brothers and I headed to the place where they found Bill.

Bill runs one of the bookie offices downtown. That's where the men found his mutilated body over an hour ago.

The soldiers are already outside when we get there.

When we step inside, I smell it.

Blood.

Fresh blood.

Manni is standing by the door to the office where they keep the safe. The expression on his face is grim.

"In here, Boss," he says pointing inside.

"Thank you," I answer and move past him. My brothers follow.

As soon as I step through the door I regret it, and even with the shit I've seen in all my years, my stomach turns upside down.

On the sofa is what remains of Bill. I'm not sure what should get to me more: the fact that half his head is hacked off, or that it's just his torso propped up against the black leather. Or maybe it should be seeing the other half of Bill on the floor in a pool of blood.

There's blood everywhere.

On his chest is a fucking note.

Stop looking for me.
Piss me off and more will die along with you...

That's all it says. It's enough. It's a message for me.

A threat on my life and others.

"Fuck..." I hiss.

"I'm sorry," Tristan breathes.

I look at him. "No. This isn't you." This is what rocking the nest means.

This is just more to add to it and more will die, *along with me*, if I don't stop looking.

This threat is real. I take it very seriously, but giving up the search for Vlad isn't an option I'm gonna take.

The defeated look in Tristan's eyes is what grips me and wills me to continue. More and more I feel bad for him. More and more I find myself imagining what it must be like to be in his shoes. He wants vengeance for what was done to Alyssa. It won't bring her back but it will mean something to him. I can't give up for that reason, because I'd do the same thing if I were him.

I now have a woman I feel deeply enough for that I would do the same.

———

Days later I sit on the terrace and watch Emelia on the beach. We're getting married in a few days. In a few days it will be official. She'll be my wife and I will be her husband.

She's far away, but I know she can sense me watching her.

Things have been weird between us again because of me.

I made it so. I've been distant on purpose. As if that will help me feel less for her.

Idiot.

The joke's on me. I concocted this plan to get my enemy's daughter, and this is what happened to me. I look at my bride-to-be and confliction filled my soul. I'm conflicted and caught in emotions I never thought I'd have.

I turn when the shuffle of footsteps catch my attention. It's Tristan. He sits on the chair opposite me and looks out to the beach too, seeing Emelia.

A gentle smile washes over his face briefly. "I see you took my advice..." he states.

"You tell me many things; which advice are you talking about?" I ask, playing stupid. I'm like a fucking teenage boy.

"Massimo, I'm not in the mood for shit. I'm not." The smile recedes from his face. "You know what I'm talking about. You started changing when you realized *what* she was. But you know what, the *who* and the *what* are the same thing. You weren't wrong when you said that. It's just how you see it. She's Emelia, and she's a woman you're falling for. Doesn't matter whose daughter she is."

"Tristan—"

"No, I'm being serious here," he cuts in. "Of all of us, I think you hated Riccardo the most because it was you that found Ma in the river, and you blame him for that memory. It's enough. We blame him too, but it's never going to be the same for us. We didn't find her. And it wasn't us that Riccardo held a gun to at Ma's funeral. It was you. Then there was what he said at the funeral, blaming Pa for the hard life Ma had. Riccardo was the man who took everything from us, and you included Ma in the mix."

I'm listening and he has me speechless.

"I'm here to tell you to stop looking for Vlad," he adds. "I want you to leave me to do it. You saw the message. The man is serious as fuck. That message was for you, Massimo. This has gotten out of control. We can't find Vlad, and he's gotten to two of our best guys. I don't want you putting your life, or your girl's life, at risk for me. I've never seen you like this with anybody. It would break me all over again if you lost your girl the way I lost mine. So leave it to me."

I stare at him long and hard and shake my head. No way in hell am I allowing him to go after Vlad by himself. I'd lose him, and I can't let that happen.

"No," I say.

"I'm telling you to stop."

"And as boss and your brother, I'm saying no. I always back you up the same way you're there for me."

"You can't drag people you care about into this," he argues.

"She's already involved, Tristan. It's already too late," I point out.

He knows I'm right and I hate that I am.

"What the hell are you gonna do? Continuing is reckless and careless."

"For Alyssa, it's not," I answer, and appreciation comes into his eyes.

"I'd do the same for you." He nods with conviction.

"I know. That's why I'm gonna ask you to get Emelia somewhere safe if something happens to me." That is what it's come to. There's no other way around it.

It will be the best thing I can do for Emelia.

Even if I let her go now and continue my pursuit of Vlad, she'd still be in danger just for knowing me.

Guilty by association once again; a different monster this time.

Me, her husband-to-be.

Not her father.

CHAPTER THIRTY

EMELIA

It's my wedding day...

The moment is finally here. The moment I've been counting down to.

I'm down to the last few minutes of being Emelia Balesteri.

A hush falls over the congregation in the cathedral as the organist starts playing Mendelssohn's traditional *Wedding March*, heralding the start of the ceremony.

Everyone looks at me as I make my way up the aisle, by myself.

In the wedding I imagined when I was little, my father would be walking me up the aisle. I imagined flower girls and a page boy. I would have gotten married on the beach. Not that I have anything against being in a church. I just wanted the beach. Somewhere in Italy, where it's gorgeous. Since I imagined Mom at my wedding too, it fits that it would fall part of a dream and right up there with things that will never happen.

At the altar stands Father De Lucca, the priest who will be marrying us, and possibly the only real thing about this wedding. When he came to the house to go over the ceremony details, there was pride in his eyes for Massimo. The same type I'd seen displayed in most of the people who'd known Massimo as a boy.

At Father De Lucca's left stands Massimo, with his father and brothers as his best men.

Massimo looks perfect in his tux. He looks like the prince in every story, the heartthrob of every movie. The lover in every story told. He looks like the dream, and once again, I can't deny what I feel for him.

It's just everything else that feels wrong.

I've feared this day for weeks, right from the word *go*. Right from that night I signed that contract.

Darkness settled over me the minute I put on this dress earlier this morning. This beautiful wedding dress should have been worn by a bride who was ecstatic to get married. A bride who couldn't wait to skip into her groom's arms.

When I look at Massimo standing ahead at the altar, Dad's warning plays out in my mind.

He will never love you...

That's knowledge I already had and feared. Each step I take feels like pieces of me are dying slowly.

If I don't escape, I don't know what my life will be like from here onwards.

I imagine us growing apart when the wild sexual haze fades, and we'll just slip into a loveless marriage.

What I felt the other night was real, but I've come to accept that Massimo will eventually hurt me. Physical wounds can heal. Emotional wounds are another story. Those are harder to heal. I wouldn't be doing myself any favors by encouraging these feelings I have for him.

I would be hurting myself if I truly fell for him.

Such awful thoughts to have on my wedding day. Preparing my heart so it doesn't love my husband. We haven't even said our vows yet, and I'm already planning ways to break the simplest one.

Don't fall for him.

Don't love him.

I scan the pews, looking over the guests who are dressed in their finest. There are over a hundred people here. A mixture of family from my side and his. He has friends here and people who work for him. I have no friends. I already knew Jacob and his family wouldn't be invited.

Who I'm looking for is my father.

I see him now. I see Dad. There he is in the front pew. Like everyone else, he's been looking at me. Our eyes connect. The remorse and defeat in his eyes grip me. He wears the face of a helpless man who's watching his only child marry his enemy.

His eyes follow me as I walk by, and I swear I see a tear slide down his cheek. I look back and realize I'm right. He wipes it away quickly, though, with the heel of his hand.

I turn back to face Massimo and find him gazing at Dad with that stern expression I hate.

I reach him on those shaky legs, and that's when he focuses his attention back on me.

Father De Lucca begins with a welcome to our guests and jumps right into a blessing on us. Nerves fill me, and I find myself switching to autopilot. I haven't been to many weddings, but I know ours will be quick.

When the priest finishes the blessing on our marriage and I know it's time to say our vows, the gravity of what I'm doing hits me full force.

I'm getting married. *Me.* I'm getting married to this man who's turned my world every way except the way it was supposed to be.

We're getting married.

I'll be his wife, and he'll be my husband.

Even if I manage to escape, those things will never change until death do us part.

"When you're ready, you may say your vows," Father De Lucca says, slicing through my thoughts. He looks to Massimo first, who straightens and starts to recite his vows.

"I, Massimo D'Agostino, take you, Emelia Balesteri, to be my wife. I promise to be true to you in good times, in bad, in sickness and in health. I will honor you all the days of my life."

I pull in a little breath and focus on what I'm supposed to say. "I, Emelia Balesteri, take you, Massimo D'Agostino, to be my husband. I promise to be true to you in good times, in bad, in sickness and in health. I will honor you all the days of my life."

Father De Lucca smiles and switches his focus to Massimo. "Do you, Massimo D'Agostino, take Emelia Balesteri to be your lawful wife, to have and to hold, from this day forward, for better or for worse, for richer or for poorer, in sickness and in health, until death do you part?"

"I do," Massimo says, and I wonder if he means to keep that vow to me. I wonder how many women he'll have. Will he still be with Gabriella? At least she's not here.

"Do you, Emelia Balesteri, take Massimo to be your lawful husband, to have and to hold, from this day forward, for better or for worse, for richer or for poorer, in sickness and in health, until death do you part?"

"I do," I say, and there's a moment when Massimo and I stare at each other.

Don't...

That one word comes back to haunt me, and my heart squeezes.

Don't love him. Don't fall for him. There was no mention of love in our vows. That was done on purpose, *by him*.

The sting of that realization makes me hate him so much right now I wish I could run through that door and make my escape.

Tristan steps forward with the rings, slicing into my thoughts. Father De Lucca blesses mine and hands it to Massimo.

Massimo takes my hand and says, "I take this ring as a sign of our union and faithfulness in the name of the Father, the Son, and the Holy Spirit."

He places the ring on my finger. I do the same to him when Father De Lucca gives me Massimo's ring.

"I now pronounce you husband and wife," Father De Lucca declares.

I look at him as if I can't believe what he's saying. Just like that, I've become Emelia D'Agostino.

"You may now kiss the bride."

Massimo leans forward and kisses me. His kisses always feel real to me, like it's us, like he truly wants to kiss me. This kiss, though, is supposed to be the one that matters, yet I feel nothing. I can't feel him anywhere. Even his lips are cold.

He pulls away and takes my hand to lead me away as everyone stands and applauds.

A shout from the back suddenly catches my attention. It's

near the door. There's a commotion. I look ahead to see what's happening.

"I object!" comes a strangled cry from a voice I recognize.

Jacob?

Massimo and I stop in our tracks as Jacob comes into view, fighting against the guards. He's shouting the same two words over and over again.

"*I object.*"

My blood runs cold. Ice takes residence in the pit of my stomach when I look at Massimo and see his features darken with rage.

Oh my God. No.

Jacob's cries catch the attention of everyone in the church. He doesn't know what danger he's put himself in by doing this. Or maybe he does. He's my best friend. He'd do anything for me, no matter what.

He runs in, and the men rush him with guns. I let go of Massimo's hand and run with everything inside me, throwing myself in front of Jacob.

"No, please, don't kill him!" I wail.

Jacob grabs my arm, his face panicked. *Terrified.* More terrified than I've ever seen him. He's holding on to me so hard it hurts.

"You're in danger, Emelia. If you stay with him, you'll be in danger," he cries.

A stone drops in the pit of my stomach.

"What's happening?" I ask.

"Leave him. Run away. He and his Syndicate won't be able to save you."

My God.

Syndicate? He knows about the Syndicate.

I don't get to ask him anything else. Someone grabs me from behind. It's Manni. *Him again.*

The guards position their guns again as Massimo and his brothers step forward.

"Get him out of here," Massimo commands, and the guards take hold of Jacob.

"Run away, Emelia, run far away," Jacob cries as the guards take him away, back the way he came. "I love you. I love you. I love you."

His voice echoes through the church, along with the whispers of the shocked guests. Jacob's voice is all I hear until the large oak doors close and sucks out the rest of the sound.

I love you...

It feels like the continuation of that conversation we were having at the diner. That's what he wanted to tell me. Now that he has—in the worst place possible—what will happen now?

Massimo looks at me, and I see the rage again. His hands are fisted by his sides. He's not a man you embarrass the way Jacob just did. No one would dare, but Jacob tried to warn me I was in danger. Danger would come for me if I stayed with Massimo.

"Take her home," Massimo orders Manni, and before I can blink, I'm carried away.

My heart squeezes when Massimo walks ahead with his brothers, following down the empty trail Jacob and the guards left. He's following them.

Oh my God...

What will Massimo do to Jacob?

"Massimo, no!" I shout. My eyes water.

He doesn't look back. He continues walking like the angel of death, his three brothers in tow.

"Massimo..." I cry.

He's going to hurt him.

I'm sure he will...

After all, don't I already know Massimo's the devil?

My husband is a monster who won't think twice about killing my best friend in cold blood.

The last face I see is my father's as Manni carries me through the door and it closes shut.

CHAPTER THIRTY-ONE

MASSIMO

I land a fist in this fucker's stomach. He tries to double over, but my soldiers hold him up.

I already messed up his face. That was me trying my best not to kill his ass.

Act and show my wrath, then ask questions later. That's what I plan to do. And my, do I have questions for this little prick.

"Stop..." Jacob wails. Tristan gives me a stern look.

Andreas and Dominic, however, are on my other side and seem to be in favor of the beating.

What the fuck am I supposed to act like after that little display? Under normal circumstances, I would have popped a bullet in this fucker's head right there in the church. Of course, I didn't do it because of her... *Emelia*. And *fucking fuck*, Father De Lucca has never seen me kill before.

I wasn't about to end this guy on hallowed ground with everyone watching.

Taking him out back is just a little better, but still bad.

"Stop? Really?" I roar and pull my gun. I hit him on the side of his face with the butt of it. Instantly, the skin cracks and blood pours down his cheek. "You motherfucker. It seems like you don't know who I am. Or maybe you have a death wish. You think you can just burst into my wedding and do shit like what you just dished to me and live to tell the tale? Fuck no."

When I get up in his face he flinches, but schools himself quickly to hold his own and glare back at me.

I have to give this kid credit. Maybe he has more balls than me. After all, he did just declare his love for my wife from the rooftop for all to hear.

"I don't care who you are, Massimo D'Agostino," he answers through the blood running from his teeth. "Kill me if you want. All I care about is her. This marriage wasn't real. You took her away and crushed her dreams. She was supposed to be in Florence, not here on this day, marrying you."

I hit him again, but this time, I hit him because he's right.

He spurts more blood and starts panting but stares at me head on. I don't know what infuriates me more. The fact that he loves my girl, or that he loves her so much he's willing to put himself in danger and die for her.

"Think you're brave?" I ask. It's a useless question.

"I don't care. She's in danger, and when danger comes, it will take all of you. Your Syndicate won't be able to do anything against the people coming for you. You will die, and I don't want her to go down with you."

"What are you talking about?" This fucker knows something. Something that made him risk his life to try and save Emelia.

"Find your own information," he shouts, trying to kick me.

I take the kick so I can rush him. The guards drop him when I do, and I land a one-two punch in his face. I have half a mind to beat his ass, but I hold back. Jesus Christ, do I ever hold back. He can't tell me what I need to know if I mess him up too badly. Instead, I grab his face and hold his jaw so he can stare me in the eye and see I'm serious as fuck and need to know what he knows.

He can act all ballsy if he wants, but we'll see what he says when I break his fucking jaw off for pissing with me.

"Listen to me, you little shit," I begin and grit my teeth. "You tell me what I need to know right the fuck now. If you fucking love Emelia the way you say you do, you will tell me everything. Tell me so I can protect her."

It must be a miracle that falls on us, but his eyes soften somewhat on hearing my words, and he seems less adamant to hold on to information.

"Members of the Circle of Shadows are here," he says, which is enough. I don't need to look at my brothers to know they've tensed up at the mention of the group. "There was a guy. Russian guy. He was talking in a bar on the underground. I heard a conversation I shouldn't have heard."

"What did he look like?"

"Long black hair and a tattoo on his face of a snake, the fire crest of the Shadows tattooed on his cheek."

Vlad.

"What did he say?" I demand.

"He said he'll take back what you stole from him," Jacob answers.

I release Jacob and narrow my eyes. What the fuck is he saying to me?

Stole?

Me?

I haven't stolen shit.

"I haven't taken anything from him," I rasp.

"He seems to think so. He said he'll take it back, and he'll take pleasure in killing you, your family, and anybody linked to you when the plan is complete. He said you can look for him all you want. You won't find him, but he'll come for you when he's ready."

"What bar were you in?" I ask.

"The Crow. I've seen him there three times now."

I bite down hard on my back teeth. The fucking bar is a place I've been to twice already since we learned of Vlad's return. Nobody knew anything, yet Vlad had been there three times. *Lies.* They'll pay for that.

"When did you last see him?"

"Last night. Miguel, the owner, was talking to him," Jacob explains.

I stand and glare down at Jacob. He's looking at me like he doesn't know what to expect. My brothers are doing the same. What I'm going to do is completely unexpected.

"Get the fuck up and get gone. Don't say shit to anybody. This conversation never happened."

Now he stares at me like he can't believe I haven't killed him.

He stands up and continues to stare. "What will you do? You know those men are above you. They're assassins who work differently. Too strong for even the Syndicate."

"Never mind about me."

"Emelia... What about her?" His brows knit together.

A cruel smile lifts the corners of my mouth. "My *wife* is none of your concern. She's mine now, and if I see you again, you're dead. And so is anybody else you care about." His eyes snap wide when I say that. The fool never thought of his family. "Count yourself lucky for disrespecting me and being the only guy *ever* to walk away. Now go."

He's definitely lucky. Lucky my feelings for Emelia are that strong that I couldn't hurt him more than I did.

Jacob knows not to say any more shit to me. I watch him as he hobbles away.

I turn to the guards once he turns the corner of the alleyway and I can't see him anymore.

"Get out of my sight and make sure my wife is safe," I order, and the guards move.

Wife...

I have a wife now. And what a way to start our marriage, with another man telling the only woman I've ever gotten close to that he loves her. And this shit.

I turn to my brothers. They all look ready to kill.

Pa hung back to go home with Emelia. I wish he were here now.

"What the hell could Vlad think you stole?" Tristan asks.

"I don't fucking know," I answer. I can't think of what the hell it might be. "I need to find him."

"We've looked everywhere for that prick," Andreas adds. "What the hell is he planning?"

"Whatever it is, we weren't supposed to know he's alive," I say, swallowing hard. "Then Pierbo saw him. He knows we're looking for him, and the reason we can't find him is because of this plan. He has help. People who can help him stay hidden."

"What now? If no one's talking, it means they're not scared enough of us," Dominic says. "What should we do?"

I grit my teeth. I already know the answer to that.

It's always the same.

Be ruthless and heartless.

"I think it's time to fix that, and we know where to start."

The Crow.

I turn and walk down the alley. My brothers follow.

Blood will stain the streets before the sun goes down.

I walk into the house with bloodstains all over my face. It's late, bordering nine.

Pa emerges from the sitting room looking worried. I sent a message to him earlier letting him know what was happening. Priscilla walks out of the kitchen and stops short when she sees me, then turns back in her habitual way to grab stuff to clean me off.

In silence, I walk back into the room with Pa and take off my shirt.

"You okay?" he asks.

"No. Not a damn bit. I got nothing." Nothing but the blood of the owner of the Crow on my hands, and a bunch of people who fled.

Can't talk, run. I don't blame them. Many would have been dealt threats on their family's lives if they spoke.

"Stay focused, my boy. Focus on what we need to. All we can do is keep our eyes open and look around."

"Yeah." It's ironic. I thought taking Emelia and screwing with Riccardo wouldn't make me feel useless, helpless, or powerless.

This is the first time I've truly felt all of those things.

"Pa, I can't just sit around and wait."

"No, of course not, but you can't go crazy, either, looking. You have to stay calm and focus."

I run a hand through my hair and think of Emelia. "How is she?"

Pa sighs. "Not good. I think you should go to her."

"I will."

Priscilla walks in with a bowl of warm water and some

cloths and leaves us. I start cleaning off the blood on me. I'm going to take a long shower, but I want to see Emelia first. And I don't want her to see me with evidence of death on my body. The first thing she'll think is I did something to Jacob.

"I'm gonna head out. Call me if anything happens. Sorry for the shit today, my son." Pa rests a reassuring hand on my shoulder.

"Thanks. At least I know more than I did yesterday."

Pa nods and leaves.

I head upstairs and gear myself up for an argument with Emelia I don't want.

When I get in, she's exactly in the mess I expected her to be in. She's still dressed in her wedding gown, and she's sitting in the corner of the room with her back against the wall. Tears have made the makeup stream down her face.

"Did you hurt him?" she asks.

I delay answering, which hurts her all the more. I don't like hurting her, but what about me? How the fuck am I supposed to feel about Jacob? I'm not convinced she doesn't have feelings for him.

Look at her. A mess for... What was he? A potential lover? I just happened to get there first.

"Massimo," she cries. Her voice cuts through me.

"I didn't hurt your little boyfriend, Emelia. I wanted to, but I didn't. Instead of killing his ass for daring to piss with me, I roughed him up a little and sent him on his merry way." I wish my voice didn't hold so much emotion.

"Roughed him up? What did you do? What does that mean?" She looks freaked.

"He's not missing any teeth." She wouldn't know how truly lucky her friend was, or she wouldn't push me.

Her hands fist at her sides. "You are such an asshole. What is wrong with you?"

I see red. That's the color I see before me, and it's the first time it's ever happened with her. I don't know how she can ask me shit like that.

"What the fuck did you expect would happen? You think what he did was okay?" I throw back.

"No, it wasn't okay. Of course, it wasn't okay. But did you have to beat him up? He's my best friend."

Jesus Christ, I can't do this shit with her right now. "Correction, he's your former friend. You aren't seeing that fucker ever again."

"You can't tell me what to do," she argues. It seems like she's definitely forgotten how things work.

"Yes, I can. When last I checked, I own you. You are my wife, Emelia, and you will not disrespect me with this boy. We'll see how you like it when the tables are turned."

Her eyes go wide. I know I was an asshole for saying that, but right now, I don't care. I tried to learn to be gentle for her, and it's not working, so I'll play hard.

"*When?*" she asks. "When the tables are turned, Massimo?"

Good... Let her worry that I'll cheat. But the fucking joke is on me. Even if I wanted to, I couldn't cheat on her. But she doesn't need to know that. She can stew in her thoughts.

I'm too hyped up on rage and jealousy to be around her, so I turn and walk away. Before I reach the door, I hear something break. I turn back and see that she's smashed a vase against the wall.

"Where are you going?" she demands, but I don't answer. "Are you going to her? *Gabriella?*"

I walk away and close the door. Once outside, I hear her break down, but I keep walking.

I spend my wedding night at the strip club.

In the office.

I order a pizza and beer and watch classic films until I fall asleep at the desk.

The phone wakes me early the next day. It buzzes right beside my head on the desk. It's Tristan.

"Hey, man," I answer, trying not to sound like shit.

"Hey, we got a problem," he replies.

I bolt upright. My first thoughts go to Emelia. "Is Emelia okay?" I blurt. It's a stupid question since I should be with her.

"It's not her. It's the kid, her friend. He's dead."

My mouth goes dry.

"What?" I stand, knocking the pizza box to the floor.

"Bullet to the head. Cop associate said they found him in the back alley of the Crow."

CHAPTER THIRTY-TWO

EMELIA

The second I see Massimo's face, I know something's wrong. Something happened.

The look in his eyes and the paleness in his olive skin are enough for me to push aside my fury over where he spent our wedding night.

It's late afternoon, and he's just coming home. I push past the fact that his hair is scruffy, like it would look if he spent the night in bed with that woman.

He walks into the bedroom, moves right up to me by the window, and takes my hands.

When he holds my gaze, I know for sure something really bad must have happened.

"What happened?" I ask, afraid to hear it, not knowing what he's going to tell me to break me.

"I'm sorry," he says. "I'm so sorry, Emelia. Something bad happened."

I stare back at him trying to preempt what he's going to

say. He wouldn't look so broken if something happened to my father, and I don't think he would look like that either if he cheated on me.

I don't think he would say sorry.

"What happened?" I ask again.

"It's...Jacob."

I pull my hand from his, and a breath leaves my lips. "Jacob... What happened to Jacob? You said you let him go."

"I did. I did let him go, but I don't know what happened after. I got a call this morning. Um... Emelia, he's dead."

My knees give, and I fall to the ground with my mouth open. A gamut of emotions swarms my body and shock flies through me, slamming into every crevice of my being.

"No... No." I shake my head. "It can't be true."

He gets down on the ground and stares back at me. "I'm sorry..."

My hands fly to my mouth as the tears come hard.

Jacob.

My Jacob is dead?

It can't be true.

"He can't be dead. You told me..." My voice hitches when I remember in perfect clarity what Massimo told me. "You monster. You told me I'd never see him again. This is what you meant?"

When he left here last night, he looked enraged. Ready to kill. I back away from him on my hands until I can stand, then I back out of his way.

"No. I didn't kill him. He was shot. He was...somewhere he wasn't supposed to be and knew things he shouldn't."

I cry harder. Poor Jacob.

This can't be real. My poor friend. And why did he die? For me...

Massimo reaches out to touch me, but I back away.

"Where did you go? How convenient that you should leave me after the way we argued, and then my best friend turns up dead today? Where did you go, Massimo?"

"I was at the club all night," he answers.

"Club. You actually went to a club on our wedding night?" I shriek.

"My club. Renovatio."

My eyes snap wide. I know that club, not because I've ever been, and not because I knew it belonged to him. I heard Jacob's friends talk about it. It's a strip club.

I raise my hand and slap him so hard my fingers leave a mark, just like that day weeks ago.

"You bastard. Not even a full day of marriage and you spoiled it. I hate you. I shouldn't know you. I don't know why you couldn't have found some other way of getting even with my father. Fuck you."

I don't care what I say to him. My soul is broken. My best friend is dead. Jacob tried to warn me I was in danger, and now he's dead.

"Emelia—" Massimo reaches for me, but I rush away from him.

"Get away from me. Get the hell away from me."

The door opens, and Candace stands there looking in to see what's happening. I run straight into her arms and cry, feeling my body break when I think of Jacob.

He's dead. I can't believe it. I just can't.

And it's my fault.

It's my fault he's gone.

I hear his words now. Him telling me he loved me. I didn't say anything in return. I couldn't because I gave my love to the wrong man.

The monster.

"Do you want some more?" Candace asks, glancing at the empty cup of hot chocolate.

She made it extra sweet, and Priscilla made cookies. They both said sweet things were good for shock. Mom used to say the same thing.

"No," I croak. It hurts to talk.

We've been out on the terrace for a few hours now. I've already gone through a box of tissues and a plate of cookies that I know were delicious, except my taste is off and I couldn't taste the sweetness.

I ate just to do something with my hands, and chewing seemed to distract me from the pain of loss.

"Can I do anything for you?" she asks.

"No, thank you for sitting with me. I...don't have many friends. I just had him. All my life, it was just the two of us."

"I understand. I'm so sorry he's gone. I'm so sorry," Candace says.

She knows I think Massimo did it. She also knows I know she doesn't believe he did.

"Thank you."

"Emelia, talk to me. I think this is the one day when you can truly talk to me and not a damn thing will be said against either of us. I'm all ears." She nods.

I dip my head and bring my arms in, as if I'm trying to hold the rest of my heart together. When I look back at her, I see nothing but genuine care in her eyes.

"I just wish I never got dragged into this mess. Jacob would still be alive. He was from our world. He knew not to do certain things, but he got freaked because he thought I was in danger. He would have done anything for me."

"You can't blame yourself, Emelia. If he was from our

world, then he knew the risks. I feel like an asshole for saying that to you, but it's true, and you can't blame yourself for something you have no control over."

"I just feel so awful." I stare at Candace and decide to ask the question on my mind about Massimo. Maybe I just don't want to believe he could hurt me so badly. "You don't think Massimo killed him?"

She shakes her head. "I don't. Maybe if this was a few weeks ago, I mean, before he knew you, I wouldn't question it. It would be my first thought. Something changed him when you came along. Yes, he was hard working, and yes, he's still a hard man to deal with, but... I don't think he killed him. It would hurt you too much."

I shake my head at her. "He doesn't think of me like that."

"I can't speak on that, but I've known him long enough to know him as a person. I don't agree with most things he does, but if there's one thing you can count on Massimo for, it's telling the truth. Either he'll tell you the truth, or he'll say nothing. It's his one saving grace. He's not a liar."

I press my lips together and gaze out to the sea as the gentle breeze touches my cheeks.

Massimo isn't a liar...

I can't think right now to process anything, even if I know she's right.

In all the time I've known Massimo, he's never lied to me.

Sleep never came last night. I spent the time re-reading Jacob's messages.

The ones I never answered.

All one hundred of them.

I went to the room and sat by the window, never moving except to go to the toilet and get a drink of water.

Massimo didn't come back to see me. I don't even know if he was home or if he left and went back to his club. *God...* I can't believe he owns *that* club.

I push it all out of my mind. Shit like that means nothing given what's happened to Jacob.

I need to see his family. Even if I have to swim across the sea, I have to see them, see how they are. I can imagine his parents and his brothers being devastated. Everyone loved him.

The door creaks open and I look over to see my *dear* husband walking in.

So, he is here.

I accepted in my mind that maybe he didn't kill Jacob, but I'm still mad because this is still his fault. He walks over to me as I look at him. I don't know what we'll argue about today. I want details, though. I want to know more.

"I came to check on you," he says.

"Did you just get back from the club? Were you there all night, *again?*" I ask, unable to hide the fury in my tone.

"No, I didn't. The other night, I wasn't with anybody. I went to my office, and that is where I stayed all night. I have footage of me being there, but I'm not going to take it that far. When I tell you something, I expect you to believe me," he says, cool and even.

I look away from him. He, however, chooses to sit in front of me so I can't escape his hard blue gaze.

"I didn't kill Jacob, Emelia," he says. "I don't have an alibi in regard to the proposed time of death because I would have been driving, so unless a camera picked me up en route to the club, I'm a little screwed when it comes to whether you believe me or not, but that's my word. When I said you weren't going to see him again, I didn't mean this. Can I please ask you to think about what I'm saying?" His gaze clings to mine.

I draw in a breath and nod slowly. I'm not ready to be okay with him yet, because things are far from okay. They were never okay to begin with.

"What do you need?" he asks.

"I need more information. You said he was somewhere he wasn't supposed to be and knew things he shouldn't."

"Emelia, I wanted to give you some context. But I can't tell you more than that."

"Why?"

"There's a reason we keep women out of business. There are some things you shouldn't know."

I've heard that mantra before when my mother would ask my father questions.

"Would the Syndicate have killed him?" I want to know that.

"No. I don't think so. But I'm looking into it."

I hold his gaze. Hearing that lessens the tension.

"Thank you... Can I see his family? Please. They're like my own. I just want to see them."

"Yes." It's the first thing he's ever agreed to so quickly. "Do you want me to go with you?"

"No. Thank you, but maybe I should go by myself, if that's okay."

"Okay, but you have to go with the guards. Now's the time to be more careful than we ever were."

I can't argue with that.

CHAPTER THIRTY-THREE

MASSIMO

I sigh with frustration as I step through the door to the house and take off my jacket. It's not even midday and my head is already all over the fucking place. The guys and I have been on the streets trying to get answers and coming up with shit. It's becoming quite clear now that we're not going to find anything until trouble comes to find us.

Even before Jacob confirmed I had something to worry about, I was already riled up about Vlad and his threats. Then Jacob got himself killed.

It's harsh to think of it that way, but what else am I supposed to think?

Even after I told him to get gone and keep his head out of shit, he must have gone back to the Crow to snoop. Then Vlad caught up with him.

I walk into the hall and see Candace in the living room polishing the furniture. Sometimes it grieves me that she can't move on to become who she was supposed to be.

After her parents were killed, she wasn't the same. Her family has always worked for mine in some way, but she was never supposed to end up in my house polishing anything. When she went to college, she lived here, though she didn't have to. I thought that by giving her a ridiculous amount of money, she'd leave. But it's not about money when it comes to her. It's the fear from that night. She would have died too. That type of fear leaves you with all kinds of shit and anxiety. That's what happened to her. She only feels safe with me. Her family was always loyal to us, even after we lost everything. So, this is my way of helping and taking care of her. The way they used to take care of me.

I walk in and she gives me that look of disdain she's been sporting since the wedding.

I lean my head to the side and shake it. She ignores me and looks back to the vase she was about to dust.

"Can you stop doing that, please?" I ask.

"Stop doing what, *sir*?"

"Acting like you're my servant. We've known each other for too long to be like this."

"These days, one might be scared to talk, could die." She still doesn't look at me.

I walk closer to her, and she sets the dust cloth down.

"Candace... Say whatever's on your mind."

"It's best I don't, Massimo. I would prefer, as per usual, to keep my comments to myself, like I always have. Emelia is back from seeing her friend's family, and I don't think it went well. Your efforts are best placed with tending to your wife, not me."

My shoulders slump. I hoped that Emelia would find some solace seeing Jacob's family, but then what did I expect to happen? They just lost their son, and I'm sure they heard what happened at the wedding. They're probably casting blame my way.

I still want to talk to Candace, though. She's clearly upset with me.

"What's going on, Candace? Talk to me," I insist.

"You've changed."

"I had to."

She shakes her head. "We all have to change, but that doesn't mean going to extra lengths to be cruel. Massimo, did you have to go to the strip club on your wedding night? Couldn't you have just gone for a walk or something?"

"I didn't do anything there," I justify, but I know what she means.

"Massimo, seeing those naked women might be so commonplace to you that they look like part of the furniture. They're there the second you walk in," she chides.

I stifle a groan knowing that even if I didn't do shit, I saw enough.

"What do you want me to do? Move the stage?" I smirk. I already dealt with the matter of the strip club.

"Massimo, that's not funny. Your wife was just as horrified to find out you have a strip club as she was to hear you spent the night there. I couldn't have been more disgusted."

"Well, maybe you'll be less disgusted when you hear I gave the club to my brother," I inform her.

I said my brother because I know she'll assume I gave the club to Tristan or Andreas. I actually gave the club to Dominic yesterday, but since Candace has always had a thing for him, I don't think she'd be too thrilled to hear it's him who now owns a strip club.

Candace looks visibly surprised at my answer. "You did what?"

"You heard me."

She looks proud of me now and taps my shoulder. "Thank you."

"What for? I'm the one who just lost a quarter of my income."

"For being the boy again," she answers. I know what she means. She means me before Ma died. I give her a nod.

"Emelia's sitting on the terrace."

"I'll go see her."

Pulling in a breath, I leave her and make my way outside. When I step through the door, a gust of wind lifts my hair and it smells like rain is near.

Emelia is sitting on the little wall with her knees hugged to her chest. I move to her, and she looks at me. The sun glistens off her wedding band, a reminder that she's my wife. A reminder of the feelings I have for her that scare me.

I sit next to her, brushing my shoulder against hers, and she offers me a little smile. It's more for pleasantries. But it says she's at least willing to talk to me.

"Hi," she says.

"Hey. Candace said your visit to Jacob's family didn't go so well. What happened?"

She gazes out to the sea, looking lost. Her lips tremble and her skin goes pale.

"They didn't want me there. His mother...she didn't want me in the house. It was his father who came out and asked me to leave. I got the feeling he wouldn't have minded me being there, but it was her. I heard her. She was shouting and crying for her son. She said it was my fault he's dead."

"It's not your fault," I say.

She looks back at me. "I might not have pulled the trigger, but he was doing whatever he was doing because of me. I know I can't blame myself. I know there was nothing I could do, but I feel so bad. Now his mother is blaming me. She thinks you killed him. I told them you didn't."

"You believe me."

She nods slowly. "You've never lied to me."

"No. I haven't, and I won't start now."

"The funeral is next week. They won't want me there."

"You want to go? Can you handle it?" I ask.

"I should be there. I can't handle it, but I should be there."

"Then I'll go with you."

"Thank you, but they'd hate me even more if I brought you."

"That doesn't matter. People's opinion doesn't matter in times like this. What matters is who you're there for. You're going for Jacob, not his family. And I will take you there personally to make sure you get to say goodbye to him."

"You would do that?" Her gaze desperately clings to mine.

"Yes," I answer with conviction.

I'm surprised when she moves to me and slips her arms around my neck, holding on to me like she's trying to garner strength. I circle my arms around her and pull her closer so I can cocoon her in my arms as she rests her head on my chest.

"Thank you, Massimo," she whispers, grabbing my shirt. I cover her hand with mine and see my ring too.

Mine and hers.

When I wrote our wedding vows, I took out all traces of the word *love*. At the time, I was thinking of my hatred for her father. I wasn't thinking about her.

I should have been.

I hold her now and find myself at that point again, when I know that the moment I accept what I feel for her, it will make or break me.

It's the first time in my life where I actually don't know what to do.

She's my enemy's daughter.

Loving her is wrong. But she feels like my something good.

The only good thing in my life.

CHAPTER THIRTY-FOUR

EMELIA

It's raining.

Not hard. Just a light spray that trickles over the cemetery.

Massimo holds my hand as we walk across the pathway toward the gathering of mourners.

We didn't go to the church service.

Not knowing what was going to happen, we just came here. As I look ahead, I'm grateful to have caught the coffin before they lowered Jacob into the ground.

Like at my wedding, I scan the crowd looking for my father, but he's not here. I'm not sure if that's because he was told not to come. Maybe Helena, Jacob's mother, didn't want him here either. I don't know.

The priest finishes a prayer, and as Helena lifts her head she sees me coming. She freezes her stare on me, causing everyone to look at Massimo and me.

I have a single red rose in my hand that I want to give to

my friend. I want to say goodbye properly. Then she won't see me again.

I understand her grief and her pain. I understand that she's upset with me, but what I won't allow her to do is make me feel worse than I already do.

I look at Massimo as he pulls me to a stop just ahead of the crowd.

He dips his head, and a lock of hair falls over his eye. "Out of respect, I'll keep my distance. I'll stand right here, and if anyone says anything to you, call me. You understand?" he says with a hardened gaze that flicks between me and the family.

"I understand... Thanks for coming with me."

"Don't mention it."

He releases my hand, and I continue the rest of the way. I head straight up to Helena, but Nero, Jacob's father, steps forward, probably gearing up to ask me to leave.

"Emelia—" he says, but I stop him. I shake my head firmly and stare him down.

"No, do not tell me to leave. Don't do it. All of you." I look at each member of Jacob's immediate family and some of his cousins, aunts, and uncles I know. "All of you know me. You've known me since I was born, and you know how close I was to Jacob. You know I should be here. You can't tell me to leave."

"What about him?" Helena points to Massimo. "Are you going to say the same for him? Your *husband?*"

It still feels so weird to think of Massimo as my husband, but it's the first time he feels like he is.

"He didn't kill Jacob, Helena. It doesn't matter what you believe, though. He's here to support me, and I'm here to say goodbye. I'll do that, and then I'll go. You'll never see me again." It's hard to say such a thing to a woman who was close to me, like my own mother. But it's harder to have her look at me the way she is.

Turning away from her, I face the glossy chestnut casket where my best friend will lay in rest forever. I never thought I would experience this day. Jacob had so much to live for. Gone far too soon.

I walk right up to him and lay the rose on top of the casket.

"Thank you for being my friend... Thank you for being who you were. Thank you for being everything. I love you too, Jacob," I say and place my hand on the cool surface of the wood.

I stay like that for a few moments. Then it really hits me that he's gone. My legs start to shake, and I tremble.

When warm fingers caress mine, I lift my head and find myself staring deep into Massimo's bright blue gaze.

He covers my hand with his, giving me a gentle squeeze, and that's how I find the strength to walk.

Walk away.

The next two weeks follow, and I grieve by spending my days in the hall, painting. I paint to forget, to cope, and to try and move on. It helped me when Mom died. When I paint, I escape, and I don't think about anything else. The images that fill my mind replace my worries and fears. This is the first time in my life when I've had so much on my plate.

I've been purposely avoiding thinking about my less-than-perfect relationship with Massimo because it's too confusing right now.

He's been nice to me, and nice is what I've needed. My brain is trying to keep me grounded and my head screwed on.

Although, my heart misses the man it fell for. I'm aware, though, that each day that passes gets stranger than the last.

Today is Saturday again.

It's a month since Massimo and I were married, and two months since we've been in this arrangement.

He leaves in the mornings, weekdays and weekends, and most days he's home by dinnertime. As to where he goes during the day, I don't know. It could be work, as in D'Agostinos, or the strip club, or something more dangerous. He never says. Though I can't imagine that he could receive a warning of danger without doing anything about it. He said he would keep me safe. That was all I needed to know.

At night, we lie next to each other until we fall asleep.

That's the routine we've fallen into. We don't even kiss anymore. All that steam and wild sexual energy we shared before the wedding is gone. Not that I've had time to think about sex with everything that's happened with Jacob.

In the periods of time when I've allowed myself to think, I contemplate what must have happened to Jacob. What he saw and heard that he shouldn't have. What more could have happened?

Today, Massimo left a little earlier than usual, so I decided to change up my routine and spend the day on the beach reading one of the thriller novels I was going to read in Florence.

Every time since the fundraiser when I've gone to the beach, I've thought of my conversation with Dad and making that escape. Every time. In the back of my mind, I've been waiting for that moment Candace suggested. The right time. The moment when I knew I'd earned Massimo's trust.

I think I have it now. I am at the point where he trusts me.

The last two weeks have seen that change I was waiting

for. Since the funeral, Massimo has eased up on the constant supervision. Maybe it was just as simple as him thinking I needed time to myself to breathe and to heal without having someone always looking over my shoulder. That small change, however, could mean a clear path to leave. A clear path to take the boat and escape.

I've been out here today for six hours. Only once has someone come to check on me. That was Priscilla with some lunch. Just her. No guards.

Unlike all the times I've come out here before, when the thought of escaping crossed my mind today, I didn't know if I could do it.

I didn't know if I could leave Massimo. I didn't know if I could betray him like that, or my heart.

Things are different from when Candace put the idea in my head. *I'm* different. It would have actually been easier to run away when we first talked about it than to wait it out the way I have. Doing so changed me.

Massimo and I have this continuous up-and-down cycle. We're back and forward, and he changes like the wind. My heart, however, clings to something it wants from him. Something I only feel with him.

I finish reading my novel and head back inside when it gets dark. Covered in sand, I start taking off my clothes when I step into the room.

I don't see Massimo until he comes out of the walk-in closet and startles me. Instinct makes me reach for the beach towel to cover my nakedness.

With my hand at my heart, I try to calm my breathing.

"I didn't know you were in here," I say, feeling foolish. This is his room. He's usually home by now, except typically he'd be in his office or the study, on the phone making business calls.

A sensual smile slides across his lips as he gives me a once-over that makes my nerves scatter and tingle with heat.

"That a problem? When last I checked, it shouldn't be. This is our room, after all."

Our room... It's a nice thought.

"No. It's not a problem. I was just going to shower," I reply.

"I'll join you," he answers, stepping forward.

When he walks up to me and stops a breath away, he feels like the Massimo I'm used to. He definitely becomes himself when he tugs the towel away from my body, revealing my nakedness.

He looks me over with appreciation. My cheeks burn. I haven't been naked in front of him in over a month.

"Come, let's go," he says, then, with one hand on my ass, he ushers me into the bathroom where he takes his clothes off and we both step into the shower.

With the water on a light spray and his arms placed on either side of me, it feels like I've stepped back in time to the people we were weeks ago.

I gaze up at him as he stares at me like he's expecting something.

"What are we doing?" I ask, barely above a whisper.

"Waiting."

"Waiting for what?"

"You."

I narrow my eyes, not understanding. "What do you mean? Why are we waiting for me?"

"Emelia, I won't be with you when you have another man on your mind. When I kiss you, you're kissing me. When I'm inside you, I want you to be thinking of me only. So...*we're* waiting on you, *Princesca*." The words roll off his tongue.

When he leans forward and looms before me, I feel it.

That wild sexual energy that always consumes me when I'm with him floods me, and I'm paralyzed by the need and desire.

I reach forward and lightly run my finger over the tattoo of the angel inked on his heart.

I trace the outline of the wings and trail down to his navel, lingering by the fine dark hair of his happy trail.

He touches my cheek and turns his smile up a notch. "You want me."

I hold his gaze. "Do you want me?"

"Always... I always want to fuck you."

He moves forward to kiss me, but I turn my face away, causing his lips to brush my cheek. It's the first time I've ever done that, and it surprises him.

He catches my face, holds me tight so I can't look away, and presses me into the wall, pushing his cock into my belly.

"What? I can't know what you're mad at me for if you don't tell me. What are you pissed at me for today?"

"How often do you go to the strip club?" I ask. I already know it pisses him off when I talk like this, but he's right. I'm still pissed that he even owns a strip club and that he goes there.

"Why?"

"I don't want you to go back there," I answer and steel my spine, readying myself for some crude remark about me being jealous or some shit he'll say to hurt me. I'm definitely surprised when he releases his hold on me and chuckles.

"I gave it away weeks ago," he answers, surprising me further.

"What? You gave it away? You—"

He steals my words with a heart-stopping kiss. The type of heart-stopping, bone-tingling kiss we used to share. The one we didn't have on our wedding day. I missed this. I missed his lips crushing mine the way they are now, devouring me, like he wants to take me whole.

"Mrs. D'Agostino, just shut up and let me fuck you," he groans, and I nod.

He slides his fingers inside my pussy, checking if I'm ready for him. I am. I'm always ready for him. He smiles when he feels his way around my passage and pulls his fingers out to lick off my juices.

Greedily, he lifts my leg, takes hold of his cock, and drives into my pussy, plunging in deep. So deep I gasp and grab his shoulders.

He fills me up completely with his thickness, and my body yields to him. I savor that feeling of him being inside me, and I know from the satisfied look on his face that he can see that I do.

My muscles squeeze around his cock from the intense pleasure when he starts pumping into me. Slow then fast and faster, and oh. My. God.

I arch my back and scream his name.

"That's right, amore mio, scream. Scream my name, because only I can make you feel like this," he groans, pounding into me. "Only I can fuck you like this because I know exactly what you need."

He does. That's why he knows to pick me up so I can wrap my legs around his waist. Fucking me in this position reaches every inch of my body, sizzling my nerves with fire. It burns, it scorches, it incinerates. It wipes my brain clean of everything that isn't this wild man before me who's shaken my world in so many ways.

Time freezes, and all I feel is passion and pleasure, desire and carnal, primal need that drives us to take all we can from each other. He smiles wide when I start to move against him too and we crash back into the other side of the wall, tearing down the shower curtains. Something smashes and breaks. We don't know what it is.

We don't care what it is.

Then it's like we both go crazy on each other. I remember coming harder than I ever have, then us leaving the bathroom and heading to the bedroom. Night turns to day. Then we switch from sleep to fucking until it's night again.

We're so engrossed in each other that the next few days pass while we barely eat or sleep. I get to a point where I almost believe we could be like this forever, and I have a hard time believing we weren't like this before. I have a hard time believing that his lips weren't always touching mine, and I lived my life for nineteen years without my body touching his.

I don't know what day it is when I eventually conk out into a deep sleep where my body feels heavy, like I'm sinking into a state of blissful pleasure. Then a buzzing sound wakes me. It sounds far away, but as I come to, I realize it's not that far.

I open my eyes and momentarily forget where I am, but I see a phone buzzing on the nightstand. It's dark, pitch black outside, and I hear Massimo inside the bathroom.

Instinct must make me reach for the phone believing it's mine, although I haven't slept with my phone nearby in months and the person who would have contacted me at this hour is now dead.

I'm about to put the phone back when I realize it's Massimo's. I almost feel afraid for him to catch me with it, but what stops me from all but throwing it far from me is the preview of the text that's just come through.

It's from Gabriella.

A stone drops in my stomach when I see her name, but fury flies through me when I read the preview.

My pussy misses you. Come to my place, and we can fuck for the rest of the night. I'm sure that girl can't be pleasuring you the way I can. See you later x

That's what the message says. This bitch knows we've been married for over a month and thinks it's appropriate to message my husband this.

Under normal circumstances, I'd call her. I'd call her and tell her to delete his number and never call again. I can't do that, though, because she must be messaging him because she thinks it's okay to do so.

Massimo's footsteps echo off the bathroom floor. I set the phone back down quickly, falling back onto the pillow, pretending to be asleep.

He walks in, and the phone buzzes again. This time it's ringing, but it's on silent. He picks it up and answers it.

"I'm on my way," he says in a low voice, careful not to wake me. I press down hard on my back teeth to keep myself from screaming.

He's going to see her.

Fuck.

He's actually going to see her.

He walks out of the room, and when the door closes, I open my eyes and wonder what the hell I'm supposed to do.

CHAPTER THIRTY-FIVE

MASSIMO

Emelia is the last thing I should have on my mind right now as I walk down the alleyway leading to the chamber. That's what we call it.

It's the place where we question people.

Question? That's a mild way to put it since most people we question don't make it out alive. In fact, I can't remember when last that happened.

My brothers found a guy who's been working with Vlad.

They have this fucker now chained to a wall, waiting for me to interrogate him since he has decided he's not talking. I'm here to make him talk or pay with his life. We'll see about defiance when I get there.

It's going to be one of those difficult nights, so I need to put my mind in the right frame.

I continue down the alley, my gun in my side pocket at the ready in case some wise guy thinks he can take me out.

Most don't mess with me when they see me, and most stay

clear of this area, gangsters and mobsters alike. They know it belongs to us.

I get to the door and steel my spine when Dominic steps out from the shadows. It was he who called me to come down here.

"Hey," I say.

"Massimo, this fucker is one crazy son of a bitch. Tried to gouge my fucking eyes out with a knife." He smirks.

"Fuck. You alright?" I still think of him as my kid brother, but he can more than take care of himself.

He nods. "Don't worry about me, bro. Let's do this."

We continue down the path and head down into the basement. Above is another bookie office we own.

It's busier during the day. At this time of night, we have just one guard on site by the front entrance. Tonight, we have three, just in case any shit happens.

I push open the metal door, and Dominic and I walk into the room, where our guest is indeed chained to the wall. He's been beaten badly. Tristan is standing in front of him, sharpening my knives.

The fucker on the wall is a fat balding asshole with two missing teeth. I don't know if that came from his encounter with my brothers or if he already looked like that when he got here. It doesn't matter to me either way. Missing teeth will be the least of his problems when I finish with him.

"Knives are ready, Boss," Tristan says with a dark smile.

I tip my head. "Wonderful, now on to business," I state, looking back at my guest. "Name?"

"Yev Lobochev," Dominic replies. "Age thirty-seven, although he looks like shit. He's from Russia, of the Pelov Brotherhood, or so he used to be until he joined the Circle of Shadows."

"Motherfucker!" Yev shouts at Dominic.

I answer him with a kick to his stomach, which makes him howl with pain.

"Speak when you are spoken to," I hiss and eye him sharply. I look back to Tristan and hold out my hand. He passes me two knives. Throwing knives. I have a set of ten. Usually, the victim dies on the tenth, but by then I have the intel I need.

I focus on Yev, and the room goes quiet.

Clearing my throat, I move a few paces forward, keeping my gaze trained on this fucker the whole time. I don't even blink.

"Tell me, Yev, where is Vlad," I demand.

"Fuck you," he snarls. "I'm not fucking telling you shit. You can go fuck yourselves, all of you."

That's it. My patience is gone. I throw one knife into his thigh. He screams, howling like a wild animal trapped in a snare.

A wild animal I would show mercy. I have none for him.

As blood pours from his thigh, Yev looks back at me like he can't believe what I just did.

Just as he's about to catch his breath, I throw the second knife into his other leg. Not only does the motherfucker scream louder than before, he pisses himself too. Piss trails down his leg and runs onto the floor, pooling around his shoes.

"Fuck, man," Dominic says with a chuckle, looking at Yev with disgust.

"If you shit yourself, you're dead," I tell Yev. "I will put a bullet in your fucking head if I even smell anything more than the stench of your piss."

My tone and my words are hard, and I get the desired effect when he starts to tremble. From the sneer on his face, though, I know I don't have him where I need him to be just yet.

"You animal, I will not tell you anything," he says.

That's what I thought. I put my hand out, and Tristan passes me two more knives. I send both into Yev's left arm. He heaves like he's going to vomit after the screams and cries of agony.

"Ready to talk yet?" I taunt. "We can do this all night. I don't mind, and neither do my brothers. We'll be here until you draw your last miserable breath if we have to. Know why? Vlad is an enemy to us. He's killed our people."

Yev wrenches and the chains clink. He looks like shit and worse for being covered in blood.

"Ready to talk, *Yev?*" I ask, readying to throw another knife. I'm aiming for his stomach. He sees that and starts sputtering.

"Wait, please...no more," he wails. More tears seep out of his eyes. "Please. I was just hired to set up some computers for a job. Surveillance. That's what I do."

"What kind of job?" I demand, holding the knife out to slice him up.

"Vlad is working with Riccardo Balesteri," he blurts and my eyes nearly pop out of my head.

"What?"

"Riccardo Balesteri has been working with him. They want to take down the Syndicate."

I look at Tristan because he's the closest to me, then Dominic. Both look shocked.

"You're certain of this?" I demand.

"Yes."

Riccardo wants to take down the Syndicate? Holy fuck. What the fuck?

I recall what Jacob said. He mentioned a plan. Vlad was

going to come for me when the plan was completed. Fucking Riccardo. They've been working together on this plan. A plan to take out the Syndicate. I don't know anybody who's successfully gone up against the Syndicate and managed to take any of the members out. They're practically invincible. Then again, so are the Circle of Shadows. No one's ever enlisted them to take out the Syndicate before.

How the fuck did Riccardo manage to do it? They don't work with Italians.

I push past the shock in my mind and try to focus. I need to get everything I can from this fucker.

"What is he planning?" I ask.

"They're waiting for some important transaction to take place, then they'll unleash the plan."

"What transaction?" That could be anything. They have transactions taking place daily. Everything from million-dollar to billion-dollar deals in drugs or diamonds, or some other shit.

"I don't know what it is," Yev rasps.

Fucking Riccardo. Damn him. This goes right back to all that money he owed. I should have guessed he would be up to shit.

What the hell is he fucking up to, though?

Yev starts to laugh. "Look at you, caught in a net. I hope Vlad wipes you out. Maybe take that pretty little wife you have and fuck her while you watch. Maybe chop off her head, too, like the last girl. Pretty girl. She begged for her life before he killed her. What was her name? Alyssa?"

I pull my gun and fire one bullet, getting to him before Tristan can. The bullet lodges right between his eyes and blood splatters all over me.

Four more bullets echo next to me, leaving my brother's gun. Tristan shoots, firing one bullet after another until the life leaves Yev's body and all that's left is a bloody mash-up of blood and gore.

Fuck, he was one of the guys who took Alyssa, and he was talking about my wife. I understand Tristan's pain now more than ever. I understand his loss. I understand how he must blame himself, because neither he nor I could stop them from taking Alyssa.

They killed her because she married him.

I don't realize I'm shaking, seething with rage with the gun in my hand, until Dominic rests his hand on my shoulder.

I look at him and grit my teeth.

"Focus," he says, but I can see the storm brewing in his eyes. "We need to focus."

Shit. How can I focus after hearing that?

I turn to Tristan, who lowers his gun.

"I need to cool off," he says and walks out. I allow him to go.

"I have to contact the Syndicate," I say to Dominic. I'll call Pa first. "I need to find out what transaction Vlad is waiting on."

"I can look into that and see what I can find out," Dominic says.

"Thank you, brother."

"Don't worry. Try not to worry about Emelia," he tells me.

If anyone can see straight through me, it's him. He has a way of seeing past my hard exterior. That's why he needed to be my consigliere. Even if it's just to calm me the fuck down.

I won't allow anything to happen to Emelia.

Once again, Daddy Dearest strikes.

Pa has been going over the Syndicate creed of protocols and policies. I think of them and know straightaway what the fucker is up to.

You keep what you kill. The Syndicate has a protocol called

Code Ten. It's a way of preserving the wealth accumulated and keeping it within the group.

It provides that when one member dies, the remaining members receive their shares and wealth. Ten percent of yearly earnings are put into the Syndicate funds. That currently stands at five hundred billion. That's just the money side of it. There is also the value of services and business specialties the group owns together. If Riccardo wiped out the Syndicate and was the last man standing, the fucker would get everything.

We screwed with him, but little did we know he must have been planning this shit for a while. When his cartel deal went bust and we shit all over his plans, that must have really pissed him off.

Now I know what's going on.

He wants to kill us all. Me included. And take everything.

That will be how he gets his daughter back.

CHAPTER THIRTY-SIX

MASSIMO

Phillipe's hands tense as he gazes down at the image of Vlad laid out on his office table. He looks enraged.

It's the image we got from Pierbo's camera.

Pa and I are sitting before him, waiting for him to say something. We've just filled him in on what's happening.

He looks up and aims a cold stare at Pa.

"I have no idea what transaction Riccardo's waiting on," he states. "It could be anything. There are a number of things happening over the next few weeks that amount in the billion-dollar region. Obviously, though, he must wish to enact Code Ten. Kill us fucking dead and take everything."

Pa nods. "Yes, it could only be that."

Phillipe looks at me now, then back at Pa. "What is going on between you and Riccardo? I'm asking as a friend, Giacomo."

Pa glances at me. I don't know what to do here. We've

accomplished our own mission, but what will it mean? It could mean all kinds of shit.

"As your friend, I will tell you that I'm not at liberty to discuss that. As my friend, I will expect you to respect my wishes and those of my son."

Phillipe gives him an exasperated sigh. "Fucking hell, Giacomo, shit has always been brewing between you and Riccardo. Something happened between you two recently. Something to make him give up his voting rights in the Syndicate and his daughter. That's one hell of a debt repayment. You have more dirt on him. More than this, with this madman from the Circle of Shadows. Dirt you definitely weren't supposed to stumble over. I think it's to do with the Syndicate."

"We signed in blood, and I'm a man of honor. I am not at liberty to tell you anything. I took care of the shit, and this is new shit you have hanging over your head," Pa tells him firmly, homing in on his old self as boss.

"So, what should I do? My allegiance is to the Syndicate. Just for this shit I should recommend the blood death to the Brotherhood."

I bolt to my feet and rush Phillipe, grabbing his neck and shoving him hard against the wall. He gasps for breath and stares back at me with terror in his eyes.

He's fucking right to look terrified. I'm about to knock his teeth down his throat or kill his ass. The blood death means killing Riccardo and his family. He means to kill Emelia. That's who they would start with.

"Fucking bastard, you leave my wife out of this. Leave her the fuck out of this!" I shout. "If you even think of hurting my wife, I'll slit your throat right the fuck now, and you won't get the fucking chance to recommend shit to anybody. I didn't have to tell you anything. I could have taken my family and fled. I could have run away with my girl like a motherfucker and leave you to die."

"I...won't do it," Phillipe coughs. "Let me go."

Pa grips on my arm and I glance over at him. "Let him go, son."

I release him but the look of terror still lingers in his eyes.

"My apologies," Phillipe says, coughing to clear his throat. "I am, however, recommending death to Riccardo. He'll have the chance to come and plead his case and we'll issue his sentence."

I clench my jaw. "You think Riccardo's gonna turn up?"

"No, so we'll be looking for him. I think it goes without saying that we're all in danger until we figure out what transaction he's waiting for. So we'll be looking for him, and when we find him, we'll lock him up and then give him the chance to talk."

"He could pull this off, couldn't he? He must think he can."

"The significant thing about the Shadows is that they always have help and you never know who's helping them," Phillipe answers. His pale blue eyes look even paler. "They are enemies who have allies that may be close to you, and you would never know until it is too late. We are powerful, but even the mighty can fall. I'll get the best men working on it. I suggest you do the same. More hands, less work."

I already have my best man working. *Dominic.*

"Okay, we'll check back in when we can," Pa says.

Phillipe nods and we leave. I'm the first to go through the door. When we get outside, I throw a fist in the wall.

"Son...calm down," Pa says.

I turn to face him. "Pa, I don't fucking trust him. What if he does come for her?"

"We have to protect against everyone and all eventualities.

I don't think he will. He's just pissed we won't tell him what Riccardo did initially. If we do, it's death to us too. No question about it. When I found out Riccardo was stealing from them, I should have reported it, but I decided to screw with him."

"*We*, not just you. Now that it's done, I can't feel the redemption I sought." I shake my head at him.

"I know. Don't let it get to you. Go home to your wife and cool off. You've been back and forth for hours."

I sigh. I'm fucking exhausted, but I don't think I can rest until I have some plan in motion. I saw Emelia earlier. She could tell something was up with me. I hate being around her when I feel like this.

"Pa, I'm sick of this shit with Riccardo. I don't know how he got a man like Vlad in on this."

"Eventually, all things will reveal themselves." He dips his head. "Keep your ears to the ground, Massimo."

"I will."

One last look at me and he heads to his car.

I jump on my motorcycle and ride home, wanting to see my girl. All I want to do for the rest of the day is spend time with her. Then I'll get back on track tomorrow. Maybe Dominic will have found something. Thank God I have Andreas holding the fort at the company. I can't do business when I'm like this either.

I get home. I'm about to make my way upstairs when the sound of ice clinking against crystal has my head turning.

Gabriella stands in the doorway of the sitting room. The broad smile on her face suggests she's here to cause trouble. What she's wearing does too—a little kimono—and I'm pretty sure she's naked under it.

"Hello, lover," she says with a smile.

CHAPTER THIRTY-SEVEN

EMELIA

I've been on edge since last night. And...conflicted.

I'm a mess. Massimo came home in the early hours of the morning. I had to put on that stupid act, like everything was okay, when all I wanted to ask him was where he'd been all night.

We had breakfast together, then he left for work with the promise to be in and out of the house today.

Needing to be alone, I stayed in the room to gather my thoughts. I've been thinking of how I'm going to talk to him about Gabriella. I can't think of anything that won't cause a really bad argument.

And realistically, what am I arguing for?

I shouldn't have to stay with a man who leaves my bed in the middle of the night to go to another woman's.

I sit in the room for hours, contemplating what to do, trying to calm my anger. Deciding to head down for lunch, I make my way downstairs. When I walk past the sitting room, I hear raised voices. It sounds like Massimo, and...a woman?

I wouldn't normally stop but the door is ajar, and hearing a woman talking has my nerves spiked and my curiosity piqued.

Who is he talking to?

I divert my path and walk closer to the door so I can peek in.

My damn heart squeezes when I see her. *Gabriella.*

It's her, with her luscious blonde waves, wearing a kimono.

"I don't have time for this shit, Gabriella," Massimo says to her. He takes a seat. In his hands is a large manila envelope.

"You used to make time for me." Her voice sounds just like it did when I first met her. Sugary and slick. *Seductive.* "You used to always make time for me, Massimo D'Agostino. I'm just reminding you that all work and no play is never a good thing. We used to play a lot. Remember the hours of fucking in the hot tub in Switzerland?"

I bite down so hard on my lip I swear I've pierced the skin. My back teeth press down so tight I think they might break.

"Gabriella, like I said, I don't have time."

That's all he's saying. Any man who was truly mine would send her packing. They'd throw her out. Fuck. They would even say something as simple as *I'm a married man.* Not him, though. Not him. Because he's not mine. He never was.

He's just my husband on paper. *Business.*

God. I've been so stupid. Dad said I'd eventually just become a thing in the house. He was right.

"Make time," she coos with seduction, and as her kimono floats down her back, revealing her nakedness, my mouth falls open.

When she walks over to Massimo and sits on his lap and

he does nothing to get her off him, an uncontrollable tear slides down my cheek and my heart shatters.

I back away from the door and fight the tears that threaten to come. I will not stay in this house another minute. I'm leaving now.

I'm leaving right now.

Rushing back up the stairs, I return to the bedroom and get my phone to call Dad.

He answers on the first ring—unusual for him. He's always in a meeting or something business related. Answering shows he must have been waiting on me, waiting desperately.

"Dad, I need to come now," I blurt, trying to hold the emotion in. "I need to escape now."

"Emelia, stay calm. Are you okay?"

"No, I need to leave."

"Okay, tell me what side of the beach the boat is on."

"The south side."

He sighs. It sounds like he's relieved. "Okay, we need to get this right. We have one shot. Go now, and I'll send someone to get you. Just try to be okay once you get on the water. Call me again if you can, but go now. They'll wait if they don't see you, but they won't wait for too long."

I nod even though he can't see me. "I'll go now. Thanks, Dad. I love you."

"I love you too, sweet girl. I love you with all my heart. Go now, quickly," he says and hangs up.

I won't take anything other than the phone. Massimo has a door leading out to the beach, so I leave through it.

I walk down the steps on the terrace and head down the sandy path, walking like I'm just enjoying the weather, like I usually do. There aren't any guards around, but there will be someone on surveillance watching this part of the beach. I walk along and pretend I'm picking up shells until I reach the camera Candace told me about. The one that's not working.

The docks are just ahead of me. I start to run when I get past the camera and run up the ramp leading to the boardwalk. The rowboat is right at the end, bobbing on the water that already looks rough. I pray I'll be okay once I get out on the open sea. Earlier, it looked like a storm was brewing. The angry gray clouds rumbling in the sky do nothing to calm me, especially knowing the waters are dangerous.

I rush along and try to focus, pushing aside the sight of Massimo with that woman. I can just imagine what he's doing with her now. I saw what she looked like. I can't imagine him saying no to her, and why would he? For me?

I'm a fool.

Exerting extreme caution, I step into the boat. It rocks from side to side, making me unsteady and I almost fall. Luckily, I stabilize myself. I look at the large wooden oars, take a deep breath of courage, and unhook the ropes holding the boat in place. As soon as I do, the boat drifts away, pulling out with the current, which is quite strong.

As I drift, I think of what I'm doing. *Escaping.* I'm doing it. I'm actually doing it.

God...

I'm leaving my husband. The man I was forced to marry. Forced? It feels weird to think of it being forced now, given all that I've done with him and the way I felt. I loved him. The sad thought hits me. I fell in love with him. It was the stupidest thing I could have ever done.

I can't think of that now. It's my fault my heart is shattered. My grandmother used to say that a snake will always be a snake, no matter what you do. Shame on you if the snake tells you it's going to hurt you, yet you refuse to believe it.

Massimo warned me. He told me he was the big, bad wolf.

The devil. That I shouldn't want him. He told me *don't*. That *don't* was in reference to everything. Look what he did today with that woman.

I gather my strength and start rowing. I've never done this before. It looks much simpler in the movies. Granted, it looked a lot easier when I've seen people rowing on the river as opposed to the sea. What I think of as I pull out and row out to sea is *Titanic*.

Huge waves roll toward me, fueled by the oncoming storm. The boat lifts high. I yelp when water splashes inside the boat and rocks it so hard I think it's going to capsize.

I row hard, but it's like trying to move concrete. It's not working. I'm not strong enough. Ahead, another wave flows toward me. It's what Jacob would call a surfer wave.

It comes for me, and I row harder, As it slaps the boat, I fall and drop one of the oars. It's gone. I made the mistake of looking and nearly fell over the side. I have one paddle now, and I don't think it's going to be able to do what two paddles would do.

The angry sea takes me farther out as the water turns fiercer. I can't imagine Massimo using this boat on these rough waters.

Jesus, it's too rough.

The boat rocks hard from side to side, carried by the waves. Whatever I do with the remaining paddle counts for shit. Water soaks me, and I start to cry. I can't see anybody coming for me.

Dad, where are you?

Jesus, where is Dad?

I glance back to the docks when another wave hits me. I'm shocked that I can barely see it. I didn't realize I was that far away.

I'm so far away, and the waters are getting more turbulent.

Another high-rise wave rolls toward me. I scream when it hits the boat so hard it twists me right around and makes me feel sick, like I'm going to vomit.

More waves are coming, higher and stronger looking than the last. So high they seem to touch the sky.

I don't think I'm going to make it.

CHAPTER THIRTY-EIGHT

MASSIMO

God, I don't have time for this.
Arguing about fucking shit.
I've never met a more stubborn woman. It's because I know her why I'm sparing the time to have this fucking argument.
I'm not violent toward women. It's not my way, but fuck, this woman has me all riled up in ways I can't describe.
It took all of ten minutes just for me to get her fucking clothes back on.
"Something is wrong with you," she snaps at me, setting her hands on her hips.
"What? What the fuck could be wrong with me? I told you we can't play this game anymore," I retort. I'm loud, and I know I could be causing a scene. What I'm mindful of is Emelia coming in here after hearing the argument and seeing Gabriella.

I know what Gabriella is like. If that happened, she'd find some way to make Emelia feel bad about shit.

"Massimo, you're saying this because of the marriage. It's not real. It's an arranged marriage to conquer an enemy. You and I are more than that. Look how many years we've been together," she says, giving me an incredulous glare, like I should see her point.

The thing is, I do see it. If I was going to be with anybody, it should have been her. We've been screwing around the way we have for the last ten years.

I look at her and know she can see what everyone else who's close to me is seeing when it comes to Emelia. Some show me respect. Some keep quiet. She wants to ruin it.

Gabriella came here and tried to seduce me again, and I couldn't do it. I couldn't do shit because I want Emelia. I want my wife. If that is who I want, I have to tell Gabriella straight that she's to stop this shit.

"Listen to me," I say, walking up to her. I get close, real close. So close I see the tremble in her skin she tries to hide. She's always been afraid of me, never knowing if I just might snap if she pushes me the wrong way. Today came damn close. "Listen to me, Gabriella, and listen well. Today is the last day you do this. You are not to come back here, and you are not to message me about shit again. You are not to come anywhere near me or try to pull shit like you did today ever again."

She can no longer hide the shaking. Her eyes brim with tears, but I know she won't cry. She's not a crier. It's not that she's strong. She just doesn't want to reveal that vulnerability.

"So, this is it? The end of us." Her voice quivers.

"We ended when you thought it was a good idea to jump in bed with Senator Braxton. That was it for me. We ended a long time ago." That is the truth, and more emotion than I would normally reveal. It tells her I was hurt by what she did.

"You will never love her. You loved me."

"Just go." I can't talk about this anymore.

She cuts me a crude glance, gathers her purse, and storms out at the same time Tristan and Dominic walk into the sitting room. She almost bumps into Tristan as she makes her exit.

Dominic's eyes widen, and Tristan gives me a look of disapproval. From what Gabriella was wearing it was obvious she was naked under that kimono.

"Massimo, did you?" Tristan asks, pointing after the empty trail Gabriella left. Dominic looks on curiously.

"No, I didn't do shit. She came to drive me fucking crazy," I seethe.

"Well, you're about to go crazier," Dominic says, chewing on the side of his lip.

He has news. More pieces of the puzzle.

"Hit me with it," I say.

"I hacked, and from what I could see, I think they're waiting on a shipment of diamonds that's supposed to come in the next three days. It's blood diamonds worth a shit load of money. There were references to Africa and mines in emails I saw between Riccardo and Vlad. They have a deal and they have a buyer. The conversation showed Riccardo was trying to hang on to his membership in the Brotherhood until the transaction took place. Vlad has been taking care of negotiations with various people. That's what I got so far."

Fucking fuck. I grit my teeth. *Diamonds*.

Before I can open my mouth, the door opens and Priscilla rushes in. She knows never to interrupt when it looks like I'm in business meetings. But I'm not about to talk down to a woman who's like a mother to me.

"Massimo, we can't find Emelia. She was supposed to come down to lunch. She didn't. We've been looking around everywhere. The cameras show her on the beach, but then she just disappears."

My blood runs cold, and my throat goes dry

"What? What do you mean, disappear? She couldn't just disappear. The cameras should pick everything up," I say.

"Where on the beach was she?" Tristan asks. "Did she go in the sea?"

Oh my God. What if she did?

Ma's cold dead eyes come to my mind. Would Emelia do that? Go in the sea and die?

If they can't find her and she was on the beach, there's only one place she could have gone and that's in the sea. Someone would have seen her.

"She was just walking on the beach picking up shells. She didn't look herself," Priscilla says.

"How long ago did the camera pick that up?"

"Twenty minutes."

"And nothing more?" I ask. My fucking voice waivers.

Priscilla shakes her head.

"I think I know where she went," Candace says, stepping forward. Her face is ghostly pale, her eyes heavy with sadness.

"Where?" I demand.

"She would have taken the rowboat. The cameras don't work on that side of the docks," she confesses. I glare back at her. Candace is a woman I trust nearly as much as my brothers.

"The cameras don't work?" I growl. I wasn't aware of that, but clearly, security has been keeping things from me. Someone will die tonight.

"No. I'm sorry. I'm so sorry."

"And how did Emelia know about the cameras and the

boat?" I've guessed it, but I want to hear it for myself. From her lips. How she helped Emelia escape. So clever to betray my trust.

"I told her."

I roar, and she starts crying. I lunge for her. Tristan and Dominic grab me to hold me back.

"Massimo, there's a storm coming, and Emelia isn't a strong swimmer," Priscilla says quickly. "I can't imagine a young woman rowing a boat on the sea the way it is. And to where? Where is she going? She won't survive water like that."

Panic and terror already have me moving. I don't care why she left, or how she left, or who helped her leave. Fuck, I don't even care if she does manage to escape. I just don't want her to die.

I run with everything inside me. It's not until I get outside that I realize Dominic and Tristan are following me. We rush across the terrace and down the boardwalk on the docks. The rowboat is indeed gone.

We jump into the speedboat, and I shove the keys in the ignition. Once we pull out, I instantly see how turbulent the sea is. I usually take the rowboat out on calmer waters to fish. I would never venture out in these types of waters in that boat, not with the sea wild like it is.

Tristan grabs a pair of binoculars while Dominic starts looking around at the ropes and other things I have stashed under the dashboard.

"Can you see her?" I ask Tristan.

"No," he answers.

I'm trying to calculate the timing. Priscilla said Emelia was seen twenty minutes ago on the beach. So maybe she's been out here for at least thirty minutes, give or take. My guess is as good as shit, though, because it doesn't count for anything.

I don't know how long Emelia's been out here. I don't know if I'm too late. If she's thirty minutes ahead of us, then she's far away. I speed faster and faster.

"Massimo!" Tristan cries. "Over there. Look!" He points, and I see. I see the boat rocking on the water.

"There's another boat coming," Dominic states. He points farther out to a speedboat heading toward Emelia. There's no mistake it's going for her. It's going to crash into her.

I accelerate and get the boat going as fast as I can. When we get closer, I see her crying inside the rowboat. She doesn't appear to have any oars. I'm not surprised. The boat rocks violently on the waves and water splashes inside.

Dominic starts waving a flag to the other boat to warn them of a hazard ahead so they can turn, but they keep coming. They keep coming fast, and they're heading straight for her.

They get close, then a fucking bullet whizzes by my ear.

"Holy fuck!" I shout.

"Fucking hell, this is some kind of plan," Tristan cries, grabbing his gun. As the boat gets closer, I see the guy who's shooting at us. He's a bulky-looking Russian guy. Who I see next, though, emerging from the cockpit with a shotgun, has my blood turning hot and cold at the same time. It's Vlad!

"Oh my God," Tristan gasps and starts shooting back.

Emelia screams. She's in the middle of this and could get caught in the crossfire.

Vlad's boat gets closer to her. He has men readying themselves to get her. Tristan manages to shoot two of them, and they fall into the water. Vlad dodges the bullets but goes to the side to get her while two men cover him by shooting back at us.

I don't want him to touch her. I don't even want him to look at her. The panic has stalled my mind. My brain can't function right now to process what this means. I just know that if he gets her, she's dead. I just know.

When a twenty-foot wave bounds down on her and the boat flips over, I die a thousand deaths.

"Fuck, Massimo, get her! We'll handle them and cover you!" Dominic shouts.

I kick off my shoes and jump into the water. As I dive in, all I hear around me is bullets flying and the water slapping against my body.

I push, swimming forward like I have lightning attached to my feet, my arms slicing through the water.

I catch a glimpse of obsidian hair and speed that way. She's right at the bottom amongst jagged rock trying to push up, but she can't. I could breathe fire when I see her foot is clamped between the rocks and she can't get out.

I swim to her. She's doing the worst thing she could do by screaming. As the water fills up her lungs, she reaches out to me.

I head for the rocks and try to free her foot, but she's clamped in like a fucking vice. She must have pushed the rocks out of place. Her foot is so small that it slipped right in. I kick at the rocks but stop when her body stills. Swimming back up to her, I see her eyes go wide as I grab her and shake my head. All she does is stare at me. Her eyes remind me of that deathly terrified look I saw on my mother's face. Her lips move. I make out an M. Then she stops.

No.

I can't let this happen.

Even if I have to break her foot, I will do this.

I push back down, feeling lightheaded because I should have already come back up for air and haven't.

One kick to the rocks makes them crumble, but her foot

is still stuck. I do the only thing I can think of doing and throw myself into her. It's then she comes free.

Grabbing her, I push back up to the surface and swim with her to my boat. And I pray. I can't remember the last time I prayed. I can't remember the last time I thought of God, but I do now as I swim back with my love.

The bullets have stopped flying and the other boat is gone, but I can't think of what's happening outside the cold, still body of the woman I'm carrying in my arms.

Tristan lowers himself over the side and reaches for my hand. He takes hold of me. Horror fills his eyes when he sees Emelia.

We get up on the boat, and I lay her down, positioning her to clear her airway, then check her to see if she's breathing. She's not. She's not fucking breathing, and there's no pulse either.

Fuck. This can't happen. Not to her. I can't allow her to die.

Panic and adrenaline force me to focus on what I need to do. I snap into action, press my lips to hers, and give her five breaths to try and resuscitate her.

When nothing happens and she's still not breathing, I start CPR immediately.

I do the compressions and rescue breaths, yet still nothing happens. One minute passes, then two, and I've done two sets.

I count, and I breathe into her mouth, and I press on her tiny chest, willing her to come back to me.

I count, and I breathe, and I press, but nothing happens. She won't move. She's not moving.

In my mind's eye I remember the time we spent together after the dinner at Pa's house. We laughed and I carried her down the road as we talked. That was the most normal we'd been. We were just a guy and a girl talking. She wanted to know about me. Then, before the night ended, I did what I always do and fucked things up.

Can't we go on a real date? I hear her ask in my mind as her lifeless eyes stare back at me and a tear tracks down my cheek.

"Emelia, come back to me," I wail.

"Massimo," Tristan says, resting his hand on my shoulder. "I'm sorry."

"No, leave me!" I shout, shoving his hand away. He's messing this up. I can't let her go. I won't stop trying to pull her back from where she's gone. I won't. I can't be too late. I *can't* be too late.

I pump and I breathe into her lips, but I stop and keep my trembling lips against her. Love flows through me. I don't want to deny it. I don't want to fight it. I don't want to fight that I love her. I have from the moment I saw her.

That's what this is about.

I love her, and I can't let her go.

"Emelia...come back to me!" I shout and press down so hard I think I've broken her.

A gasp leaves her body. What comes next is water sputtering from her mouth. She brings it up, all of it, and starts breathing. I think past the haze in my mind and flip her onto her side so she can bring all the water up.

When she finishes and is coughing, I reach for her and hold her in my arms. I hold her like I never want to let her go while she grabs my shirt. The fucking tears come. I remember the last time tears left my eyes.

I was twelve. It was just after I found Ma.

CHAPTER THIRTY-NINE

MASSIMO

We get her back to the house and call the family doc, who can be here on my word. He comes quickly and tends to her.

Emelia keeps looking at me with fear in her eyes. We haven't spoken.

No one has said anything to me because I look like I'm going to snap.

I know what happened. I know now what shit must have been concocted. The answer is the one-worded answer that has long since plagued my mind. Riccardo.

The pale-blue-eyed devil.

Motherfucker.

If we hadn't seen Yev and heard that Vlad and Riccardo were in cahoots, I would have thought this was something else.

And…how did Emelia get everything together so quickly? Her fucking phone.

Betrayal.

I've killed for less than this, but this woman has my heart and my love. But she doesn't know that. She doesn't know I would never hurt her. That I can't.

Doc continues to check her out, but she looks at me as tears roll down her cheeks. I have to walk out when I see that. I can't stay. I have one more thing to attend to, and it's not going to be nice. I walk past Tristan and Dominic in the hall. They both rush to me when they see me turn the corner and must know I'm heading for Candace's room.

"Don't," Tristan says, grabbing my arm. "Don't you fucking hurt her, Massimo."

He shakes his head. Dominic glares at me too, his eyes pleading with me.

"She betrayed me, and look what could have happened," I snap.

"It's Candace," Dominic hisses. Instantly, I think of the painting Ma made of the five of us playing in the meadow.

Us four brothers and the little girl who used to play with us. We treated her like a sister.

"Calm down, Massimo," Tristan says. I wrench my arm free of his grasp.

They won't do more than that. Out of respect, they won't do shit because I'm boss, and regardless of who and what we are, they know what crossing me as the boss could mean.

I head down to the room and all but break the door to get inside.

Candace is sitting on the bed with her head hanging down, hands in her lap. She hasn't flinched from my rage.

"How dare you do this to me?" I demand.

"Just kill me," she says. "Just kill me now, Massimo. I won't speak to you when you're like this, so I won't speak at all."

She raises her head, stands up, and walks up to me.

"Go on, Ruthless Prince, take out your gun and end me. It

would be easier if you did that. It's always easy if a stranger takes your life over someone you know."

My hands are fisted at my sides.

"We've known each other since we were kids," I bark.

"And yet I don't recognize you. I look at you, and I don't know you. I don't know this version of you, who you've become. You're not the boy I used to play with in the meadows. You're not the boy who promised to take care of me after my family was killed. So, please, just kill me. Don't I already owe you my life? Take it." As the last word leaves her lips, her eyes water.

She looks at me like she really thinks I'm going to do it. The look is expected, and I can't believe I'm not, but her words halt me.

Her family was killed. She would be dead too if I hadn't killed the fiend who came to kill her mother and father.

She was fifteen years old when it happened. I came in and saved her before he could rape and kill her. He was my first kill. I chopped his head off when I saw him on top of her naked body. Her mother lay just across from her, half burned, as well as her father with his head paces away from his body. Somebody put a hit on their family. We've never been able to find out who it was.

She's the oldest friend I have. To hear her say she doesn't know me grips me to the core.

"Why did you do it?" I hear myself say.

"Because what you did was wrong. Regardless of what you feel for Emelia, you went after Riccardo through his daughter. You held her captive like an animal locked in her room. She didn't deserve that. She was innocent in your game of vengeance, and I couldn't stand by and allow her to not have a choice," she answers.

I gaze back at her and press my lips together.

She's...right.

"I didn't know when she was going to do it, and I don't know why she chose today. We spoke about it months ago," Candace adds.

I harden my stare on Candace. I need to do something. I need to punish her. As I look at her, though, I feel the same way as my brothers do when it comes to her. She's like family to us.

"How did you know about the cameras?" I ask. She knows that question means I'll be drawing blood tonight.

She shakes her head. "Kill me, Massimo. Kill *me* instead."

I grab her and catch her face, holding it so tight my nails dig into her skin.

"Fuck you. I can't kill you. I love you like a sister. Candace Ricci...if you don't answer my question, I'll kill the whole security team. Forty men dead because you won't give me a name. Or was it two?"

The tears come. I know it can only be a minimum of two of my guys. Manni is my right-hand man, and Jake takes care of the cameras. The men watch the house and have a strict rota to keep things tight. That's why people like the Shadows can't just walk onto my property without a big fight.

"Please...don't make me," she begs. "We were just seeing each other, and it's over. I was never supposed to tell anybody. We'd sneak out to the boats."

As she says that, I know who it is, and I feel like a bastard for it.

Manni. It's him. I remember the way he looked at her.

I release her, but she knows I'm not stupid and I know exactly who's to blame.

"No, Massimo, please," she cries.

Reaching for my phone, I storm out of her room and call

Manni. She runs after me, trying to grab my arm. Every time she touches me, I wrench my arm free of her grasp.

Manni answers the phone.

"Yes, Boss," he says.

"Get here now. Get to the main floor right the fuck now," I demand and pull my gun from my back pocket. When Candace sees it, she screams and starts crying harder. Manni would have heard her.

"Yes, Boss... I'm on the way." At least the prick has the sense to sound wary. He should.

I bound forward down the stairs. Candace follows. Her cries have everyone's attention. Priscilla comes out of the kitchen, and Tristan and Dominic come rushing down the other set of stairs, panic on their faces.

I zero in on the one fucker I want as he walks in through the door. Manni stops in the foyer when he sees me, his face pale, his body tense.

I walk up to him and land my fist straight in his face, knocking him to the ground. Before he can right himself, I aim my gun at him and cock the hammer.

"You fucking prick. I hire you for a job and you screw with me," I roar.

When he sees Candace, he knows what the fuck I'm talking about.

"Massimo, please, don't kill him," she begs.

I can't listen to her. I can't look at her. All I see in my mind is Emelia lifeless in my arms.

She could have died. That's the fucking bottom line. Emelia could have died.

"Boss, I'm sorry. I should have had the cameras fixed. I didn't mean to—"

Rage makes me shoot the Ming vase by the door. It shatters.

I hate when people use that excuse. *They didn't mean to.* Of course he did. If he didn't mean to do it, then he wouldn't have done that shit to me knowing the risk.

When I aim the gun at him again, Candace throws herself on top of him. I look at them both and seethe.

"Massimo, no, please." She shakes her head. "Don't do this."

"Candace. There is always trouble. Remember Vlad? Remember how he killed Alyssa?" I shout at her.

She knows the past, so she remembers well.

"That's who came for Emelia today. Him. He's working with Riccardo. The cameras are for our protection. I can't be everywhere, and I can't keep my arms around everyone to protect them from shit. Something as simple as a fucking camera not working and me not knowing for fuck knows how long could have changed the tide of what happened today." I'm shaking as I speak.

"I know. I know," she answers. "But this is my fault. I could have told you about the camera too. I shouldn't have told Emelia anything. I shouldn't have. Manni didn't do it. It was me, and I promised him I wouldn't say anything. You can't kill him for something I did just because you can't kill me. If you do, you'll be no better than those monsters. Please..."

I narrow my eyes and press down hard on my teeth.

I'm not a fucking monster. Her words get to me. They get me good and my finger loosens on the trigger.

Footsteps sound behind me, and I turn to see my father. I didn't even know he was here. He shakes his head, and I lower the gun.

Returning my focus to Candace and Manni, I straighten.

"Get up," I tell both of them.

They do as I say.

"Manni, get the hell off my property. Get the fuck off and don't come back. You better hope I never see you again."

"I'm sorry, Massimo—"

I hold up my hand, cutting him off.

"Don't. I don't want to hear it. It counts for shit. I trusted you, and you know my trust is hard to come by." I look at Candace too when I say that. I'm including her in that because she's right.

She shouldn't have told Emelia anything. She knows how dangerous those waters are and that Emelia can barely swim.

Manni leaves. Candace looks at me, expecting me to throw her out too. However, the same way I couldn't kill her, I can't kick her out.

With that, I leave everyone.

I need to be by myself for a little while to cool off.

I still haven't spoken to the person I need to speak to most.

Emelia.

It's late…

I must have been in the study for quite a few hours now. It's getting later with each passing second, and I'm still unable to bring myself to see Emelia.

I don't want to talk to her feeling this way. The sting of betrayal and fear is too fresh.

I want to know what happened, why she suddenly decided to do this today. I'm afraid of the answer, though. Things have always been shit, but more shit since Jacob's death.

Was she planning this all along? It had to be a plan, since the only time she could have seen her father and spoken to him was at the fundraiser. Unless she called him.

God, I need another drink.

I walk to the drink cabinet, grab a glass from the little shelf, and toss some ice in from the mini fridge. I pour myself some scotch and knock it back as soon as I swivel it around in the glass and get it chilled.

A knock sounds on the door. Dominic comes in. He has that look again. I bite the inside of my lip when I see he's carrying another envelope.

"What now? What the fuck more now?" I ask.

"I found more paperwork. The diamonds are for the Circle as a group. Riccardo plans to give the Shadows forty percent of the wealth he'll get from the Syndicate resources. But this is how he enticed Vlad in the first place."

"What is it?"

"Just have a look, Massimo." He walks up to me and hands me the envelope.

I set the glass down and open it. I'm getting tired of opening envelopes with bad news. This one, though, is the mother of bad news. I look at the first page and my heart stops when I read over the first few lines. Pieces of the fucking puzzle are coming together. Now I know exactly why fucking Vlad thought I stole something from him. Enraged, I look back to Dominic.

"Where did you get this?" I rasp.

"Massimo, you know me," he answers. "That's just one more piece of the puzzle falling into place. I guess we know now all that Riccardo was up to and how he enticed Vlad to help him. Riccardo definitely had plans for Emelia. Big plans."

My mouth goes dry. "Fuck," I hiss and move past him.

It's time to see Emelia and show her exactly the kind of devil her father is.

CHAPTER FORTY

EMELIA

I've been waiting for Massimo. It's been hours. The doctor left a while ago, so I expected him to come and dole out his punishment.

My mind told me he would, but then I remember him saving me.

He called me back from the dead.

I heard him.

I remember the man who cried as he held me. His heart beating so close to my ear speaking of love.

Then we got back here, and it was like I entered the *Twilight Zone*. Everything felt abstract and surreal. Things have been happening around me, and yet I don't quite know what.

What I'm certain of is that Massimo is furious. I just don't know what he's done with that fury. He would have known that either Candace or Priscilla told me about the boat, and since I've seen Priscilla twice in the last few hours but no sign of Candace, I'm inclined to believe he knows it was her. I just pray he didn't do anything to her.

I've been in here going crazy with worry, my mind all over the place. I haven't even thought of the fact that I'm alive. I'm alive, yet the plan went to hell. Dad sent those men to get me. They were shooting at Massimo and his brothers. People died. I never expected that to happen. I'm sure Dad must know by now that we failed.

I recognized one guy. His name was Vlad. I met him at the charity ball. Dad introduced him as an investor.

The door smashes open, and I jump with fright, leaping off the bed.

Massimo stands before me like a raving lunatic, eyes red and face blotchy. Rage and fear are all over his face.

I've never seen him look afraid until today as he held me. This is worse.

"Tell me what happened. Tell me everything. And don't you dare lie to me." He raises his right hand and balls it into a tight fist. In his left is an envelope. "Skip the parts about Candace. I know that part. She's already filled me in."

I start to shake.

"Talk, Emelia, tell me what happened!" he demands. "Things were good between us, then you suddenly decided to do this today?"

"I saw you with Gabriella. She was sitting on your lap in the sitting room. *Naked.*"

"I didn't do anything with her."

"You didn't push her away, either. And what about last night? Where were you? I saw the message she sent you telling you to go to her, and you went."

"I didn't. *Fuck*, Emelia, fucking hell. I think I've proven to you more than once that I will only tell you the truth. I didn't see her until today. I would never cheat on you." He grits his teeth. "I threw her out and made sure she knew to never try anything like that with me again."

"I'm sorry. I didn't know what to think..." I manage, but rage still fills his stare.

"Tell me what your father had to do with this. You called him."

"At the fundraiser, he said he was trying to get me back and that I shouldn't trust you. He said you would never love me. Then I saw you today with Gabriella. I...thought he was right."

He runs his hand through his hair and shakes it. "Well, Emelia, it's time you got a rude awakening on who your father truly is. I will tell you exactly who that man you're calling Father is."

I tense right up, my body so rigid I can't breathe.

"When I was ten years old, your father stormed into my home with his men and threw us out. No warning, no nothing. No time to pack a fucking bag. Dominic was six years old, practically a baby. As he clung to my mother's side, I watched your father tell his team to destroy everything inside the property and get everyone out. Us and all the people who worked for us. My father went broke overnight. Literally. Your father cleaned him out. Took everything and turned people who could have helped us against him. He threatened the others. If they helped us in any shape or form, they'd die. Them and their families. That is who your father is." He tightens his fist and continues spewing out the vile words of a man I don't recognize. Dad said he did things he wasn't proud of, but this is awful.

"For years, we struggled just to have a place to live. Everywhere my father went, no one would help him, and you know why? It was because your father was in love with my mother and she wouldn't choose him. That's why. Then it ended with her death. He dealt his last blow when he held a gun to my head at my mother's funeral. I was twelve years old, Emelia. I was standing a breath away from my mother's grave. We'd just buried her, and your father came to the cemetery and thought he should do that to me. Threaten to kill me and my whole family. How the fuck can you do that to a twelve-year-old?"

My cheeks burn and my hands fly up to them. I pant as I try to catch my breath.

"Oh my God…" I breathe.

"That's the summary of me. How about we skip to you. He only took you to that charity ball with him because he wanted to sell you. It's the kind of ball where you do things like that in a covert way, to secure a business deal. A business marriage."

I continue shaking my head. "What?"

"Did you meet anyone at the ball?" he asks.

"Yes…the man on the boat today who was shooting at you, Vlad." I feel sick, and Massimo looks worse for wear.

He gives me a crude laugh. "Your father is one nasty piece of work. But please, do not take my word for it. After all, you can't trust me, *remember*? He told you not to trust me. Don't trust me. Trust yourself. Trust what your eyes can see."

He pushes out the document to me to take. I walk to him and reach for it.

I don't actually have the strength to do that, but good old curiosity moves me to see what I'm supposed to see.

I look at the document and can't believe what I'm reading.

It's a contract for sale.

Sale of me.

This Sales Agreement is entered into on November 17, 2018 by and between Riccardo Balesteri (the **"Seller"**) and Vladimir Kuznetsov (the **"Buyer"**) to agree to the sale of Emelia Balesteri for $30 million dollars.

Terms of contract
The parties agree as follows:

Ownership of the Balesteri inheritance once Emelia turns the age of twenty-one.

Ownership of assets and shares that are currently in Emelia's name and those she will receive from her inheritance.

Emelia will be delivered to the Buyer's residence in Florence, Italy on July 10, 2019.

Emelia will join the other women in the brothel and conduct all services requested by its clients. Her body will belong to the Buyer to do with as they choose.

The Buyer agrees that she will be able to go to art school when she isn't required to work...

I stop reading. I can't read any more.

At the bottom is my father's signature, with two blank spaces next to it. A space for me to sign, and another for Vlad.

"Oh my God," I gasp, my hands shake so much I drop the contract.

"Vlad would have only wanted you in his brothel to replace one of the women he killed, Emelia. You know what he does to women?"

I wish he wouldn't tell me.

"Don't tell me." I shake my head.

"You need to hear this. He rapes, and he tortures, and he makes you beg for death. When he gets his eye on a prize, he doesn't stop until he gets what he wants, and it's all for fun. That's what he did to Tristan's wife. Then he thought it would be funny to send him her head in a box with a note and her wedding ring."

I cry out from the horror.

"Your father sent him today to get you to fulfill the fucking contract. That's who your father is, Emelia. I... I won't get my girl's head in a box."

It's the second time I've seen him cry. I wouldn't believe it if I weren't looking at the tear rolling down his cheek and nestling in his beard. I wouldn't believe it. But I'm so overwhelmed by what I just heard and read that I can't stop crying.

"I won't, Emelia. I *can't* get my girl's head in fucking box," he adds.

Bile rises in my stomach when the image comes to my mind so vividly, and fear rushes over my skin, burning everywhere it touches.

I run to the bathroom, heave, and start throwing up. My poor body wrenches forward, and everything I ate since I got back from the boat comes up.

Massimo follows me. He takes hold of me and holds my hair back.

I start crying hard while he holds me.

This horror truly is a nightmare. Dad was going to sell me to this man, and there I was, angry at him because he sold me to Massimo.

"I'm sorry," Massimo says. I look up at him, trying to see him through tears.

My legs give out and I crumble to the floor in a flood of tears.

Massimo keeps holding me as I cling to his shirt and hold him back.

I kept asking myself who the monsters were in this story. This nightmare fairytale. I wanted to know so badly because I didn't know who to trust.

The monster was the person I've known my whole life.

Dad.

My father.

He's the devil.

———

I don't remember falling asleep. Or lying on the bed.

I'm here, though, and the only light that's coming through the window is that from the moon.

Massimo is sitting by the window, shirtless, in just his boxers, staring outside. He looks like he's watching over the house. Watching over me.

I shuffle and see that I'm naked. Since I can't remember taking my clothes off, I imagine he must have done it when I fell asleep. When I sit up and pull the covers up to my breasts, he looks at me.

"Massimo," I rasp.

He walks toward me and gets in the bed.

"Go back to sleep, Princess," he whispers, brushing his lips over mine.

I feel so fragile, but I don't want to sleep anymore. I just want him.

"Can I just spend time with you?" I mutter.

"You went through a lot today. I nearly lost you. You need to rest." Pain still lingers in his eyes, but his voice is gentle and it feels like I'm talking to that part of him again that wants me.

"I don't feel tired anymore. You were looking out the window."

"Just keeping an eye out," he replies, and I know for sure then he was watching for Vlad.

"You think he'll come back after what happened?"

He takes my hand and gives it a gentle squeeze. "I don't want you to worry about that."

"He will, won't he?" He made it sound like he would.

"I won't let him take you, Emelia. I won't let anybody take you, not even death. I'll keep holding on. I'm stubborn that way. They'd have to pry you from my cold dead fingers to try and take you from me. Or tie me up to try it." He brushes his finger over my cheek. Warmth spreads over my heart.

"You'd do all that for me?"

"You're my wife." He offers me a weak smile that shows his exhaustion. "You are mine. My girl."

"I'm sorry... I'm sorry for everything, for all that my father did to you, and for betraying you."

He shakes his head. "You can't apologize for your father, Emelia. You can't."

"Then I apologize for me. My part yesterday. I saw Gabriella, and I just lost it," I answer, but I think it's time to be honest. "Before I saw her, when I first got here, I was planning it. I stopped after we got closer... Then, when I saw my father at the fundraiser and he said you'd never love me, I believed him."

He reaches forward and cups my face. As he lowers to my lips, I move toward him too. Our lips meet for a kiss that seeps into my veins and heats my blood. It flows through my body, and for the first time, I feel alive.

I'm alive, and every inch of me awakens when he starts touching me. We fall back onto the pillow, into the heat of passion and that primal force that always comes for us.

We kiss hard, with the emotions that weigh in heavily on us. It feels like he's tasting me. The way he touches me and kisses my body is a mixture of need and longing. Sweet and strong, soft and hard. Lovingly and ravenous. Ravenous, like he's hungry for me and craves me. I crave him too. I need him too. Want him too.

Need and want are on the same level in this moment. His lips nip the hard bud of my clit. His tongue thrashes up inside my pussy as he eats me out. I moan, coming on his face, then he rises, taking my arm to pull me forward.

"Get on your hands and knees and look in the mirror," he

commands. His voice is hard and demanding. Just like him.

Arousal has my head spinning, but I do as he says. He switches on the light as I get on my hands and knees and turn toward the long mirror on the wall so I can see myself. My hair falls forward, and my breasts hang before me like pillows with the nipples hard and pebbled from his wild sucking.

He gets behind me and takes his cock into his hands, pumping along the length. He does it so I can see him in the mirror. I look at him, beautiful and gorgeous, all male and muscle, pumping his cock while I submit on my hands and knees beside him.

"Remember, Emelia, trust what your eyes can see. People can tell you anything, but when you see it, you know. When you feel it, you can believe it. When you believe it without seeing it, you're unstoppable," he says and grabs my hips.

I manage to take a breath before he plunges deep inside me. So deep I feel the length of his cock touch my soul—if such a thing were possible, that's how it would feel.

He starts pumping into me, and I moan from the pleasure.

I dip my head, but he growls. "Look at us. Don't look away."

I listen and do as he says, watching him fuck me in the mirror. The sight makes my mouth water and sets my body aflame with fire that scorches me all over.

My breasts bounce with every thrust. My hair tangles, hanging before me like strands of silk. All I can see through the river of black strands that flow before me is us. Me and Massimo.

Then I see what he means. *Us.*

Us like this. It's the first time I truly feel like this wasn't about a contract.

This is us as a couple, doing what we'd do if it were just us

and nothing else mattered.
    I see and I know.
    I feel and I know.

CHAPTER FORTY-ONE

MASSIMO

"How are you feeling?" Pa asks

"Like shit," I answer. "Pa. How did you do it? How did you manage to take care of the family when we had so much shit happen to us? We're grown men now, and it's bad, but it must have been worse when we were kids."

He gives me a little smile. It's not one of humor, though. It's the kind that attempts to reassure. There is nothing to smile about today.

"I had your mother. Always, even when she was no longer living. I carried her in my heart knowing what she'd say and do when I needed her," he answers and holds my gaze, studying me.

He loved my mother dearly, never remarried, never even got close to anyone. It was maybe five years after Ma died that I saw him with a woman, and it was just a date. She seemed nice, but it didn't last. Nothing ever lasted. He always stopped anything from getting past that mark where anybody could get as close as my mother.

"Pa, everything is shit."

"I know."

"I'm worried as hell about all of this. I wish we'd killed Riccardo," I say. Of course, the fucker is nowhere to be found.

We got the update from Phillipe this morning. My guess is someone knew we got Yev and knew he'd talk. Riccardo would have gotten the heads up and headed for the hills. Add the failure of yesterday into the mix, and he would know for sure we want his head on a spike.

"Me too. I fear that our greed to watch him suffer meant that we didn't treat him the way we would if he were anyone else."

"Pa, I'm going to hunt those bastards down."

"I don't doubt you, son," he says. "But take some time to think about strategy. Maybe take the day to cool off from yesterday and regroup. The worst thing you can do is go after people like Vlad and Riccardo when you can't think straight."

Maybe he's right. I'm too hyped up on emotion to concentrate.

"Yeah maybe I do need to regroup," I agree. "We don't know what will happen next."

"No, we don't. Get the men on the streets and have some downtime. I'm certain the Syndicate will summon us tomorrow at some point, one way or the other, for the next steps. Whatever that might be."

I nod. I'm expecting a meeting too.

The door opens, and Andreas walks in. I'm relieved to see him. He's been holding down the fort for me at work.

"You guys okay?" he asks.

"Yeah, son. I'm gonna leave you two to talk," Pa says with a nod. "Call me if you need me."

"I will."

Pa walks toward Andreas, gives him a pat on his shoulder, and leaves us.

Andreas sighs and looks me over in that big brotherly way that used to get on my nerves when we were kids.

"I'm pissed at you for not calling me," he says, coming close to give me a one-shoulder hug, and I hold on for a little longer.

"I'm sorry. Too much shit has happened, Andreas."

"That's why I should have been here, not pushing paper in the office. We have extra men. We have eyes everywhere, so try to relax," he assures me.

"Thanks, Andreas, thanks for having my back."

"That's what brothers are for. Do you need me to do anything else?"

An idea comes to my mind.

I do need a break. I think Emelia does too.

It's early enough to get away from here for the day.

"Could you be boss for the day? Just be boss. I just want to be Massimo D'Agostino."

"Massimo D'Agostino is boss," he replies.

"No, not that guy. I just want to be myself for today. Take a break from shit and return to the days when we used to appreciate the simple things in life."

I think he knows what I mean when he nods.

"Well, I'm starting in here. You have better bourbon than me, and Cheetos," he jokes and ruffles my hair the way he used to when we were kids and I was much shorter than him.

"Knock yourself out."

He chuckles, and I head out to go back upstairs to Emelia.

I get to the base of the stairs and stop when I see Candace. She has a packed bag in her hands.

Nerves fill her expression when she sees me, and when I walk up to her, her breathing stills.

"What are you doing?" I ask, looking at the bag.

"I'm...leaving," she replies nervously. "I thought I should leave. I know you won't ask me to, so I'm taking the awkward decision out of your hands."

"No," I tell her before she can continue. "I don't want you to leave."

"Massimo, I...betrayed you. We both know if I were someone else, I'd be very dead. Manni's alive because of me. You showed compassion because you knew what it would do to me. I really hurt you, and my actions could have resulted in much worse. I think I just need some time away. A break."

She's never been away from me.

"Where?"

"Well, knowing me, my anxiety will make sure I don't go that far. I don't really know where I'm going yet. I just think I need to get gone for a while."

"For how long?"

She shakes her head. "I don't know. Good luck with everything. I saw you. The way you were with Emelia yesterday. You proved me wrong. Take care of her. She's come to be a friend to me."

She releases a little breath, stands on the tips of her toes, and plants a kiss on my cheek.

I watch her leave, knowing she's right. We do need a break. I'll worry about her, but maybe it's best if she's away from the shit that's happening. I'll send someone to watch over her, just to be sure.

I head to the bedroom. To Emelia. She's sitting by the window, gazing out.

She gives me a little smile when she sees me, but it doesn't reach her eyes. Finding out the truth yesterday definitely took its toll on her.

Everything she knew was a lie.

Everything she knew about her father was a lie.

We keep finding out more shit. I can't help but feel there's still more. There always is.

Not today, though.

I walk over to her, pull the chair from the dresser and sit on it backwards.

"You alright?" I ask.

"No...but I'm trying to be."

"I will protect you."

"Thank you. I feel like I need more than just protection, though. My world fell apart in one breath when I saw that contract. What's happening now? I know you say you can't tell me certain things, but I need to know."

We always keep women out of business, but as I look at her, I feel I can't honor that. She does need to know.

"Vlad is working with your father to bring down the Syndicate. That was the danger Jacob was trying to warn us about, but he didn't know specifics. He didn't know about your father, or that the two were working together. I don't know what happened after I let Jacob go, but the other night, when I went out, I got the confirmation they were working together."

I don't need to elaborate. Her face goes ghostly pale. She's a clever girl. I can almost see her mind working. She'll think the same as me that the reason Jacob died was he probably saw too much. Maybe he saw Vlad and Riccardo together and learned about the plan. That's what got him killed.

She releases a sharp sigh. "Oh my God... Massimo, do you think my father had anything to do with Jacob's death?"

"Emelia, I don't know." It's best to say that. Best to leave unconfirmed shit speculative and not cause more stress. She's already had too much shit happen. "What I do know is that I have to take precautions and protect what's mine."

That means her as a priority, and anybody else who relies on me.

"What about the Syndicate? You told them about my father's plan."

I nod. She knows that means death.

She's an angel. A being of purity. So I expect the look of remorse that flickers in her eyes. I can't even be angry at her for it because that's who she is.

I reach out for her hands, and she gives them to me.

"Things are going to be hard. I think we have some difficult times to face, some tough things to come our way, but... we have each other. I want to take you away today."

A slight twinkle returns to her eyes. "Away?"

"Yes, you know, like a normal couple. We're gonna go out, and we'll be gone for the night. Just you and me."

"Really, Massimo?" She smiles.

"Yes, Princess."

"Where are we going?"

"Stormy Creek..." I say the words. She smiles, but I get that wave of apprehension that always fills me when I think of the place I grew up.

After Ma's death, I never wanted to go back there. I wanted to leave the first chance we got, and when Pa was able to, we did. It was a long time after, though. I was a year away from college.

I hated the place because of what it represented, and I only visit to tend to my mother's grave, yet it was home because she made it home.

If there's anywhere I'm going to find strength today, it's there.

"I've never been there."

"You'll like it. It feels like home. Pack a bag. Let's leave as soon as possible."

CHAPTER FORTY-TWO

EMELIA

Massimo drove the convertible with the top down.

As we sped along the freeway, I allowed myself to get sucked into the scenery and the time spent with him. Both helped with pushing yesterday from my mind.

Though I can't quite forget, and when I think of what is to come and what other truths I might learn, my heart hurts. My soul quivers and my being quakes when I consider Dad having anything to do with Jacob's death.

I know Massimo was holding back. When we spoke earlier, it felt like that day when he got angry after I told him he and my father were the same. Now I know why he was so furious.

That day, though, he made me none the wiser about the truth of who Dad really is. What he would have known back then was enough to turn my stomach. The way Dad treated his family was unbelievable. All because he was in love with Massimo's mother.

There's something I haven't mentioned, but I thought about it. About my mother. She would have been with my father during the time Massimo and his family lost everything—and when Massimo's mother died.

My parents would have been married for five years at that point. To hear that Dad was in love with another woman and behaved that way because she wouldn't choose him shocked me. I must have been a toddler during that time. Or certainly during the earlier years, my mother would have been pregnant with me.

I always thought my parents were in love with each other. That was a lie too. This man I've come to know as my father isn't the man I grew up with. He's not. He's evil. My world is different for knowing that.

It took us a little under two hours to get to Stormy Creek. It's just past mid-day.

Massimo merged onto a country road an hour ago, and we followed it all the way to the end. What we're approaching now is a cottage surrounded by a little bit of land and a woodland area that seems to lead to the creek. A river flows along our route that looks amazing.

When we pull up in front of the cottage, I'm surprised by the way it looks. It's so quaint and cozy. It looks like a home in a fairytale book. Like somewhere Snow White would live.

"This is it," Massimo says. He draws in a breath and seems to savor the air.

The air is different here. Pure and refreshing.

"This is beautiful." I smile at him.

"I'm glad you like it." He gets out of the car and opens the door for me.

I watch him. He's different. He's not the ruthless mafia boss I've come to know. As I observe him, I get the feeling that this is the real him.

He looks around the place with a reminiscent expression. His lips press together, and a line etches in his jaw. Not one of tension, like I've seen. It's looser, just an expression.

When he looks at me, the strangest thing happens. I notice that he looks different too. It's his eyes. They twinkle like they do in his mother's painting. I recognize the boy she was trying to depict. The light showing appreciation shines in his eyes. It's more than happiness.

It brightens when he reaches out and touches my cheek. He kisses me briefly, and when we part, I suddenly understand it all.

That painting was a memory. A moment of happiness when they probably had nothing, but they had each other. I've seen him with his brothers and his father, with Priscilla and with Candace. If it's one thing I know, it's that this man takes care of the people in his life who are close to him.

He values them.

He's looking at me like that now. With that same twinkle in his eyes. It's a look that makes me feel foolish for thinking he would have done anything with Gabriella. A look like that can only speak of love.

"I see you," he says, brushing his nose along mine.

I smile. "I see you too."

"Yeah? Well, I'll let you see me here. All of me."

"You're happy here," I state, and he nods.

"This was our home. Some other little houses used to be around, but they were damaged in a fire. It never spread to our house, but we had a shed, and that went. I bought the land and the cottage a few years back. I wanted to preserve the memory of the home my mother created."

"That's beautiful. All of this? You bought the whole place?"

"Yeah. Back then we used to pretend it belonged to us.

Like one big playground full of adventure. The cottage was our base, the meadows, the river and caves by the creek—a different adventure for different days."

"That sounds amazing."

"It was. Ma was amazing. She never once allowed us to slip into sorrow over what we lost. The house we lost should feel like home, but maybe it's because I felt like I grew up and became who I was here. Even when she wasn't around. She left the magic behind."

"Magic," I breathe.

"Magic. Emelia, today I want you to forget everything. All the bad parts. When we take the next step, I want you to leave everything that happened back in L.A. It's not going anywhere, but we can leave it all behind for a day and enjoy being a couple. I can be your husband, and you can be my wife." He lifts my hands and kisses my knuckles. "Can you do that?"

"I can. I can do it."

"Great. So, wife... I'm gonna cook you lunch."

I giggle. I can't imagine him making a sandwich, let alone cook. "You're gonna cook? You? *Boss?*" I laugh. I can't believe I'm laughing.

"Yeah, me, Mrs. Boss."

"And we have food here?"

"We do. I have a custodian. I let him know we were coming by, and he got everything we need for today."

It sounds great. I haven't seen much yet, but I wish we could stay longer.

"Okay, I'm looking forward to seeing you cook."

"I promise you the best meal you've ever had." He intertwines our fingers and leads me toward the house.

Massimo was right. He made me the best meal I've ever had.

Steak. I've had some amazing steak in my life, but his was definitely the best, and the best meal too. He made me eat my words and impressed me further with an afternoon filled with talking and laughing.

I couldn't believe that we spent the afternoon in such a way.

To think that I might not have been here at all if he hadn't saved me yesterday hurts. But I'm pretending that this is our life. In this version of us, we escape here for a break. We live in the gorgeous mansion on the beach and come here when we need a breather. In this version of us, he's been listening to me talk about art and Florence and what I would be learning at the Accademia.

In this version of us, I look at him and get lost in the beauty of him inside and out. I like it. It feels like this could be our future.

Today it is.

It starts to get dark, which saddens me because I know tomorrow we'll have to leave and return to the real world.

We clear the table and unpack our stuff to get comfortable for the night. We didn't bring a lot. Just enough to change our clothes. It all fit in a carry-on.

"One more thing to do before the sun goes down," he says, tugging on my hand.

"What? What are we doing?"

"You'll see. This is the highlight of this trip."

I'm intrigued to find out what it is because everything about this trip so far has been striking.

Taking my hand again, he leads me away. We walk across the meadow and down to the river. I tense when I see a little rowboat as memories of yesterday come rushing back to me. I don't know how I managed to stay alive when the boat capsized. It was the most horrible feeling. A moment of doom and helplessness in which I knew I wouldn't be able to save myself.

"Are we going inside the boat?" I ask because it sure looks like we're heading that way.

He smiles and slips his arm around me. "We are, but don't worry. You'll be in this boat with me, and we're going on the river. It's a lot calmer than the sea. Trust me, I won't let anything happen to you."

I believe him, so I nod. As we step into the boat, I hold onto his hand for dear life.

"Sit, you'll be okay," he promises.

I carefully lower to sit. The boat feels sturdy. He sits, too, and releases the boat from the dock. He rolls his sleeves up his thick forearms, and we set off down the river. As he rows with the oars, I see exactly how it's supposed to be done.

It's vastly different from what I did yesterday.

He rows with strength and surety. He makes it look easy. He chuckles when he sees me watching.

"You make it look like it's nothing."

"Trust me, it's not nothing. What you're looking at is years of practice and definitely not easy on the sea. When my father taught me to fish, we'd either use the rowboat or sailboat. He preferred rowboats, though, because it doesn't disrupt the water. If you want to catch the best fish, you do the least thing possible to blend in."

"Really?"

"Yes. I can't refute his claim, since he's always been right. That's why I had the rowboat."

"I'm sorry I lost your boat," I say, raising my shoulders.

"Don't worry about it. It wasn't even a thought. I'm just glad you're okay and here. Not anywhere else."

Dead or alive. Although I think if Vlad had gotten me, my life would be worse than death.

"Here...this is where it happens." He looks around as we drift deeper into the woods. It gets darker suddenly because the trees enclose the area.

"What?" I ask.

"You'll see, but I suspect you'll see more than I do. My mom used to bring me and my brothers out here. Every time we came, she saw something different. I guess that's the way artists think."

I smile at that. I'm about to say something when I see it. A flow of pink light ahead of us.

It gets brighter and brighter as we approach, and I wonder what it could be.

Moments later, I get my answer when I see a flock of flamingos resting on either side of the riverbank. There are so many that the color they create together against the setting sunlight looks like a glow of pink light.

It's not long before I'm transported into a beautiful fantasy.

"Oh my God... This is beautiful," I breathe. I can't resist the smile that fills my face and the warmth that covers my heart.

"Yeah. It is." Massimo nods. "What do you see?"

"All kinds of things."

"Tell me."

I'm touched that he wants to hear about the creativity that sparks my mind.

As I talk, it feels like sharing pieces of my soul.

With him.

CHAPTER FORTY-THREE

MASSIMO

I listened to her talk.

All day, I've found the sound of her voice soothing. Hearing her talk about art and what she sees when she looks at the beautiful surroundings I shared with my mother calmed my soul.

I'm grateful we took this trip. I needed it.

Night falls, and the pink light fades. The moonlight and stars take over the night, and we head back.

I wouldn't normally be out so late on the river because the woods can attract all kinds of people. Today was an exception. There's only one person who knows we're here, and that's Darius, my custodian.

I didn't even tell Pa.

I wanted today to be about Emelia and me, and I want tonight to be about us too.

We get back to the riverbank, and I help her get out of the boat. I never expected it to start raining. It does when we're halfway back to the cottage, and by the time we reach the door, it's pouring. We run back inside, soaked. I'm so wet my clothes cling to me and my hair slicks down my face.

Emelia, on the other hand, looks like an erotic mermaid with her slick, wet hair and her white tank top clinging to her breasts. Completely see-through. Her rose-tipped nipples press against the fabric of her clothes, begging to be sucked, and the flowery scent of her arousal hardens my cock.

She sees me looking at her, and I'm pleased when she doesn't try to hide from me.

Instead, she steps forward with a seductive look in her eyes that's sexy as fuck.

She tugs on the edge of my shirt, pulling it from the waistband of my pants.

"Be careful, Princesca. You keep looking at me like that, and there's only one thing we'll be doing tonight."

"As long as we don't just do it once." She smiles and I cup her beautiful, beautiful face.

"When have I ever fucked you just once?"

She shakes her head. "Never. I just don't want us to start tonight."

"We won't," I promise before I steal her next words with a kiss. I taste her sweetness. I want it all. I want her and everything that makes her her.

I run my fingers down her neck and over her elegant shoulders, trying to commit the feel of her to memory. When she tugs on my shirt again, the buttons pop and clatter on the floorboards.

When her fingers touch the bare skin on my abs, I know we won't make it upstairs to the bedroom.

I move us into the kitchen and practically tear off her top and bra, leaving her in the little skirt that looks sexy as hell right now with her breasts on show and her hair wet.

Shoving everything off the breakfast table, I pick her up and set her down like a rare, exotic meal I'm getting ready to feast on. *She is.*

She absolutely fucking is to me.

"Spread your legs wide for me, Mrs. D'Agostino. Let me see your pretty pussy."

This woman has changed into one sexy goddess who'll have me eating out of the palms of her hands if I'm not careful. When she gives me that lascivious smile again and spreads her legs, I nearly embarrass myself and blow my load.

"With pleasure, Mr. D'Agostino," the goddess says, then goes one step further by holding open her pussy lips for me.

Holy fuck.

Lust wipes my brain clean of everything. Need makes me greedy, *selfish*, so I dive in and feast on my girl. My wife.

I lick over the sweet bud of her clit, listening to her moans and groans of wild pleasure. All from what I'm doing to her. *Me.* I have her coming undone in my arms, and she knows I want her. I see it as she comes and her sweet nectar flows into my mouth. The knowledge that I want her shines in her eyes. The look intensifies as I drink and take everything until there's nothing left.

With her juice on my lips, I kiss her so she can taste herself and she moans into my mouth.

I'll have to play with her breasts later. I need to be inside her. I've been eager to get back in there. I need her now.

Quickly, I strip out of my clothes, take my cock, and slide into her deliciously wet opening.

She gasps, setting her hands behind her on the table to take me. I hold her still to make sure she doesn't slide around, because I'm owning this pussy again tonight. Fuck damn, she feels so good. The sensation of being inside her heightens with this new sense of understanding that's between us.

"Massimo...ahhh..." she moans.

"I'm going to make you feel good," I promise and start to fuck her.

My mouth falls open and her eyes go wide, pleasure filling every inch of her face.

Infernal heat cascades over me, making me drive into her harder, faster, *furious*. Fuck.

My balls tighten painfully in response to the squeeze of her walls around my length. I try to hold on and control my movements so I can last longer, but she feels too good. Everything about her feels too good.

Mercilessly, I pound into her until I reach my limit and my climax comes at the same time as hers. The table shakes, scratching against the floor as I blow into her and she screams. It's the most glorious sound I've ever heard, yet I want to hear it again before the sun comes up.

I pull out of her, pick her up, and carry her upstairs where we fall into that cycle we got lost in nights ago.

We don't sleep; we just indulge on each other. As the sun rises, I watch her as that feeling overwhelms me again. I see her. I see who she is, and I don't feel scared anymore by what I feel for her.

The sun bathes her in its bright light as her misty gray-colored eyes stare back at me.

Suddenly I get it. I get love. I understand the risk and what my father meant when he said he carried my mother in his heart.

That's where Emelia is for me. She found her way there all by herself, found the key and unlocked the door to a cold heart that's been closed ever since that day I found my mother in the river.

"I see you," Emelia says, touching my face.

"Because...I love you," I answer. It feels so easy to say.

Shock suffuses her pretty face and her eyes go wide. She looks at me in disbelief at first. Soft strands of silk fall onto the pillow as she straightens and eases herself up onto her elbows to stare at me, lips parted.

"I love you, too," she replies, and I swear to God they're the best four words I've ever heard.

I take her hand, the one wearing the two rings I gave her, and kiss her ring finger.

As I do, I realize that if I love her the way I do, I have to change things. If I make it through this threat her father and Vlad pose, I need to make changes.

I want to.

The minute we got back home, reality caught up with us. A call from Pa summoning me to an emergency Syndicate meeting heralded that things were about to change big time.

Riccardo would be in attendance. He made contact on receipt of the numerous messages left for him and agreed to come in for us to speak to him. I don't understand how these people work. If I'd gotten that call, I would have tracked his ass and killed him. Maybe they did track him, but they still want him to come in.

I left Emelia almost as soon as we stepped into the house. I'm here now, at the high-rise building where the Syndicate meetings are held.

The whole group is here. Everyone except Riccardo.

He's late.

Riccardo is now close to an hour late.

Pa and I have just gone into the lobby to get coffee and to talk between ourselves.

"I don't think he's coming, Pa. This is suspicious as fuck," I point out.

"I know. And I agree, but this is their way. Talking out shit first while God knows what the fuck's happening. Maybe I'm just being paranoid. The enforcers and soldiers are on high alert in case he tries anything."

"Pa, this is shit. We've been here for an hour. He's not coming. We know what he's like. This isn't his style. He wouldn't be late," I say with insistence.

"I'm gonna talk to Phillipe," Pa says and leaves me.

I grab a cappuccino from the coffee machine and sip on it. I need something to keep my mind occupied. I hate being in a risky situation where I have to trust people who aren't part of my team. This right here is exactly that. I don't know these people, and I'm not really one of them yet. Everything has been spoon fed to me. I understand there are reasons for that. They have an old-school process they've been following since the dawn of time, but fuck, emergencies are emergencies. I don't think they've faced a situation in which one of their members has gone rogue.

A little ticking noise makes me look over my shoulder. It's like a clock or some sort of timer that just switched on. It's coming from the meeting room. When it gets louder, someone asks what the sound is, then panic flies through me when I realize what it truly is.

A bomb!

As soon as the thought enters my mind, an explosion rocks me and I find myself flying backwards. My body slams hard into the wall. So hard I feel broken. Something stabs through my stomach. I open my mouth to call for Pa, but darkness blurs my vision.

I must have blacked out for a few seconds. When I come to, I look around and see the devastation before me. One whole wall is gone, and fire is burning around me. The meeting room is...it's gone. It's fucking gone.

Pa...no!

Terror makes me try to lift my body. The pain that courses through me as I try to move is excruciating. I look down and see one of the spikes from the wall impaling my side. Pain shoots through my body. There're shards of glass embedded in my arms and legs. Smoke and dust are everywhere.

A bomb.

A bomb went off. Where's Pa? Where is my father? I didn't see which way he went to find Phillipe.

I try to get up and barely manage it. I need to see where Pa went. I pray it wasn't the meeting room. I try to remember if Phillipe was inside. The men had dispersed to take a break from waiting. I was talking to Pa and Levka, one of the Bratva leaders, before we came out here. I can't remember if Phillipe was inside the meeting room, and I don't know what direction Pa turned when he left me.

I take a few steps forward, but footsteps crunching against glass cause me to turn my attention to the corridor on my left.

A shadowed figure emerges from the dust with a smile on his face.

The devil looks at me with pale blue eyes, exactly the way he did on the day of my mother's funeral. Riccardo hasn't changed one damn bit. Maybe there is just one thing, though: he looks more powerful than ever before.

"Well, look at this. My, my, my, how the tables have turned the shift of power back to me," he gloats.

I open my mouth to speak, but blood trickles down the side of my chin.

"Motherfucker, you did this. Where is my father?" My

voice shakes, and so does my body. I try to lunge for him, but I can't. I can barely move, so I stumble.

He raises his gun and cocks the hammer. "You piece of shit. You thought you had me. Threatening me with the Syndicate. Where the fuck are they now? When you're gone, I'll be the last man standing, and I'll take back everything you took from me, including my daughter."

"You aren't getting my girl. You aren't selling my girl, you motherfucking dog. You'll have to tie me up to beat me. You're a poor excuse for a father." Listen to me talk. I wouldn't even be able to draw my gun quickly enough to point it at him before he ends me.

My vision is already starting to flicker as if I'm about to black out.

I can't. I have to kill him. Find Pa and get Emelia.

"All talk, no action. I'm bored now." He fires the bullet, but something slams into me, knocking me to the ground again. At the same time, another bullet echoes almost simultaneously.

Riccardo shouts, and I manage to shuffle to see that it was Pa who slammed into me and he's been hit. Riccardo got him straight in his stomach. Blood is seeping through his white shirt.

"Get out of here," Pa says to me.

"No," I rasp, holding him. "No, Pa. Come, let's go."

"No one is leaving!" Riccardo roars, holding his arm.

Fuck. The fucking bullet seemed to have hit the top of his shoulder. It's bleeding and he's holding it, but he doesn't seem fazed.

Pa's hand shakes as he tries to feel for his gun. He dropped it. I can see it, but I hold him because I can feel him slipping away from me. His body feels limp, like he's trying to hold on but is failing.

"Fools," Riccardo laughs. "The two of you. Giacomo, you look as shocked as Sariah did that night when I laid down the law."

Pa and I both snap our gazes to him at the mention of my mother's name.

What is he talking about?

"What? What are you saying to me?" Pa asks.

"The week before she died, I made one last attempt to get her back. I told her if she slept with me, I'd make sure you got back in with the Syndicate. Your family would be taken care of. No more poverty. She did. She slept with me to save you, but I wanted more. I met her on the cliff and informed her of the new terms of our arrangement." He smiles wide. My head grows light. I almost know what he's going to say next. I know even before he says it. "I wanted her to come with me and be mine. But she chose poverty over me. She still chose *you*, Giacomo. I couldn't believe it, so I threw her off the cliff."

There...

That's it.

That's what I've known deep down all these long years.

I sensed it. Every time I saw this man after my mother's death, I sensed that he had something to do with her death.

He did.

Pa shouts, crying out. I can't hear what he's saying, though. I can barely see through the fucking tears that have welled up in my eyes.

In my mind I see Ma. Her eyes. That wide, terrified expression on her face. I was right. She was crying out from beyond the grave. Calling to me, screaming out to me for justice.

Riccardo killed my mother.

"You bastard," Pa says. He feels cold in my arms.

"Yes, I am."

"You won't get away with this."

"Looks like he already has," a voice says across from us. When Andreas steps into view, shock slams into my chest.

"*Andreas*," I gasp in utter disbelief.

Pa shakes his head. "No, Riccardo. You didn't turn my son against me."

"No, Pa. He didn't turn your son against you. You did that all on your own." Andreas looks from me to Pa. Riccardo smiles wide. "I worked hard. I worked so damn hard to get the business. Day and night. And who got the credit? Massimo. I push it aside and continue to work tirelessly day and night, and who gets to be boss? Massimo. Not me."

"So you betray us because I chose Massimo. I am your father!" Pa grits, sounding like he's talking with his last breath.

"No," Riccardo says, straightening up. "You aren't. You aren't his father. I am."

I don't know how many shocks I can take in this one spell of shit. I don't know what door I walked through that landed me in this dimension. This can't be real. None of it. None of this shit is real.

It can't be.

"It's not true."

"But it is," Andreas answers. "And now I'll get everything."

"How could you—" Pa doesn't get to finish. Riccardo fires a bullet straight into his head, and as my father's blood splatters all over me, a piece of me dies.

Inside, I'm screaming and shouting. The sound doesn't escape, though. I tremble and quiver from deep within, unable to believe that I'm holding my father dead in my arms.

Pa...

"I have an idea for this one," Riccardo says. "He said I'd have to tie him up to beat him. Let's do that."

Andreas lunges at me. I try to block his moves, but I'm already too weak. He gets on top of both Pa and me then hits my temple hard twice with the back of his gun.

Powerless, helpless, useless. I go down.

Emelia is my last thought. They're going to take her. I promised I'd protect her. I can't.

Darkness surrounds me.

CHAPTER FORTY-FOUR

EMELIA

I'm starting to worry.

Massimo has been gone for hours, and I'm on edge again. Like a ghost, I roam the house from one room to the next trying to calm myself and find something to do to distract myself.

Painting usually does that for me, but I can't even think of what I might paint to take my mind away.

That has never happened. I've never been in a situation before that painting couldn't fix.

This is a first.

Maybe it's because I'm about to lose another parent. One who is already dead to me in my heart.

The other night as I read that contract, all the love I had for my father died. It faded into the ether. I couldn't believe how truly despicable he was.

I just wish Massimo was here.

The place is heavily guarded. Guards were stationed at the

front door when we got back this morning.

I'm supposed to be safe here, but to me there's nowhere safer than with him.

It's strange how that happened. Oh so strange.

Deciding to go see how Priscilla is doing, I make my way downstairs. Earlier, she invited me to bake cookies with her, but I wasn't feeling up to it. I'll gladly do it now to take my mind off what's happening.

I enter the kitchen and stop in my tracks by the door when my gaze lands on Vlad sitting at the breakfast table, eating cookies.

Oh my God… What is he doing here? *He's inside the house.*

His appearance gets to me the same as it did the night I first met him at the charity ball.

Little did I know then what was in store for me.

He looks up at me and smiles.

"These are really good. Want one? I'd love to feed it to you," he says, holding out a cookie for me to take.

Panic makes me back away to run, but I stumble into a wall. I turn to see Andreas, and relief washes over me.

"Andreas, Vlad is inside the kitchen," I say, grabbing his shirt. My hands are shaking so much I can't stop them.

"Now, now, Emelia, don't you worry. You see, he got inside the kitchen because I let him in. We arrived in the same car and stopped for a bite to eat," he explains with a smile and my jaw drops.

I release my hold on his shirt and backpedal. He walks toward me as I back right into the kitchen, right into danger.

I don't know what he's saying. He's Massimo's brother. He must know that Vlad is a dangerous man.

As I take in the sinister expression on his face, it dawns on me.

Of course... He does know Vlad is a dangerous man. This is something else.

"What's going on here?" I look from Vlad to Andreas and shake my head.

"I'm going to tell you a very interesting story about secrets, and I'm gonna give you the major spoiler."

"Is the spoiler that you betrayed your family?" I throw back. I can't believe this. Not at all.

"No, it's not that. That's not news since I've always been the odd one out. There's a reason for that. The reason is, they're my half-brothers, and the spoiler is...you and I have a lot in common. Like how we have the same father."

I gasp and bring my hand up to my heart.

"What!" I don't understand.

"Ready for the story?"

"I am," Vlad says with a smile. "Nothing like a juicy piece of news to get the blood going."

"I like this guy," Andreas states, and Vlad tips his head.

"Thanks. It's great to be appreciated." His eyes lock with mine, and a shiver runs down my spine. I only look away when Andreas clears his throat.

"Ready for the story, *Princesca?*" he asks with emphasis on the last word. "That's what Massimo calls you, isn't it?"

I stare back at the man claiming to be my brother. Yes, indeed, I'm ready to hear the story. I'm fucking ready to hear it. Another secret revealed.

"Tell me," I answer.

"It started with the death of my grandfather. That's what started this whole thing. The man I thought was my father doesn't favor tradition in the least. Or I'd be boss and king of the empire, not Massimo," he says with a chuckle, and I remember my thoughts about him that night at the dinner. He didn't look happy when Massimo received his ring and everyone raised their glass to accept him as the new leader. "When I was told Massimo was chosen, it knocked me. In my life, when shit happens, I've always sought the company of my mother's belongings. That day, I went searching through her stuff and found a journal I don't think she wanted anyone to find. It carried her secrets. There I learned that she was with your father before Giacomo D'Agostino. She found out she was pregnant with me after she got together with him and never told him I wasn't his. She couldn't bring herself to ruin the relationship she'd always wanted."

I start to shake. I don't want to believe it. I want to tell myself it's a lie, but I know it's not. It feels like the truth.

"I went to your father, and we got tested. The tests confirmed he was my father. Then we planned. I lived a hard life I shouldn't have because she decided to stay with Giacomo D'Agostino. You had everything, while I had to go through shit my other brothers didn't have to go through because I was the eldest. I took care of everything. The last blow was Pa giving Massimo the empire. And to spit in my face further, Massimo chose Tristan to be part of the Syndicate, not me."

"So, you want to wipe them out? How could you be so cruel?" I seethe.

He grabs my face and squeezes hard. "Don't talk about things you don't understand. You haven't lived my life. You don't know me, and you don't want to. I have no desire to know you either. I accepted some hard truths when I found out my mother didn't kill herself, but it was your father, *my father*, who threw her off a cliff, all because she chose Giacomo D'Agostino. I can accept your death too."

My mouth falls open, and I stare at him wide eyed.

My God... I can't believe what I'm hearing. My father is indeed evil, but how can Andreas just accept it?

"How can you be okay with that?"

"I never said I was. I said I *accept* it. I loved my mother to no end. I hate her choices, but my love for her will always be there." His jaw tightens. "I wanted to kill your father when I realized it was him who killed her. I wanted to end him. But it would achieve nothing for me. She is dead and gone, and I'm still here. There are things I want. Things I'm owed. Things only he can give me. You do what you have to do, *sis*, to get what you want. You suck up shit feelings of remorse and anger, push them aside, and don't cut off your nose to spite your face. That is what I'm doing."

"Let go of me! Get your hands off me!" I cry, trying to free myself from his grasp.

"No, I'm afraid I can't do that. You're needed as payment. Part of the grand plan. There's one more contract for you to sign. Cross me, and you'll end up like her," he jeers, flipping me around.

He forces me to walk around the counter. I scream when I see Priscilla lying on the ground in a pool of blood. Bullet holes riddle her body.

I scream and cry, shaking my head.

"No! How could you? How could you do this to her?"

"Save your tears, Emelia D'Agostino. There's worse to come. Wait until you see what I did to Massimo."

Terror claws its way through me when he laughs, crude and hard.

I'm taken away, taken off the property, and no one says anything. Of course, they wouldn't. I'm with Andreas. Massimo's brother, one of the most trusted people who could come and go as they please.

Vlad disguises himself with a large pair of Oakleys and a hooded sweatshirt. He slips into the back of the black sedan quite comfortably. Any of the guards or soldiers who saw him wouldn't have seen his face properly, but again, they wouldn't dare question Andreas.

When Andreas tells the men at the gate that Massimo asked him to take me to see him, no one questions him. It makes sense that I would be with his brother. That he got his older brother to escort me with *his guard*.

I keep wondering where the guards on surveillance are. Who's watching? Then it hits me that Andreas could have easily done something to stop anyone from seeing what he was up to. That's the only thing that makes sense. It will only be when someone discovers Priscilla's body in the kitchen that they'll know. Even then, they'll never guess that Andreas could have killed her.

I'm still in shock. People I get close to keep dying. I can't take it anymore. What will I do if something happens to Massimo?

That's why I keep quiet as Andreas leads me away. I'm too afraid to breathe.

The leverage they have over me is death. Not to me. No, they have plans for little old me, so I mustn't die. They're threatening to kill Massimo. I don't know if they even have him, but I comply because I can't go on what I don't know. I have to take this risk, throw myself in harm's way to make sure nothing happens to him.

We drive off the property easily. I'm quiet for the whole journey, trembling under Vlad's creepy stare as he looks at me the whole time.

I endure two hours of his leer. Him looking at me, licking his lips as he stares at my breasts, undressing me with his eyes. He says nothing the whole time. It's when we pull up outside the entrance of an old mine shaft that he suddenly grabs my arm and pulls me to him so he can smell my hair.

"I'm going to have so much fun with you, my pretty," he says, licking my ear. "I will fuck you all six ways to Sunday on your knees. I'll fuck every hole in your body and make sure that pretty little mouth of yours is always full of my cock, and whoever else I tell you to suck."

I shake and try to hold back tears.

It's him who practically drags me out of the car. We're near the mountains, but I don't know exactly where we are. There's a sign ahead saying *Danger Keep Out*, yet they both usher me inside the mouth of the cave.

While the outside of the cave looks like it should be deserted, I see that a whole operation is set up inside. We walk through a metal door. There are men everywhere. Some sitting at computers, others milling about. Everything so organized. They look like they've been in this hideout for months.

I'm led up a set of stairs and into an office space. The man who wears the face of my father stands by a bookcase and turns around to look at me.

When he smiles, I shake my head at him.

"Welcome, my daughter. I told you I was working on a way to get you back. Good news, here you are," he declares.

"You evil bastard!" I scream. "I can't believe this is you. What happened to you?"

He laughs. "Nothing, my child. Nothing happened to me. I haven't changed one damn bit. I guess maybe I was different when it came to you. But needs must. Being successful means knowing when you have to make certain sacrifices to increase wealth," he explains, as if that's a good enough explanation.

"So, you wanted to sell me to this madman," I snap.

Vlad tightens his hold on me. "Watch it, girlie. You don't

know who the fuck you're dealing with. I'll cut out your tongue and feed it to you," Vlad threatens.

Andreas chuckles and walks inside to grab a drink of scotch.

"Emelia, you will do as I say. I'm lucky to have found a buyer for you who won't mind that you've been defiled by that scum," Dad says, and my heart squeezes. "I trust you've met your brother," he adds, as if we're talking about the weather.

Andreas tips his head and knocks back his drink.

When I don't answer, Dad pulls out a contract from an envelope on the desk and holds it up. When Vlad marches me over to him, I see it's a copy of the contract Massimo showed me the other night.

A contract for the sale of me, my body, my assets, my inheritance. Everything linked to me.

"I'm not signing anything," I bark. Disgust churns my stomach as I recall the contract's wording.

"You will sign it," Dad says with confidence.

I've wondered how he thought he was going to get me to sign it in the first place. That was what was supposed to happen to me if Massimo hadn't come along.

"No, I won't. You can't do this to me. I'm not a thing." Déjà vu. I've said this before several times. It's happening again. "I'm married."

"We'll see about that. Give her to me. We'll see what she says after she sees what I've done to her *husband*," Dad states.

There's a difference about him that's terrifying. Even his voice sounds different.

Vlad hands me over to Dad, who takes hold of my arm roughly. We walk through another door, and I see an open space that looks like an area where people used to work in the mines.

There's a pit. Dad takes me to the steps leading into the

pit, and I gasp when I see what's down below. It's Massimo. He's attached to two metal poles with chains around his wrists. He's shirtless, but there's so much blood on his chest that it covers all his tattoos. He looks like he's been beaten near death. His face is battered and bruised.

"Massimo said I had to tie him up to beat him. That's true," Dad states. "I did, but I did it in a more clever way. Everyone has a price, my girl. I got a man he trusted with his life and his empire to betray him. His own brother, who was so neglected and overlooked. That is the only way you can get to a man like that. Full of hate and rage it almost makes him invincible. *Almost and never.* You will sign the contract because he is your price."

I turn my head and look at Dad. He nods, and I burst into tears.

"If you don't sign, I'll kill him. Sign, and he might have a chance if we let him go."

He releases me, and I run down to Massimo.

"Massimo!" I cry.

He lifts his bloodied head and his eyes widen at the sight of me.

"No, you can't be here," he manages.

I touch his face. Blood stains my hands. "I'm so sorry."

"I'm sorry I couldn't protect you, Princess. I love you."

"I love you too," I breathe. I didn't know that when he left this morning, it was going to be the last morning we'd spend together. I won't let him die. I won't allow him to suffer if I can do anything about it.

"I—" He cries out when a whip lands hard across his back.

I scream, shaking my head vigorously when I look up and see Vlad behind him getting ready to strike him again.

Another powerful blow lands on Massimo's back, causing his knees to buckle. Dad laughs and comes closer.

Vlad strikes Massimo again, and again, and again.

My breath stills. I feel like I might fade away.

"Want it to stop?" Dad asks. "He's strong, but even he has a limit."

"I'll sign," I answer weakly.

Dad makes a mockery of me when he places his hand to his ear and leans in closer, pretending he can't hear me.

Massimo gets another hit and cries out loud.

"What was that, Emelia?" Dad says.

"I'll sign!" I scream. Dad takes my arm again.

With a bright smile on his face, he takes me away from my love. I look back at Massimo.

That's the last time I'll see him. The last time I'll tell him I love him.

The last time I'll feel love for anybody.

My father leads me away to the fate that awaits.

Death.

It can only be that. I'll be sold to a madman who will kill me when he decides he wants my life to be over.

CHAPTER FORTY-FIVE

MASSIMO

At least I got to see her again.
One more time.
I'll take that as my final memory. Her beautiful face. Her beautiful tear-stained face and misty, gray-colored eyes. Love filling those eyes for me as she told me she loved me. I can't believe I fought so hard not to fall for her. I tried my best not to love her.
I kept seeing her as the enemy's daughter. She was never that. Who she is and what she is was right there in front of me the whole time. The woman I love. The girl of my dreams. They're the same person.
And no more.
That was it, the last. Riccardo and Vlad will kill me here. No matter what shit they promise to her, they will kill me here.
Why? Because they had to tie me up to beat me.
I can't begin to process Andreas' betrayal. I won't waste

time on it. I knew he would be angry that Pa didn't choose him to take over as boss, but I never expected this. He stood there and allowed Riccardo to kill Pa. And he would have known that the devil was responsible for our mother's death.

That makes him dead to me.

A crude laugh makes me lift my head. I see Vlad's face looming before me.

"Motherfucker," I hiss, and he laughs louder.

"Look at you thinking you're still king. You aren't," Vlad taunts. "You people couldn't kill me the first time, and you definitely won't now."

"How the hell did you escape the first time?" I can barely talk, but fuck, do I ever want the answer to that.

"We Russian men are tough. But sometimes you have to lose to gain," he says, rolling up the sleeve on his left arm.

My eyes narrow when he reveals a robotic arm and smiles. His hand looks normal, but the rest is titanium similar to what you'd see in a *Terminator* movie.

"In the Circle of Shadows, we never give up on our own. The Circle found me, patched me up, and turned me into a freaking cyborg. Making me stronger than ever before." He laughs as he glares at me. "I'm going to have fun torturing you to death, then I'm going to have fun fucking your wife to death. Then I'm going to have fun with all the wealth we currently own. Diamonds and money. *Power*."

"Fuck you," I snarl.

He sends a kick to my midsection. I double over, pulling against the chains on my wrists.

"I'd love to see you try and fuck me, bastard dog. Come and try it. Make my day," he jeers. He moves forward and pulls a knife from his pocket. "You people can't leave well enough alone. Always taking what isn't yours. This is the second time you people have done it to me."

Again, he's talking about Alyssa. Alyssa and Emelia, both angels. My brother's love and then my girl. *What will he do to Emelia?*

"Neither of them belonged to you. Not Alyssa, and not Emelia."

"Wrong, always wrong, and I'll get to prove it to your dead body every time I fuck your girl. The same way I fucked Alyssa until she couldn't even move." Again, he laughs.

He inches closer and lowers his head to me but stops short when something pierces through his chest.

I look and see the silver tip of an arrow poking out with blood on it.

Before he can grab his chest, another arrow pierces through him in the same spot, and when I lift my head higher, I see Tristan leaping down into the pit. He launches himself into the air, folding into a somersault, and as he comes out of it, he pulls two knives out at either side of his legs and stabs Vlad right in his heart.

Seconds, that's how long it took to have the demon on his knees with blood pouring from his body. He looks up at my brother with the same disbelief I do because I can't believe the stunt I just saw him pull off. I can't believe he found me. He found me, and he brought company.

Dominic and a team of men storm the platform above. My gaze lands on Manni, who I nearly killed only days ago and threw off my property. The soldiers rush in with them. I hear bullets flying as my brothers and my men take down the bastards who are working for Riccardo and Vlad.

But my eyes are locked on the scene before me of Vlad bleeding out.

"You fucker," he says to Tristan.

"No, it's you. This time, I'm going to make sure I kill you fucking dead. This is for my wife. You will not do the same to

Emelia," Tristan cries, and with that, he uses those same knives he plunged deep in Vlad's body and cuts his head off his miserable body.

Both head and body fall to the ground in a bloody heap.

Tristan spares him no time. He comes straight to me and shoots off the chains binding my wrists.

Dominic joins him, and together they steady me as I stumble upon release.

"Guys," I rasp, feeling the deepest gratitude. "Thank you." I look from one to the other.

Tristan nods. Dominic looks worried at my appearance.

"How the hell did you find me?" I ask.

"The ring," Dominic says. "There's a tracker on it. Pa had it installed for safety. The guards alerted us after..." His voice trails off.

"After what?" I ask.

"Priscilla... She's...dead. And we think something's going on with Andreas. He's being used. He took Emelia. And there was a man with him."

I don't know how I can tell them this truth, but I have to.

"No, he's working with them."

Both look shocked.

"What?" Tristan says, shaking his head.

"Andreas is working with them."

"Fuck."

"Where's Pa, Massimo?" Dominic asks, ignoring what I confirmed about Andreas.

It's then that Tristan focuses on me.

I shake my head. "Riccardo killed him. There's a lot to tell you, but I have to get Emelia."

Riccardo has her.

"Can you walk?" Tristan asks.

"I can walk," I answer, baring my teeth. I *will* walk.

I can't allow that bastard to walk out of this place with my girl and sell her to the next bidder. She's my wife.

I will die trying to get her back. Then I'm going after Andreas.

He has a lot to answer for.

CHAPTER FORTY-SIX

EMELIA

I signed the contract.

One more contract of sale. This time as I sign, all traces of humanity leave me.

Dad watches in excitement. Of course he would. He's going to be a rich man.

He must be on cloud nine.

Thirty million just for selling me, and all the Syndicate's wealth. I heard him talking to someone on the phone. I don't know who it was, but they sounded like they were in on it. On this grand scheme of shit.

"Wonderful. My dear girl. I never knew you'd be such an asset to me," Dad says.

"I don't know how you could do this to me. How were you going to get me to sign this before? I was supposed to go to Florence. What would have happened there?" I really want to know.

"Your uncle was going to take care of it."

"How?" I push.

"By threatening to kill you. Getting you to Florence was the easy part. You were so excited to go. At least you would have gotten to go to school." He raises his palms and shrugs.

"My God. You are truly despicable. I don't know you. I don't know who you are. What else did you do, Dad?" I ask, narrowing my eyes. I have questions. *Questions* I want answers to before I'm taken away and there's no one left to give them to me.

"I did many things, Emelia."

"Were you responsible for Jacob's death?" I ask outright. That's the most important question on my mind. "Did you know he was going to die?"

"Emelia, Jacob always had a habit of sticking his nose where it didn't belong. I think he was my toughest kill," he reveals, and a cry falls from my lips.

I'm so stupid. Here I am, asking him if he knew Jacob was going to die when he was the one who killed him.

My God...

"You killed Jacob! Dad, *you*? It was you?"

He actually looks a little sad.

"I prayed at the wedding that he'd keep his mouth shut. I prayed he'd keep his nose out of shit it didn't belong in, but when it comes to you, that kid couldn't see straight. Friendship and love. That was what he had for you. Even when he was warned by your beloved husband to keep out of trouble, that very same night, he went hurtling himself back into trouble's arms. He heard too much. Saw too much when he saw me talking to Vlad. He knew about my plans to wipe out the Syndicate. He had to die."

"You shot him. You killed Jacob."

"Sad... But I had to."

The door flies open, and Andreas rushes in.

"We've got to get out of here," he urges in a hurried voice. "My brothers are here with a team of men. Think we might be outnumbered. Backup won't get here in time."

"Fuck!" Dad snarls. "Where is Vlad?"

"Dead," Andreas answers and Dad's face grows pale. As pale as Andreas'. It's understandable because of who Vlad is.

Vlad's death means that contract of his no longer exists. No promise of thirty million to buy me.

Dad gazes back in disbelief. "Damn it, damn it to hell."

"You go. I'll keep them occupied to give you a head start," Andreas promises.

Dad seethes, grabs me with one hand and his briefcase with the other. Without another word, we leave through the side door leading out to a narrow tunnel.

As he pulls me along, I know Vlad's death means nothing. All this man has done is sell me from one man to the next.

He'll do it again.

He's got his back against the wall and greed running through his veins. It didn't escape me that Dad completely snubbed Andreas' offer to stay behind while we escaped. Without so much as a thank you.

Dad rushes down the tunnel, pulling me along. He's using his bad arm now, which is just as strong as his good one.

When we get to a set of stairs leading up to an even darker tunnel, I try to wrench my hand free of his grasp.

"Let go of me!" I yell, but he takes pleasure in squeezing my hand until it feels like it's about to break. I scream so loud the sound seems to be pouring from my soul.

He's hurting me just like that day back in his office. I was so foolish to ever consider that Massimo and Giacomo were forcing him to do anything. They weren't. That was the first time he showed me his true self, but I failed to see it.

"Stop it, Emelia. Fucking stop it," he snarls, shaking me. I realize he's too strong. I can't fight him.

Fighting him is only going to result in me hurting myself. I glance back at the tunnel we walked down thinking of Massimo, wondering if he made it. I wish I could do something to save myself. I can't, though. I'm too weak.

Ahead, the tunnel is dark. It looks like somewhere we shouldn't be going. Dad stops when we get to a crosscut, confusion filling his face.

He looks from left to right. We both hear a sound, like someone running, and Dad decides to go left.

He pulls me along frantically. When we see a light ahead, he starts running. The worst thing we could ever do in a place like this, where everything is unknown. Dad runs forward on shaky ground as the earth beneath us gives. There's a rail track ahead, with a rusty mining cart with some old ropes attached to it.

Twice we nearly fall over because the earth is moving so much. He's heading to the rusty cart. I think that's a bad idea. The track ahead looks old. Who knows when it was last used or even checked?

"Dad, where are we going?" I cry. "It doesn't look safe."

"Shut the fuck up!" he yells.

Before we can get to the cart, the track we step on breaks. Then we're falling. The briefcase Dad was carrying goes flying past me, and I scream and scream as we go down, certain this is it. I'll die now. But then I'm jerked to a stop and hanging in the air. Dad's still holding me. He's hanging from a rope. A rope so old it looks like it used to be white but is now brown with age and raggedy.

I manage to grab a part of it and hold myself up.

"Come. It won't hold," Dad urges impatiently.

He releases his hold on me and tries to climb up, slowly.

He's right. The rope won't hold. I don't dare look down. Terror has me panting and thinking of pulling myself up as fast as I can. Out of danger. Out of *fear*.

The rope jerks and starts snapping.

Shit, shit, fuck. We're nearly there. So close, but it can't hold the two of us.

Dad stops midway and looks back at me as I try my best to make my way up when the rope gives again. It's our weight. The rope can't hold both of us.

"I'm sorry, Emelia. I can't die here," he says. "I have too many plans."

Before I can process his words, he pulls a knife from his pocket and starts cutting the section of the rope beneath his grasp. The section I am holding onto.

"No, please. Please don't do that," I plead.

He ignores me and continues sawing through the twine.

"Dad, please, no!! Don't kill me," I cry.

A wicked look washes over his face as the twine pulls apart. Just a few more, and I'll fall right to my death. I'll die.

Tears blind me as I look up at the man who's supposed to be my protector. My father. He really is evil incarnate.

I scream when the rope jerks, and now I truly feel like this is my end. I see parts of the rope snap away. Then a roar pierces through me.

Massimo comes launching through the air, hurtling himself at my father. His foot connects with his jaw, snapping his head back with a bone-crunching sound. While Massimo grabs the rope, Dad falls backwards, screaming as he tumbles past me. Falling.

Falling to his death.

At the same time, the rope snaps and I fall too, but Massimo catches me.

With a strangled cry, he lifts me and secures an arm

around me. I don't know where or how he finds the strength, but he manages to lift us both back up onto the platform and move us away from the shaky track.

I throw my arms around him and hold him, crying and shaking.

"I got you. I got you, Emelia," he says, hugging me hard.

"Oh, Massimo," I cry into his chest. I never thought I'd have this moment again, when we'd be holding each other like this. "Thank you so much."

"Don't thank me. God, Emelia." He cups the back of my head and holds me close to him.

Turning my head, I look at the dark abyss my father fell into, and that's when I see Andreas stepping out from the path with his gun aimed at us.

CHAPTER FORTY-SEVEN

MASSIMO

It's not fucking over yet.

Not by a long shot.

I see him too. Andreas. But not quickly enough. My brother managed to pull his gun on me first.

"Stand the fuck up," he demands.

Emelia and I stand. I push her behind me.

"How noble of you. Always thinking of pussy first."

"Fuck you. Fuck you, Andreas, and everything you are. You have no justification for what you've done. I split the empire four ways so we could all be equal."

He shakes his head. "I don't want equality. I wanted it all. I would have had it all, if not for you."

Everything about him shocks me to the core. I wonder how it was I missed these changes in a man I'm supposed to be close to. These changes didn't happen overnight. They existed long before Grandfather died. They would have had to for him to become like this.

"What happened to you? Why didn't you tell me you found out Riccardo was your father?"

"What can I say? I must take after our dearest mother. She kept me a secret in her diary. My origins locked away. I only happened upon it after Grandfather's death. You don't know what it's like to be me, Massimo. So, fuck no to this conversation. Sign over everything: D'Agostinos Inc. and the Syndicate's wealth. Sign over everything to me and I'll let the two of you walk out of here."

That's not happening. I won't do it, and it's not because I'm a selfish bastard. It's because there's no way I trust him to let us go.

I rub my finger over Emelia's hand on my waistband. I'm going to have to hurt her to save her.

"What's it gonna be?" he demands.

Whatever I'm gonna do has to happen now, or it won't at all. He's unstable. His ticket to reach his goals just fell into the abyss of hell, exactly where Riccardo belonged, and now I'm all he's got.

The longer I take to answer, the more agitated he gets. The tic in his jaw is a tell.

On three. I need to move.

One. Two. Three.

I shove Emelia out of the way, and he fires the bullet. Thank fuck I dodge, and she scrambles out of the way and covers herself in the crevice of the cave.

I throw myself on him with the rage of a wild animal spawned from the depths of hell, consumed by the fury over what he's done. I manage to knock the gun out of his hand when I push him to the ground. What follows next is a series of punches between the two of us. Two brothers fighting to the death.

I give my all, blow for fucking blow, and as I do, I unravel any love I had for him and replace it with my last images of my father and every sentimental memory that comes to my mind.

If not for Andreas, Pa would still be here. Not dead. He would have lived a long life, just like Grandfather.

Andreas' hands are as dirty as Riccardo's. Riccardo pulled the trigger, but Andreas might just as well have given him the gun.

I roar as I come down hard on him with my fist until my knuckles are raw and start to bleed.

It's his strength that gives him some leverage. He's always been strong, so when he flips me over and I land on my back, I'm not surprised. But I'm strong, too. My father taught me to be strong. My mother taught me to be stronger.

That's why I'm ready for him when he manages to retrieve his gun. He's gearing up to end me, but that window his movement gives me is an opening to attack. I grab him and flip him back onto the ground. Grab and twist his hand holding the gun, so when he fires the bullet to kill me, he shoots himself instead of me.

The impact is so intense it shakes me. He doesn't make a sound. It's not what I expected. It's as if the pain is too great for him to scream or shout. His eyes go wide, and a whimper leaves his lips.

He's a traitor to our family. A traitor to me. Yet as I stare at him, I see my brother. I see my big brother. The guy who always looked out for me and had my back.

Andreas D'Agostino.

The light leaves his eyes, and he goes too.

Dead.

In this one day, I've watched two people I love die in my arms.

Warm fingers rest on my shoulder, and I look up to see Emelia.

The sound of footsteps approaches, and Tristan and Dominic come into view. They stop in their tracks when they take in the scene of me and Andreas on the ground.

As I look at them, all I know is that everything will be different now.

Our lives will have changed forever.

In just this one day.

The next month flew by within a flicker of an eye and was the hardest I've lived in a long time.

Three funerals occurred: Pa, Andreas, and Priscilla.

Andreas was the hardest because I felt I shouldn't be there.

We decided between us that we wouldn't make people aware of his treachery. Those who knew, knew.

We held a private ceremony for him with just the three of us. Me, Tristan, and Dominic.

Pa had close to a state funeral. People from far and wide came to honor him.

Pa's funeral was hard in another way. A way I can't describe to anyone.

As his body was placed in the earth, I realized how much he meant to me. I looked up to him as a boy and as a man. He was my everything.

Priscilla's was another tough one because of the place she'll always have in my heart. She was a woman who was there for me when I needed a mother.

Hers was the last, closing off last week.

This week is the first clear week I've had. The first time

I've had to stop and think about the things that still don't add up.

There's a lot. A lot about what happened weeks ago that makes no sense. The Syndicate is no more. I'm the last boss left. Everything automatically came to me. I have their lawyers meeting with me left, right, and center to sign this and that or making contact to discuss what I want to do next.

The only thing I've done outside all that was track down Leo, Riccardo's brother. I didn't have to do much to him, though, because my men found him with a bullet in his head. A bullet he put there.

Everyone else in the Balesteri family is aware of the shit Riccardo got up to, and they know to tread softly with me. Since the rest of them seem to have no apparent involvement with the plans Riccardo had, I left them alone. I don't think I'm going to have any trouble with them.

I've put everything else on hold for the moment because there's one thing I need to do first, and I plan to do it later today when Emelia gets back from the stores.

I've been in the sitting room gazing out to the sea. Just thinking.

The door opens, and in walks Candace, the bag on her back she carried weeks ago.

She's been around for the funerals, but I assumed she'd be heading out again. I don't know if this is goodbye again or hello.

"Hey," she says.

"Hi."

"So, I got this job at a school as a teaching assistant. It's a few hours a day. I'm kind of back and I thought I would check on you," she says. "I also thought you might need me here for a little while. I think Priscilla would want me to take care of you. You and Emelia."

I stand up and walk over to her. She gives me a hug, and as I hold her, she feels like a good memory from the past.

"Thank you. I think I do need you."

"Then I'm here for you."

"Means a lot."

"I think my parents would want me to be here too. Maybe there's a reason why the Riccis have always taken care of the D'Agostinos. We work well together."

I smile at that.

"We definitely do."

"I guess I'll go unpack, then." She gives me a nod and leaves.

Emelia will be happy that she's back. Candace was a good friend to her.

Things have definitely not been the same without her and Priscilla around.

An hour later, Emelia arrives and heads out to see me on the terrace.

I decided to do some paperwork out here and enjoy the weather. I'm still cautious about her going out by herself, even with a guard, but I'm gonna have to suck it up and trust that she'll be safe for the next part of my plan.

She went shopping to get some special paintbrushes. The bag is so small it fits in the pocket of her purse. It probably didn't warrant a trip into the city. I understand, though, if she wanted to get out of the house.

"Hi," she bubbles as she reaches me. She plants a kiss on my lips and sits opposite me.

"Hi, Princess. Have fun in town?"

"Yeah. I did. Going to the art shop was nice." She nods with a smile and reaches out to touch my hand. It's the most innocent of touches, but it's a sign she wants me again. The same way I always want her.

We have each other. That's what came out of all of this. My thirst for vengeance sated by my love for her.

I love her, and she loves me, but I know there's something more her heart wants, and she won't be happy until she has it. So, we have a lot to discuss.

"I'm glad you went."

She looks at the documents before me, and the smile on her face recedes.

"Does this mean you'll be busy for the rest of the day?" she asks.

"No, but there are a few things we need to talk about. I think it's time."

"What do you mean?" Worry fills her pretty face.

I pull out a document she'll recognize when I unfold it. It's the contract from our first meeting.

She studies me when she sees it. "The contract."

"Yeah, the contract." I hold it up and she gasps when I tear it down the middle.

"What? What are you doing?"

"That's not how I want you. So, I'm giving you your freedom back, and all that you own. Your family's inheritance, the business and assets now belong to you. It's yours," I say, then hand her an envelope. One more envelope. This one holds good news. "That is a gift from me."

She takes it and opens it. When she pulls the document out and reads through it, her eyes fill with tears of the deepest gratitude.

"Massimo, this is an acceptance to the Accademia. You're sending me to Florence?"

"Isn't that where you were supposed to be? Emelia, you are an incredibly talented artist. I know you missed out on summer school and the first few weeks of the semester, but they're cool with it. I got you covered for however long you want to be there and wherever you want to stay when you go to Florence. You just do what you want. Whatever that is..." I hold her gaze. As happy as she is, she knows by me saying so, where my conversation is heading to. She knows what that means for us.

She presses down on her lips, and her cheeks flush.

"I've never been able to do what I want before," she states.

"Now you can. That means deciding whether or not you want to stay married to me." I pull in a breath. "I'm a mafia boss, and now I'm the Syndicate. I still don't know what that means yet. All I know right now is that when it comes to you and me, I'd start over again if I could. Take it back to nine months ago when I first saw you at the charity ball."

"Would you?" she asks, and I nod. "What would you do?"

"I would ask you out, then we'd date, and I'd ask you to marry me. I would write better vows for you." I focus on her and gaze deep into her eyes so she can see I'm serious. Everything I say next I mean from the bottom of my heart, but she needs to feel it.

"I'd say something like this." I pause. "'I, Massimo D'Agostino, take you, Emelia Balesteri, to be my wife. I promise to be true to you in good times, in sickness and in health. I promise to protect you until the day I die. I will love and honor you all the days of my life, and for all eternity because not even death can keep me away from you.' That is what I would say to you. Because I love you. I would do everything properly because you deserve that."

I truly mean that for her, whether or not she chooses me. We started things backwards.

I can declare her mine all I want, and to me she will always be.

But I want her to choose me.

CHAPTER FORTY-EIGHT

EMELIA

I stare at the beautiful man before me and think of how far we've come and what we experienced together.

So much has happened in the handful of months we've known each other.

We lost our fathers and had terrible secrets revealed.

I can't express how awful I feel when I think of how my father truly damaged him and took away the things that mattered most to him. *Family.* Both his parents were killed at the hand of my father. My father threw his mother off a cliff and shot his father dead.

And yet this man still has love for me.

We exist outside everything. He is it for me. There's only one answer I can give him.

When I smile, he gives me a hopeful look.

"I, Emelia D'Agostino, take you, Massimo D'Agostino, to be my husband. I love you, and I'm staying with you. It means so much to me that you did this." I hold up the letter from the Accademia. "You have no idea how much it means. I worked so hard to get in, and I'm so grateful for the chance to go. But more than that, I'm grateful for you. I want to be with you more than anything else. I promise to be true to you in good times, in sickness and in health. I will love and honor you all the days of my life."

He reaches for me and slips me onto his lap, pressing his forehead to mine.

"You choose me?"

"I choose you, and everything that makes you you." That means I choose this life too.

"You are mine, Emelia D'Agostino."

"I think we should go upstairs now."

I giggle when he lifts me up, pushes aside the documents on the table, and sets me down. As usual, this man never fails to shock me.

"I'm having you here," he declares, shoving my skirt up my thighs. "I'm going to feast on you right here on the table and enjoy making you come over and over again. *Then* we'll go upstairs, and I'll tie you to the bed and have you screaming my name all night."

"I like that plan," I answer, and he kisses me hard.

"Great, now spread your legs for me."

EPILOGUE

EMELIA

Six months later...

"Just feel me, Princess. Feel me and enjoy me. I plan to enjoy you," Massimo whispers against my ear.

His nose brushes mine and he kisses me. Hot, fiery kisses are placed over my cheek, then down my neck.

Against the silky blindfold, all I can do is imagine what his handsome face looks like. Because I can't see him, all my senses are heightened. His touch seems to reach me everywhere. His voice washes over my skin like a gentle caress. His scent tantalizes me. And the feel of him thrills me.

Today is my birthday. This morning we got married, *again*, on the beautiful coast of Sicily. It was just the two of us and the priest, Father De Lucca.

Massimo said the only thing real about our first wedding was the priest. So we got him to marry us again. Here, where we could declare our love and honor for our union.

What I got that I didn't have the first time was the dream and true love's kiss. I had all the emotions, too, that I always imagined for such a special day.

Now we're in the beach house living out another fantasy.

His this time. In it, my wrists are bound to the bed with silk ties and I'm blindfolded so I can feel all the pleasure he wants to give me.

As he kisses his way down my body, I writhe against the silky sheets, cool against my skin, the perfect balance to the fire from his lips.

Just like always, it doesn't take long for me to get lost in him. I do within a few moments as I feel all that he has to give me, all at once.

The wild suckle of my breasts, the intense tasting of my pussy, the luxuriating sensations that make me surrender to one orgasm after another.

I feel amazing, but nothing feels better than his cock inside me. As he sears into me, my body welcomes the thrilling sensation of his thick cock filling my passage.

Pleasure explodes inside me when he starts to fuck me. I writhe against him, hot and wild, arching my back into the bed, the thrill wilder due to the restraints around my wrists. I'm completely and utterly under his spell with every secret part of me screaming his name.

The savage energy storms through my body like liquid fire, and as I come, he does too. Our bodies join together to share the mutual surrender of the unexpected thing that came to claim us, starting from that first moment we saw each other.

It takes a few minutes to climb down from the high, but my brain is still buzzing and reeling with delight.

He pulls out of me and releases the bindings from my hands. The blindfold comes off next, and when I see my handsome prince, I smile.

We kiss, and he pulls me into his arms, where I always feel safe.

It's dark outside. We've been in this bed for hours, right from the minute after we said, "I do."

"You must be tired, Emelia," he whispers to me.

"I'm not. I don't want the day to end. It was perfect." It was the most perfect day I've ever had.

"It is perfect. I promise you many more days like this." He turns to face me and takes my hand.

"Thank you. I promise you perfect days, too." I always try to show him that I want to do things for him too.

"Every day I have with you is perfect."

I've been in Florence now for the last six months. He comes to see me every weekend. Not one weekend has gone by when he hasn't come. Even though I'm living my dream, I miss him so much when I'm not with him.

This visit was extra special because of our wedding plans and my birthday.

We'll be flying back to L.A. together for the Easter break. I have another eighteen months to finish the program. Then I'd love to open a gallery in L.A. But I have other dreams I want with this man.

He looks down at me and searches my eyes. "What are you thinking about?"

"Our future."

His smile turns up a notch. "What do you see in this future of ours, Princesca?"

"Everything. I want everything with you. That includes the ten kids you said we'd have." We have this running joke I don't actually think is a joke. But I like it.

"That sounds like a great future."

I reach up and touch his face. "Thank you for giving me my dream and being you. You are my happiness."

"You are my happiness too, Emelia." He presses his forehead to mine. I know he truly means that.

Our journey led us to this moment. We're exactly where we should be. We belong to each other.

I'm his, and he is mine.

Nothing is more perfect than that.

MASSIMO

I look from Tristan to Dominic sitting before me and rest my hands down on the table.

I have to reread the letter in my hands again just to process it in my head. Dominic brought it to me. It was left at D'Agostinos Inc., slipped under my office door.

It says:

Dear Massimo,

You do not know me. But I know you, and I feel compelled to contact you in light of the information I've recently discovered.

There was so much more to what happened seven months ago when the Syndicate was obliterated.

There were more people involved than who you think. So many more who were responsible for the deaths of our loved ones. So many got their hands dirty to end our fathers.

Riccardo Balesteri was just a pawn in a bigger game to eradicate enemies. I urge you not to stand alone but to reform the Syndicate and lead. Be a leader.

It is only with the strongest alliances that you will be able to hunt your enemies, or war will come.
Good luck.
A friend

Rage I've tried to calm fills me at the thought of more people involved in Pa's death.

This letter answers questions I had on my mind.

I should have known that day when the bomb went off in the Syndicate building that more people could be involved. I should have known that more people must have been involved right from the time when we raised the alarm that Riccardo was involved in a plot to wipe out the Brotherhood and no one could find him nor Vlad. It didn't make sense for that to happen given who the Syndicate was.

Now it's clear as fucking day they had help.

I ball my fist and slam it down on the table.

"What are you going to do?" Tristan asks. "Reforming the Syndicate is not a bad idea, Massimo. They formed for a reason, and we have the next generation of leaders we can look to."

I've purposely avoided talk of it because I didn't know what to do. Many have contacted me, but I placed it on hold. Tristan is right, though. The Syndicate was formed for a reason. The wealth and assets I've accumulated are so vast it blows my mind. It was designed to be shared and used. But there was more to the Syndicate than wealth. The alliance of powerful men was solid and existed for generations. For the most part, though, they trusted each other.

"There are few I trust," I reply.

"Maybe that's why this guy suggested you take the lead. People you select to join you will be more trustworthy," Dominic joins in. "And they've never had a leader. Maybe it's time to change that."

"I agree," Tristan adds.

I think about it. About being a leader. The first thing I'd want as leader is vengeance.

It doesn't take much for me to remember how it felt to hold my father dead in my arms. Knowing that more people were responsible for that makes me want vengeance.

"I want to hunt the fuckers responsible for Pa's death."

"Me too," Tristan says through gritted teeth.

"And me," Dominic adds. "I'm sure the remaining families from the Syndicate members will feel the same way *when* they find out more people were responsible for murdering their fathers that day."

I look at the letter again. I'd have to inform the others. I don't think anyone would decline my leading to get blood for fucking blood. I'd have strength in numbers.

"Reform and lead, Massimo," Tristan imparts with a firm nod. "We'll back you up like we always do."

I gaze out to the beach and see my girl off in the distance, painting.

I promised I'd protect her from everything so we could have this life.

I don't want the threat of war or anything to threaten our family. I want everything with her. The future with her and the children we'll have.

She chose me to be her husband and protector. Pa chose me to take the lead on the business and the family. My brothers chose me because they believe in me.

It's time to become who I'm supposed to be and take the lead, indeed. On everything.

"I'll do it."

*Thank you so much for reading.
If you enjoyed Massimo and Emelia's story
you will love
Tristan and Isabella's in Dark Captor.*

ACKNOWLEDGMENTS

For my readers.
Always for you.
Thank you for reading my stories.
I hope you continue to enjoy my wild adventures xx

FAITH SUMMERS' COLLECTION

Faith Summers Collection

Series

Dark Syndicate

Ruthless Prince
Dark Captor
Wicked Liar
Merciless Hunter
Heartless Lover
Ruthless King

Dark Odyssey

Tease Me
Taunt Me
Thrill Me
Tempt Me
Take Me
Original Sins

Dark Odyssey Fantasies

Entice
Tease

Play

Tempt

Duet

Blood and Thorns Duet

Merciless Vows

Merciless Union

Novellas

The Boss' Girl

The Player

ABOUT THE AUTHOR

Faith Summers is the Dark Contemporary Romance pen name of USA Today Bestselling Author, Khardine Gray.

Warning !! Expect wild romance stories of the scorching hot variety and deliciously dark romance with the kind of alpha male bad boys best reserved for your fantasies.

Dive in and enjoy her naughty page-turners.

Connect with her by joining her reading list at:

https://www.subscribepage.com/faithsummersreadergroup

Printed in Great Britain
by Amazon